BROKEN ROADS

Victoria Lynn

To all the people who believed I could,
when I didn't believe in myself.
But more importantly,
to all the people who believe they can't.
If I can do it, so can you.
Believe in yourself.

Broken Roads

Victoria Lynn

ONE
ELIZABETH

I could feel them boring into me. A gaze so icy and cold it shot chills through my body. They were watching me, following my every move, studying me. I kept my gaze trained on the large, uncovered windows in the manor library; refusing to blink or move, I was frozen to that spot like a deer caught in the oncoming headlights of a semi. With all the lights on, I knew they could see me; but I was struggling to find the strength to stand as my breathing became more shallow. If I didn't move, though, I was a sitting duck; just waiting for whatever was coming.

Forcing myself up, I shoved out of the chair I'd been sitting in. Slowly and lacking the poise I was known for, I stumbled back a step or two until I collided with the old oak shelves that lined the room behind me. I couldn't bring myself to look away from the window; if I looked away for even a second, they could make their move. I knew they were out there. Every fiber of my being screamed that someone was in the shadows just beyond the patio. A shiver wound its way down my spine and through my entire body at the very thought of someone being in the darkness, hidden by the cover of night.

As much as I wanted to, I knew I couldn't call the police anymore; they were done with me. They had made that much perfectly clear the last time I had called them in a blind panic. I'd called them one too many times; they didn't believe me anymore. They didn't think there was really anyone after me. They said there was nothing they could do for me without proof, but there was definitely someone out there in the darkness every night, watching every move I made.

There wasn't a room in this manor where I felt safe. If they got in once, they could get in again. Reaching out to my right, I fumbled for the light switch. My heart rate spiked when it wasn't there. I knew this room like the back of my hand; it was there. It had to be there! The longer it took to find it, the more frantic my reach became, grasping wildly until my shaking fingers finally made contact with the smooth plastic.

 Flipping it down, I plunged myself into darkness too. At least now we were even.

Maybe it was all in my head; maybe the nightmares that kept me up at night had pushed me into a state of total delusion. I didn't want to be faced with the possibility that I was going crazy, but no matter how I tried, I couldn't shake the feeling. Someone was watching me continuously. It had become this constant fear that thrummed through my body, this relentless vibration. I couldn't catch a break from it. They were coming for me, too, just like they had come for my parents.

I knew what I needed to do. I needed to ground myself. That was what the internet told me. I needed five things I could see. But that meant looking away from the window. I could see trees and the edge of the patio. I could see the moonlight and… I could see what looked like someone moving just beyond the fence that lined the verandah. I wasn't crazy. There was someone out there.

The panic continued to rise and flow through my veins like poison; with each rapid pump of my heart, it continued to spread. Each breath came quicker as I tried in vain to make myself smaller. I wanted to disappear into the bookshelves behind me. It was hopeless, though; fighting back wouldn't get me anywhere. If my parents couldn't fight back, how was I supposed to stand a chance?

They were coming for me. Someone was out to end the Richfield name. I was the last one standing. I was the only one standing between them and their goal; I just wish I knew what it was all for. Why my parents? Why me?

I'd walked in seconds too late. I could still hear it. The shot rang out through the otherwise empty house. I could smell it, the blood potent in the air. The gunpowder, heavy and lingering in the air, the closer I got to the room. They were moments that would forever be etched into my subconscious. I would never fully be able to escape the nightmare.

A weight settled in on my chest; the air around me grew thick as I tried to pull in each breath, but it only continued to come in short gasps. I continued watching out of the window, waiting for it, waiting for something. Part of me screamed to run, to get away from the windows and hide somewhere safe, but I was frozen to my spot, and there was nowhere safe on this property. I tried not to blink, but the harder I stared at the darkness outside, the more everything started to spin around me.

I wouldn't dare look away. If I took my eyes off them, they could get me. They would get me. I wasn't fast enough to outrun anyone. Then what? What would they do with me once they had me in their grasp? Would they kill me too? Would they torture me? Would they...

I couldn't catch my breath. The tears streaked hot down my cheeks, and my eyes burned, but I still couldn't bring myself even to blink. If I blinked, it would be over. A hysteria was growing within me; I could feel the way it was rolling through me. It was tightening my stomach, weakening my knees until I couldn't hold my weight anymore.

Slowly, I sank down the wall to the floor. A blackness hinted at the very edges of my vision as the dizziness worsened. It was starting to feel like I was on one of those amusement rides; I could barely see straight, and what I could make out was blurred by tears. But it didn't matter; I couldn't give over to it. I couldn't do it. I couldn't look away. They were coming. They were going to get me; if I dropped my gaze, blinked, or ran. There was no escaping it. I didn't know what to do. The blackness encroached further, taking over all of my senses until I felt nothing more than complete and total darkness.

My head hurt.

I suppose that was to be expected, though. I had grown accustomed to the post-panic attack hangovers. The headaches that lasted all day, the sensitivity to all forms of light, the way my throat felt like I'd swallowed sandpaper.
Unfortunately for me, these episodes were growing more and more common. Everything felt fuzzy; even my fingers felt like I was wearing a rubber glove, like I wasn't really touching anything.

The trouble was I couldn't always recall the specifics, what exactly had sent me over the edge, spinning out of control, but I had a pretty good guess. The feeling was a constant in my life now. That feeling that someone was watching me. It was worse at night when I was in the manor alone, when I noticed my parents' presence more. I always ended up in the library, too, thinking I was smelling the sweet aroma of my father's cigars. I could almost hear my mother's laugh. It pulled me to the library. We'd spent a lot of time there together as a family.

Maybe the police were right. After the second or third false call, they urged me to seek professional help. I'd been through a trauma like no other. It was one thing to lose my parents the way I had, but the fact that I was the one who… No. I couldn't think about that. I couldn't start down that path again. I could already feel the icy grip of the panic rising again as it flowed through me. I had to remember what those videos online had taught me.

Deep breaths.

In through the nose.

Count four.

Hold.

Count six.

Out through the mouth.

Count eight.

One by one, I could feel the icy claws pull from my chest as it subsided again. My heart rate started to steady as I finally peeked my eyes open just enough to take in my surroundings. I sighed, blinking back against the bright light streaming in through the open window.

It was morning. I was safely in my bed. I could hear the sounds of the house staff hard at work. I could smell breakfast cooking. I was okay. I just had to keep telling myself that, and maybe sooner or later, it would actually sink in. I would be okay. I had to be okay.

Pushing upright, I looked around the room. This room personified who I'd been for the last twenty-five years. The sweet little princess who thought her father had hung the moon and stars just for me. The spoiled teenager who wanted it all, because I'd always had it all, and nothing was ever good enough unless it was exactly what I wanted. The party girl that had landed herself in the headlines more than once and never for anything good. I'd even gone as far as finding myself in jail more than once with the attitude that Daddy's lawyers would get me off like they always did, no questions asked.

The truth was I was an embarrassment to the Richfield name. I always had been. My father had done his best in the last year of his life to straighten me out, to groom me into the person I needed to be to take over the company. But I wasn't ready yet. I wasn't sure I'd ever be ready.

How was I supposed to carry on the name and the company now that the two strongest people I knew were no longer with me to support and guide me? I wasn't fit for any of this. I couldn't be who they wanted me to be. I wasn't built for this. I couldn't run a multi-million-dollar business.

I just...

I couldn't do it.

My father's vice president could step into the role. He could keep things going; they didn't need me. I had to get out of here. I couldn't keep living this life knowing someone was waiting for me to slip up, watching my every move. What if I stepped up, took over, and they came for me? Alive and alone was better than being the dead Richfield heiress.

Shoving the covers to the side, I pushed to my feet. My gaze flitted around the room, looking for anything I needed to take with me because I didn't belong here anymore. I didn't know where I belonged; I just knew I needed to disappear.

I knew if I wanted to pull this off, I had to travel light. The designer clothes and runway handbags were bound to give me away wherever I ended up. It was best that I left it all behind. Besides, if I genuinely wanted a fresh start somewhere else, I couldn't be holding tight to the past. I had to let go of everything.

I had thrown a few casual outfits, boots, and sunglasses into a bag. I didn't know where I was going, but it was only mid-June. The whole summer was stretched out before me. I would have time to brace for fall and winter if necessary. I could figure it all out. I would figure it all out because no matter the fact that I was running now, I wasn't one to buckle. My father made sure of that. I had to believe he would understand why I was doing what I was doing now. It would be better for everyone involved if I just removed myself from the equation altogether.

With my bag slung over my shoulder, I glanced around the room one last time, looking for anything I may have missed. I was about to turn and leave when I saw it lying on my dresser by the door. The little angel figurine my mother had given me one year for Christmas when I was a child. She'd promised me that my angels would always watch over me as long as I kept it close. As a child, I believed her story, but the idea became more unrealistic as I grew. However, if there was ever a time to start believing in those angels again, now was it. I grabbed it and pulled my bag around enough to place it in with one of my shirts. That should keep it nice and safe. Reaching for the light switch, I turned it off. This was it.

Without so much as looking back, I ran down the stairs to my father's office. I paused momentarily at the door, unsure if I could handle opening it without seeing them there, lifeless on the floor, but I had to risk it. With a deep breath and shaking hands, I pushed open the door. I didn't look at the desk or the carpet. They were still stained despite the staff's best efforts. Instead, I set my sights on the safe in the corner of the room.

My father liked to believe that I didn't know the combination to get into it, but if there was one thing I knew beyond a shadow of a doubt, my father loved me. I was his everything. So it hadn't been hard to guess that the passcode to get into the safe was none other than the very day I turned him into a father.

4·3·93.

Easy enough to crack. I quickly typed in the code, the heavy door clicked open and I pulled it toward me. Sure enough, the money for a rainy day. When I was younger, I didn't know what that meant. Why did we need to set anything aside when we already had so much? But now I understood. This was the rainy day he was saving it for. Grabbing the cash, I shoved it in the bag with the rest of my stuff. It would be enough to take me anywhere in the country. It would get me a place to stay and get me started in this new life.

The idea of actually working was foreign to me, but I would make it work. Somehow. Because I was a Richfield, it was just what we did. Sighing to myself, I closed the safe again, hearing the locks fall back into place. I headed back out of his office and to the front door, shouldering my bag again. It was weird thinking there was a chance I'd never see this place again. This was where I'd grown up, but too much had happened here. It had changed more than I could handle. It wasn't my home anymore.

Running out to my car, I jumped in and sighed when the electric engine came to life. There was one stop I had to make before I could really be gone for good. If I had any family left at all, it was Abraham and Elisa. Abraham had been my father's valet for as long as I could remember. But they were more than that to me. Elisa had taken me into her home, taught me how to cook, sew, and do all the things my mother didn't know how to do. Abraham had been the one to teach me how to ride a horse right alongside his own daughter. They were all I had left, and I knew it wasn't right to leave without taking the time to say goodbye.

They only lived a short distance from the manor, less than a ten-minute drive. Pulling into the small driveway, I climbed from the car and ran to the front door. Knocking once, I pushed the door open. I didn't want my last interaction with Elisa to be her scolding me for acting like I wasn't part of the family. I could smell breakfast cooking as Elisa poked her head around the corner and smiled at me. "My Elizabeth, you're just in time for breakfast."

There was part of me that knew I needed to get going, but there was another part of me, a firmer part, that longed to have this one last meal with them. To sit down and talk with them. "I don't want to intrude," I returned her smile. She waved a hand at me at that. Of course, she knew I already knew there was no such thing.

"We haven't seen you much since the news broke," she noted as I followed her back into the kitchen. Abraham had come by the manor to check on me, but the press had had a field day with my parent's death. There'd been no escaping them. It was easy to talk to Elisa; it always had been. But nevertheless, I found myself struggling to say the words to her that I needed to say.

We talked about a lot of things as she cooked until Abraham returned to the house from tending to the chickens they kept. We all sat down and ate together, and I couldn't help but shake the feeling that this was precisely what I needed. I needed them; I needed a family. I knew if I stayed with them, though, I would only put them in the line of fire too. I was barely handling losing my own parents; I wasn't so sure I could handle losing Elisa and Abraham too.

After we'd eaten, I helped clean up. It was the least I could do before I broke the news to them. Then, sighing to myself, I turned from the sink and looked at both of them. I wasn't sure I had it in me to break their hearts, but it was my only choice.

"There's something I need to tell the both of you," I started slowly. "You know I've had panic attacks since everything happened. They've only gotten worse, and I can't tell if I'm just creating this paranoia or if it's legitimate. But either way, the police are tired of hearing from me, and I just… I can't stay in the manor anymore. But as long as I stay here, I feel like I'm a target, that whoever killed mom and dad will be back for me. So maybe it's irrational, maybe it's not, but I have to start over. Somewhere else, somewhere where I'm not the Richfield Heiress." I looked at both of them, tears in my eyes. "I'm leaving today, I'm changing my name, and I'm not coming back. But I couldn't leave without saying goodbye first."

Elisa stood up and stepped into me, wrapping me in that warm hug she'd always been so good at. "We'll always be here for you, sweetheart," she said softly. "But we understand. You have to take care of yourself."

I nodded against her shoulder, not able to find my voice. I was glad they could find it in their hearts to understand. "I have a question before I go," I started. "I can't be Elizabeth Richfield anymore. And I mean, I've always loved my middle name. So I was thinking of having it changed to Oakley Morgan, if that's okay with you?" I asked.

Elisa's breath caught at that, "Of course, it's okay, Elizabeth," she smiled. "We'd be honored to have you be a Morgan too." She pulled back from me, going to grab a pen and paper. Writing down both a phone number and an email address, she handed it to me. "As a Morgan now, that means you have to keep in touch," she instructed. "Please. So that we know you're okay."

I nodded at that. I could do that much. It wasn't long before I was back out the door; I'd called a cab, giving my car to them. When it pulled up, I grabbed my bag, hugged them each, and jumped in. I didn't know where this road would take me, but I had to follow it through until the end. Making one more quick stop with a notoriously shady man, I had new papers in hand and the promise that Elizabeth Richfield was no more.

To say I had no real plan was a monstrous understatement but standing in the airport looking at the board of departures, I was suddenly overwhelmed by the possibilities. I could go anywhere. I was scared out of my mind. Closing my eyes, I took a deep breath and pointed. Wherever it landed, that's where my new life awaited. Peeking one eye open slowly after my finger made contact with the cool screen, I took in my destination. Philadelphia, Pennsylvania. Well, that could make things interesting. I didn't know much about the east coast, but it held one major appeal, it was on the other side of the country. I wasn't sure I was much for city life, but maybe I could find some small town off the beaten path. Somewhere no one would ever think to look for me.

With a sigh, I moved toward my future. Things would be different now; I didn't know how I knew that. I didn't have much of a plan at all. But things would be different. Stepping up to the desk, I smiled my best smile, "One ticket to Philadelphia, please. The next flight you have."

Almost six hours and no sleep later, I stepped off the plane in Pennsylvania. Setting my bag at my feet, I sighed and tried to get my bearings; I felt a pang in my chest for my home, Abraham, and Elisa. I just had to keep telling myself this was for the best. If I could start over fresh, somewhere new, I could shake all the ghosts haunting me. I could go where no one would ever find me. I could shake that feeling of being watched, and I could take my life back.

I heard a gasp as I bent to reach for my bag again. "That's not…" a nearby voice whispered.

"I'd recognize that blonde hair anywhere," another added.

I sighed; I was the face of the Richfield family. Ever since I turned twenty-two and graduated from Stanford, my father had groomed me to take over the family name. He wasted no time putting my image out there for the world to see. He wanted everyone to know who the next successor to the Richfield fortune was.

This meant now, when I was trying to hide; everyone would know who I was. Pulling my sunglasses back on, I ducked my head, grabbed my bag, and did my best to ignore them. I let a veil of blonde hair fall between them and me as if that were enough to protect me as I moved through the airport and straight out the security doors. I would have to do something about that; I hadn't thought of people recognizing me on the other side of the country, but that was a stupid error on my part. It had to go.

I jumped in the first cab I saw, not knowing what to tell the man driving. I didn't know where I was going; I couldn't tell him where to take me.

"Just drive," I asked him before digging two hundred dollar bills out of my bag and tossing it into the front seat, "however far that will take me." I knew I had to have some kind of plan. But for now, I settled back against the seat as the taxi driver pulled out into traffic.

"Any particular direction?" he asked me, glancing in the rearview mirror at me.

I sighed and closed my eyes, "somewhere no one will ever find me."

TWO
OWEN

"Why the fuck do I even bother?" I called down the hall after my partner, Ethan Jacey, who only waved a hand over his shoulder in farewell at me. From the distance, I couldn't quite tell if he was giving me the finger or not. Knowing the jackass, it was highly likely. He was well known around town for being a complete and total pain in my ass.

It came with the territory, though; we had been friends since grade school. He was more like a brother to me at this point; he sure as hell knew how to annoy me like my brothers did. It didn't change the fact that I still questioned the sanity of whoever thought it was a good idea to pair us up on the job. Yeah, we watched out for each other, but one of these days he was going to push the wrong button, and I was going to retaliate. On more than one occasion, I had to remind myself that revenge on the idiot wasn't worth losing my job over.

Given that Gratin was a small town of just over a thousand residents, we were often the only two in the office working the night shift. But that was just part of the gig. Plus, we had both grown up here; we were the veterans. That didn't mean we weren't good on the job. We got the job done. Somehow, we worked well together; there were plenty of people in town who questioned the decision to put us together.

I guess we actually balanced each other out in some odd way. He liked to go on gut instinct and, as he so often put it, 'wing it.' I needed a little more structure. There were rules and protocols for a reason. Sure, it didn't always play out in a way that followed the books, but sometimes that was better than throwing caution to the wind and just seeing what happened.

Not that it mattered, really; it wasn't like Gratin saw that much excitement, especially at night. We were usually lucky to get any calls at all. Turning around, I trudged back to my desk and dropped into the empty chair. On the one hand, I loved working the night shift. When the town was asleep, everything was quiet. It was a great time to get some work done at the station.

However, on the other hand, on nights like tonight when I didn't have a damn thing to do, it was fucking boring. Leaning back in my chair, I sighed and pushed my fingers through my hair. Jacey was off on a coffee run; we had one late-night diner in this place. I should have gone; it would have given me something to do. Instead, I was the one that got to sit around the office with my thumb up my ass.

The coffee at O'Dell's wasn't the greatest at this hour, right before they closed, but it was at least better than the jet fuel they served us in the station. Plus, making a run out offered some level of socialization, which at almost one in the morning with no one but a coworker to stare at; even Liv's clipped attitude was a welcomed interaction. Sighing to myself, I sat up in my chair and reached for the files sitting on my desk. I knew I was looking for something that wasn't there, but that didn't stop me from looking again.

Most of our cases were open and close; they were easy to solve. For the sake of Gratin, that was a comfort. It meant this little town nestled in the Pocono Mountains of Pennsylvania was safe, at least for the most part. We weren't without our troubles; a gang liked to roll through town with fair frequency, but we'd also discovered that they weren't worth going after until we had something to hold them on. Sometimes they caused trouble; sometimes, they just passed through. They hadn't caused problems in a while, and I often preferred it that way; our little two-person nightshift police team was enough to handle anything that came along.

Though, at some point, I found myself wishing for something more to do, almost regretting that I didn't take that job in Philadelphia. I could have been chasing down killers and carjackers and thieves all night long. Or at least that's what I liked to try and convince myself. The reality was, though, that killers, carjackers, and thieves came with a shit ton of paperwork. If there was one thing I truly hated about my job, it was fucking paperwork. Which begged the question of why I was staring at the collection of case files sitting on my desk. I just wanted something to do.

I grabbed my phone and my keys and headed for the door without giving it another thought. Dispatch would know where to find me when, or rather if, a call came in. I sent Jacey a quick text telling him I was heading out on patrol before hitting the office lights and turning for the door.

Driving around town when it was dark and completely deserted was almost relaxing. A certain level of peace came with seeing the town at night. With one hand on the steering wheel, I followed my usual route through the center of town. I was browsing through my regular radio stations, looking for something to listen to. I glanced down at the radio for a moment before looking back to the road when something caught my attention. Slamming on the brakes, I stopped just shy of her. Long blonde hair, wide eyes staring at me with a look of shock plastered across her face, her grip flexing on the strap of her bag slung over her shoulder.

I knew almost everyone in Gratin; that came with the territory of having grown up here, along with the fact that I was one of the few officers on the Gratin Police Force. But this girl was new; I had never seen her before; I knew that because I would remember that face: those heart-shaped lips, that long blonde hair.

Slamming the patrol car into park, I moved to get out of the car. However, it was almost as if my movement startled her. She took a cautious step back away from the nose of the car as I opened the door. "Is there anything I can help you with, ma'am?" I questioned, putting forth my best 'you can trust me, I'm a cop' voice. It was something my brothers made fun of me for mercilessly.

She shook her head and took another step back, "No, I'm okay," she answered. "I wasn't paying attention, so preoccupied with everything. I'm just...."

She motioned to the old Inn I only now realized I was parked in front of. Well, that made sense. If she were new in town or just passing through, of course, she'd be stopping in at Rudy's place. "You may have to really ring the bell a few times; Rudy's hearing is shot. He never hears those bells anymore," I explained, smiling at her. She seemed jumpy, which alone piqued my curiosity about her. But the goal here wasn't to scare her off. "I could come in with you if you'd like, get Rudy's attention, make sure he treats you right. He doesn't like newcomers. Which makes his choice of business rather… ironic."

"The Innkeeper doesn't like newcomers?" she asked, giving the Inn a wary look.

I stepped away from my car, "I don't want to scare you off; he's just an old grump who likes things the way they've been for the last sixty years. He still does all of his bookkeeping by hand. He refuses to update with anything. He pays his bills in cash. Which I hope you have; he doesn't trust credit."

She nodded slowly, "I have cash," she confirmed. "I should be okay," she backed away from me again. Her mannerisms were peculiar, to say the least. She watched me closely, seemingly gauging every move I made. She was tense; the way her fingers flexed against her bag strap told me she was ready to run with less than a second's notice. Though she did her best to keep her gaze on me, she did flick her eyes away from me every minute or so, checking her surroundings too. She was afraid of something. Of me? I couldn't place it for sure. "But thank you for your help, Officer…." She leaned forward slightly as if she were trying to read my nametag, but we were too far apart for her to see it in the dark. She looked back up at me, a question in her eyes.

"Hale," I answered, "Owen Hale."

She nodded, trying her best to keep her composure, "Thank you for your help Officer Hale, but I should be okay," she repeated.

I dug in my pocket for a card before holding it out to her, "Don't hesitate to call if you need anything." She stepped forward enough to take the card from me. "Even if it's just Rudy being his typical pain in the ass self."

She gripped the handle of her bag again, "Thank you," she shook her head, "I should stop saying that. Well," she paused, taking another step away from me. "Good night."

I nodded in farewell; I would hang out here and wait to ensure she could wake old Rudy up. Something about her intrigued me: the way she hadn't told me her name, the way she kept distance between us, and the way I couldn't quite tell in the dark if her eyes were blue or green.

I watched her as she turned and headed the rest of the way across the street and pulled open the front door to the old Inn. It wasn't long before the office light turned on, and Rudy came ambling out, scratching at himself. I shook my head; this town had quite the collection of characters, there was no doubt about that. But it was home. Spinning on my heel, I walked back to the cruiser door and jumped in just as my phone lit up in the empty seat next to me.

E. Jacey:
Where the fuck are you?

O. Hale:
On my way back.

I wanted to know more about my town's newest resident, but theoretically, there was police work that needed to be done. Logically, it was now closing in on almost one-thirty in the morning. I'd have to save the mystery for another day, preferably when the sun was actually up.

I wanted to know more about my town's newest resident, but theoretically, there was police work that needed to be done. Logically, it was now closing in on almost one-thirty in the morning. I'd have to save the mystery for another day, preferably when the sun was actually up.

Strolling back into the station, I shook my head at the questioning look Jacey gave me from his spot behind his desk.

"Dude, this town is like five miles wide; it shouldn't take you thirty minutes to do a patrol," he laughed.

I sighed, "Newcomer in town, she was looking to get into Rudy's place. You know how he is; I wanted to make sure she got in okay. Our streets may be about as threatening as a fuzzy little bunny rabbit, but that doesn't mean I want anyone spending the night on them."

"Fuzzy little bunny rabbit?" he inquired, amusement smothering his gaze. "Have you ever tried to catch one of those little shits? They will seriously fuck your day up if you get caught on the wrong end of those teeth and claws."

I chuckled slightly at that, "Don't tell me you're afraid of a sweet little runny babbit, Jacey?" I mocked, effectively dodging the pen that came flying at my head, knowing it was coming.

"They're not sweet, and you damn well know I don't like them," he accused. Half the fun of being partnered with someone I had grown up with was that I knew all the dirt. It gave me something to pass the time in the middle of the night. The only trouble with that was that he knew every little secret about my childhood, and he was always prepared to use it against me.

"Don't even go there," I warned before the words could come out of his mouth, and he just grinned. All it took was mentioning it, and the image popped into my head. Ever since my seventh birthday, clowns freaked me out. To be fair, though, the clown my mom had hired was a little sketchy. He claimed the red stain on his outfit was icing from the birthday party before mine, but as a cop now, I knew better. Icing wasn't that color, and if it was, I could guarantee there were a lot of worried parents the next day when it all came out the other end. Either way, clowns freaked me out, and the jackass sitting across from me wasn't above sending me clown pictures on the regular to see if he could get me to jump out of my seat. It worked once.

Jacey held his hands up in a show of total Innocence, "I said nothing," he challenged, "But you might want to check under your bed when you go home. Never know who might be lurking. And here I thought you had outgrown the 'monsters under the bed' cliché, Hale," he mocked with a smirk.

I mumbled a string of curse words under my breath at him as I moved to straighten out the files on my desk again. There were seriously only so many times a man could straighten the same pile of file folders. I was definitely pushing that limit.

"So tell me about this girl," Jacey changed the subject as he tapped his pen on the edge of his desk. He leaned back in his chair as if he were counting on a good story.

I shrugged, "There's nothing to tell. Probably just someone passing through. You know how it is, we see tourists, sure, but we don't get a lot that stick around. It was late; she probably just needed a place to crash. And well, our options are Rudy's, Rudy's, and Rudy's. So she got stuck with the old pain in the ass for the night. Probably be on her way out come morning." Jacey smirked at me in that self-assured way, making me want to knock him in the head. He seemed to be under the impression that he knew something I didn't, which was impossible given the fact that I was the one who had almost run her over with a cruiser. I knew I would regret asking, but the question danced on the tip of my tongue anyway. Apparently, I was a masochist. "What?"

His smirk only grew at that, "Nothing. Nothing at all," he swiveled back and forth in his chair as he contemplated what to say next. I couldn't quite tell if he was trying not to piss me off or if that was precisely what he was doing. "Just thinking, you seem rather preoccupied with this new girl. Could have just said that she was staying at Rudy's, but you got all weird."

I huffed, "I did not get weird; I was just explaining."

He laughed at that, "explaining shit I already know. I grew up here too, dumbass."

I knew there was no use arguing with him; he knew all the buttons to push. Again, he might as well have been my brother. The younger brother, that is. He wasn't younger by much, but it definitely showed in maturity. It seemed one of us forgot to grow up. "Isn't there something you could be doing?" I asked him, "What's the matter? Your diner owner wasn't in tonight? Get the evil twin instead?" I questioned.

It wasn't exactly a secret that he still held a candle for Fiona O'Dell. But any time he dared to try and flirt with her, he ended up looking like a complete and total dumbass. I didn't know why he tried; she'd already dumped his dumb ass once. I had to admit though despite their history, she seemed to enjoy their back and forth. She did an excellent job at keeping him guessing. I didn't understand their little dance around each other, a lot of people didn't, but it was more than obvious to anyone with eyes that there was some sort of unfinished business between them.

The remaining five hours of my shift seemed to drag by even worse than usual. I usually could find things to keep myself busy, to keep going through the night. If we were lucky, we'd get a call for minor disturbances. Mrs. Reilly had even called in about once again believing someone was skulking around her property. Just like every other time, it turned out to be nothing more than shadows, but even that didn't help pass the time. It felt like I was searching her property for at least an hour, only to have returned to my car and realized the whole thing had only taken fifteen minutes.

I found that every time I let my mind wander, even just a little, it went back to that meeting in the street. I couldn't get her eyes out of my head. They looked troubled, but there was a life in them that couldn't be snuffed out. Clearly, she was a tough one; that much was evident from our short interaction, but it was weird to say there was something about her. I wanted to know more.

Though, I had to keep reminding myself that what I had told Jacey was likely true. She was just passing through. The chances of seeing her again were rather slim. Finding a way to move past it all would do me good.

As I stepped outside, the wind kicked up. It wasn't abnormal for storms to blow through during the summer; I could see the threat of dark clouds and rain on the horizon. I would make my usual stop at the diner for breakfast before heading home to bed. As I got into my car to head that way, I found myself turning down the main road leading in the opposite direction, back towards Rudy's place.

It was seven in the morning; I didn't know what I thought I could accomplish by going back to Rudy's. It wasn't like she'd had a car the night before, so I could check to see if it was still in the small parking lot or not, and Rudy sure as hell wasn't about to give up anything on his guests. He believed that it was no one else's damn business who stayed at his Inn; I had to give the old man credit for that because he never cracked. Not even for family members of people staying there. He always claimed that everyone had a right to their privacy, and if we ever wanted a glance at his books, we would need a warrant. Thankfully, we had never had a reason to call in a warrant. So, I knew there was no way he would tell me if she had checked out already or not.

I slowly drove by the old Inn, looking for any sign of life within the brick walls. There was nothing, no movement, no cars out front. If she was still in town, she was safely inside. I had to admit, I felt like a bit of a creep for even trying to check up on her; I didn't even know her. Unfortunately, I would just have to wonder, which sucked because the only thing I loved most about mysteries was solving them. If they remained open and cold, they drove me crazy. And that girl, with her long blonde hair and blue-green eyes, was a mystery I had a feeling I wasn't ever going to be able to solve.

Three
Oakley

Picking up the scissors off the counter, I could feel my hand shaking. I was not a hairstylist, but it was the middle of the night, and there was no place open. I wanted to be rid of anything that resembled who I used to be. It was bad enough that my face would be plastered across every news outlet and gossip magazine the moment they realized I was gone. I couldn't change my face, but I could change everything else in hopes that no one would recognize me.

Sucking in a deep breath, I closed my eyes and counted to ten. I know it sounded vain, but my hair was everything to me. I had spent hours caring for it and ensuring no hair was out of place. I paid top dollar to have professionals cut it. My identity and self-worth were rooted in looking perfect. I had to have the right shade of blonde; it had to curl perfectly. My hair was who I was, and now, standing in the four-by-four bathroom of some smelly Inn room, I was going to cut it myself.

Opening my eyes, I met that striking light green in the mirror and nodded to myself. It was only hair; it would grow back. Eventually. The long blonde hair with soft beachy curls was Elizabeth Richfield. I was Oakley Morgan now. I didn't know who she was, but the reflection staring back at me wasn't her. Lifting the scissors, I willed my hand to stop shaking before pulling a lock forward and squeezing the handles together. The blonde curls I loved fell to the floor, but there was also something oddly liberating about watching it all slip away. I pulled another lock forward and did the same thing. I knew I had no idea what I was doing, but I had stared down stylists in the mirror before, watching their every move to make sure they never messed anything up.

Maybe I learned a thing or two because, by the time I was done, I even had to say it didn't look half bad. It didn't exactly look good, but I did a better job than I had anticipated. Instead of waves and curls running down my back, I now had a shoulder-length bob. I couldn't bring myself to cut it any shorter than that; maybe later on, I could have someone fix it for me. Though, I also had a box of hair dye sitting on the counter. If I had no idea what I was doing with the scissors, I really had no clue what I was doing with the dye. Part of me just wanted to wait for a salon to open in the morning and let someone who actually knew what they were doing do it for me, but I had already bought the dye, and I had cut my own hair.

I was in a place out in the middle of nowhere, where hopefully no one knew me. So what if I looked like a total train wreck? It would undoubtedly throw anyone looking for me off the trail. Elizabeth Richfield was known for looking put together in designer clothes and hair and make-up that looked like I had it done by professionals every day. To have a choppy hairstyle and color from a box, no one would believe it even if they did recognize me. Maybe it was fitting. Oakley Morgan was a hot mess.

I opened the box with one more deep breath and set to work. By morning I would look different; maybe I would actually wear my glasses, too, instead of my contacts. The goal was to look like a whole new person, and if I succeeded, I could finally let my past die.

Staring in the mirror once again, I didn't even recognize myself, which was kind of the point. At the same time, though, I didn't feel like myself anymore. Without my trademark blonde hair, I just looked like any other girl. Again, though, that was kind of the point; it was just hard to wrap my head around.

I hadn't done a terrible job with the dye, but I could tell it was a little uneven and blotchy, and my forehead looked like someone had tried painting me. It was nothing make-up wouldn't fix in the morning. I couldn't dwell on it now; I was tired, I needed to get some sleep. Taking out my contacts, I threw them in the trash rather than putting them back in their case. Fumbling for my glasses, I slipped the dark frames on my face and caught myself smiling slightly. Aside from the uneven cut and the mess I made with the dye, I had to count this as a success. I was a mess, and somehow, that was precisely what I was going for all along.

The next afternoon, after sleeping in much later than I had intended, I cleaned myself up and ventured out into the tiny town where my cab driver had dropped me off the night before. First, I had to get my bearings with my surroundings and learn the lay of the land, and hopefully, avoid any further awkward encounters with the local law enforcement. I needed to keep my head down and stay off the radar as much as possible.

Turning to my right, I set out on what appeared to be the main road in town. I found all the usual suspects, a grocery store, a diner, and a clothing shop – that would be handy. I needed new clothes that would make me blend in a little more. I had left most of my belongings behind, and while what I'd brought was plain, they were still designer.

I kept moving until I found the corner store; it appeared to have a little bit of everything. Opening the door, I stepped inside and went directly to the counter. I didn't want to waste my time. I needed a new phone, and if I couldn't get one in this shop, maybe the owner could point me in the right direction. Except there was no one at the counter. "Excuse me?" I called into the seemingly empty store.

"Be right out!" a deep voice called from the back room, making me jump. There were a few bangs, crashes, and cuss words before a man appeared in the doorway. "What can I do for you?" he asked, but I froze. Those eyes looked familiar. It took a second to place them; why I recognized them, the officer from the night before. Though, unlike the officer's clean-cut look, with his uniform perfectly pressed and his dark hair combed back out of his face.

This man was almost more rugged; his dark hair was messy like he didn't even know what a brush was, let alone the fact that he may actually own and use one. He sported a beard and a rumpled flannel shirt with the sleeves rolled up over a white t-shirt. All the same, there was a definite resemblance between the two. Just what I needed, a possible connection to the cop who had almost run me over.

I shook my head, trying to clear away the thoughts. It wasn't like he was the officer from the night before, and even if he had been, I had changed so much in the last twelve hours I highly doubted that he would recognize me anyway. "I was just wondering what my chances were that you might be selling cell phones here?" I asked him, stepping closer to the counter.

He shook his head and shrugged, "Sorry, nothing anyone would be after. We have a couple of used ones. But in today's age of all that smart technology, the little flip phones I have here won't do you much good."

A flip phone. It wasn't the smartphone I was used to, but maybe that was precisely what I needed. I needed to stay away from social media, and as long as it could make a couple of calls and maybe send a few texts, it didn't have to be anything special. "Actually, that sounds perfect," I told him, smiling slightly at the look of total shock that transformed his face.

He seemed to shake off the surprise quickly, though. "Right then," he nodded, "The selection isn't that great." He pulled a couple of phones from a nearby case. "Take your pick. Do you need a number to go with it?" he asked.

I dipped my head in a slight nod, "I can call a provider," I told him, but then paused. "Except I don't have a phone." I could just go back to the Inn. The room I was staying in had a phone I could use.

He smiled slightly at that, "I have a phone here you can use," he pointed out to me, amusement coloring his gaze. "Just pick out a phone, and we'll get you all set up," he promised.

I nodded, he seemed a little perplexed by my predicament, but there was also a level of amusement in the way he looked at me. Like I was some kind of sideshow act. I realized the ridiculousness of my situation. Believe me; it wasn't lost on me. A young woman with a bad dye job buying a flip phone from the early 2000s. Yeah, I knew how absurd I looked, but he seemed content to help me anyway. He was probably excited to finally be moving a product that should have gone the way of the dinosaurs.

He set a cordless phone on the counter in front of me, along with my new phone, "I can make the call for you; I've dealt with them before; I just need some information first."

I didn't like the sound of that, "What sort of information?"

"The usual: name, address, how you'll be paying for it," he smiled at me again, a spark lighting up his brown gaze.

Well, shit.

Standing out on the street a little while later, I stared down at my new phone. Except nothing about it was new. It was practically an antique. I had thought phones like this didn't even exist anymore, but as I had told myself in the store, I didn't need a smartphone. I only had one number to put in it. I had thrown my old phone away. I was starting fresh, and I didn't need things like social media getting in my way.

Tucking the small device in my back pocket, I resolved that it was only temporary. I needed to start figuring out this new life of mine. Austen, the man from the shop, had helped me out by setting me up with a post office box until I could find a place to live. If I was even staying in Gratin. He also directed me to the nearest bank; it was all the way out on the edge of town and my only option unless I wanted to drive toward the nearest city. Which, without a car, would be a little tricky. I would have to set up a new account if I wanted the phone to work. He told me to set up the account and then come back to see him.

I really had no clue what I was doing out in the real world. My whole life had been sheltered; we were a family of old money, my great-great-great-grandparents were the ones to place the Richfield name in the Valley. They opened the winery that was now synonymous with royalty. It was top shelf; they prided themselves on only the absolute best. It was a vineyard built by love and sweat. The vineyard and the family had survived everything thrown at them, the phylloxera epidemic, prohibition... but it hadn't survived the deadliest thing to come crashing through.

Me.

I started down the street again, trying to make sense of everything I had been through in the last six months. Between my parents' death, all the media coverage, the survivor's guilt, and the endless parade of questions. With a high-profile case like my parents, I would have figured that the police would have been all over finding who was behind it. With each dead end they came to, though, the more they seemed to give up. Until finally, they shoved it aside, claiming my father had so many enemies they weren't sure they'd ever truly figure it out. Hell, at one point, they even considered the possibility of murder/suicide. They had theorized that one of them snapped; the only thing that kept them off that trail was that no gun was left at the scene.

Not that it mattered; the team leading the case was full of real *geniuses*. There was still a detective on the case who looked into any possible leads, but it was also painfully apparent that it wasn't a top priority anymore. Especially, since they seemed to be under the impression that I was at no risk. If only there were some way to prove it to them, but it didn't matter now. I was likely soon to be declared a missing person by someone in my father's company that would only show false concern for my well-being.

The truth was no one wanted me to take over the company. They all thought I was unfit for the job. I guess my leaving worked in their favor then. Unfortunately, that didn't make the decision to leave any easier on me; I'd been part of a legacy that had now ended with me. I sure knew how to make my family proud.

A few hours later, I had taken care of everything to get my new phone up and running. Austen had proven to be of more help than I had anticipated too. By the time I had returned to the shop, he had also pulled up all the local listings for houses for rent. None of which were exactly in my price range if I didn't want to deplete my savings too quickly. It would be hard to go through a couple of million dollars, but I needed that money in case I was actually right and the police were wrong in assuming I was safe. I would need to be able to make a quick escape. I was not too fond of living my life on the run, but I didn't know what else to do at this point. I had moved, I changed my name and everything about myself.

If only my parents could see me now. I wasn't the daughter they'd raised anymore. I'm sure my mother would have been critiquing me, my hair, my clothes, anything. My father would chastise her, telling her none of that mattered if I couldn't run the company and that she was too hard on me anyway. I could hear every word as if they were standing right next to me.

It was another reason I had to leave; I felt them no matter where I went in that manor. That wasn't something that was easy to explain to anyone, feeling haunted and trapped in your own home. Richfield Manor held so many good memories too, but everything was overshadowed now. I couldn't sleep; I couldn't eat. I had spent most nights terrified, hiding in a corner, anything to get away from those prying eyes.

Without the love of my family, without my father's boisterous laugh and the soft click of my mother's heels as she moved about, it was empty and almost cold. It would always be home in some respect; but the circumstances, the paranoia – if that's what it was, had become too much. I just needed a fresh start.

I shook my head to clear the torrent of thoughts. My mind really wandered these days. I had to focus. I needed to get something to eat before heading back out to a small apartment space over the local flower shop. According to Austen, it'd had someone in it until recently, but she had just gotten married and was expecting her first child. He pointed me in that direction because not only was the apartment open and at a fair price for the space, but a job was open as well.

Apparently, he was the one to go to for these sorts of things. He claimed he just knew the happenings around town because his shop was a frequent stop for most of the inhabitants of Gratin. People talked. Though the way he spoke about Buchannan Flowers, I could only guess there was more history there than he was letting on.

However, he had also pointed me in the direction of this place. The diner I was standing in like an idiot while the waitress gave me a confused look. "Ma'am?" she asked again as if this were her third or fourth time trying to get my attention. Great, so now I wasn't only the new girl in town the local law enforcement had almost run down, but I was going to be the crazy one too.

"Just one," I did my best to smile at her, but smiling wasn't easy these days. She nodded and led me back to a booth in the corner, thankfully. I didn't want to be in the path of prying eyes. I had already made enough of a spectacle of myself at the front. However, as I went to step around the waitress who was placing a menu on the table for me, I all but crashed into someone. Two strong hands wrapped around my upper arms to steady me.

"Whoa," he chuckled, and I immediately recognized that voice from the night before. It was the officer that had almost run me over on my way into town. "Are you okay?"

I nodded, keeping my gaze downcast as best I could. The way he had seemed to study every feature the night before, I was suddenly worried that my appearance changes wouldn't be enough to prevent him from figuring me out.

Then, all of sudden, the waitress was speaking again, "You're always in my way Owen," she sighed. I could see the look of exasperation on her face. Clearly, they had done this dance before. Of course, that wasn't all that surprising in a small town like this. "Seriously, move," she ordered. Her tone was clipped with him, but he hardly seemed phased by it.

His hands still hadn't dropped from my arms; his touch was almost burning through my shirt. His skin felt like it was several degrees warmer than it needed to be. I wanted to find a way to pull away without him noticing, but that would be easier said than done. Before I could make a move, he spoke again, "Maybe you're the one always in my way Liv," he challenged, "Starting to question why Fiona even lets you near the customers." A teasing hint to his tone caused my gaze to snap back to his face.

"Stop manhandling the customers and get back to your boyfriend; he looks lonely over there without you," she shot right back at him without skipping a beat.

His hands still didn't drop from my arms. Instead, he was once again staring at me with such intensity I felt like he could see right through me. It was like he was reading every line of my story, drinking it in.

He shook his head, the spell broken for a fleeting moment, "I'm sorry, but have we met before?"

FOUR
OWEN

I was instantly caught in her gaze. Her eyes were a green that seemed to pierce right through me and strike me right at my core.

They were the shade of a spring morning, just as the sun started to rise, its rays glistening off the dew-covered grass. They were comparable to the mountain trees in the full swing of summer. They were a shade of green I had never seen before, not in person. They were a hue only ever created in the mind of an artist. They pulled me in to the point where I wouldn't even notice or care if I were drowning.

I'd never really been into all that poetic shit before, but now I understood what they were always going on about. It was so easy to get caught in the moment, but then she looked away, and the curse was broken. My brain started firing again; I could feel the old cogs groaning as they were forced back into high gear. This girl had stopped me dead in my tracks.

I felt the words coming; I couldn't stop them before asking her if we had met before. Because every fiber of my being was screaming at me that we had, but I didn't recognize her when I stopped to take in her whole image. It wasn't until I took a second to take a closer inspection that I saw the faint stains of hair dye along her forehead, close to her hairline, and masked with makeup. I recognized the choppy, slightly uneven cut of an amateur. I would know; I had sported a similar DIY style myself before I was old enough to know better.

Was it possible this was the same girl from the night before? Before she could answer my first question, I felt the second one bubbling for release.

"Rudy's treating you alright at that old Inn of his?" I questioned. My gaze met hers again, and this time I somehow managed to keep myself from falling under their enchantment. At least enough that I saw them widen slightly in alarm. That spoke louder to me than any words ever could. She didn't like that I recognized her. Why was that? I could only guess the reason behind the sudden arrival in a small town and the dramatic changes to her appearance. She was hiding from something. Or someone. I couldn't gather more than that, not without actually talking to her. Though, she didn't seem the type that would readily open up to some stranger.

Holding her gaze, I could see fragments of pain shining within their depths. I had to give her credit; she tried to cover it up. She did her best to recover from the surprise, but I could still see it. She was young, early to mid-twenties, if I had to place a guess. Young enough that she shouldn't have those small wrinkles right at the corner of her eyes. Not yet. Her makeup was done well, but I could still see traces of the bags under her eyes too. She was exhausted.

Something inside of her was broken, and something in me called out to fix it. I wasn't generally in the habit of trying to fix people. It never worked out the way it was planned. It was a known fact that there was no helping someone who didn't really want the offered help. That was the trouble here; I couldn't tell if she wanted my help or not. I had to take a leap of faith. "No one should eat alone," I told her, dipping my head slightly to catch her eye again as she dropped her gaze. "I'm here with my partner, come join us." I phrased it more as a statement of truth than a question. A question gave her too many ways to back out of joining Jacey and me. If she had her heart set on eating alone, I also wouldn't stand in the way.

She paused for a moment; I could see the wheels turning in her head. I couldn't tell if she was actually contemplating my offer or if she was trying to formulate some kind of escape plan to get the hell away from me. When she nodded, albeit slowly and barely noticeable, I felt myself smiling at her. I motioned to the table over her shoulder where Jacey was giving me this strange look, almost as if he were watching something unfathomable happening right before his eyes.

There was truth to his stunned look; it wasn't as if I dated much or showed interest at all in meeting someone. I mainly worked and then went home to my two dogs, Justice and Roscoe, where I worked some more. Sometimes I watched movies before turning in for the day. That was the struggle of a night cop, sleeping during regular human hours.

By the time we had reached the table, Jacey had managed to wipe the stupid look off his face. I shoved his shoulder to get him to move into the booth more, giving her the other side to herself. I didn't want to crowd her. Jacey looked at me with this smug countenance, "Who's your friend?" he asked, the question directed at me.

I stared him down for that, I didn't know her name, and somehow it was as if he knew that. He wanted to point it out and make me look like some weirdo stalker. Though I suppose, if I were a stalker, I would at the very least know her name. I looked to her for assistance, trying to find a way to express that I had not a damn clue what her name was. I don't know what she saw in me that made her take pity, but she sighed. "Oakley," she answered. "Owen and I met last night when he tried running me over just outside the Inn."

Oakley. The name suited her the way any name could. It just felt… right, hearing her say it. I felt myself breathe a sigh of relief at the knowledge; it was another missing piece of the puzzle to this mystifying woman. What worried me, though, was that Jacey's smile only grew at that information, "So you're the girl from last night then," he stated simply.

She shot a pointed look right at me, "You're talking about me?" she asked. "I didn't know coming to town would be police business."

I didn't get the chance to respond before the bell over the door jingled. Most of the afternoon lunch rush had passed at this hour of the evening, and it was a bit on the early side for dinner. Aside from the few stragglers like myself, Jacey, and Oakley, the place was mostly empty. I glanced up just in time to see my brother walking towards us. Austen reached out and messed up my hair, "Hey, little brother, shouldn't you be home in bed?" he queried, but then his eyes settled on Oakley. "Hello again," he nodded. "Any luck on that apartment hunt?"

She shook her head, "I haven't ventured over there yet, thought I'd get some food first." She looked between us, and it seemed everything was clicking into place for her. What confused me, though, was how Austen seemed to know more about her than I did when she had only arrived in town the night before. Noticing the confusion, Oakley glanced back at me. "I knew you two could be brothers. The fact that you are makes so much sense. Austen helped me out earlier this afternoon. I lost my phone in my travels, so he set me up with a new one. Also gave me a few pointers on places to rent and work."

"You know he only sells antique phones, right?" I asked her, a smirk tugging at my lips. Austen moved to sit in the booth next to Oakley, and his mountain man stature made her look tiny in comparison.

"You know these are only two of the four, right?" Jacey cut in, "The Hale boys have a bit of a reputation around here."

I wished I could tell her he was lying; I didn't want her asking too many questions. We had all been young, stuck in a small town. Our antics never seriously hurt anyone; I was a cop now, after all. It wasn't like we killed someone or something. Choosing to acknowledge his statement, I rolled my eyes at that, "Like your name wasn't tagged with ours every single time," I challenged.

Oakley's gaze shifted to him, "I actually didn't get your name," she told him.

He held out a hand to her, "Ethan Jacey," he answered, "But the only people who call me Ethan are my family," he chuckled. "Everyone just calls me Jacey."

There was a crinkle of amusement around her eyes before she shook her head, "I think I'll stick with Ethan," she told him. I was surprised when he only shrugged in response.

While the whole exchange was happening, my mind was reeling. Oakley was this puzzle that I couldn't figure out. The longer I focused on it and studied it, the more confusing it became. Her mannerisms were muted, almost like she was reining herself in, folding in on herself. She was like a turtle, retreating inside her shell for protection. What I couldn't figure out was why.

She was open enough with the conversation; it seemed to flow easily between the four of us. She was even willing enough to poke fun a little. I still noticed things, though: the way she leaned against the wall next to her and away from Austen, her eyes occasionally darting to the door behind me, to the aisle next to the table, to the kitchen, which had a back door. She was studying possible ways to get out.

She had come to the table willingly enough; she spoke openly with Austen as if he were an old friend. It was hard to explain. She was hard to figure out. And I knew I wouldn't rest until I figured out the next piece to the puzzle.

Lunch had turned into more of an event than I had initially planned. I had already gotten a few hours of sleep, but now, I was tired enough to know I would be able to pass out fairly quickly for the rest of the day after taking care of the two dogs. Roscoe and Justice both sat patiently at the back door, waiting to run out and chase whatever poor woodland animal happened to fall within the perimeters of my fence. They'd never hurt any animal; in fact, Justice was known for bringing me baby rabbits held gently in his mouth. Roscoe simply enjoyed the chase. I was pretty convinced he wouldn't have the first clue of what to do with a squirrel should he ever actually catch one. They were both rather thick-headed, but they were both good dogs.

I watched them bound around the backyard like a couple of puppies before heading for the bathroom. I scratched at my jaw, where a fine stubble was appearing again. If I let it go, I would have a full beard in a matter of a few days, but beards weren't my thing. However, instead of reaching for my razor to start shaving, I got caught in my own gaze in the mirror.

No surprise, I found myself thinking about her again. I wouldn't say I liked leaving things unsolved. It was one of the reasons I had become a cop in the first place. Once I latched on to something, I needed answers. I didn't have Oakley's last name, though, and I tried to tell myself there was no good reason to go digging around and looking into her. So Gratin didn't get newcomers very often, but that didn't mean this girl had anything to hide.

Maybe every instinct I had about her was wrong. Maybe I was reading too much into things. Maybe I was looking for something that wasn't there because things had been so slow around the station. My instincts were rarely wrong, but that still didn't give me license to look into the file of a seemingly innocent woman because I couldn't quiet the nagging voice at the back of my head.

Coincidentally, that voice sounded an awful lot like my mother. I had to leave the poor girl alone, but the more I tried to convince myself of that, the more questions came to mind begging to be answered.

If she was moving here on the up and up, why didn't she have a place to stay lined up?

Furthermore, why hadn't she already looked into the job climate?

She also walked into Rudy's with only one suitcase. She would have had more things if she were moving here, right?

Why had she gone through the effort of changing her appearance so drastically?

If she was here for no other reason than wanting to enjoy life in a small mountain town, why did everything about her scream that there was something more at work?

I wanted to believe that everything with Oakley was perfectly normal, and most of those questions could have logical answers if enough thought were put into it. I just couldn't shake the impossible feeling that everything wasn't on the up and up. I wanted to look into her further, but I also didn't want to be the cop that came sniffing around without good cause.

There was a chance that if I talked to Austen, he would give up some information on her, but I also highly doubted that. He would tell me to leave her the hell alone; she wasn't some game that needed to be won. I didn't get a prize at the end if I figured out what she was hiding. Maybe, though, if I was right in assuming she was running from something, just maybe she was the one that needed some help and just didn't know how to ask. Maybe, if I were lucky enough, I could be the one who helped her figure everything out.

It was stupid and cliché, but I had a thing for damsels in distress. It was part of the reason I had become a cop in the first place. I loved a good mystery, and I couldn't walk away from a woman in need. It was a deadly combination. Every tragic love story seemed to be focused around that. The foolish man who thought he could save the day and win the girl in the process. Unfortunately, life didn't work that way. I was likely in for a world of hurt getting involved with this girl in any capacity. I also knew there was no way I would be able to stay away from her either.

Either I spent my life wondering about that mysterious woman who breezed through Gratin, or I looked into it and maybe found things I wasn't so sure I wanted to find. I just had to decide which was more important to me, solving the mystery or saving my sanity.

Walking into the station later that night, I sighed. I wasn't expecting much of anything to happen throughout the night; that was the way of Gratin, after all. I loved my small town. It was home; but I would be lying if I tried to tell anyone that my job was anything other than boring as all fuck most of the time. Luckily, that didn't seem to matter much to me most nights. Tonight, I at least had something worth looking into.

After a bit of prying with my older brother, who mercilessly taunted me for my curiosity, I managed to get Oakley's last name from him. Of course, he wouldn't give me anything else, but it was a start. It was something that I could focus on. I wanted to know more about her; I wanted to try to understand her. Plus, she was new to town. I was a cop. It was for the safety of the town that I knew who walked the streets.

For all we knew, she was a serial killer on the lam from New York. Not that I had heard any whispers of a serial killer, but it made my point. I had to make sure she wasn't someone I needed to be keeping an eye on. Gratin didn't see a lot of crime, and I intended to keep it that way.

Yeah.

Sure.

I was doing this for the town.

I couldn't even convince myself to believe that bullshit.

I sighed as I dropped into the chair behind my desk. Jacey barely looked up from his paper. "So your mystery girl pulled up no results," he said, turning the page down enough to look at me. I could feel my eyes narrow on him.

"You looked into her?" I accused. I had no room to talk; that was precisely what I was going to do. I just didn't like that he had somehow gotten her name easier than I had. "You don't even know her last name," I pointed out bluntly.

"Morgan," he answered as he folded up his paper. "While you were too busy staring a hole through her head, I saw the name on her license. She pulled it out to get to her money to pay for her food before you went all caveman and told her to put it away. Oakley E. Morgan. For a cop, you're shit at your job."

"I got her name too," I argued, slumping back into my chair.

Jacey laughed, "How? What'd you do, shakedown Austen?" he joked, and I could only guess my expression gave me away because he only started laughing harder at that. Picking up a pen off my desk, I chucked it across the room at him, but it did little to deter his hysterics. "Sometimes I wonder how you even got a job here," he poked fun after his laughter had sobered. "But man, I have to tell you, what I found, or rather what I didn't find, kind of worries me a little."

His expression changed; he was more serious now, which had me sitting up a little straighter in my seat. It was a rare occurrence that Jacey got serious about something. Even when faced with an armed suspect, he was still known to crack jokes. So even a meager ounce of seriousness from him was a big deal. "I didn't find anything. No birth record; she's not on any census record. If I had to take a guess, she's early to mid-twenties. Which says she should be on at least one if not two census records. Nothing came back. There are no accident reports, not even a damn traffic citation. She has no credit cards in her name; the only bank account I could find she opened today. Her license was a California-issued license, but there's no listing of her in the Cali DMV; there's nothing. She's blank, man. She's a ghost."

I sighed again and pushed my fingers through my hair; I didn't like the sound of that. So maybe my serial killer theory wasn't so far-fetched after all. "Are you sure?" I asked him. A name like Oakley wasn't exactly the most common name, though. At least, not that I knew of.

"There are plenty of Oakley's that came up, but no Oakley E. Morgan. At least not around here. It's not exactly painting a pretty picture because no one is that clean. Even you and I have shit from when we were younger. Everyone has a past, except for her apparently," he answered plainly.

"Which tells me one thing," I shook my head, "She's running from something. The question is, what?"

Jacey shrugged and shook his head, "I poked the bear; I should have known better. You're not going to let this one go, are you?"

I just stared at him for a long moment. Of course, I wasn't about to let it go now. Jacey's search confirmed one thing for me. There was, in fact, a mystery at hand, and I was going to solve it.

Who are you, Oakley Morgan?'

FIVE
OAKLEY

I had managed to lay low for a few days and stay off of Officer Hale's radar. It didn't take long to figure out his schedule, and when I had to avoid the diner. The only issue was that this town was small, and the only way to completely guarantee that I wouldn't run into him was to stay put at the Inn. I couldn't sit in that room staring at the same four walls any longer, though. It hadn't taken long for me to learn that no matter where I was, whether I was back home at the manor or here in some outdated Inn, I couldn't entirely escape the feeling that I wasn't as safe as I wanted to believe.

Glancing at the time on my phone, I sighed to myself. It was twenty-to-one in the morning. The diner was closing a lot sooner than I wanted. I wasn't looking forward to the walk back to the Inn by myself in the dark in the middle of the night. It wasn't far, but it hadn't taken me long to realize just how dark it got in a small mountain town in the middle of the night.

I didn't even have the benefits of someone being at the front desk when I got there. Rudy seemed to turn in early most nights, leaving the front desk unmanned, and there was something unsettling about walking into that place when it was empty like that. He had made it more than abundantly clear to me since my arrival to town that the night I appeared, I was a "damn lucky little lady" that he was still in the office working on the books so late.

Something hadn't been adding up right. I had thought about it several times now that I could offer him my services. I was computer savvy. I could do it by hand the old-fashioned way, but technology made everything faster and smoother. Rudy was an old grump of a man, and his absolute refusal to step into the twenty-first century baffled me to no end, but I was starting to learn that under the gruff exterior, there was a kindhearted older man just very set in his ways.

Sighing to myself, I reached for my coffee cup and drained what was left of it in one sip. I was putting off leaving for as long as I possibly could, but I knew my time was ticking away quickly. Even though I kept trying to convince myself that it wasn't likely anyone would find me here. Under cover of darkness, with shadows surrounding me and a thousand and one places to hide, my anxiety was really good at convincing me that nowhere was safe. I just had to keep reminding myself that no one knew where I was, and the people of Gratin didn't know who I was.

That didn't change the fact, though, that the police hadn't had any leads on my parents' murder. Not that it was really a surprise, but that meant, in no uncertain terms, that their killer was still out there. I had found myself on more than one occasion since leaving the manor feeling like I was caught in the crosshairs. They were out there, they were watching me, and they were waiting for their chance to put an end to the Richfield name for good. I shivered at the thought that I just might have someone gunning right for me, and I had no idea who they were.

My fears didn't change anything, though. I couldn't hold up the girls who worked in the diner and keep them from going home. They had lives, things to do. It wasn't fair to keep them because I was afraid of the dark. There were actual monsters out there in the world, and I had gotten a good taste of what they were capable of. The truth of the matter was, no monsters were hiding on the streets of this small Pennsylvanian town; at least none of the caliber I had encountered. If I had to take a guess, the last murder this town had seen was probably decades ago.

I was safe here, but I could still feel those cold eyes boring into me. Maybe they weren't real, maybe they were nothing more than the figments of my frightened imagination, but that didn't stop the very thought from making the hair on the back of my neck stand.

"Will that be everything for you tonight?" the waitress asked, causing me to jump in my seat. I had been so caught up in my own thoughts and the fictitious monsters my head was creating that I hadn't heard her approach the table. I looked up at her wide-eyed, and she simply smiled tiredly in return. "Sorry," she apologized, "Didn't mean to sneak up on you like that."

I had gotten her name; she had told me her name when I sat down, but for the life of me, I couldn't remember it now. I felt terrible that it had slipped my mind so easily. That was a shadow from my past too. I had once been that girl, the one who didn't bother learning the names of those beneath me. I wanted to know these people, though. As much as it scared me that they might figure me out, I was one of them now.

I shook my head. She was staring at me, clearly waiting for a response from me. "It's fine," I managed to mutter. "I know you guys probably want to get out of here. I'll just… take the check, please."

She waved her hand at me, "We're here until one of the boys come in," she explained. "They certainly take their good ol' sweet time doing it too."

I knew it was none of my business, but I felt myself asking anyway, "The boys?" I questioned, looking at her. I was curious; sure, this was a small town. It might be good to know these things if I planned on hanging around. It was also, in large part, an attempt to stall my departure from the safety of the small diner just a little bit longer.

She smiled slightly at my question; this time there was a touch of something else there, though I couldn't tell what. "You may have met them, our night cops, Owen Hale, and Ethan Jacey." Her smile seemed to grow ever so slightly at the mention of Ethan.

Good.

Good? Wait, what? Why did I care if she had something going with Officer Hale or not? It wasn't as if I had some kind of claim over him. I mean, I had been avoiding the man like he had the damned plague or something. It wasn't safe for me to get too close to anyone anyway. I was better off if I did my best to let go of whatever random infatuation I had with him and move on.

There was something about the way he had looked at me the last time I saw him at the diner, though. It was almost like he was analyzing me in some way. I knew I should have felt naked and exposed with his eyes on me, but I didn't. It was weird. I nodded all the same, "I've met them," I answered. "Officer Hale tried running me over my first night in town."

She bobbed her head in a slight nod, "That sounds like Owen. You'll have to talk to Liv over there about that; Officer Hale is her problem," she teased before glancing back to the other woman.

"He's not my problem; you gotta get it out of your head that something is going on between Hale and me," she rolled her eyes, "Not with a ten-foot pole, Fi."

She smiled again, "Don't act like you don't enjoy your twisted back and forth. Like some demented form of foreplay," she reasoned.

"Not gonna happen, Fiona," Liv shook her head, "Besides, you're one to talk. What about Ethan? Follows you around like a lost puppy dog, clearly he…" she challenged.

"We're not talking about him," she cut her off, her tone suddenly changing.

I watched their back and forth, and despite their snappy tone, there was a whisper of a smile on either's face. "Are you two…?" I started to ask.

"Sisters," the one across from me nodded. "Twins, actually. She's the evil one."

I couldn't help myself; I laughed at that. It felt so good to really laugh and know it wasn't forced for once. Ever since finding my parents, I hadn't had much to smile about, let alone laugh at. "Well, okay then."

She held her hand out to me, "I'm Fiona, and that's Olivia. But don't call her that, you know, unless you want a fork through your hand." She shrugged. "She goes by Liv."

I took her hand and shook it, "Oakley," I introduced myself.

"I love that name!" she told me before releasing my hand. "I wish I had a name like that. You know?" I shook my head. "Just…interesting. Fiona O'Dell. It's just so… bleh." She shrugged.

"Well, my last name is nothing special," I tried to comfort her. The truth was, before everything, my last name had been the source of all my power. It was what carried weight; it got me into the hottest clubs and dinner reservations at all the popular restaurants. Unfortunately, it had also brought on a lot of fraudulent dates, guys looking to marry into the Richfield fortune; but I wasn't a Richfield anymore. "Morgan," I told her, "Oakley Morgan."

She sighed, "Even that has a nice ring to it."

Liv walked over to the table, "Quit your bitching," she shook her head at her sister, "you got the better deal, Olivia O'Dell, not sure what Mom and Dad were thinking. Too many O's going on."

"Nuh-uh," Fiona argued, "Yours has the alliteration thing going; that's a hot commodity these days."

"Whatever." Liv turned to walk away just as the bell over the door rang. Fiona glanced around me, only to sigh when she saw who it was. "Hale," Liv greeted.

I couldn't help myself; I glanced back over my shoulder at his name. I was drawn to him like a moth to a flame, but much like that moth, I knew if I dared to get too close, I was going to get burned.

When he turned his gaze towards me, it felt like every nerve ending in my body came alive all at once. I didn't understand the pull this man had over me. I barely knew him. That didn't change the fact that I had never experienced something so totally all-encompassing before. I was used to being the one in control. When it came to Officer Owen Hale, though, he held all the cards close to his chest, and I really didn't like it.

I didn't breathe again until his blue gaze shifted off of me and to the woman that had been sitting across from me. "Don't look so disappointed to see me, Fi," he joked, "You're going to give me a complex."

Liv scoffed from her position behind the counter, "I know you're used to women faking it with you, Hale, but around here, we only deal in brutal honesty."

Owen sighed and shook his head, "Can always count on you to keep a man modest, Liv," he answered. I stayed rooted to my spot in the booth watching the exchange between them. I couldn't help the bubble of jealousy from rearing its ugly head again at the way they seemed to interact. Maybe Fiona was right; perhaps they were into each other in that pull-on-the-pigtails playground way. Maybe I stood no chance at winning over a man I knew I couldn't let close anyway.

Why was everything always so damn complicated? So what? I was on the run from a cold-blooded killer, and he was a cop. He was trained for this kind of thing, but to admit that also meant admitting who I really was, that I had lied to him in the first place. Most importantly, it meant possibly giving up the location of my little sanctuary if he started poking around. As tiny as it seemed the night I arrived, I was growing quite fond of Gratin, and the last thing I wanted to do was bring down the hellfire of the media on the people of this town.

So again, I was forced to ask the question, why did everything have to be so damn *complicated*?! I had to remind myself that, cop or not, he didn't ask to be part of my problems. I couldn't bring myself to ask that of him either. Because from the brief interactions I had with him, I knew he was the kind of man who would never say no to a woman in need.

Realizing that I was intently watching the back and forth between the three of them, I shook my head and turned back around to face the table again. I toyed with my coffee cup, running my finger around the smooth rim of it as I tried to figure out how I could sneak out without anyone noticing me leave. I wanted to minimize my interaction with him to save any overthinking later. My hopes of any of that were dashed when that voice came from behind me again.

"Rudy toss you out or something?" he asked, the amusement evident in his tone. I'm glad my situation with the old Inn owner entertained him. Every muscle in my body locked up at the direct contact. I was pathetic. I knew if I turned around, his blue gaze would be zeroed in on me again. He made me so weak-kneed that it was much safer if I just didn't turn around. I could pretend like I didn't hear him.

I had been raised better than that, though; that was about as rude as I could be. My mother would cringe at the very thought of me being that cold towards someone, especially someone who had been nothing but nice to me: him and his brother. I took a breath before slowly spinning back around and meeting that gaze.

"N-no," I answered, my cheeks flushing at the way I had stumbled over my words slightly. I cleared my throat and sighed, calming the bundle of nerves in my stomach. "I hardly see him," I continued, "and when I do, he's usually whining about all that damned technology."

He laughed at that, "Sounds like Rudy."

The truth was, I didn't like being in the Inn more than I had to be. I was reasonably sure I was the only tenant of the Inn. I didn't like being there alone. Left to my own thoughts like that, my imagination tended to run a little wild.

Okay.

Maybe it was more accurate to say a lot wild.

It was as if I could feel eyes on me, piercing through me. I knew it was ridiculous. No one knew who my parent's killer even was. No one from my old life knew I was in Gratin. There was no way someone was watching me; but anytime I walked outside, especially at night, it felt like a million tiny ants were marching their way across my skin. The hairs on the back of my neck stood at attention like little soldiers guarding me. Every muscle in my body tightened as I prepared to run. The eyes were cold too. I could feel their icy caress as they carried through the darkness, causing a shiver to wind its way down my spine.

I wasn't about to tell Officer Owen Hale any of that, though. I didn't want him to think of me as some damsel in distress. I had made it this far on my own. I could keep moving right along; I didn't need his help. I shouldn't *want* his help. To be perfectly honest, I was so back and forth about how I felt about him thinking of me at all, in any capacity.

On the one hand, it fell into the same realm of reasoning as me thinking of him in any way. It shouldn't be happening, simply put. On the other hand, the very idea of me being the thing to tangle his thoughts sent my heart racing in my chest. There were butterflies in my stomach.

Butterflies.

I couldn't begin to say when I last felt butterflies for someone. It wasn't fair that that man could turn me, Elizabeth Richfield, heiress and playgirl, into such a bumbling, stuttering idiot. The truth was, I wasn't Elizabeth Richfield anymore, I lacked the power and confidence that came with the name. I was Oakley Morgan now, and I was still discovering exactly who she was. For all I knew, she was someone who had no idea how to talk to a man as drop-dead gorgeous as Owen Hale.

I felt something tickling at the edge of my mind when I realized I had been zoned out and caught up in my own thoughts the whole time. I blinked a few times to refocus myself again, only to be met with that gorgeous blue gaze. There was a look of amusement coloring those eyes, a half-smile playing at his lips. I felt like a dancing monkey. Only here to amuse the people of Gratin with my tricks. "W-what?" By the look on his face, I could tell that he had said something I clearly missed. Great.

My question only seemed to amuse him more. His lips stretched out into a full smile. "I said, they're closing up shop here, are you headed back to the Inn?" he repeated slowly as if I simply hadn't understood the words coming out of his mouth.

I looked around the small diner. Both women were busy cleaning up, stacking chairs, and wiping down. Owen had two coffees in his hand, ready to leave. I had no other choice at this point. I nodded slowly in response. Everything else in Gratin was now closed. I had to go back to the Inn where it was just me and my shadow-cast demons. "Yeah, I guess I am," I finally answered. It was only a few blocks up the road, but I dreaded every step of that walk. Being out in the open made my anxiety worse. At least deadbolted in the safety of my room, I could close the blinds and do my best to attempt to lock the world and all its horrors outside.

He nodded towards the doors, "Do you want a ride?" he offered, "I have to drive right by Rudy's place to get back to the station."

A ride? That meant being in a confined space with him, all alone. Yes, the drive would be short, but I knew it would be the longest two minutes of my life. Which was worse, though? Walking, exposed to any one of my numerous nightmare creatures, or getting a ride from the friendly officer who had taken over my thoughts. Both offered endless possibilities for overthinking and anxiety. The scales were definitely tipped more in his favor when weighing the two options. "Don't lie to the poor girl, Hale," Liv called from the counter, making me look up. She smirked when I met her gaze. "It's the complete opposite direction," she pointed out.

Owen sighed at that, "This town is fucking tiny Liv, I can drop her off and still make it back to the station before Jacey starts bitching," he countered.

I shook my head, "I don't want you going out of your way," I started, "I can…" I struggled over the last word before finally forcing it out. "…walk."

He zeroed that perfect gaze in on me again, and I suddenly found myself completely unable to tell him no. "Let me give you a ride," he asked, "please?"

I dipped my head in a nod before I realized what I was doing. It was too late to take it back now. "Okay, yes, that would be great," I forced myself to say. "Thank you."

This man was going to be the end of me. I could feel it.

I was honestly surprised when she agreed to let me drive her back to the Inn. From what I had learned so far about her, Ms. Oakley Morgan was fiercely independent. She didn't seem the type to let anyone do anything for her unless it was on her terms. Looking at her, I saw the trepidation in her eyes. Something was bothering her.

I wasn't sure in the two-minute drive down the street that I would be able to get her to talk at all, but I could certainly try. She was this mystery that just kept getting more mysterious. I knew it was utterly stereotypical for the cop to be enthralled by the new, mystifying woman in town, but I couldn't help it. I was a walking, talking stereotype. At least I owned that fact.

I watched as Oakley left the money for her coffee on the table with the check, but before she could leave, Fiona came up to her with a to-go coffee cup in her hand. "Here, it's on the house," she offered. She gave a thankful nod before taking the cup, but then Fiona set her sights on me, and I sighed. She stepped in front of me and held up a bag. "Doughnuts for our favorite annoying cops," she smiled. Like I said, walking, talking cop stereotype.

"Thank you," I answered, "But you know Jacey is the one who's gonna eat them."

Fiona shook her head at me, "Make him share," she demanded, "Or he'll have me to deal with."

I laughed at that, "You know he'd enjoy that a little too much," I warned her.

"Well then, he can answer to Liv," she answered.

I smiled, "One of these days, one of you is going to cave," I told her, "But I gotta go." I nodded towards Oakley before she could argue with me.

She nodded, "Go, get outta here, we got work to do."

We said our goodbyes, I called out to Liv too, but she only waved a hand at me as she counted down the register. The sisters couldn't be more different sometimes, but their dynamic worked well for the diner.

Turning towards Oakley, who was huddled by the door holding her coffee cup with both hands, I smiled slightly. She was definitely uneasy. That much was evident in the way she carried herself, but right then, I could tell it was far worse. I nodded towards the door, pushing it open for her to walk out into the cool summer night air first. Neither one of us said a word as we approached my squad car. She waited for me to climb in first and lean over to unlock her door for her before she dared to climb in with me. Then, after she had buckled her seatbelt securely, I turned the car on.

Glancing over at her once, she had her hands in her lap, still holding her coffee cup securely, with her eyes cast down. "Everything okay?" I asked, but the sudden break in the silence made her jump slightly, her coffee sloshing out the hole in the lid and over her hand. Reaching for a napkin in the cupholder between us, I held it out to her. The question hanging in the air between us.

She looked from the napkin in my hand to meet my gaze, her eyes wide like a deer caught in oncoming headlights. Frozen with fear, knowing the collision was coming but unable to do a damned thing about it. "Y-yeah," she stumbled.

Taking the napkin from me, she wiped at her hand. Anything really to keep her gaze off of me. Was I really that bad? It hadn't escaped my notice, though, that that was the third time she had stuttered over her words since I had entered the diner. Did I make her nervous? It was something I could only assume. The deeper question here was, was it me, or was it my badge? She had been squirrely with Jacey too that day at dinner.

"Look, Oakley, I know we don't really know a lot about each other," I started as I easily shifted the car into reverse. "But if you need to talk about anything, I'm happy to listen," I offered. I knew it was likely a useless offer, but I had to do something. She merely shrugged in response. I didn't know what else I could do.

I backed my car out of the parking spot and turned onto the empty street, sighing to myself. At this hour of the night, there was no one out on the roads. It was almost peaceful. Night has always been my favorite time of the day. I felt like I did my best work after the sun had gone down, which was probably why the lieutenant had put Jacey and me on the night crew in the first place. The drive back to the Inn was silent save for the soft music coming from the radio. Oakley didn't look my way once after that initial glance, which was fine. If I had felt her eyes on me, I would have been compelled to meet her gaze. They were gorgeous, and as much as I hated seeing that fear in them. I couldn't seem to look away.

Pulling into the parking lot of the old Inn, I put the car in park. I expected her to jump from the car before it came to a complete stop, but she didn't move a muscle. Not even to reach for the handle to get out. She was undoubtedly a curious creature. "Oakley?" I coaxed softly.

She didn't look at me. Instead, she looked out the passenger side window at the building. "Is it just me, or does this place give you the creeps?" she asked. "It's just… I don't know. I feel like someone is watching me when I'm here. Even now, sitting in the safety of your cruiser, with a cop, I can still feel someone's eyes on me."

Well, that was interesting. It was something that I could help with, at least. "Do you want me to check around?" I asked her. "I can make sure the area is safe. It might give you some peace of mind." She didn't turn to look at me, but in her reflection in the glass of the window, I could see how haunted she looked. This ran deeper than just a simple case of nerves and anxiety. I knew there was more than met the eye with her, but I wasn't sure how deep it went. Something was troubling her.

"That might help," she finally answered me. Her voice was so soft I almost missed it, but I could hear it, the doubt coloring her tone. She didn't think it would help at all. What else could I do? If she wasn't willing to talk to me about what was going on, there was only so much I could do for her. All the same, it didn't stop me from wanting to try. I had to do something to calm that troubled look in those green eyes.

I nodded once and reached for the handle of my door. "I'll be back then," I told her. "I'll lock you in," I added as I pushed the door open. I hit the lock on my way out of the car before closing the door. I didn't even know what I was looking for. For all I knew, I was looking for some kind of ghost that was haunting her.

I headed for the left first, toward an alleyway that lined the side of the Inn. If someone was actually hiding out, it was the most logical place. Pulling my gun from its holster, I held it close to my side as I pulled my flashlight from my belt too. I clicked it on and stepped into the empty alley, shining the light in every possible hiding spot. I knew she could be imagining the eyes on her. It wasn't uncommon for the victims of some kind of crime to feel like the perpetrator was still out there, watching them.

Victim.

I don't know why I immediately went to that, but everything about Oakley's posture, the way her gaze was downcast, the way she tried to make herself smaller in the seat. Especially tonight. It all screamed victim to me. I lived in a small town, and I had always worked for the Gratin PD. As the city cops liked to point out, we had never truly witnessed actual crime here, but I knew the difference between the victim and someone who had committed a crime.

Either Oakley deserved the best actress award, or my gut was right. She had been through something. There was nothing out there after her. Nothing more than a haunting past. Maybe that was why there was no record of her.

I checked the last corner of the alley before turning back to the entrance. I scanned the front of the Inn and across the parking lot. I looked across the street for any sign of movement, and there was nothing. Going back over to my squad car, I knocked on the window once, and she jumped in her seat.

Seeing it was me, she scrambled across to unlock the door for me. I slid back into my seat before putting my flashlight and gun on the dash. "It's all clear," I told her, glancing her way again. "There's nothing out there."

She nodded, her gaze finally finding mine again. She didn't seem to convinced that there was nothing out there. "Are you sure?" she breathed. "I can't explain it, Owen, but I just… someone is watching me. I know I sound crazy," she shook her head and pushed her fingers through her dark hair. When she met my gaze again, tears were smothering that beautiful green. It was like a stake straight to the heart.

I took a chance; I reached out and put my hand on her knee, "You're not crazy," I promised. "I don't feel comfortable leaving you here in this state," I said. "I don't want you freaking out like this. Rudy's a good guy, but he's not the best with emotions. At this hour, he'd be your only option and he'll call in the whole damned calvary before trying to help you himself. We have a cot back at the station that Jacey and I sometimes crash on when we have particularly slow nights. You can come back with me; no one will touch you if Jacey and I are both there."

I knew it was crazy to offer up being her personal security guard, but I couldn't in good conscience leave her to fend for herself. There was no telling what levels of hysteria she might reach if she thought someone was after her. The last thing we needed was her snapping and doing something crazy.

She studied me for a long moment, contemplating my offer. I could see the wheels turning in her head as she must have run through every possible outcome. Then, slowly she nodded, just the slightest dip of her chin. I almost missed it. I would have if I hadn't been staring at her so intently, studying every flicker that crossed her gaze. "Okay," she whispered.

"Yeah?" I questioned, and she bobbed her head again, this time a little more forcefully. "Okay. Is there anything you want to grab while we're here?" I asked. She turned back and looked up at the Inn. She seemed to study every crack in the stucco, every hint of discoloration. "I'll come in with you," I amended. She really didn't want to be left alone.

Plus, if I took her back to the station with me, it would give me a chance to talk to her. It didn't appear as if she would be sleeping any time soon. In fact, I wasn't sure when the last time she even blinked was. I pushed the door open again on my side. When she didn't get out, I grabbed my gun and flashlight from the dash and tucked them both away before walking around and opening her door for her too. Holding out my hand, I wanted to offer her some kind of comfort. I worried about what being so close to her would do to my sanity, but it was a risk I was willing to take. This gorgeous woman needed someone.

She had come to Gratin completely alone; there was no telling if she had anyone else that could be there for her. If I could find a way to help her, I was going to. I couldn't bring myself to leave her to fend for herself. She looked up at me before slipping her hand into mine. The contact was electric. My heart jump-started in my chest; I could feel my palms tingle with the possibility of sweat. Something passed between us in that moment, a silent understanding. I would do everything in my power to help her, and if I were lucky, she would let me.

I dropped her hand as soon as she was safely out of the car. I didn't want to push any of her boundaries more than necessary. Tonight had already forced her to the limits of her comfort zone. I could tell by the way she watched me that she was studying me just like I did her. She was trying to decipher my every move, figure out a motive behind my actions, trying desperately to discern if the good guy image was real or not. I couldn't blame her for her interest. She was wary of me; after all, I wasn't anything more to her than a kind stranger at that point.

Motioning for her to lead the way into the building, I followed closely behind, my hand coming to rest on the butt of my gun as I scanned the area for anything remotely suspicious. I honestly believed that there wasn't anything she needed to fear in my tiny town, but I didn't want her to think I thought she was crazy.

Sure, her fears were unfounded at the moment, but that didn't mean to her they weren't real. Something was scaring her, whether it was all in her head or not. Which meant I had to find a way to get her to talk instead, to get her to admit to what was really going on inside her head. She was only letting me in so far, though. Those walls still stood just as strong around her as they did the night we had met outside the Inn almost a week ago. I may have breached the very perimeter, but I was hardly any closer to getting to the truth of who she was. She was playing her hand very carefully.

I stared down the hall as she unlocked the door and immediately moved to gather the things she would need for the night. With a passing glance around the room, I could tell there was nowhere for someone to hide. There was no closet; the underside of the bed was boarded off. The window didn't even have curtains, just those cheap plastic blinds. There was hardly a bathroom for her to use.

No wonder Gratin never saw much in the way of long-term tourism. It was mostly day trips in the summer, people who wanted to escape for the day. If this were the lodging offered, though, I could see why they often chose not to stay the night.

I made my way around the room, coming to a stop in front of the only window in the place. "That's where I feel it most," her voice surprised me. Glancing back over my shoulder at her, I nodded for her to explain. "I close the blinds, but there's a few missing in the middle. So someone could still get a rather good view in here, you know?" Again, I knew all of this could possibly be a very vivid creation of her imagination, but I turned my gaze back out into the darkness all the same.

This time I looked at the buildings across the street with a different perspective. I scrutinized every window, looking for the slightest movement, anything to give away that someone was indeed over there. I was about to turn away when something reflected off the streetlights in one window as if something had shifted behind the panes of glass. I turned to face it more; I didn't even want to blink in case I missed it, anything to validate her demons, but it never happened again.

I knew what I saw, though; something had been there in that window. It was yet another thing to add to my to-do list for the next few days. I was going to check it out and figure out what was or wasn't there. "Owen?" Her voice startled me again; it always surprised me when she spoke, no matter how soft. I turned away from the window, annoyed by my almost discovery, but I could see the worry creasing at the corners of her eyes. I tried to relax enough to smile at her.

"You ready to go?" There was no need to tell her about what I did or didn't see. If it were something, I could look into it, I could fix it for her, and she could move on with her life. There was no reason to get her all worked up if it was nothing.

She nodded slowly, not sure how to take the shift in my demeanor. Finally, she held up her bag, "We can go," she answered. "Please."

Even with me in the room, my hand now gripping the butt of my gun, she was still so unsure. I consciously uncurled my fingers from the metal; she didn't need to see that. It would only heighten her panic. If I stayed calm, I could hopefully get her to calm down too. I dropped my chin in an affirmative nod before offering a hand to take her bag. She seemed to understand the gesture and almost anxiously handed it over to me. I shouldered the backpack-style bag before walking out into the empty hallway first, standing guard while she locked the door.

We walked in silence back out to my cruiser. I opened the door for her and allowed her to slide in before shutting the door behind her. I could feel a twinge in the air as I rounded around the front of my vehicle. Immediately my gaze shifted back to that window, the one where I had seen that flash not ten minutes before. I stood next to the car, my hand instinctively going back to my gun.

Now there was no question in my mind that Oakley didn't imagine it. There was someone in the darkness watching us. This town, much like most, had its crazies, but we knew who they were and where they resided. For the most part, they were harmless. This person, whoever it was, they meant to harm. Even through the distance and the darkness, it felt like we locked eyes for a moment. I didn't know what they wanted with Gratin's newest resident, but I did know that I would do what I did best. Being a cop and protecting this town was everything to me. Oakley was part of that now. If I had my way, no one was going to touch her.

I tossed her bag into the back seat before climbing into the driver's seat, ignoring Oakley's questioning glances as I threw the car in reverse and pointed it towards the station.

The way he froze up, his hand going to hold his gun, had my heart hammering away in my chest again. Was it possible that everything I had been trying to convince myself wasn't real actually was? Before I could dwell on it for too long, he jumped into the driver's seat and expertly backed out of the spot.

The quick drive to the station was mostly silent. His posture remained rigid in his seat. From my spot next to him, I could see his blue eyes darting back and forth, surveying the area as we drove. I didn't know what had set him on edge back in the parking lot, and I wasn't entirely sure I wanted to know. If it had been enough to make him so tense, there was no telling what it would do to me.

Turning away from him, I stared sightlessly out the passenger window. Too caught up in my own thoughts to really register everything around me. I wasn't sure what to make of the complete one-eighty in his demeanor. He had gone from Owen: a sweetheart of a guy I was having a hell of a time keeping at a distance, to rigid, almost cold, and calculating Officer Hale. It was better for all involved if I just stayed quiet for the remainder of the drive, giving him the peace he needed to do whatever it was he was doing.

It wasn't until we pulled into the station on the north edge of town that he finally breathed a sigh of relief, and I turned back in time to see his shoulders slump forward as he relaxed in his seat. There was a part of me that had decided I wanted to know. Whatever had caused him to tighten up the way he had, it could mean all the difference to me. It was better to know my demons were out there after all. Ignorance wasn't always bliss. For me, it could mean the difference between figuring out this life or being buried next to my parents with an epitaph stating how a young life was lost too soon. I sure as hell didn't want that to be my legacy. Yeah, it was better to know.

"Owen?" His name passed my lips before I had fully given my vocal cords permission to speak. The curiosity in me had swelled to exponential heights. I had to know.

He swiveled his blue gaze to focus on mine, his eyebrow over his right eye arched ever so slightly in question. I couldn't help the slight squeak that escaped me at that adorable look. My fingers burned to reach out and run over that peaked eyebrow to smooth it back down.

No.

I had to focus. Now that we were back where he felt comfortable, it was apparent he was more relaxed, having switched back to the aforementioned 'good guy Owen.' "Yeah?" he answered, that same amusement from the diner playing at his features. I didn't want to take that away.

The way he was looking at me was more than clear that he didn't have the first clue what I was about to ask him. "Back at the Inn…." I started, and I saw the understanding cross his gaze. The amusement vanished. "Outside, when we got in the car," I pushed a little more. His whole body instantly stiffened again at the mere mention of it. "You saw something, didn't you?"

He dropped his gaze from mine before clearing his throat. He was trying to come up with a cover story. I didn't want some line to try and make me feel better. I wanted the truth. He didn't realize just how imperative it was to my well-being, and I couldn't explain that to him. "Please," I added before he could speak, "tell me the truth."

He sighed and looked back up at me, the indecision still playing across his eyes, but he nodded so slightly that I thought I had imagined it at first. "Yes," he answered. "Across the street, there was something in one of the windows. But this town is full of nosy neighbors. So I have to look to see specifically whose house that was. I could explain it all away, Oakley. You're new in town. The neighbors want to get to know you, even if that means spying on you through your hotel room window." I watched him for a long moment trying to decipher if he was telling me what he really believed. All I saw in that cool blue was total honesty. "I was going to go back in the morning to check it out."

Okay. I could live with that. It wasn't as if the answers would be found right then and there. He was clearly taking it seriously enough to have the forethought to look into it and make sure it was honestly nothing. That was more concern than I had gotten from the cops who had run my parents' investigation. I leaned back in my seat, my head coming to rest against the headrest while I studied him. "Thank you," I answered softly. "It's just nice to know that maybe I'm not crazy after all."

He smiled again, and the pitter-patter was back. God, this man would be the death of me. When he determined that no more questions were coming from me, he pushed out of the car and grabbed my bag from the back seat before meeting me on my side of the vehicle. "I hope you're ready," he exhaled. "Jacey is going to be a pain in the ass about this. Just warning you now."

"Tell him I have a stalker, and you're just protecting me like any white knight would do," I teased as he locked the car. He had the coffee from the diner in one hand and my bag slung over his shoulder. Dammit. I knew I had forgotten something in the room back at the Inn. My coffee was sitting on the nightstand next to the bed. Oh well. It was too late now.

"Trust me, that will only make it worse," he laughed as he opened the door to the station for me, ushering me in ahead of him.

I glanced back over my shoulder at him. A grin played at my lips. "And why's that?" I inquired.

He shook his head, "Top secret, I can't tell you," he joked. With the tension slipping from both of us, I was surprised to find that I was actually looking forward to spending the night in a police station. The last time I had done it, it hadn't been nearly as much fun as I was hoping this could be, and I had only just arrived.

The longer I spent in Gratin, though my time here had been short so far, the more I found that I didn't miss my old life. I missed my parents, I missed Abraham and Elisa, and the jury was still out on whether or not I missed the other vineyard socialites that had masqueraded as my friends, but I didn't miss my old life. I didn't miss going out every night and getting so drunk I could barely stand. I didn't miss getting picked up by the cops and the tabloids splashing my picture all over the cover of yet another magazine. I didn't miss the look of disappointment in my father's eyes as he tried to make me understand that I was meant to take over Richfield Winery one day.

Sure, I had come to my senses a little since then, but my parents' murder really brought everything into perspective for me. I only had this one life. I really needed to make the most of it. I needed to make it count. I wished there had been a way for me to save the company too. I had known, though, that if I had stayed and taken over the family business, they would most definitely have come for me next. Maybe we didn't know the specifics of who *they* were, but I didn't have a doubt in my mind that they were after the business in some respect.

"Oakley," Owen's voice broke through to me, my eyes widening as I refocused on his face. We were still standing in the lobby of the station. I really had to stop getting so caught up when he was around. "Thought I'd lost you there for a moment."

I pushed my fingers through my hair as I tried to make sense of things again. "I'm sorry, what were you saying?"

He smiled, the right side tipping up slightly more than the left. "It was nothing important." He motioned for me to start down the hallway to my right. "The office space is at the end of the hall and to the left. The room with the cot is to the right. Which I guess will be your room for tonight."

I followed his directions to the end of the hall, my hand coming to rest on the door handle to the room with the cot. I knew I needed to try to sleep. I hadn't been sleeping much at all since I had started feeling those eyes watching me. But now, in the safety of the station, I could feel how much I needed it. Yet, at the same time, I was buzzing with this weird energy that only seemed to happen when Owen was close to me. I knew I needed sleep, but sleep meant walking away from him. "I guess I should...." I opened the door a little.

Owen nodded, "If you need anything, Jacey and I are both right across the hall," he promised.

"Thank you again," I stated as he handed me my bag. I slipped into the room and closed the door behind me. I could hear the ribbing he was taking across the hall, Jacey questioning what he was doing bringing a girl to the station. I stepped away from the door before I could hear Owen's answer. I wasn't sure I wanted to know the truth about how he felt about me. Not yet anyway, I wanted to live in my little fantasy that someday everything would work out, and he would know the truth about me, and we could be together. I knew that wasn't possible. The lies ran too deep. A girl could dream.

I took in my surroundings for the night, feeling oddly comforted by the fact that there were no windows in the room. I was safe here. That was an odd feeling for me. I couldn't remember the last time I had actually felt safe. I walked over and sat on the edge of the cot before changing slowly into the pajamas I had grabbed, a pair of fleece bottoms with an old t-shirt. Maybe I could bring back Elizabeth Richfield just long enough to teach Oakley Morgan a thing or two about how to dress. Especially now that there was a hot cop involved. I looked down at my attire for a long moment. This would just have to do.

Slipping my shoes back on, I walked over to the door and opened it a crack. The two men's voices carried easily into the room. I needed sleep in case that needed repeating for the third time, but I couldn't bring myself to try to sleep just yet. I stood silently for a moment; I knew I shouldn't be eavesdropping, but maybe there was a chance Owen would tell Jacey more about what he had seen than he was willing to say to me.

"Well, what about Fiona?" Jacey asked. "She's got that spare room since Liv moved out. It would give her a roommate, and it would get her out of that Inn."

Out of the Inn? Were they talking about finding me a place?

"She'd have to get a job, but Austen said he pointed her towards Mama Buchannan. She's been saying for a while she needs an extra set of hands around the shop," Owen answered.

I pulled open the door a little more, the hinges creaking in protest. I cringed as both men stopped talking. Well, my cover was blown. This was why I wasn't the one who was a cop. I stepped out into the hall and walked over to the office door. "I can't sleep," I told them, "Mind if I hang out here for a little while?"

I barely caught the smirk on Jacey's face because I was almost immediately swallowed by the ocean blue again. It was Jacey who answered my question, though. "Sure," he laughed – for what reason, I wasn't entirely sure. "I was thinking of going out and patrolling again anyway." At the very least, that seemed to snap Owen out of his momentary daze as his stare snapped from me back to his partner. It was my turn to smile; at least, I wasn't the only one.

"I was just out there," Owen pointed out to him. Jacey only stared back, waiting for understanding to dawn on him. After a few silent seconds, he nodded and mumbled, "Oh. Yeah. Right." Maybe there was part of the conversation that I had actually missed while I had been in the room that was serving as my bedroom for the night.

Jacey pushed back from his desk and stood up, stretching his arms up over his head. If I hadn't met Owen first, I would really understand why Fiona was into him. She tried to deny it, but it was fairly obvious. He was tall and lean, his blond hair was kept tousled and messy, and there was a spark of mischievousness in his dark brown gaze. It was also abundantly clear with the way his uniform shirt pulled tight as he stretched; he hid a nice body beneath it. Plus, he was fun, at least from what I had seen so far. He was clearly the more amusing of the two.

I couldn't help it, though; in my opinion, he just didn't compare to his partner. "You can have my seat," he offered, "more comfortable than the chairs we put the perps in."

"Perps?" I queried, my amusement heavily tinting my tone. "I find it hard to believe Gratin has *perps*." This town seemed too small and quiet even to begin to imagine there being some sort of seedy underbelly.

"We take jaywalking very seriously around here," he kidded. I couldn't help it; a laugh bubbled from somewhere within me at that.

Owen shook his head, "Don't laugh at him. Then he'll start thinking he's actually funny."

"Shut up, Hale," he shot back, "I'm hilarious. If you removed that stick from your ass, you'd see it." As he stepped by, he smacked Owen on the back of the head, causing a few strands of hair to fall over his forehead. I wanted nothing more than to push them back into place gently. My fingers curled into the hem of my shirt at my side as I tried to resist the temptation.

"You know, I just feel so safe knowing the two of you are protecting this town when it's at its most vulnerable," I retorted sardonically, but I couldn't fight the smile that was desperately pushing its way back across my lips. Of course, I wanted them to believe I was actually serious, but there was no use in fighting it.

"You should really watch how much time your girl spends with Liv," Jacey gave Owen a rather pointed look, but all I could focus on was those two words now seared into my brain, *his girl*. I really shouldn't have loved the way that sounded as much as I did. I had always despised those couples who were so proud to say they belonged to someone else. I hated it even more when a guy called me his, like he owned me in some fashion. I didn't belong to anyone. All the same, though, I liked the idea of being his. It went against everything I had ever stood for, but likewise, me being his, wouldn't that make him mine too?

I could feel the heat from a blush creeping up my chest and neck and across my face. That only seemed to amuse Jacey more. He was poised to say something when I fixed my best withering stare on him. By some miracle, Owen had missed the whole exchange. And I wanted nothing more at that moment than to keep it that way.

"Don't you have somewhere to be?" I asked Jacey.

Wrong move.

"Looks like someone wants her one-on-one time with Officer sweet ass," he remarked, staring me down, silently daring me to challenge him. That comment took me by surprise. I guess I just hadn't expected him to be so forward about how he viewed his partner. "Next time you get the chance, check it out. He's earned the nickname. Maybe if you ask nicely, he'll even let you feel it."

Owen huffed, "That damned nickname needs to vanish, just like you." He waved Jacey off. "She's right, Jacey; you've got somewhere to be." He shot him with a knowing look and a pointed nod to the lobby, and the man standing near me sighed. Yeah, I definitely missed something. By the way they weren't really saying anything; I could hazard a pretty good guess what it was that Jacey had to run off to do in the middle of the night. That seemed to snap him out of his taunting of us, and he turned for the door, grabbing his keys on the way by. We got nothing more than a wave over his shoulder in farewell.

I glanced toward Owen, not really sure what to do next. I didn't want to interrupt any of the work he had to get done. Just because it was the middle of the night for me didn't mean it was for him. We were smack in the middle of his workday. Night. Whatever. Before I could worry myself over it too much, though, he motioned to the empty desk chair behind Jacey's desk. "Have a seat," he offered.

Thrilled that I didn't have to go back into the pseudo guest room anytime soon, I dropped into the vacant chair. Jacey was right. At the very least, it was more comfortable than the chairs sitting in the corner of the room appeared to be.

I sank back into the chair and looked across the desks to Owen, who lounged comfortably in his seat. How had I hardly noticed how good he looked in his pressed uniform? The lines were so crisp and clean; he looked so put together. That was yet another surprising fact about all of this, though. Back in the life and ways of Elizabeth Richfield, I had migrated to men in uniforms; they had always been my biggest weakness. This man, however, I never seemed to make it past his eyes. I met his gaze, and I got stuck.

I hated that my life had become a Before and an After, but if this had to be my After, I was glad I had seemed to find a friend. Sure, he played to every weakness I had ever known, but it was nice all the same. I could do this on my own. I knew that. I had to believe that if I wanted to survive, but it was also nice to know that maybe I didn't have to.

EIGHT
OWEN

At first, neither one of us said anything. The truth was, I didn't know what to say. The silence hung in the air between us, but it wasn't awkward. There was a mountain of paperwork sitting on my desk, forms that needed to be filled out, incident reports that needed to be written, and a shit ton of old case files that needed to be filed away, but I couldn't bring myself to do any of that. Not with the gorgeous woman sitting across from me, studying my every move.

Oakley was a curious creature; I had already determined that much. I knew she was running from something but determining what had proven to be a bit more of a challenge. The way she wasn't totally afraid to stand her ground signified that she wasn't running from an abusive ex. Abuse victims tended to wear their scars a little more visibly. They weren't always physical scars that could be seen, but the signs were there if someone was trained enough to spot them. They weren't there with Oakley. The shadow in her eyes, though, the way her smile never quite seemed to reach them, that told a story. She was strong and independent, but she was haunted by something.

I wanted to know more. I wanted to know everything I could about this woman. "So…" I started slowly, not wanting to spook her back to her makeshift room.

"So…" she repeated, kicking her feet up on Jacey's desk. Damn it, why did she have to be so adorable?

"Tell me about yourself, Oakley," I requested. "Doesn't have to be anything huge. I'd just like to get to know the mysterious woman who showed up in my town in the middle of the night," I smiled at her to show I meant nothing by it.

She shrugged, "There's not much to tell," she tried. "I'm jobless. Homeless. But those aren't surprises to you," she clicked her tongue as she fell silent again. I could tell she was trying to determine what was safe to say to me.

I leaned forward on my desk slightly, studying her every feature. This woman would be one hell of a poker player with how she mostly managed to keep a straight face. She had tells, but nothing I could actually work with. It was more than evident that I wasn't going to get anything from her unless she decided she was ready to talk.

I sighed and sat back again, looking across the desks at her. "Jacey and I were actually talking about that," I allowed the slight change in topic. "Instead of getting that apartment above the flower shop. Fiona from the diner has a spare room. We were thinking of talking to her to see if we can get you out of the Inn. Maybe having someone around will calm those anxieties you've been having," I suggested. "Plus, she lives in one of those row homes just off the main street through town. She's a middle unit, which severely cuts back on windows."

She sighed and glanced down at her hands for a second, fiddling with her fingers. "That would actually be a good option for me, I think," she admitted. "And Austen suggested that flower shop. Said the owner was getting a little older and looking for some help?"

I nodded, "Mama Buchannan," I smiled. "Her name is actually Meredith, but a few of us just call her Mama Buchannan," she looked at me curiously, wanting me to explain further. "Meredith has one daughter, Bailey. She and Austen were high school sweethearts. So Bailey was always over at our place, and Meredith took to him, took to all of us really."

She tilted her head to the side slightly, her dark hair barely brushing her shoulder. "How many of you are there again?" she asked me.

"Four, all boys. Austen is the oldest, then me, then Mason – he's an EMT here in town," I explained. "And the youngest is Wyatt. He took off as soon as he was old enough, and he hasn't really been back since. Visits here and there, but that's it."

She genuinely seemed interested in my family dynamic. At first, I would have pegged it as an attempt to put the focus on me to take herself out of the hot seat, but she really seemed to want to learn about me too. "And you all stayed?"

"We all went away to college; as you can tell, Gratin doesn't have one of our own. Austen actually joined the military right out of high school. It was what ended his relationship with Bailey. She couldn't handle him leaving. But we all came back as soon as we could. This place is home; it always has been." The chair creaked under her weight as she shifted slightly. Not that she could weigh that much, to begin with. "What about you? Any siblings?"

She shook her head, "No, it was always just my parents and me." There was a twinge of melancholy in her tone when she mentioned her parents. That could mean a lot of things, but I guessed that they weren't in the picture anymore. "They passed away not all that long ago," she admitted softly. "It was sudden, and I lost both of them at the same time."

I reached across and touched her hand where it had come to rest on Jacey's desk. "I'm sorry, Oakley," I told her sincerely. I couldn't imagine losing both of my parents in one go like that and to not have any siblings to lean on through it, I could only imagine what she had been going through. Everything she was doing now, maybe there was no big secret behind it. It was entirely possible that she was just looking for a new start, and Gratin happened to be her place of choice. I wasn't sure I believed that, though. Too much remained unanswered, but I had to acknowledge the possibility. There was a chance that losing her parents was the tragedy I was seeing in her gaze. It could very well be something that haunted her.

She shrugged at my condolences. Then, pulling her hand away, she wiped at her eyes a little, trying to hide the tears that had suddenly formed there. "I'm just trying to deal, you know?" she asked.

I nodded; I didn't know, though. Both of my parents were still alive and happily living in the warmth of the Florida sun. They had packed everything up and said goodbye to Gratin as soon as Wyatt was out of the house. They had said they had done their time here, that it had been long enough, and it was due time to move on. I hadn't seen it that way; seeing my childhood home go up for sale like that had been more challenging than expected. I wasn't the focus here, though.

Slowly but surely, Oakley was starting to let me in. I wanted to ask how her parents had died. That would open up so many avenues in my curiosity. The truth was, though, I was coming to care for her, at least a little. I could see how much talking about all of it was hurting her. I couldn't bring myself to keep prodding at something that was so clearly painful for her. The answers be damned. I would find out everything in time; I was sure of that much. It didn't have to be right then and there.

I leaned back in my chair, at a total loss of what to say next. I knew if I didn't say something soon, she would likely pull away again, the walls would re-erect themselves around her, and I would have lost my chance at learning anything. I couldn't make my mouth form the words needed, though. Sighing to myself, I pushed my fingers through my hair. When I looked back at her, I found that green gaze was staring right through me.

She was studying me again; I could see the wheels turning. She was trying to figure me out as much as I was trying to figure her out. Neither one of us was going to get anywhere if someone didn't just say something. "So…" I started, "Austen was trying to help you find a job, right?" I asked. I knew he had been; he had pointed her toward the flower shop. She nodded once, "Maybe I can help get you in with Mama Buchannan tomorrow?" I suggested.

She nodded again, "Okay," she answered softly. "Do you think we could talk to Fiona too?" she asked, "After tonight, I honestly don't know if I can go back there alone. I know it sounds crazy, Owen, but there was most definitely someone out there watching me. I don't know who," she was telling the truth with that. "I don't know why," she dropped her gaze and fiddled with her nails. That was a lie. She knew why someone might be following her.

I sat up again, "Oakley, look, I don't know what's going on. But I think you do," I told her gently. I was running the risk of her completely shutting down on me, but it was a risk I had to take. If I wanted to be able to help her at all, I needed to know all the facts. "And anything you tell me, it stays between you and me in this office. I promise you that. But I can't do anything to help you figure out who might be following you if you're keeping quiet about things."

She stared at me for a minute, her green gaze skimming the top edge of her glasses as she watched me over the frames. She hadn't been wearing glasses the night she had come into town. Her hair had been long and blonde. Not that this new look didn't suit her, it was just very consistent with someone on the run. I knew all the signs. I could piece together this kind of puzzle in my sleep. "I just…" she started, trying to find the right words. My guess was she wanted to answer my inquiries, but she didn't want to give me too much information. "There are people out there that I'm afraid might want to find me," she tried to explain. "But I don't know who they are…."

That was a whole mess of not-fucking-helpful. Didn't change the fact that I couldn't let her see my exasperation at her non-answer.

"Okay…" I tried prompting her. "What makes you think there would be people after you? Has anyone ever threatened you?" I asked. She shook her head. I was starting to think that her previous statements of me thinking she was simply crazy were right. If I hadn't felt it too, standing outside the Inn, I would have thought this was all in her head. Some self-created tragedy to distract from what was really going on. The thing was I *had* felt it. Someone had been watching us, both when we were in the building and again when we were getting into the cruiser to come back to the station. Someone had their sights set on her, and the way the air had stilled, I wouldn't be entirely surprised if they had had her in the crosshairs waiting for their chance to fire.

As crazy as she sounded, I couldn't help but believe that she was in legitimate danger. And if she were, I couldn't just walk away because I was getting nowhere with her. Then she'd eventually turn up as an unidentified in the morgue, and it would all be on me for not figuring it out sooner. I had to trust my gut here. Oakley Morgan wasn't a danger to anyone, but someone in the shadows was most definitely a danger to her.

I could tell she wasn't really going to answer my questions, so I needed to let it go and just figure out a way to move on. "We can talk to Fiona in the morning," I said randomly, jumping back to her living situation. "Liv moved out because she's all about having her own space, but Fiona doesn't do as well on her own. She's been kicking around the idea of looking for a roommate." It was apparent to pretty much anyone that she didn't like being left alone at night. No one in Gratin hung out in the diner until close if they had anywhere better to be. The O'Dell girls were nice and all, but Liv was surprisingly good at scaring people off.

"Are you guys sure she'd be okay with me being her roommate?" she asked; there was a touch of apprehension in her tone. "I mean, it would be amazing if she said yes, but I don't want to pressure her into it."

I simply nodded, "I think, from what I do know of you, and I've known Fi since we were kids. You two would get along. It would give her someone to talk to at home because she needs someone to talk to outside of her sister and Darian – the cook at the diner. But it would also get you out of Rudy's place. And she lives on the main road, part of our patrol route," I hinted. "She's in to open the diner. As I said, we'll ask in the morning."

Oakley looked at me, confused. "But she closed the diner; why would she be in again to open?" she asked.

I laughed, "You'll learn, Fiona never sleeps. She occasionally makes this whining noise and temporarily shuts down," I joked. "Usually once every couple of weeks." That only seemed to confuse her further, but she shook her head before resting it back against the seatback. I could tell she was tired. She, unlike Fiona, needed to sleep. "You don't have to stay up with me, you know. I'm kind of used to being up and about at this hour."

Her eyes widened slightly, "I'm not... no... actually..." she stumbled over her words. It was actually kind of adorable how easy it was to call her out like that. "It's not you I'm worried about," she finally found her footing again with what she was trying to say. "Ever since my parents died, I get these nightmares. They've been worse since I've been here and feeling like someone is watching me almost every night. And really, I just, I'd rather not be alone. If that's okay?"

Of course, it was okay. I stood up, though, and started moving the pile of boxes off the covered couch that we had in the room. No one ever used it as anything more than a messy filing cabinet. Though, if I could offer her somewhere more comfortable to lie down than the awkward position she was sitting in Jacey's chair, I would. I stacked each box in the corner of the room. The more I moved, the more it finally started to look like a couch again.

Finally, everything was out of my way enough to pull the plastic drop cloth from over the top of it to reveal the nice black leather couch. I turned back to her, "Go grab your blankets and pillow from the other room. You can lay on the couch." She looked poised to argue with me, but I held up my hand. "You're tired, but you don't want to be alone," I reminded her. "This way, you can lay down, and if you fall asleep, you fall asleep, but Jacey and I will be here the whole time," I promised her. That seemed to appease her, at least enough to stand up to retrieve the blankets and pillows from the next room. I fully expected her to fight falling asleep. I doubted she would go down easily, but at least she would be lying down.

When she returned with the blankets, I spread one out over the leather so that she didn't stick to it. That was the worst thing about that couch. Taking her other blanket, she curled up on the couch before focusing those green eyes on me again. God damn, it was so easy to get caught in that gaze. Everything else just seemed to disappear. I knew I was in trouble with her. I knew I already liked her, and even I knew how ridiculous that was, considering how little I knew about her. It was something so much deeper than just surface stuff. Something in me screamed to help her. I just wished she'd let me.

The only downside to getting so easily swept up in her gaze was that I never heard Jacey come back into the office. I didn't even know he was there until he flicked me in the back of the head on his way by making Oakley laugh slightly. She was desperately trying to fight the smile. Of course, she would laugh at my plight. I sighed before turning to look at my partner and dropping back down into my chair. "So, is this a slumber party now?" Jacey asked, nodding to the new setup. "Because honey, I call first dibs on the hot one," he jokingly pointed to me.

"Shut it," I grumbled, "Did you find anything?" I asked.

"All work and no play Hale, no wonder you haven't seen a naked woman in years," he retorted as he sank into his office chair. I knew if I put up with his games, he would get to the point eventually if I was lucky. "There was nothing there. A few new cigarette butts; collected a few of those, figured we could send them down to the city, see if they can pull anything from them. Run it through the database. But there was nothing there. Whoever was watching the two of you cleared out as soon as you did, I'm guessing," he sighed.

Oakley focused her gaze back on me. I knew what she was thinking, so I just nodded. "There's your confirmation," I told her, "Someone was definitely watching us tonight. Now we just have to determine if someone intends to hurt you." I knew chances were it was just some nosy neighbor looking to find out anything they could about our newcomer. I also didn't want to risk anything, either. I wanted to be sure of that. "We'll run the cigarette butts like Jacey said, see if we can figure out who it is. But until then, there's not much we can do. Do you think this person wants to hurt you?" I asked her, trying to determine the severity of the situation.

She shrugged once, "It's possible," she answered. "I think I'll be okay, though, if I get that job your brother was talking about at the flower shop. And if Fiona is okay with me being a roommate. No one has tried anything yet, and up until now, I was pretty convinced I was making it all up."

I wasn't sure I liked how calm she was about all of this. If she wasn't willing to give me anything to work with, there wasn't much I could do, and I couldn't begin to express just how much that fucking sucked.

NINE
OAKLEY

At some point throughout the night, I had fallen asleep curled up on the couch in the police station office. I wasn't entirely sure when I had nodded off. Everything from the night before was a bit fuzzy. I could hear murmuring nearby, but I couldn't quite understand what they were saying. There was a mysterious third voice in the mix, though, that didn't belong to either Owen or Ethan.

I peeked my eyes open slowly, only to find that I was facing the back of the couch. On the one hand, that meant I couldn't see who the new voice belonged to, but on the other, it allowed me the chance to listen more intently to what was being said. I could only make out every other word or so, though.

"She… truth… covering up…." I heard Jacey say. I could only guess they were talking about me. Owen had been particularly inquisitive the night before. I could tell he knew I was hiding something. The truth was, I couldn't tell him. Yes, protecting people was his job, but I couldn't bring myself to put that on him. I knew he wouldn't only want to do what he could to save me; he would also want to solve my parents' murders.

The way these people moved, they hadn't set off any alarms in the house, they had gotten in and out without Abraham's notice, and they had dodged every security camera we had. It was like trying to catch smoke. As soon as the police thought they had something, it dissipated right from their clutches. Owen was just some small-town cop; he didn't stand much of a chance against these people.

That's why I needed to make sure nothing was standing between them and me if they came for me. If someone's life was going to end, it was going to be mine and only mine. I wasn't going to let the sweetheart of a cop I was coming to care about take the fall for me. At this point, it wasn't like anyone would miss me anyway. Which begged the question, why was I still here? I knew I should be running again if they had already found me. It was my only defense.

Rolling over on the couch, I looked towards the door. Even with his back to me, I knew it was him. His lean form leaned against the doorframe. I could admit that much to myself; he was the reason I wasn't running. If this had all gone down in the first few days in Gratin, I would have turned around and taken off for the next safe haven, hellbent on running for the rest of my life if that was what was necessary to stay alive. The issue was I had taken the time to get to know him a little. Men like him didn't come along more than once in a lifetime. I couldn't let him help me; I couldn't stand the idea that something could happen to him because of me, but I also couldn't bring myself to run away from him.

I was stuck in this twisted limbo between the life I wanted and the life I was doomed to. It would have been foreign to me before to ever consider a life in this tiny town, but I could see it now. Getting that job at the flower shop, being roommates with someone like Fiona, maybe dating and falling in love with the cute night cop. We'd meet for breakfast at the diner every morning before he headed off to bed, and I headed off to work. It would be challenging, but we would find a way to make it all work for us. Eventually, we would cave to the need to see each other whenever possible, and I would move in with him. Maybe one day we would get married and have a couple of kids. I would never have to worry about the Richfield name coming back to haunt me again because all of that would be behind me.

It was a nice dream.

That was all it was, though. That was all it could ever be, just some pipe dream. Even if I could have him like that, there was no reason whatsoever that he would ever want that with me. I sighed to myself before sitting up on the couch and letting the blanket fall away. I didn't remember covering myself with that. Sure, I had carried it into the office, but it had been lying on the floor when I had laid down. Which meant...

"Your slumber buddy is awake," I heard Jacey say. Looking up again, I watched as he turned around and caught my gaze. A slight smile pulled at those perfectly full lips. God, what I wouldn't give to kiss him just once; they looked like they would be as soft as down pillows. Shit, I was horny in the morning. There was no denying it though, I wanted those strong hands on me. I wanted him to hold me. I wanted…

No.

I needed a cold shower and to get the hell out of there before I jumped him. He didn't need some lunatic latching onto him because she couldn't control her wild desires.

I blinked, realizing that I had been staring at him since he had turned around. Fuck, I really needed to stop doing that. He probably already thought I was crazy; I didn't need to add to it by staring at him like he was some hunk of irresistible man meat. Truth was, I was learning quickly he was so much more than that. If it were only the fact that he looked like he belonged on the cover of a magazine, I could walk away. The struggle was the idea of walking away from a man with such a good heart. Those weren't so easy to find.

I dropped my gaze, remembering the one thing everyone always told me. I couldn't hide anything for shit. What I was feeling was always plastered across my face, which meant that the smirk on his face was because he'd read me like an open book. I could keep secrets, only give away what was necessary, but when it came to men that got me all hot and bothered, I didn't stand a chance at keeping it under wraps.

I pushed myself up off the couch, busying my hands by smoothing down the pajamas I was wearing. "I should go get dressed and get out of your hair," I muttered, "I'm sure you boys want to go home and sleep."

"I thought we were going for breakfast," Jacey answered. "Don't tell me you two are canceling breakfast?!"

I could feel the weight lift off of me as Owen's gaze moved to his partner. I could finally breathe again. I needed to get a grip on whatever this man was making me feel. Sure, I hadn't been with a guy since before my parents' death. And *before,* I certainly hadn't been known for my celibacy pact. That didn't mean I could dump all my raging hormones all over the friendly police officer who had saved me from a night of total paranoia, though. "Don't cancel breakfast on Jacey," Owen warned me, causing my gaze to snap back up to meet his. "Any chance to eat."

"I'm not canceling breakfast for everyone," I amended, "I'm quite sure I don't have that kind of power. You guys can still go; I just think I should get a jump on the whole job thing. Go out to the flower shop."

He glanced down at his watch, "Meredith doesn't open for another three hours," he pointed out. "And Fiona is at the diner, opening everything up. So if you want to talk to her about her spare room, you have to go there."

Jacey grinned at that, "Which means breakfast!"

I sighed at that; I was stuck. Silently I folded up the blanket and placed it neatly on top of the pillow still sitting on the couch. "I guess I should go get dressed then," I shrugged.

Clearly, I wasn't going to get out of whatever breakfast ritual these two had every morning. I woke up in their office, which meant, for the time being, I was part of their crew. With the thoughts still running red hot through my mind about the one officer, in particular, I wasn't sure I could handle being in a small booth with him, but I would have to do my best. God knew I couldn't dare ruin breakfast for Jacey.

An hour later, I was finally calm enough and put together enough that I dared to step out of the small room that had been allocated to me the night before. I had my bag thrown over my shoulder as I stepped to their office door again.

"About time," Owen laughed when he looked up and saw me standing there. "I was starting to take bets on how long before Jacey here withered away from starvation."

"You could have gone without me," I tried, but when I looked at Jacey, there were remnants of doughnut on his face. "For someone so fit, you eat a lot. You don't even need breakfast now."

His eyes widened at that, "Don't you talk like that to me," he warned. "I need sustenance!"

I shook my head at him, "well, then get up," I smiled slightly. "I don't have all day, Jacey."

That made Owen laugh again, "I think I'm really starting to like having you around Ms. Morgan," he joked. "Always nice to have someone else so quick to put him in his place."

Ms. Morgan?

Why was he calling me that now when, just the night before, he had been staring at me so intently; my name nothing more than a whisper on his lips as he took my hand? I could still feel the warmth of it wrapped around mine.

Dammit!

I needed to shake these feelings. I needed something else to focus on. "Well, he makes it easy," I nodded. Both of the men stood up then. It was only then that I noticed they had both changed from their uniforms. And on closer inspection, Owen's hair was wet. Every muscle begged for me to reach out and brush back the stubborn strands that fell over his forehead.

This was a whole new sight to take in, though. His jeans hugged him perfectly. The nickname Jacey had given him the night before was no joke. A tight t-shirt stretched over his arms and chest. This man was going to be the death of me. I couldn't have breakfast with them. Not when I was panting over him like some kind of dog in heat. Waking up to the sound of his voice, him being the first face I saw in the morning. It was doing things to me. The whole situation was Innocent. He had merely taken care of someone who needed his help. I needed just to breathe.

"So I'm thinking, we go to breakfast before Jacey has a conniption. We talk to Fiona, I'll take you out to see Meredith, and then we'll hopefully get you out of that Inn and into Fiona's place today," Owen explained as he grabbed his keys and wallet from his desk. Wait, what?

"Don't you have to sleep?" I asked him stupidly. It seemed obvious, he had worked all night, and I could only guess he had to work again later on. He needed to sleep at some point.

He smiled at that, "I'm off tonight, and as you know, we were quiet last night. After you fell asleep, I caught a couple of hours sleep in my desk chair."

"Slacker," Jacey joked as he stuffed the last bite of his doughnut in his mouth. "Let's go! Breakfast awaits!" He led the way out the door, and for a moment, I was left dumbfounded. Apparently, today I wasn't going to catch a break. I was going to spend it with Owen Hale. Who knew what that was going to do to my already mounting lust for the man. If I couldn't control it, he would have a restraining order against me by day's end.

Straightening my shoulders, I took a deep breath before following them outside. Jacey jumped in his own car and had it started before I knew what was going on. He rolled down the window enough to yell out to us that he would meet us at the diner. Which meant I was riding with Owen.

Of course, it did.

I turned to find him standing next to a convertible. I knew nothing about cars. I couldn't tell anyone what make or model it was. What I did know, though, was that it was almost the same brilliant blue as his eyes, accented perfectly with a black top and two black stripes running down the nose and rear. It was gorgeous, just like the man that would be driving it.

He grinned at me, "If you hurry up and hop in, I know a shortcut to the diner. We can beat Jacey there. Always pisses him off when I get there first."

That made a laugh bubble up inside me as I reached for the door. "Let's do it," I nodded. Maybe I couldn't touch, but that didn't mean I wasn't allowed to have a little fun.

We pulled into the diner a few minutes later, and I couldn't help but notice the van parked next to the front door. It looked familiar, but I couldn't quite place why. I tore my gaze away from it and looked back to Owen just as he took his seatbelt off and lounged back in his seat like we had been sitting there for a while already when Jacey pulled into the diner parking lot. "This is the fun part," he laughed. This was the first I was really getting to see more of Owen and less of Officer Hale.

At that point, I had heard both Jacey and Owen refer to each other as the partner with a stick firmly implanted in their ass, but seeing them like this was like watching brothers pick at each other. It made their relationship make that much more sense. I glanced around Owen as Jacey pulled in next to us, his hand banging on the steering wheel.

He jumped from his car, hands above his head, "How the fu-?" he shook his head.

Owen laughed again before getting out of the driver's seat, "Never," he answered, playfully slapping him on the cheek on the way by.

"But you let her in on your little secret?" Jacey turned to face me as soon as I closed the car door. "We're friends, right?" he asked, and I shook my head. If Owen wanted to let me in on a little joke he played on his friend, I wasn't about to ruin it. "Right, because the two of you have a hard-on for each other, can't possibly give away the source of this newfound bonding moment."

I felt my cheeks starting to warm at that. I didn't have some hard-on for him. The way I had woken up that morning, though, I could deny it all I wanted. It was true. So very painfully, obviously, true. Of course, when I looked up again, Owen's blue eyes were firmly planted on me. This time, I saw a hint of something there before he recovered. He wasn't meeting my gaze; instead, his eyes were roaming down over my body. And I hated how much I liked that. I had to force my legs to move when I saw he was also holding the door open for me. I had to ask the question, though, why did the cops in this town have to be so fucking sexy?

I slipped by him, trying not to let it show that I had seen him checking me out the way he had been. We were here with a purpose. I had to remind myself of that. I needed a new place to stay. Fiona possibly had something for me. This wasn't some sort of date with the pretty cop. I could get through this. I just had to focus. Hopefully, I could catch Fiona for a minute to talk to her and explain my situation. All of that was blown to hell when she came dashing by me; she grabbed my hand and shoved a key into it.

"You can move in today; Jacey and Owen can show you where it is unless you want to wait until noon when I get done here. Then I can take you myself," she relayed as she delivered plates to nearby tables. "Enjoy," she smiled at the customers before looking back at me. "Your room is at the top of the stairs and to the right," she paused for a moment to smile at me, "Don't argue; I'm happy to help," she added before she breezed by me again, leaving me dumbfounded, staring after her. That hadn't been the conversation I had been hoping for. Now there was nothing left between me and my pulsing attraction to the man that was now standing way too close to me.

"Well, that was easy," he nodded.

"Too easy," I shook my head before looking at the two men I was with. "Did one of you...?" I started to ask, and Owen just shrugged.

"I sent her a text last night explaining everything after I left the station. I figured having her on board would make it harder for you to weasel your way out of it. She's obviously all for it, and she said you could work out specifics later," Jacey explained.

"Specifics like I have no job to help pay the rent?" I asked him, which wasn't entirely a lie. I had enough money stashed under the bed at the Inn to buy the house Fiona was living in. That wasn't the issue. No one in Gratin knew that about me, though, and my discount outfit choices leaned more toward the "She doesn't have any money at all" image.

Jacey waved his hand at me before turning me around and nudging me toward an open table. "Breakfast first, then you can yell at me," he sighed. I shrugged off his grip. I didn't appreciate being manhandled in the middle of the diner. Especially by him. If anyone were going to be manhandling me at all…

No.

I stopped that train of thought before it could finish. Heading for the table, I slipped into the booth, studying Owen's every move to see which side he went to. I was both surprised and not surprised at all when he slid in next to me.

"This is good, Oakley," he tried to reason with me, "Fiona is already on board, we can get you moved in today, and you don't have to stay at the Inn anymore. We can talk to Meredith this afternoon, and you will have a job," but his voice was nothing more than background as the blood started pounding in my ears.

My heart began racing in my chest; my palms began to sweat. Everything was closing in on me as my vision began to blur. Out on the very edges of my consciousness, I could hear them speaking to me. Their words were all garbled and washed out by the thrumming, though. I couldn't focus on anything else; I couldn't make my brain zero in on what they were saying.

Those words kept reading through my mind, playing on repeat like some sort of broken record splashed across the headlines for all to read. Most incriminating aspect was the pictures. They weren't old. They were from the night before. Me with Owen, getting into his car.

RICHFIELD HEIRESS FOUND WITH FORBIDDEN LOVE!

They knew where I was.

TEN
ASH

Leaning back in the chair, I flicked through the channels on the TV. Leave it to the media. It hadn't taken long for them to notice she was missing, at least, not after I called them to inform them that she'd run off. If there was anyone out there better at finding people than the FBI, it was reporters.

I knew if I tipped them off to her departure that it would only take a few weeks at most before they were hot on her trail, I had to say, though, I was impressed with how quickly they'd caught on to where she was. Some small town in Pennsylvania.

Lizzie… did you really think you could escape me that easily? She was the one I was really after. Her parents had merely been in the way. She was the one that needed to pay for what she'd done.

"Ash…" Elisa managed to cough behind me. Fucking hell, didn't that woman know when to shut the fuck up? I glanced over my shoulder at her, finding Abraham struggling against the knots that tied him to the chair. Placing the remote down, I stood up slowly and turned to face them.

"Let me guess," I started as I stepped towards her, "You don't have to do this!" I mocked her tone. She had this irritating squeak in her voice that I swore only fucking dogs could hear. "There's another way! We can get you help!" I continued as I moved closer to her. "Like I haven't heard it all before," I sneered at her. "Don't hurt me!" I had heard it all before. "Jonathan said the same thing. He made the same promises. He stood in front of his wife and swore he'd pay for any help I needed. But money doesn't buy happiness, does it, Elisa?" I pressed. "That's what you always told your precious little Lizzie, right?"

"Ashland," Abraham warned from his spot. Fuck I needed to figure out a better way to tie those gags.

"Stop saying my fucking name!" I yelled, turning to look at him. I was getting really fucking sick of hearing their voices, hearing them say my name over and over again like that was going to fucking change anything. There was no going back now; no amount of help anyone promised would actually amount to anything. The media had already handled the only help I was interested in. I didn't want anyone else's fucking help. I didn't need their help. I had gotten this far on my own, after all. "Fuck! Is that the only thing the two of you can fucking say?" I asked him as I turned toward him. "Ashland!" I mocked. "Learn a different song."

I was done playing games with the two of them. They'd been no help to me since I'd arrived a week or so ago. I had tried to get them to crack, but despite my best efforts, they hadn't been willing to spill on their little princess. "You know, this game is getting tiring. And your pretty little princess Lizzie is pissing me off. Did she really think she could run from me? That I wouldn't find her?" I reached for the remote that I had set aside before. "She can't fucking hide from me!" I yelled, turning up the volume on the news station so they could hear it. I whipped the remote at Elisa, grinning as she cringed.

Reaching for the knife I had sitting next to her, I watched the blade for a moment. It was tempting just to drive it in and end my torment. I couldn't take hearing them whine anymore. I smiled again, stepping forward enough to reach out and grab her face with my free hand. She whimpered in my hold, her dark eyes widening in fear. "I guess that means you were wrong then, doesn't it?" I questioned. "Money can buy happiness. Amazing what money can get you, pay off the right people, and suddenly our little runaway isn't so hidden anymore." I shoved her head back as I stepped back from her again. "Which means we're going after her. The thing is, I guess that means I don't need the two of you anymore."

Turning away from them, I left them there, tied to their chairs, before slamming the knife down on the counter and storming out the back door of their small home. I had to come up with a plan. I couldn't keep winging this shit like it was nothing. I wanted Elizabeth to pay for what she'd done to me, but it wasn't enough to just kill her, no. I wanted to torture her. I wanted to make her scream and cry, and I wanted her to understand exactly how it felt to have everything ripped from you at the hands of someone else, someone *better*.

I looked back at the house; it would only take me a few days to get across the country. The question was what was I going to do with dear Abraham and Elisa? I couldn't just let them go, not now; they knew too much. They would have the cops on me so fucking fast. I was good, but not good enough. I was never fucking good enough. I slammed my hand down on top of the chicken coop, the birds inside squawking and flapping their wings.

It was going to be a bitch to drag both of them across the country with me. Sure, I could admire the fact that they would serve me well once Elizabeth found out I had them. They carried certain leverage, but they weren't going to go willingly. Elisa didn't know when to fucking stop. I had a feeling she was going to be the problem child. She wasn't going to give up until she'd successfully taken me down or warned her precious little princess. She had spunk; I had to give her that. That just meant she was a liability.

The truth of the matter was that Abraham would be far more pliable without the strength his wife offered. I was betting he'd fold like a house of cards in a slight breeze if he didn't have Elisa there pulling the strings. The saying was true, behind every good man... I knew what needed to be done, but I didn't like the idea of adding more blood to my hands. Not unless it was hers. It was only ever supposed to be hers! Of course, she had to go and make this a whole big fucking mess for me. Why could nothing ever be easy?

Turning back to the house, I sighed. I had gone to the manor that day looking for her. My sources had told me Jonathan and Winnie were out of town. They must have returned early; I didn't know for sure. When the opportunity presented itself, though, how was I supposed to say no? It had been easy pulling the trigger that day. One bullet to the head for Jonathan. One to the chest for Winnie. I'd heard a rumor that it would take longer for her to die. I had no qualms with Jonathan. He was merely in the way. Winnie, however, she was the reason Elizabeth was the way she was. I was okay with allowing her to suffer, lying there in her own blood, staring helplessly at her husband's wide, lifeless gaze.

The only way that moment could have been more magical was if I'd seen the look on Elizabeth's face when she walked in. Or if she'd come in, I could have put a bullet in her too. Then, it would have been over. I'd be free and the police would be writing it off as some tragedy to strike a family of fortune. Of course that wasn't the way it played out. She'd escaped me that day. I couldn't stick around to wait for her with the mess she'd caused. Then she had the nerve to run as if I weren't going to find her.

Though I had to admit, this opened new possibilities. I wonder how easy it would be to get to that cop of hers. I'd never killed one before. I was betting there was a particular rush to that. I didn't like getting my hands dirty, but there was a certain adrenaline hit when I knew I was the keeper of life and death. I decided which way they tipped when I knew I held the scales.

Walking back into the house, I grabbed the knife from the counter on my way through the kitchen. I could hear Abraham's pleas in the background, he knew what I was about to do, and there wasn't a fucking thing he could do to stop me. His cries filled the air like a perfectly orchestrated soundtrack for what was about to come. I set my sights on the prize. I slammed my knife in, hilt deep. I watched the realization strike her gaze before I yanked it back out. I stared, curious, as the life left her eyes, as she slumped forward in her chair, as he wailed in the background.

Looking down at my hand, I sighed. Of course. Stepping towards the old man sitting in front of me. "Are you ready to talk?" I asked him, pulling at the gag around his neck with the tip of my knife, the knife that still dripped with blood. He refused to budge even with tears that now streaked down his face. The old man was stubborn; I would give him that.

Despite the pain I had already inflicted, he simply stared at me. His eyes, which used to be filled with warmth and love, were glacial now. "I know where to find her, Abraham," I told him as I dragged the tip of the blade over the skin of his throat. "You just have to tell me what I need to know...." His glower didn't falter in the slightest. At least I had accomplished something. He was finally fucking quiet.

I exhaled deeply; I didn't know why I expected different results. "Have it your way then," I answered before driving the knife into his hand. I barely heard his screams of pain. "Your silence isn't going to save her anyway."

I glanced to Elisa; I would have to dispose of the body. I couldn't just leave her here for the neighbors to find later. That was easy enough. Gathering my things, I started to pack. We had to move before anyone realized what was going on. I glanced out the window; we had a few hours until sundown. I would have to use the cover of night to get out.

As I threw my stuff together, I looked back at the TV running in the background. Her picture was staring across at me. I just had to believe that my revenge would all be worth it. That once I had that pretty little throat in my hand, all of this fucking hell would be worth every second. I wanted to hear her scream more than anything, beg for her life, and then I wanted to watch as every last shred of hope in her eyes died. Then I would watch as the last breath of life left her body.

Everything was leading to that moment. I knew plenty of people who would tell me to let it go. Especially now that she was keeping company with a cop, it was a suicide mission. If that was the case, then so be it. I wasn't about to let some backwoods, hillbilly, gun-toting moron ruin this for me. I had come this far. I was damn well going to finish what I'd started. I didn't doubt she would put up a fight. Hide behind her cop. Look to him to protect her. If I could outsmart and pay off the cops around here, though, how hard would it be to take him down?

I studied his image a little closer. I now had the blood of three souls on my hands. Two of which had all of the top of the line security money could buy. I'd skirted all of it. What was one fucking cop?

Once night fell, I loaded everything into the van I'd stolen a few weeks back. Going back into the house, I grabbed my knife again and pointed it at the old man. "I'm going to untie you," I told him. "You're going to walk outside and get in the van. If you try anything, you'll end up like your sweet Elisa. Understand?" He nodded.

Untying the rope, he stood slowly. Abraham was a tall man. Not many would dare take him on, but he didn't scare me. He gave one last glance to his late wife before doing exactly as I said. I could see there was still a fight left in him. He was clearly hoping that he stood a chance at saving Elizabeth if he listened.

Once everything was loaded, I went back inside with a can of gasoline and some matches. Pouring it over her, I stepped back and struck the match before dropping it at her feet. If only I'd had the time to watch it all burn. It would be a hell of a sight. However, I had bigger dreams to make come true.

Eleven
Oakley

It was like everything around me had suddenly shifted into slow motion. My heartbeat reverberated through me, thrumming in my ears. My breathing started to come in short gasps. I could feel every fiber of my being seize up with the panic flowing through me. I couldn't do this, not here, not in public. Before I could really think about what I was doing, I turned to try and leave, but Owen was still firmly planted in the booth next to me, staring at me like I was losing my mind. "I…" I choked on the words before glancing back at the TV.

It was blasted across the screen for them to see. I had been lying to them about everything. They weren't going to want to help me anymore. "I have…" I couldn't get the words out. I just needed to leave; I couldn't be here anymore. I looked up enough to meet Owen's gaze, knowing tears were now streaming down my face, "Please?" I whispered.

His blue gaze shifted between me and the TV. "Oakley…" he started, the confusion evident across his face.

I shook my head; I had to get out of the diner. If the media knew where I was, then that meant my image was splashed across every entertainment news outlet all across the country. I couldn't stay in Gratin. "Please?" I all but begged. He relented enough to allow me out of the booth. I shoved away from the table and ran out the door.

Outside I was met with the flash of a camera coming from that van I had noticed when we pulled in. I did my best to shield myself, but I knew it was useless. I had been in the fray before; I knew too well how quickly the paparazzi came down. Right now, it was one camera, but it would be ten more by tomorrow. All clamoring to know why the Heiress of such a fortune walked away.

No one in this town deserved this. They were quiet people; they kept to themselves. They didn't need their little town splashed across the front of next month's tabloids. My feet were moving, they were taking me somewhere, but it wasn't until I was standing outside the Inn that my mind finally caught up with me. I didn't have time to come up with a plan, I needed to get the money I had stashed in my room, and I needed to leave. It wasn't lost on me that if the media had found me, it was only a matter of time before people I didn't want to find me knew exactly where I was.

Running up the steps to my room, I fumbled with the keys; I tried to unlock the door through the tears that were forming. I couldn't break down just yet. I had to get my stuff and get out of town, get back to the airport, and go somewhere else. Anywhere else. The question was how long would I have until they found me again? Was this going to be my life now? Was I going to be constantly running from my past? I had stupidly wanted to believe that I had escaped, that maybe I could build a life here in this small town, and no one would be any wiser. I should have known that wasn't how things would play out.

Grabbing the money from under the bed, I turned to stuff it in my bag, only to realize it wasn't there. I'd left it in Owen's car. I couldn't go back, though. If I saw him again, I wasn't sure I'd be able to leave. It had been hard enough running from the concerned look in those blue eyes once. I couldn't do it again. So it was just me and the money. I could buy new clothes.

When I pulled open the door to my room, I sucked in a breath when I realized Owen was standing against the wall across from me. "I tried knocking…" he explained, "Even tried opening the door." I couldn't help myself; I dropped the pillowcase with the money in it and stepped into him, burying my face against his firm chest. I could feel the awkwardness circulating through him as he froze at the contact before he slowly wrapped his arms around me in a tight embrace, hugging me to him. It didn't change anything. I still needed to leave. "Oakley, talk to me," he said softly.

I wanted nothing more than to spill everything to him. To try and make him understand why I did what I did, why I needed to do what I was doing now. I just didn't have it in me to try and form words together. This would have to serve as a final goodbye to the first genuinely nice guy I had met in a long time. Men like Owen Hale just didn't exist in my world. They saw me only for my looks and my money, a ticket to an easy life with a trophy wife. Guys who even had ill intent to try and take the company from me wanted to date me to make it easier.

Owen, though. He didn't know any of that. He spent time with me because he wanted to. Maybe he was fueled by some need to figure me out; I couldn't be entirely sure. When he smiled at me, when he laughed at what I said, the way he had talked to me the night before in the station, all of that was real. There were no pretenses with him. Which only made me feel worse about the fact that I had been lying to him from the moment we met outside the Inn.

"I should…" I started to pull away. Leaving was going to be hard enough before I had opened the door and saw him there. Now it was going to be damn near impossible.

Owen looked over my shoulder at the pillowcase I had dropped to the ground, "To Fiona's, right?" he asked me. I stepped back, shifting my gaze to my feet and the space I had just put between us. "Oakley?" he prompted. When I still didn't answer, he sighed, "What good is running like this really doing for you? They found you once; they can do it again. Wouldn't it be better to stay put where you have people who want to help you?"

I looked up at him, my gaze tracing over his skin, wanting to absorb every little feature I could. "Owen, I lied to everybody here," I pointed out to him as if he didn't already know that.

"Do you have a reason?" he asked me, his gaze searching mine. "Because in my experience, there are two reasons someone changes their name and runs away," he pushed. "They've either committed some heinous crime, and they're trying to disappear to avoid getting caught. Or they're hiding from something. And knowing what I do about you, I'm going to guess it's the latter. Which means I can help." I shook my head, but he only pressed on. "Jacey went back to the station to talk to the captain about what we can do to deal with the incoming media presence. Fiona left the diner to go get your new room ready for you. You are not alone in this. We can help. Besides, I have your bag of clothes."

I stared at him for a long moment before nodding. It would be easier to sneak out in the middle of the night when they were all asleep or at work. I really didn't want to leave like that, not knowing how many would show up before nightfall. In my experience, the paparazzi moved quickly. They came on like a swarm of locusts; one was just the beginning. Especially when they found someone they had been clamoring to get to since my parents' death.

I picked up the pillowcase from the hallway floor while Owen headed outside. Taking a moment to myself, I dropped the key off with Rudy. I wasn't completely surprised to find his car sitting outside when I walked out. He had proven that he wasn't exactly a fan of speed limits on the way to breakfast. He had even joked about getting pulled over by one of his co-workers. I climbed into the passenger seat and stared down at my hands for a long silent moment. "Owen, I…" Words really weren't my friend right then. "If I stay…." I leaned forward, resting my head in my hands. Surprising me, Owen reached across and pulled me into his arms as best he could.

"It could be hell; I don't know, I don't have much experience with the media," he acknowledged. "But would you rather face this now, when you have friends to help you or face it alone if they catch up to you again?"

I curled my fingers into his warm shirt, where my hand rested on his shoulder. And I couldn't help but notice just how nice he smelled. It was a mix of something earthy and robust black coffee. It was nice; it was relaxing. "It's not the media," I answered. "It's who the media has now alerted."

I wasn't a fool. If whoever killed my parents wanted me dead, they would be gunning right for me and I highly doubted they gave a shit about anyone that dared to stand between them and me. I didn't want someone getting hurt on my behalf. These people hardly knew me. It wasn't right to ask them to lay down their own lives for mine.

"And Jacey and I are cops," he reminded me like I had forgotten how amazingly perfect he looked in that uniform. "Let's just go back to Fi's place, and we'll sort things out from there. Who knows, maybe this whole thing will just blow over." There really wasn't much chance of that happening. I really appreciated his positivity all the same. I let him pull back and start the car. I would have to figure something out. I couldn't ask them to risk everything for me. It seemed they were willing to do it whether I asked or not. Which again meant removing myself from the picture.

I wanted to believe him when he said things might just blow over. I knew in my gut, though, that likely wasn't going to happen. It was a nice thought, but that's all it was. I leaned back in my seat, watching the trees fly by out the window as he drove us out to the outer edge of town. "Guess we should have thought of that…" he mused as he pulled into a driveway. "You don't have a car, do you?" he asked, looking over at me.

I shook my head. We were out on the end of the main street, and as far as I knew, the town was small enough that there wasn't any kind of public transportation. It would only take an hour tops to walk from one end of town to the other. "I have my mom's old car tucked away in my garage if you want to borrow it," he offered.

Well, having wheels of my own would make getting out of town a lot easier. Then I would be on the run for grand theft auto too, what was one more problem at this point. Owen was trying to help, though; I couldn't steal his mother's car like that. Before I could answer, though, the front door to the house swung open, and Fiona came out and down the front steps.

Climbing from the car, I met her gaze. She surprised me when she stepped forward and wrapped me in a hug. "I'm sorry for everything you've gone through," she said quietly to me. "After you ran out, we all kind of searched your name," she admitted. "I lost my mom too, not the same way; she was sick. But still, I get it." I nodded against her shoulder at that. I had to admit; it was kind of nice to have someone understand, even if it was only a little bit.

Of course, they had searched the internet for me. I couldn't blame them for that. I had lied about who I was. They were bound to be curious. The most common links were related to my parents and what happened to them, but if someone were determined enough to scroll back far enough, they would find the truth. Maybe a distorted version of the truth, but the truth all the same. They would know what kind of person I really was, what I used to be. Owen stepped forward just as Fiona pulled back, "We should get you in and get you all settled," he suggested. "And then maybe we can talk?" That blue gaze fell directly on me.

"Actually, if you guys don't mind, I'm kind of tired. I didn't sleep much last night," I said, looking at Owen. He knew how much I hadn't slept the night before. "And it's been a big morning so far. I'd really like to just lay down," I confessed. The truth was, I just couldn't deal with any of it anymore. I wanted a chance to try to think a little clearer and figure out my next move.

Fiona nodded, "I can show you where your room is. And then later, I can give you a tour of the rest of the house." I was betting it was all pretty self-explanatory. The bathrooms were the rooms with a toilet; the kitchen tended to have a refrigerator; the living room often had a TV and a couch.

I mirrored her nod. "Sounds great."

It had been a few days since the move was official. I had tried to sneak off a few times, but I was greeted by someone else in the house every time I did. It had become like a revolving door. If it wasn't Owen stopping in to check on things, it was Jacey. Liv was around quite a bit too, and I had since met the cook from the diner, Darian. Apparently, he was something of an older brother to the twins. I had tried to avoid Owen since that day at the Inn, but it had been to no avail. I didn't want my issues to become his problem. Everything that was going on was on me: someone was after me, the paparazzi wanted me. None of that was his problem.

Thankfully, on that front, a massive scandal broke in Hollywood the next morning, so the paparazzi weren't as severe as I'd been expecting, but people were still knocking at the door, wanting to talk to me. They were still lurking around town, trying to get another good shot of my apparent sweetheart and me.

I had told Fiona that under no circumstances was she to let anyone in that she didn't know. It was bad enough that I was still in town at all; I didn't need something happening to her because of me. Jacey would have my head. Neither seemed to want to admit it to the other, but he was around an awful lot for someone who didn't want to date her. I had just become the convenient excuse to hang around. Fiona was quickly becoming someone I cared about, though, which put a target squarely on her back. I just couldn't live with myself if something happened to her, to any of them.

I heard another knock at the front door; I sat up enough to peek out the window to inspect the car in the driveway. It was another news van; I sank back against the headboard. I knew I was the only surviving child of a high-profile murder, but if that were the reason they were here, I would make up some bullshit excuse for everything. They weren't here because of my parents, though. They were here because I was a royal fuck up, and they wanted to know what could possibly come next. They were here to keep the gossip mill turning and their jobs secure.

It didn't matter that I had gone through something traumatic. It didn't matter that the killer was still out there, possibly wanting my head on a silver platter. All that mattered to them was that my trauma would cause me to do something stupid, and they could make me look like some spoiled, rich bitch to make the rest of the world feel better about themselves.

"Oh, the poor thing...." I heard the woman at the front door say. I didn't know what Fiona was telling them now, but that was the fakest line of bullshit I had ever heard. There was no remorse for what they were doing. They didn't care as long as they got the story they were after. I heard the front door shut again, shortly followed by another car door. There was no way they were already leaving.

I leaned up again and peeked out the window for a second time. This time, seeing that familiar convertible parked out on the street. He just couldn't leave well enough alone, could he? He'd already been by earlier that morning. He was gorgeous; of course, I'd give him that much, but the boy lacked the will to survive. Being entangled with me meant getting hurt. There was no way around it. Because even if a killer didn't come for me, I was a mess, and it would only end in him getting his heart broken. He had such a beautiful, caring, sweet heart. The last thing I wanted to do was be the reason it shattered, but he was leaving me with no choice. He kept showing up; he kept calling; he was always around; he didn't seem to understand how imperative it was to avoid me at all costs.

I could hear voices again. Owen was talking to the woman from the van. He had been in those pictures too; he was being hounded about my whereabouts as if he was the reason I dropped everything and ran away. Because my parents being murdered in my childhood home, and me being the unfortunate one to find them had nothing to do with why I might want out of that life. Of course not. It was all because of some guy. Because that was all Elizabeth Richfield was interested in.

I pushed off the bed and went over to the bedroom door, taking care to both lock it and shove a chair under the handle. Damn cops, the last time I had only locked it, he had picked it open. Lesson learned, officer. He was going to have to work harder than that this time. To be fair, they had been banging on my door for twenty minutes, and I didn't answer. Both he and Fiona had started to believe there was honestly something wrong. So that justified their actions. To a degree, anyway. This time, though, he wasn't getting in.

I just couldn't see him right then; I couldn't look into those blue eyes and say what needed to be said. So I was taking the mature route and hiding in my room until he went away.

Going back over to the bed, I grabbed the pillow and hugged it to my chest. It was no match against that hug in the hallway outside my room at the Inn. The way he had held me meant something. I just wished things could be different, that we could be some normal couple and find some kind of happiness. There was no such thing as a happy ending for people like me, especially now that it was out for all to know that I wasn't Oakley Morgan after all.

As predicted, ten minutes after hearing him outside, there was a knock at my door. I didn't answer; maybe he would just go away. Take a hint and leave me there to wither away.

"Oakley…" that strong voice came through the door, and I hugged the pillow tighter, fighting the urge to start crying again. I had done enough crying the last few days. I didn't know how there was anything left to cry out. I couldn't escape and run, but I couldn't ask them for help either. Which meant I was eternally stuck in that bedroom to rot away until whoever was after me finally found me.

They would have to come in through the bedroom window, though, so that they didn't run into Fiona and Owen in the hallway. Yeah, that sounded like a solid plan. Maybe I would post a note for them on the window so they knew where to find me.

TWELVE
OWEN

I leaned forward, resting my head against the wall next to her door, when I was greeted with nothing but silence from her. I didn't understand it. She seemed to think that I would automatically hate her because she lied about her identity and that I wouldn't want her around anymore. She was so far from the truth, though.

I knew there had to be a reason. She had a reason for running; she had a reason for changing her name, and lying about her identity, and since finding out that Oakley Morgan was really Elizabeth Richfield, I had done my research. Her parents had been murdered. There were still no leads on the case, and there were plenty of reports about how she dropped off the face of the planet afterward. Which I couldn't blame her for. One police report I had managed to get my hands on even said that she'd been the one to find their bodies.

It was amazing to me that she was still fighting, still standing so strong. I understood, but she didn't want to hear that. She wanted me to tell her how much I now hated her. How I was disgusted with the woman she was, but I wasn't falling for Elizabeth Richfield. I didn't even know her; I didn't want to know her. Besides, it wasn't like I would ever get that chance because I was more than certain that she had died that day too.

The moment she opened that door and saw them both lying there on the floor, who she was changed. She stopped being some spoiled princess when reality slapped her in the face and turned her whole world upside down. The Oakley I knew, the Oakley I was really starting to fall for, she was sweet, she was caring. Sure, she had a bit of an edge to her, but I liked that. It was the kind of thing I looked for in a woman because of my job; I couldn't be with someone too soft.

I knew not a lot happened in Gratin, but that didn't mean something couldn't. Small town or not, my job was still dangerous. I needed someone who could handle that, who was strong enough to recognize why I did what I did. Oakley… she was amazing. She made me smile; she made me laugh. It was all stuff I was starting to think I would never find. That, maybe, I really would have to go out with Liv because even dating her would be better than ending up alone. None of that had to happen, though, if Oakley would just come out of her room and talk to me.

"I don't think she's going to let you in, Owen," Fiona said from behind me. I glanced back over my shoulder to where she was standing at the top of the steps. "She barely even talks to me when she does come out."

I shook my head at that, "She can't hide in there forever and avoid all of this Fi," I sighed. I just wished there was some way to make her see that.

Fiona shrugged, "She seems pretty determined," she smiled slightly, "Anyway, I have to head into the diner for the evening shift. You're good here?" I nodded. "Well, help yourself to anything in the kitchen." It sounded like she was willing to leave me to fend for myself. I really didn't plan on leaving my spot in the hallway. I wanted to be here if she decided to come out. I didn't have to work that night; I had all the time in the world.

"Thanks, Fi," I answered. She nodded once before turning and heading back down the steps. I shifted and leaned against the wall next to the door, sliding down it until I was sitting. "Oak… please, just listen to me." I leaned my head back against the wall. I didn't know if she had headphones in, if she was asleep if she was blatantly ignoring everything I was saying. It didn't matter, I had to get it out there on the slim chance she was sitting on the other side of the door listening to every word coming out of my mouth. "I get it, okay, I know why you lied. And I don't blame you for wanting to start over," I sighed. "You have every right to try and live your life the best you can after what you've been through. I just… I want to help you. I'm not the media. I don't give a shit who you were. I know who you are now. It's not worth running anymore. If you run and they find you again, and you'll really be alone in all of it. But here, if you stay, you're not alone. You have all of us."

I stared at the painting across the hall from me, hanging on the wall. It was an ocean storm. The waves were crashing; the sky was dark. There was a little boat lost in all of it. Through the haze, there was a lighthouse shining as a beacon of safety for that little ship. I knew right then that ship was Oakley. Life was tossing her all over the place. The rain made it hard for her to see, and she didn't know which way was up anymore. She was drowning in everything. She needed someone shining a light through the darkness for her to follow to safety. I wanted to be that lighthouse. I wanted to be the light that guided her home in one piece. It wouldn't do her any good, though, if she couldn't open her eyes long enough to see it shining through for her.

Once again, I found myself getting caught up in all the poetic shit. I didn't know what it was about this girl that made my whole system go haywire, but I lost all sense of logic and rules and procedures around her. All I wanted to do was help her. "I don't know how to make you understand," I continued as I stared at that painting. It was oddly fitting with everything going on. "None of us are mad at you about any of this. Well, I wouldn't go to the diner any time soon. Liv is a little pissed about the reporters. But Liv gets pissed if you look at her funny, so she's not worth getting upset over." I didn't know what else to say to her to make her open the door. I had tried asking nicely. I had now tried talking to her. I couldn't make her come out. No matter how much I wanted to get to the bottom of this and help her, I couldn't make her do anything. I never wanted to do anything that upset her, but I also didn't want her to think I now hated her for whatever stupid reason she had for believing that.

"No matter what's in your past," I started again, "you are an amazing woman, Oakley Morgan," I added on for her benefit. I didn't want to tell her what I was feeling for her, not until I could look into those green eyes as I said it. "Please just open the door."

There was some rustling around behind the door before a piece of paper slid out next to me. It simply read, "I can't."

"Why can't you?" I asked. "This house is safe; I checked it out myself. There's no one hiding here. There are no reporters outside. I threatened to arrest the last one for trespassing. Hopefully, news spreads fast with these people, so they'll leave you alone here. This is your sanctuary, I promise. No one will get you here."

"That's what my parents thought, too," she said weakly from the other side of the door. "We had every top of the line product out there, our home security was off the charts, and yet…" her voice faded out to a slight sniffle. I waited a moment to see if she would continue talking. I had made contact; that was the first step. If only I could get her to open the door too, but I knew I had to take this one step at a time with her. If I spoke too soon or said the wrong thing, she would go back to ignoring me.

"I want to help you," I finally answered her. "I may not be some top-notch security guy, but I know this house is safe. And as long as you have one of us around too, you'll be safe. I promise you, running may have worked the first time, but you don't have to do it anymore. Mama Buchannan is still willing to give you that job at the flower shop. She said something to Austen about it yesterday. Obviously, Fiona is fine with the arrangement here. And I can make sure everyone stays off your tail. Jacey and I are already on it." I heard movement again before the door finally pulled open. I guess I finally said something right. Until I looked up into those angered green eyes, they were bloodshot and red. Her cheeks were wet, her hair sticking to them slightly. It was apparent she had been crying again.

She shook her at me, though, "Owen, please don't tell me you're looking into the murder," she all but begged of me. I couldn't lie to her. Clearly, that was so important to her that she thought I hated her for lying to me about everything. I knew she would take it to heart if I lied to her about everything.

"Not exactly," I answered as honestly as I could. "After we saw the headlines and I brought you back here, I did some digging," I admitted. "But mostly just to figure things out. I did get my hands on one active case file. But no, I'm not exactly looking into the murders."

"You're just looking into me…" she sighed before trying to close the door on me again. Except I was faster than she was. I stuck my arm between the door and the frame before she could close it.

"Was I looking into you? Yes," I answered as I stood up so I could face her. My arm was throbbing from where the door had hit it, but I was doing my best to ignore it. She needed my undivided attention if I was going to make my point clear to her. "But not to prove anything. I was just trying to figure out what was going on. Oakley, that's not who you are anymore, do you understand me? The young woman I met that night outside of Rudy's Inn, she's a completely different person."

I dared to take a step closer to her. The way her eyes widened proved to me that it was almost as if I were dealing with an easily spooked horse. I knew I had to tread carefully if I wanted to avoid her lashing out at me. "I've already said it, and I'll keep saying it until I'm blue in the face and you finally believe me. You are an amazing person. I've only known you for a few weeks and I already know that," I insisted. She just shook her head at me.

"You don't know anything about me," she countered, taking a step back and away from me again. I really wanted to ask why she felt the need to push me away like this. What was she hoping to prove? That I was just going to let her go? I was starting to wonder if she'd ever had anyone fight for her rather than against her.

All of the media coverage I had found about her was primarily negative; and while I wasn't so skeptical as to refuse to believe any of it, I also wasn't naïve about how the media worked. They likely focused on every misstep she took, anything for a good, juicy gossip piece. Hell, I wouldn't be entirely surprised to find out that at least half of the pictures circulating out there were used in conjunction with stories that had nothing to do with the images at all.

"I know enough," I answered, holding my gaze steady against hers. This girl needed someone who wasn't about to give up on her when she needed them most. I wasn't going to walk away. She shook her head again, repeating the same words.

"You don't know anything about me, Owen."

"Fine. I don't know you. Then show me," I challenged, pushing my fingers through my hair in total exasperation. The saying was right; someone couldn't be helped if they really didn't want it. I was starting to think Oakley liked living the way she was. Because otherwise, I had no clue why she wouldn't accept help from someone. I didn't know how to make her understand that we all wanted to help her. She wasn't forcing this on us; she wasn't dragging us into her mess. We wanted to be here for her; she just had to let us.

"Tell me something about the real Oakley because I'm pretty sure I've already met her," I dared. Pulling out my phone, I typed her name in and pulled up a picture of the made-up blonde in designer clothes and heels. I held it up for her to see, "Because if I had to wager a guess, I'm going to say anyone who knew her, they're the ones that didn't really know you. This was your act Oakley, not who you are now. Trust me; I've seen the kinds of acts people put on. It's all fake," I shook my head and dropped the hand with my phone back to my side. "The Oakley I've been getting to know has been genuine. So please explain to me how I don't really know you."

From the look in her eyes, I could see that she didn't know what to say to that. She didn't want to admit that she had actually let her guard slip just ever so slightly around me. That I might know her better than anyone she left behind. "Owen… it's not that simple…" she tried; I could see the wheels turning in her head as she fumbled for a reason to back up her claim. She was wrong, though; it was that simple.

When she had moved to Gratin, she had shed the skin of Elizabeth Richfield – Heiress to the Richfield Fortune. She was just Oakley now, and it was obviously difficult for her to handle the fact that there was no mask for her to hide behind anymore.

I didn't know how to make her see it, though, that she didn't need to hide. She was an amazing woman, inside and out. There was no reason for her to lock all of that away. I wished I had the words to make her see that. She didn't need the blonde hair and all that makeup to be gorgeous and loved; she just needed to be herself, her true self.

What was sad was that she had played that part for so long it didn't seem like she even knew who she was anymore. I dared to take a step closer to her before tucking my phone back into my pocket. Reaching out slowly, I placed my hands on her shoulders, not sure if she would welcome the advance or not.

"If what I've seen so far honestly isn't the real you, if you've been putting on some flawless act this whole time, give me a chance to get to know the real you," I suggested to her. "Because false or not, what I saw that night at the station when we stayed up talking, Oakley, I really liked her. But I think you're having a hard time convincing yourself now that she's not the real you. But what do you say to dinner tonight? We can go back to my place, I can cook, and we can just talk?"

I had done everything in my power to convince her. Now it was all on her to decide. I couldn't force myself or my help on her. That wouldn't be right. I had pleaded my case before her, and now I had to wait for her decision. If she allowed me the chance to get to know her or not, if she allowed me in. I knew I could keep fighting for her, but if she wanted to leave, she was going to leave. To hell with what I said or did.

The truth was, we hadn't known each other that long. I had seen a spark in her eyes once already, though. I knew there was still fire in her. Someone just had to fan the flames a little to get her going again. She needed to believe in herself, that it was worth fighting to stay in Gratin, but again, I couldn't make that happen for her. She had to decide if it was worth fighting for. That all of us: me, Jacey, Fiona, that we were worth fighting for. In return, we would stand behind her, unfaltering.

"Please?" I added on for good measure. The truth was, I wanted to look into her parents' murders but because it was still an active case, I couldn't really. I knew I really couldn't help her find closure there. That would likely only come when the killer was caught. I didn't have any of the facts or evidence, so there was little I could do.

It appeared she didn't want me looking into it anyway. For what reasons, I couldn't be totally sure. If I had to hazard a guess, though, it would be because she didn't want me in the line of fire. If someone were really after her, she wouldn't want me standing in front of her. At the same time, I had to play devil's advocate, what proof was there that someone wanted her dead?

I had to turn off the cop brain. I had to stop thinking like a police officer and start thinking like a friend. Because right then and there, Oakley didn't need some guy trying to play the hero. She didn't need someone who was falling for her, fawning over her, and trying to push his way into her life.

Right then and there, she needed a friend, someone she could rely on, who listened when she spoke. I knew she could just as quickly have that friend in Fiona, and maybe she did for all I knew, but I couldn't help but want that friend to be me. I could be that friend. She really just had to find it in her to give me the chance to prove it to her.

Thirteen
Oakley

Dinner.

He wanted me to have dinner.

With him.

At his house.

So we could talk while he cooked.

Yeah, that didn't sound like a dangerous idea at all.

The way he was looking at me, those gorgeous blue eyes were all but pleading with me just to say yes. How could I, though? What would saying yes imply to him? That I was sticking around? That I would let him help me? He just didn't understand how dangerous it was. How risky it was for him to be around me, let alone actively helping me.

At the same time, how could I say no to that look he was giving me? I knew I needed to back up a few steps and close my bedroom door. Maybe even go as far as barricading it completely this time. Yes, so that he couldn't get in the room to me. More importantly, though, so I couldn't get back out to him. I knew in my head that's what I should do, but my heart was singing a different tune.

He was right on so many things. Every day I had painted on this mask back home. I had to be who my father expected me to be; I had to be who my friends wanted me to be; I had to be who the media painted me to be, but I never really felt like I had a chance just to be me. In Gratin, that's exactly what I had done. I had stripped away all the false layers and had walked into this town with my raw self showing completely.

I hadn't tried to really hide anything except for who I had been before coming to town and that was nothing more than a name and a media-appointed personality. Was I really that rich bitch who thought the world revolved around her? I thought I was until all of that was taken away from me.

I could have milked the media for all it was worth. I could have put on a good show with the giant crocodile tears. I could have gone on talk shows and pleaded with the public to come forward with any tips about my great tragedy. I could have made the world feel sorry for me, and I could have basked in that attention. The truth was, though, I wanted none of that.

After I lost my parents, I shut myself in. Mostly out of fear, sure, but partly because I didn't want to put on that big production of pity. I just wanted to deal with it on my own. I felt like I had no other choice, but it had taken time to come to the decision I had. I didn't want to be a Richfield anymore, simply put. I didn't want to be the one that everyone turned to for the latest drama. I just… I wanted to go into hiding so that I was safe.

He was right; I just wanted to move on with my life. After stripping all of the falsity away, I was just the woman standing before him. The woman who had stayed up most of the night talking to him that night in the station. I hadn't hidden anything from him. Maybe he knew me better than I knew myself anymore. I didn't realize I had started nodding until his eyes lit up. "Really?" he asked.

My eyes widened slightly. Apparently, my body had ideas of its own, but there was no taking it back. "Yeah," I answered. "But the truth is, I'm kind of tired. There was some jackass outside last night with a flashlight, kept shining it in my window. Probably just another paparazzi trolling for something good."

Owen laughed slightly, "If only," he sighed. "Jacey was here last night checking things out. Said he got out and walked around with his light to make sure no one was hiding anywhere they shouldn't be. I would have done it myself, but it was right around when Fiona was supposed to be getting home. I'll warn him to be more careful next time."

"Or…" What was with my body making decisions for me? "Or you could stick around for another hour or so and help me hang my new curtains Fiona bought me. The sun rises on this side of the house, so I get blasted first thing in the morning. She suggested those room darkening curtains. Before I had a chance to look for some, she came home with a set. But I'm not very handy with hanging things."

I wanted to sleep. Why was I inviting him to stay? That wouldn't get rid of him any faster. God, why the hell did he have to look at me like that? It made it so much harder to be able to tell him no. It had me questioning if I even wanted to tell him no. There was no denying it, though, now that he'd gotten through, I wanted him here. The problem was I knew letting him stay meant letting him in completely and nothing scared me more.

He answered before I could take back what I had said, though, "I don't mind helping," he shrugged. "You grab the curtains and the rods, and I'll go grab the tools I need," he explained before turning for the steps.

Now.

Now was when I needed to lock myself in my room. Barricade the door and bury myself under a mountain of blankets and pray for this nightmare to be just that, a nightmare. I couldn't like him. I wasn't allowed to like him. It wasn't fair. Seeing him light up the way he did, though, sent my heart racing in my chest a million beats a minute. He was gorgeous; he was sweet; he was kind and caring. He was everything I wanted more than anything.

If I let him help me, there was a very real possibility that I could lose him. I didn't want to live in a world where things like that happened to men like Owen Hale. I knew it wasn't safe for either one of us. Being around him, being with him, it painted a bright red target right on his back too, but at the same time, not being around him hurt.

I turned for my room, leaving the door hanging open behind me as I started to unpack the needed hardware. Next, I moved to the curtains, undoing those from their packaging, when then there was a slight knock on my door. I jumped; I couldn't help it. I was extra jumpy lately. When I looked up, though, the tension eased from my body at the sight of that amused smile.

"Sorry, didn't mean to scare you," he answered as he stepped into my room, holding up the bag of tools for me to see. "I just didn't want to come barging in."

I waved my hand at him. If I could just put all the worry about what might happen from my mind, I stood a chance at just letting myself have some fun. That was a scary thought.

"It's fine." I turned to assess the windows in the room; there were two along the front wall, with my new bed situated between them. "Both windows need curtains. I prefer to be a vampire when I sleep. Complete and total darkness. With a fan running." He laughed and shook his head at me before moving over to the first window.

I knew I wasn't likely going to be much help at all; I knew nothing about hanging things. We had people for that. Before. If I bought something new that needed to be hung up, I just left it out, and suddenly it found its way to where it needed to be. If I was going to be doing this whole surviving on my own thing, I knew I needed to learn these skills, though. That way, I was prepared if I decided to make a run for it again. I could stick around one more night. See what happened with dinner. He did say we would just hang out and talk. Which, in my experience, didn't spell hot date or anything. Who knew what could possibly happen, though, if I let my guard down a little more with him.

He had pulled a step stool out of somewhere; I didn't even know one of those had been in my room. I was even more confused about why he knew where to find it. I wasn't about to ask too many questions, though. I knew before me; this room had belonged to Liv. There were just some things I didn't need to know.

I stepped up behind him, though, as he climbed up onto the step stool. "Think you could walk me through the process?" I asked him. "Spoiled rich girl, never had to do anything like this on my own before. Might be a useful skill to have."

He looked back down at me and smiled before stepping back down. He held out his hand for mine, and slightly confused; I slipped mine into his warm palm. God damn, I had forgotten about the electrical currents that shot through me when he even so much as touched my hand. I wanted to know what it would feel like to have his hands elsewhere on me.

No.

I had to stop that train of thought right there. I didn't even want to know what it would do to me if I started imagining his hands on me. Every time we'd made contact, he'd been nothing but gentle with me. From the first time in the diner, he'd held me softly but still so steady. All the way to now.

His fingers wrapped around mine, just enough to guide me. I stared at our hands clasped together like that for a moment before looking back up at him. "Climb up the ladder," he instructed, and I just watched him cluelessly. "I could tell you what I'm doing, but it'll be better if you can see what I'm doing too," he explained.

With a shaky breath, I stepped on the first step, and it shifted beneath me. "Owen!" I shrieked, clinging tighter to his hand.

He chuckled, and I looked up enough to shoot daggers at him. "You're fine. I'm going to grab a chair, so we're up there together."

I shook my head, "Nope. Feet firmly planted on the ground," I stepped back off the step stool. "I'm not looking to fall to my death today."

His smile only grew as he tried not to laugh. "You were only about six inches off the ground, and I had your hand the whole time," he pointed out to me before giving my hand a slight squeeze. Which only deepened my scowl directed at him. "If you stand on your bed, will you feel safer?" he asked, amusement playing across his features. I nodded, though, before kicking off my shoes and climbing onto my bed. He returned to the step stool.

Together, we managed to hang both curtains. He talked me through every step the first time, and then he encouraged me to try the second one. He explained that it was easier to learn with that sort of thing if I did it myself with his guidance. After they were both hung, we both stepped back to admire our handiwork. "Mine's all wonky," I sighed. "Looks like it was hung in a funhouse."

He shook his head, "It's not that crooked," he argued, "Though yes, it is a little crooked," he teased. I reached out and shoved his arm. I had done my best, and it had surprisingly actually been fun. I had a funny feeling that had more to do with Officer Hale than anything else, though. If I had attempted to do it all on my own, I would have failed miserably, probably stabbed myself on one of those sharp little screwy things, and I would have ended up on the floor pissed at the world.

So I was oddly grateful that my heart wasn't paying a bit of attention to my brain. It controlled everything right then, and I was ready to let it, at least for a little while, as long as it didn't go and do anything too stupid.

I looked up at Owen, "So…" I started, only just realizing that my hand was still firmly resting on his arm. I pulled my hand away quickly as if something had burned me. "Dinner tonight. I'll come over, on one condition," I countered, trying not to focus too much on the tingling in my hand.

He raised a brow at that, "and that is?"

I grinned, "I'm cooking. That's one thing I actually know how to do. My dad's valet, Abraham, he's always kind of been like a second father to me. He was a huge help in the aftermath of everything. But when I was growing up, his wife Elisa used to teach me to cook. Her grandmother was fully Italian. She taught me all the family recipes. So tonight, I'm cooking. You've done so much to help me. From letting me stay at the station the other night to even helping me hang some stupid curtains. Dinner is the least I can do."

He sighed and shook his head, "Okay, fine, I suppose I can live with that. But we're still doing it at my place, right?" he questioned, and I nodded.

"And you have to stay out of the kitchen," I amended.

He stared at me for a long moment, "You've never been in my kitchen. You won't know where anything is."

I rolled my eyes at that, "So I'll figure it out, officer," I answered smugly. "Now you need to leave so I can be a girl and figure out what to wear tonight. I also have to go to the store to get everything I'll need," I mused. I looked him up and down, poised to ask him if he wanted to come along on that adventure too. For once, though, I was actually able to control the words coming out of my mouth. "So go away," I smiled innocently enough at him.

He laughed and shook his head, "I'll pick you up at six," he told me.

My gaze followed him as he moved to my bedroom door. "Why would you pick me up?"

"Because you don't know where I live," he shot back. "And I'm not telling you. I'll pick you up at six."

"I could always ask that pain in the ass partner of yours," I challenged, but I supposed I could allow him one small victory. Shaking my head, I smiled at him, "but fine. Six it is then." He shot me one last grin before he was out the door and heading down the steps.

Falling back against my bed, I stared up at the ceiling for a long moment before taking a deep breath. How the hell had I gone from wanting to find an escape route and getting away from Gratin and Owen for the safety of all involved; to walking straight into the lion's den and having dinner with him at his house alone? Clearly, I had lost my damned mind. That had to be it.

Or the amazingly simple fact that Owen Hale was fucking gorgeous, and when he smiled at me, I went all weak-kneed, and I would do almost anything he asked of me. Which sucked; I used to be so much stronger when it came to men. I knew men hotter than Owen. Hell, I had been with men more desirable than Owen. It wasn't all about his looks, though. It was about who he was that both completely enthralled me and terrified me to no end.

The man was gorgeous, sure. I was able to control myself around gorgeous. It was the fact that the more I got to know him, the more I really started to feel things for him. I wanted to talk to him; I wanted to get to know him; I wanted to learn more about his family and his childhood and how the hell he and Jacey had become so close. Plus, there was also an extraordinarily strong part of me that wanted to jump him. I wanted his hands on me. I wanted to know what it would be like to kiss those lips. In short, I was a complete and total goner.

I pushed up off my bed and started to dig through the one bag I had brought with me. There had to be something in there that I could wear. If not, I could always ask my new roommate for something. She knew Owen. They had all grown up in Gratin together. She would know what kind of girl he'd like. As I dug through my clothes, though, I realized something surprising to me. Everything I had brought with me was designer. And I wanted nothing to do with any of it. Which meant I had nothing to wear.

Grabbing my purse and my keys, I headed downstairs and out the front door for the first time in days. I knew the media was still likely crawling all over Gratin, but it wasn't like I didn't have practice with them. I slipped on my sunglasses and pulled a ball cap over my half-up ponytail. I could hope to blend in, but I knew they were on the lookout for me now. They knew my new look.

Maybe not everything from my old life was terrible. I had gotten fairly good at avoiding attention when I wanted to. They didn't realize it, but every picture they had of me, aside from the ones taken that night of Owen and me, had been a setup. I knew how to fly under the radar if I really wanted to.

Heading into town, I found the small boutique out on the main road that I had noticed when I first got to town and by some miracle, I had found something to wear that night. It wasn't the designer clothing I was used to, but that was the appeal. Oakley Morgan didn't care about labels. It was a freeing feeling really. I also grabbed some more subtle makeup and a nice headband for my hair.

Then, I headed off to the grocery store. I loved the idea of cooking for Owen, of being able to share something with him that had been a valued part of my childhood. I had adored those cooking lessons with Elisa. She taught me everything I ever wanted to know. It wasn't much, but it was what I could offer him.

I was still unsure about letting him in too far. I didn't want him to see all the baggage I came with, at least not right away. Because as much as I tried to convince myself otherwise, I liked him. He was the type of guy I could see myself falling for, head over heels, hard and fast. He was the type of guy a girl latched on to and stuck it out with all the way to the altar, the kind of guy a girl built a family with. It was all a dream I'd likely never get; I knew that. I had to admit, though, for once, it was nice to play 'what if' and fantasize that maybe, just maybe, one day my luck would turn around and he would be there waiting for me.

Fourteen
Owen

I felt ridiculous; I had spent the remainder of the afternoon staring at the damned clock like a teenager waiting on his first date. Even my dogs seemed to think I had finally cracked. I couldn't help myself, though; I was excited. I was also nervous. It was no secret that I had it in for Oakley, but it felt like I was walking a very fine line with her. Everything kind of hinged on tonight going well.

Not only could I lose my chance to be with her, but I could lose my chance to help her. I knew she could completely shut me out if she really wanted to. She could turn around and run again, and I would never see her again. There was really nothing I could do to stop that from happening. My only chance was to make her see that she didn't have to. That Jacey and I could help her.

It wasn't as if we were swamped with work. She had gotten to see that firsthand. Most nights, we sat around with our thumbs up our asses because there was nothing else to do. It helped that we now had a valid police reason to check out the house at night to make sure the girls were safe inside. It eased my anxieties about leaving her alone if I could make sure no one was skulking around outside.

The pictures from the night Oakley had gone to the station with me proved that the person watching us from across the street had been nothing more than a paparazzi. However, she seemed to believe she had genuine reason to fear someone coming after her. At least enough of a reason to warrant running again. I didn't think she realized that she would have to keep running for the rest of her life if she were to run again. She would never feel safe enough to slow down and actually build a life for herself. If she stayed in Gratin, though, if she let us help her, she could create that life right here in our small Pennsylvanian town. She could maybe build that life with me. At least in part, I hoped she'd want to.

I knew how crazy it sounded. That I was already falling for a woman I hardly knew; but there was something about talking to her that night, seeing her laugh and rag on Jacey the way she did. That innate need to protect the people she had come to care about. She was exactly the type of woman I had been waiting for and I had known almost instantly that night at the station that I belonged in her life, as long as she would allow me, in whatever capacity. She was going to make an amazing impact on my life. She needed to be here.

People came and went from our lives for a reason. Maybe her reason for being in my life was to finally teach me it was okay to love again. It had been three years since Chelsea left, and it had been my fault for pushing for something too quickly. Though we had been together four years when I proposed. It wasn't like it had come out of nowhere. She knew I wanted to get married, and still, she said nothing. That night I asked, she said no, and by morning she was gone.

She headed out west to follow her dreams of being an actress. Last I heard, she wasn't doing too well. Not that I wanted her to fail; I didn't, but just hearing her name still left a bitter taste in my mouth. The town had all moved on. They didn't really even talk about her much anymore. Something had held me back, though, a tether tying me to the night she broke my heart. Everyone else let go, but something in me couldn't. Not until the night I met Oakley. That night, the tether finally snapped me free. That meant something in my book. That maybe her being here wasn't just so that I could help her. Maybe it was so she could help me, too.

It had been long enough. I had once stupidly thought no one could make me feel the way Chelsea had until Oakley came along. Maybe it was selfish to put all my hopes on this when, clearly, she was going through something. I just couldn't ignore it anymore. I had to see if there was something there or if I was just pushing for something because I kind of sort of liked this girl a little.

I glanced at the clock on the stove again. I had told her I'd pick her up at six. It was just about five. Which meant I could finally start getting ready without feeling ridiculous about it. The house was clean already; after I had gotten home from helping her, that was the first thing I did. Except the house wasn't dirty to begin with. I kept pretty on top of routine maintenance. With the dogs in the house, I had to. Otherwise, the place started to stink.

I had to jump in the shower quickly and get dressed before heading out to get her. She had said she was going to the store to get things for dinner. I was curious to see what she would be making for us. The way she talked, maybe sticking her in the flower shop for a job, wasn't the way to go. It was a shame that the bakery had closed down a year prior to her showing up in town. I could only imagine she would be good there.

There were a few other restaurants in town, but they were all small mom-and-pop shops that were family-owned and operated. They rarely hired outsiders. Even O'Dell's was that way. The girls had taken over for their mother as soon as they'd been able to, but somehow, even they hadn't been forced to hire outside help. They made it work.

I pushed away from the breakfast bar where I had been sitting, staring at the clock for how long. I swear this wasn't my first time bringing a lovely lady home. Despite my nerves about it, I was usually quite good at it. I looked at the dogs, "You guys up for making a new friend tonight?" I asked them. Roscoe thumped his tail against the hardwood floor. He was the more sociable one of the two of them. Justice just stared up at me through the tops of his eyes, assessing what I was saying to him. "She's really nice," I promised them, and Roscoe's tail went into a full wag that made me smile.

I knew that Justice was the one to trust when it came to reading people. He was slow to warm up to people, but it meant they were trustworthy if and when he did. How he reacted to Oakley would be very telling.

Roscoe, on the other hand, loved absolutely everyone. A masked robber could come in, and as long as they were willing to pet him, he wouldn't give two shits if they were there to kill everyone. I shook my head at the boys before turning for the steps to get ready.

An hour later, I was running up the front steps of Fiona and Oakley's place. I stopped for a moment to smooth down my shirt before knocking on the door. It almost immediately flew open as if she had been standing right on the other side of the door. Except it wasn't Oakley. Instead, I was met with Fiona's amused gaze. Which, admittedly, scared me a little. She was definitely the sweeter one of the O'Dell twins; there was no denying that, but she had that same spark of feistiness that Liv had. The difference was Liv used it as an out-and-out weapon. Fiona was far subtler about it. Which, in many ways, made her that much more dangerous.

"She's still getting ready," she spoke as a way of a greeting. "But let me tell you, Owen, she looks absolutely amazing. Like, drop-dead gorgeous. I'm really rather hoping I don't have to call Mason to come resuscitate you after you see her," she teased. I simply shook my head at her and stepped into the house when she stepped back and held the door open for me. "You don't understand…" she laughed, "So I don't want you dying on me because you didn't heed my warning. I mean, how embarrassing would it be for you if I had to call your little brother in to give you mouth to mouth," she poked fun at me.

"Fi, she's gorgeous no matter what," I answered, hoping that would make her stop talking, but no such luck. Her smile grew at my comment.

"Spoken like a guy falling in love," she retorted. Damn it. I had thought I had done a better job at hiding the fact that I was falling for Oakley. Even at that, I wouldn't say that I was already in love with her. That was really pushing it. I was fumbling for a retort, but her knowing smirk made me sigh. There was no arguing with an O'Dell woman once her mind was made up. "So tonight, is this like a *date?*" she asked, putting way too much emphasis on the last word.

I pushed my fingers through my hair. How the hell was this more uncomfortable than waiting with my prom date's parents while she finished getting ready? I thought that was as bad as it could ever get. Her dad sat there, cleaning his gun, not uttering a word. Well, that wasn't entirely true. He threw a gruff "eleven" at me as we turned and headed for the door. Fiona shooting all those questions at me, though, was somehow worse than that prom date.

"There's no classification on what tonight is," I answered. "I told her that we'd just have dinner.…"

"At your house, all alone," she interrupted me.

I sighed, "Yes, at my place, and that we could just talk. She kept saying I didn't really know her. So I asked for a chance to get to know her."

Fiona bobbed her head once, "Well, you know, that's usually what first dates are for," she laughed. "Getting to know someone, you know, all the preliminary stuff. The precursor."

She was relentless when she wanted to be. Thankfully, I didn't have to argue any further because I heard a door close at the top of the stairs. She wasn't wearing anything remotely spectacular, just a really nice pair of jeans that fit her perfectly, hugging the curves she did have, and a plain t-shirt. Fiona was right to tease me, though, because I wasn't sure I had seen anyone more gorgeous.

I noticed right away that her hair, which had been somewhat unruly every time I had seen her previously, was now straightened and smooth. The most striking thing, though, was the fact that she wasn't wearing her glasses. They were in her hand, but this was the first time since the night we met outside the inn that I had seen her without them. Without the dark frames to hide behind, her eyes were even more stunning than I had previously realized.

All of Fiona's jokes suddenly made sense to me. "Wow, Oakley," I breathed, "You look…."

She slipped her glasses back on before she smoothed her hands down over her jeans and dropped her gaze to her feet in a shy manner that only made her even more gorgeous to me. This was what I had been talking about, that shy girl who ducked her head at a compliment. She was the woman I had started to get to know.

The woman who had been prominently featured in all those articles wasn't shy. She basked in compliments and all but begged for more. That wasn't the real Oakley, not the one I saw anyway. She finally looked back up at me and flashed me a smile. Fiona was right. It was enough to stop my heart dead in my chest.

"Thank you," she answered. "You don't clean up half bad yourself there, Officer Hale." Her returned compliment made me laugh slightly. Out of nerves, I could only guess. I was trained to stare down the barrel of a gun and not break a sweat. I had honed my skills to stay calm in absolutely any situation. Up until this moment, I thought I had reasonable control over myself. My sweaty palms and nervous laughter proved that I was no match for Oakley Morgan, not when she looked at me like that.

"Ready to go?" I asked her, doing my best to ignore the way Fiona was smirking at me from behind her. I didn't need her opening her mouth and saying something Oakley didn't need to hear just yet. I knew girls talked, and after tonight, I was sure Fiona would put her through an interrogation like no other. For now, though, I needed her to stay quiet.

She nodded once, "I just have to grab the bag from the kitchen with all of tonight's supplies," she answered.

I followed after her, taking the bags of stuff from her when she turned around with them. I may have grown up in a house with four boys running rampant, but my mother made sure we all grew up respectful of the women and people in general in our lives. Mostly women, though. She had been a damn stickler about that. She had always told us she never wanted to hear of one of us being disrespectful towards a woman, and if she did – well, she brought us into this world. She had no issues with taking us back out of it.

Oakley smiled at me as her fingers brushed against mine in the exchange. Something had definitely shifted between us while we had been hanging curtains earlier. I couldn't quite explain it, but I could only hope that it turned out to be something good for both of us. We both said our goodbyes to Fiona before we were out the door.

It was only a ten-minute drive from her place to mine. My house was situated more in the foothills of the Pocono mountains. There was a small river that ran right along the back edge of my property, and in the daylight, I knew it was somewhere I wanted to take her some time. The dogs loved going out to the river. It was slow-flowing, so they could romp in it on a hot summer day to cool off.

I could see us doing that, taking a walk out to the banks with the dogs, Oakley laughing as they splashed in the water, shrieking when Roscoe comes running back over and shakes off right in front of her.

I shook my head. I knew I shouldn't imagine a future with this woman because doing that meant giving way to hope. Which gave her the power to break my heart if she decided she didn't want to stick around Gratin. It was so easy to see all of that with her, though.

Maybe it made me crazy, but before she came blowing into town, everything about my future had been fuzzy at best. It was as if this dense fog had encumbered my life completely. I didn't know which way to go with anything, but when she appeared, it was like the sun finally broke through. Everything started to clear up again, and I knew exactly what I wanted. I just had to hope that she wanted all of it, too.

We talked idly on the way there. The roads leading back to my place were winding as we drove deeper into the wooded areas around the town. "Where are you taking me?" she asked, somewhat amused as she glanced my way. Her eyes shone with that spark I had come to love so damn much.

I grinned in response, "You'll see," I laughed. We had talked about going to my place. She knew that's where I was taking her. But it fascinated me that she was even asking the question.

Oakley shook her head at that, "See, I don't want to wait," she challenged. "I mean, how do I know that you're not going to try leaving me in the woods somewhere. You and Jacey might have some kind of twisted bet on how long the spoiled rich girl can survive in the woods," she mused. By the way she was looking at me, I could tell that she wasn't actually serious about that. "I'll have you know; I do know how to build a fire just fine. So who's ever betting against me with that will lose," she teased.

I sighed dramatically, "There goes a hundred bucks," I feigned disappointment, "I was really banking on you not even knowing what fire is." I glanced her way again, "I picked a place out in the middle of nowhere," I explained.

"Because Gratin isn't remote enough for you?" she joked.

I really liked what I saw with her. The way the comments flowed so easily between us. There was no awkwardness. At least not right then and there in the car. It was the start of something, what that was, I couldn't be too sure. I didn't want to get my hopes up. I couldn't risk another Chelsea situation. As much as I already liked Oakley, I had to tread carefully.

I chuckled at her jab at me and my town as I turned into my driveway. "I love Gratin," I answered. "But no, it's not," I explained. "I've always loved having my own space. Out here I do." She turned to look out the window as we pulled up in front of my place.

The house was nice, but it wasn't much to write home about. It was a modest, two-story log cabin-style house. It had two bedrooms upstairs with one bathroom. The downstairs basically consisted of a small office space, the kitchen, the living room, and the smaller bathroom. It was only me and the boys living there. It wasn't like I needed a lot of space.

She didn't take her eyes off the house, "This place is amazing, Owen," she breathed. "It just… it suits you somehow."

"My brothers all thought I'd lost it when I told them I wanted to design my own place," I shrugged. That had her gaze whipping around back to focus on me.

"You designed this place?" she asked.

I nodded, "With the help of a trained architect. There's this seriously talented architect based out of Maine. He was willing to design the place. His team helped put it all together at a reasonable cost," I explained. Before I could say any more, she was out of the car and looking around.

She came back over as I climbed out to meet her, "You're so giving me a tour first. I've always loved log cabins. They're just so… homey."

I laughed again at her enthusiasm. She really wasn't the young woman the tabloids painted her to be. I had been right. There was so much more beneath those masks she wore. "Okay, but first, I have to warn you," I started as I turned back to grab the bags of food. "I have two dogs. I hope that isn't an issue."

Fifteen
Oakley

"Dogs?!" I bounced in my spot. I loved dogs; it didn't matter what kind they were. They had to be my favorite creature on the planet, though I wasn't too modest to admit that most dogs loved me, too. "What kinds? What are their names? How old are they? Are they the biggest, lovable babies ever?" I asked in rapid succession.

He laughed at my quick-fire questions as he pulled out his keys to unlock the front door. "Roscoe is a Rottweiler," he started. "He's the big baby. He loves any and all kinds of attention, and in terms of guard dogs, he's completely useless," he explained. "And Justice is a German Shepherd. He's the more aloof one. It takes a while for him to warm up to people. But when he makes it clear he doesn't like someone, that's when Roscoe finally goes full on guard dog."

I waved him off, "I guarantee by the end of tonight, they'll both adore me," I promised. "See, that's a little fact you wouldn't know. I speak dog. Fluently," I joked. As soon as he pushed the door open, though, we were greeted by a bounding black and tan mass barreling right for us. Owen called a quick command, and he skidded to a stop right in front of us, sitting down and looking up at us with this wide dog grin, his tongue flopping out to the side. "You must be Roscoe," I cooed before holding my hand out for him to sniff. Instead of sniffing me, though, he immediately licked my fingers.

"Told you," Owen said as he scratched Roscoe's head on the way by, "Totally useless guard dog."

"Oh, don't listen to him," I reached out to play with his ears. "You're not useless. You're just a big baby who loves scratches, aren't you?" Knowing the dog probably weighed more than me when I was soaking wet, I did it anyway. I kneeled down in front of him, and he immediately lunged for my face with that big tongue of his. He started to lick me wherever he could reach, making me giggle before I wrapped my arms around him in a hug. His big head came to a rest on my shoulder.

"Aren't you the sweetest thing," I mumbled into his fur. "Tell me, baby boy, how'd you get mixed up with the likes of him?" I nodded in Owen's direction. "Is he good to you? You can tell me if he's mean and doesn't give you scraps. When clearly, you're the bestest doggie in the whole wide world and deserve it." I heard that unmistakably deep chuckle and looked up from the dog's fur to meet Owen's clearly entertained blue gaze. "And what are you laughing at, mister?" I questioned.

He just shrugged, "I just didn't know I'd be ditched tonight for my dogs," he sighed.

I took Roscoe's face between my hands, "When you look like this adorable young man, then you'll get my attention back." The dog seemed to bask in all the attention he was getting as I continued to scratch his ears.

I knew it wasn't necessarily safe to be hugging up on a dog I didn't know. He was giving me no warning signs that he didn't like it, though, and likewise, Owen wasn't warning me off of him either. He seemed to have trained him well.

What surprised me was when I started to pull away from Roscoe, I felt a wet nose brush against my hand. I glanced around Roscoe to meet the gaze of who I assumed to be Justice. "Well, hello, baby," I said softly.

Owen had made it clear that Justice was the more skittish one. If there was one I really needed to be careful with, it was him. I let him sniff my hand for a moment, allowing him to take the lead. I glanced to Owen, who looked completely surprised by the sudden turn of events.

"I have to say, this never happens. Justice doesn't even like it when Jacey comes over. He usually hides out upstairs. Figured that's where he'd be tonight," he watched the dog closely.

"Dogs love me. I told you, I speak their language," I turned my attention back to the dog, still sniffing my hand, when Roscoe got me with another lick right up the side of my face. I jumped, which caused Justice to back away a few steps.

"Justice is a rescue," Owen explained, coming over to crouch down next to the dog. "We're not completely sure of his history, we know he was trained in search and rescue, but we think there's a chance his handler was abusive. It says a lot about you that he's already down here." I wonder what that meant. I wasn't about to dwell on it, though. I couldn't let my thoughts wander down the path of what Justice's appearance meant to his owner. The way Owen was looking at me said enough.

"I do believe I promised to cook you dinner," I noted, slowly standing up so I didn't spook Justice even more. My moving sent him back to the dog bed I could now see sitting next to the fireplace burning brightly. "When did you light a fire?" I asked.

He smiled, "it's electric. As simple as the flip of a switch. I put the food in the kitchen," he pointed to the right. I could just make out a fridge and counter through the archway that led into it.

He turned and headed back into the kitchen, Roscoe right at his side every step. Following him, I took in my surroundings. I had demanded a tour, but that could wait until after dinner. I wanted to see what kind of house this man lived in. The style inside said a lot about him, but having two dogs like Justice and Roscoe also said a lot about him.

When I stepped into the kitchen, I made a beeline for the bags sitting on the breakfast bar. "So I opted to go for a classic: spaghetti and meatballs. However, absolutely everything is made from scratch. I made the noodles ahead of time because they're a pain to make. It would take too long. But I figured that the sauce and the meatballs shouldn't be too bad with an extra set of hands. I know I said earlier that you wouldn't be allowed in the kitchen, but I could use an extra set of hands. Think you can handle being a sous chef in your own kitchen?" I questioned, glancing back at him.

I figured if we managed to keep ourselves busy, maybe there wouldn't be any reason to delve too much into everything going on with me. At the same time, after doing some thinking on the subject, I had agreed to let him get to know the real me and a large part of that was what happened that day at the manor.

There was a very distinctive before and after in my head. I couldn't pretend like that whole situation hadn't changed me because it had. I wasn't the same girl I was before it happened. That was a pivotal point for me. Which in order to make him understand who I was now, I had to open up about what could very well be the most horrifying day of my life. I just didn't know how to approach the subject with him.

After asking him my question, I hadn't heard him answer or step up beside me. His hands were already washed, and his sleeves rolled up to his elbows. I looked up at him a little wide-eyed, "What?" He had said something, and I had clearly missed it, being off in my own little world the way I had just been.

"I was just asking where you wanted me to start," He gave me that slightly lopsided smile again.

I nodded, "Right. Why don't you start working on the meatballs," I suggested. "They're good and messy and kind of gross to touch," I smiled innocently. "The recipe should be in the bag with all the supplies," I pointed to the one he'd need. "Just don't mess them up, Hale. May never let you cook again if you screw up Elisa's meatballs." I glanced his way again as he stepped up with everything and started mixing the meatballs' ingredients. I liked that he wasn't afraid to get his hands a little dirty. It was a nice change of pace from the men I was used to dealing with.

They had always been more worried about not getting dirt under their nails or ruining their designer suits. They would never have stepped up to help me the way Owen had. A comfortable silence fell over us as we both worked on the meal prep. Every now and then, I could feel his eyes grazing over my skin before he turned back to what he was doing. I knew I had to approach the subjects we were here to talk about, but the truth was, I was having fun, and I didn't want to bring it all down with talk of my dead parents.

This time, I glanced his way, "So, tonight is all about you supposedly getting to know the real me. What do you want to know?" I asked, opening the door for him to ask anything he wanted. He sighed, keeping his focus trained on the onion he was cutting. He seemed to consider what he was about to say next carefully. "It's okay, Owen," I encouraged, "you can ask me anything."

At my nudging, he nodded slightly. "I guess my biggest question is how you went from the party heiress that the tabloids loved to gossip about to this…" he motioned to me.

I exhaled a deep breath at that. I knew he would go right for the money shot. He wanted to know all of it. At this point, I wasn't entirely sure I would scare him off. On the one hand, I kind of wished I could. It would make leaving Gratin that much easier if that's what it all came down to. On the other hand, though, I didn't want to scare him off at all. I wanted this kind, gentle man in my life for as long as I could keep him in it, which meant coming out with the truth, either way.

I focused on the sauce that was starting to simmer on the stove for a long moment, trying to piece together the best place to start. "I was starting to turn it around," I confessed. "About six months before everything happened, my father really laid into me about how I was going to be taking over the vineyard one day and the multi-million-dollar corporation that was Richfield Winery," I tried to explain. "He made a point of repeatedly saying that he wasn't going to be around forever to clean up my messes, that I had to step up or step out. And if I opted to step out, I was completely on my own." I shook my head.

I remembered that conversation with my father all too well. He had yelled at me like he had never yelled at me before. And just when I was on the brink of tears, he wrapped me in a tight hug and promised that he was only looking out for me.

My father was a businessman first and foremost, but he still knew how to be a dad when he needed to be. He wanted me to succeed. He wanted me to carry on the family legacy. He wanted nothing more than to know I would be okay after he was gone. That meant cleaning up my act and becoming an acceptable face for the company that I would one day be running.

"And I listened. That's why the stories the tabloid were putting out were more insane in the six months leading up to everything. Because I wasn't giving them anything to report on, so they were just out to make shit up completely." I couldn't look at Owen as I spoke. "But it really all changed the day I found them. Hindsight and all, now I wonder if my father knew something was coming. If he had been threatened and he was preparing me for the inevitable."

Owen reached out and wiped his hand off on a towel before he placed it on my shoulder comfortingly. He was silently encouraging me to continue. It was all something I hadn't even really been able to talk about with my shrink after it all happened. It was a memory I relived almost every night, that scene playing on repeat in my head as if it were some kind of movie purely designed to torture me.

Then he asked the two words I dreaded him asking. The two words that could change how he saw me.

"What happened?

Six Months Ago...

"You are so full of shit, Beck," I shot back at my supposed friend sitting across from me. "So I don't go out and party as much. That's not what made me fun. My dad isn't having it anymore. But I'm still me."

"Just admit it, Lizzie, you turned twenty-five, and you turned into an old hag," she challenged. "And for the good of my image, I can't be seen out with the likes of you anymore. And all this work, not like you'll get a guy now. Guess you'd better start working on collecting all of those cats," she smirked.

I was ready with the retort when my phone rang in my purse. I pulled it out to see my father's picture flashing across the screen. I rolled my eyes and hit decline before tucking it away again.

I held up my hands, "You know what, fine," I answered. "If you want to throw twenty years of friendship away because I'm no fun anymore, be my guest," I shoved away from the table. "Sorry, I actually decided to do something with my life instead of pissing it away, hoping to nail down the right dick." I didn't stick around to listen to her answer. Instead, I headed out into the street and into the nearest bar.

Four hours later, I had sobered up some, enough that I had convinced myself I was okay to drive. By some miracle, I had made it home alive. Climbing from the car, I groaned to myself when I saw my father's car parked in the driveway. He was going to bitch up a fucking storm because I ignored his calls and now I was drunk, too. When I had promised him several times now that I would stop drinking.

Well, we would see if his threats of rehab were legit or not. He'd been throwing that threat at me for years; it was always just talk. Talk, talk, talk. I giggled to myself at that as I tripped up the steps, slamming my knee into one of the stones. "Mother fu-" I bit back the words; a proper lady didn't swear like that. I was going to get enough shit from my father. I really didn't need my mother coming down on me, too.

God damn, they were such fucking buzzkills sometimes. So what if I went out and had a little fun every now and then? That was no reason to threaten to take the company from me. Since the day they realized I was all they were getting, I had been told that one day the company would be mine. I just had to wait for the old man to croak before it was mine.

I stood up again, stumbling towards the front door. When I pulled it open, something seemed off. It was quiet. Typically, my mother had that house bustling with activity. There was always some function to plan, or the ladies were over for tea.

Fuck, was I going to have to start drinking tea too? That shit was nasty. Especially with milk in it like my mother drank. Lukewarm, milky, leaf water. What was appetizing about that? I really didn't want to drink tea all the time. Now, wine I could get on board with. This family loved wine! We grew it, we made it, and we sold it. Our wine paid for everything. Wine was definitely the way to go.

Plus, there was a good chance it would liven up those stuffy old tea parties she liked to throw so much. As if the leaf water wasn't bad enough, nothing ever happened at those things. They just sat there talking at each other because god knows they never actually fucking listened to what anyone else was saying. Unless it was gossip, I caught them talking about my scandals more than once. Not that I cared what the old biddies of the valley had to say about me.

Making my way to my father's study, I tried to rid myself of the growing limp. They didn't need to know I fell outside. I stood a little straighter and attempted to smooth down my hair. The tabloids had been hammering me lately, and all I had wanted was a little sympathy from my best friend. Beck was Beck, though. I shouldn't have been surprised at that. Her image meant everything to her. Even if that image made her look like the biggest piece of trash known to man.

I just had to pretend like I wasn't still totally toasted while they both yelled at me and then I could go upstairs to my room and pass out. Bed sounded really good right then. I took a deep breath and tried to suppress a giggle. My breath reeked of alcohol. I calmed myself back down before pushing the doors open.

Everything froze at that moment as the door swung open, and my gaze swept over everything. The scream wanted to come, but it was caught in my throat. There was blood, so much blood…

I couldn't…

 I didn't understand…

"Daddy?" I managed to choke as I dropped to the floor next to him. "Daddy, wake up!" I reached out to shake him as his blood started to soak through my clothes. When I touched him, though, I must have pushed too hard, and he rolled over. His eyes were wide open, staring up at me with no life left in them.

"Daddy?" I whispered again. "Please, no. No. No! God no!" I scrambled to my feet and back against the wall. Sliding down it, I hugged my knees tight against my body, trying to ignore the blood that now stained my jeans. It was then that I noticed my mother lying there, too, next to the desk. The tears finally came as the shock started to wane.

I sat there for who knows how long, never taking my eyes off of them, silently begging for one of them to move. In the back of my head, I knew they were both gone. I was alone now in everything.

I fumbled in the darkness for my phone, blinking when the screen lit up brightly in front of me. I found Abraham's number quickly before my gaze darted back to them. What if one of them woke up? I set my phone to speakerphone before setting it back down next to me. When he answered, I struggled to find my voice at all.

"I need your help," I managed to choke out weakly.

Sixteen
Owen

I watched her closely as she recounted everything that had happened that day. I didn't want to believe that she had gone through all of that, that she had felt the need to pack up her life and start over in a place she'd never been. I didn't know anyone could be that strong, but I could also see that in her eyes, she didn't have a choice.

When I saw the tears starting to streak her face, though, I stepped into her and wrapped my arms around her. I couldn't just stand there while she cried and not offer some kind of comfort to her. She melted in against me, her fingers pulling at the back of my shirt as she grabbed it in her hands. Fuck, if there were a way for me to take away her pain, I would do it. I would find a way. On top of the fact that she carried around the loss of her parents every day, I could tell it was laced with so much guilt, too.

"If I hadn't been drinking that day, if I hadn't broken my promise to my father, I would have been there," she whispered from where her face was buried against my chest, her tears soaking through my shirt.

"And then what, Oakley?" I asked her softly. "If you had been there, what would have happened?"

Everyone always had this idea in their heads that if they had been there, if they had been prepared, they could have changed things. They never liked facing the truth, that even if the scenario played out exactly how they imagined it, it never would end the way they wanted it to. Oakley wanted to believe that she could have stopped it if she had been there that day. She could have saved them. The truth was, though, if she had been there that day, she likely would have died right there with them, too and then no one would have any insight into what happened that day. She wouldn't be around to carry on her family's legacy or tell their story.

I did have to question, though, what she was planning on doing about her family's business. Assuming the killer was caught, and she deemed it all safe to return to the Richfield name, what was she planning on doing about the company that her family had built? Would she return home to run it, following her father's wishes?

I knew it was a question that needed to be asked, something that I needed to know for my own peace of mind before I let any of this go too far. I couldn't let myself fall for someone who might pack up and leave without any notice. Whether that was to run again, thinking that was her best option. Or whether it was to return home. I didn't want to potentially get involved with someone who might turn around and bail.

I could play the what if game myself, but there was no denying I was already involved. At that moment, though, standing there with her, none of that mattered. All that mattered was making her feel better as best I could. If that meant holding her together while she fell apart, I could do that.

She didn't answer my question. She didn't have to. I knew what she needed to believe, and I knew the truth of the matter. "Oakley, I want to help," I said softly, "But I can't do that if you run again."

She pulled back enough to look up at me, those large green eyes still filled with tears, "I don't want to run again," she admitted, her tone no more than a whisper. "But I can't let you help either, Owen. What if they come for me? What if they try to hurt you or Jacey? We don't know who it was, what they want. If they're after the Richfield money, or the company, I'm now the name on all of those accounts. Which means they're coming. My father had enemies, sure, but not in the mafia, gonna shoot him sort of way. And my mother… she drank tea and planned parties. It's not like she had any enemies out there that would want to kill her off. The most logical thing is the company. Which puts me right in the crosshairs. And now with all this stupid publicity…" she pulled away from me, pushing her fingers into her dark hair.

"They know where I am Owen. I don't want to have to run. I like it here, I like the people, I like…" she stopped herself. "But if I stay, if I let you help me, they're going to come after me. After you."

"Then we'll be ready," I challenged. "Oakley, I'm a cop. This kind of thing is exactly what I do for a living. Please, if you stay Jacey and I, we have connections. We can call in some extra help, we can figure this out. But if you run, then you're out there, alone. And if the tabloids find you again, then whoever is after you will find you there too. You could spend your whole life running from some unseen assailant. But if you slow down, if you stop and fight and let us help you, we could end this Oakley. And then you can go back home, take over the company. Do whatever it is your father wanted you to do." There. It was out there. I couldn't take it back. I would learn what she intended to do.

She stared at me curiously, her expression trying to decipher what I was really saying. "Owen…" she started slowly.

That made me more nervous than I really should have been. I didn't have any right to ask this girl to stay. It was her life. She needed to do whatever made her happiest. The truth was, I didn't want her to leave. I wanted her to pick Gratin. I wanted her to pick me. I wasn't ashamed to admit to that. At least not to myself. I wanted to be with her and see where it could take us.

She turned back to the stove, wiping at her eyes as she went. I didn't like how she left my name hanging in dead air like that.

What?

Owen, what?

How was she going to finish that sentence? "Owen, I'm sorry, but no." Or "Owen, I'm madly in love with you." The possibilities were endless. I knew I needed to leave well enough alone. I needed to accept that she clearly didn't want to finish that sentence. As a cop, though, my fatal flaw was that it was impossible for me to leave things unanswered.

I stepped back over to my post with the meatballs, returning to my work in silence. We could still turn this around and make a nice evening out of it. I wasn't sure if or how we would recover from what happened.

"Oakley," I started, and she shook her head. I didn't know what that meant. "Look, we were having fun before everything got brought up. I know the mood has shifted, and that's okay. But what do you say to trying to get some of that fun back?" I asked her. "We can put on some music, grab a drink, finish making dinner…."

She didn't look my way. "I don't know what's going to happen," she said quietly, so quietly I almost missed it. "When it's all over, if it's ever over. It depends on how long it takes. Right now, my dad's right-hand man is running the company. And he would be perfect to take it over; I could just be a silent owner. My dad only taught me so much before he died. We thought we had time. And Billy knows how to run the company; he's been doing a great job of it for the last seven months. He even put out a special bottle that had my parents pictured on the label. With a little memorial dedication to them." She shrugged. "My point is, I haven't figured it all out. But I do know, I can't go back to that house. I can't… I see it enough in my head every night. I wouldn't be able to stay there again. Be in the house where they…" She started to cry again, but this time, the tears slipped silently down over her cheeks.

"You don't have to have all the answers right now," I promised her. "All I'm asking is that you let me help so that you can figure it all out in time, in a safe space." She turned the burner down low before looking for one of the bags I had carried in.

"You know, let's just stick with having fun tonight," she answered, once again wiping at her eyes. Finally, she found what she was looking for and pulled it from the bag before holding it up for me to see. "You want to get to know me; we're making my favorite of Elisa's dinners that she taught me to cook. Maybe you should understand what all the fuss is about when it comes to Richfield wine."

I dipped my head once in a slight nod. "Sounds good to me, wine glasses are in the cabinet next to the fridge," I directed.

She turned and marched over to the fridge, opening the cabinet. "Owen!" She whined, "Is this some sort of sick joke?" She placed her hands on her hips and turned to face me again. I couldn't help but smile at that; she was so damn adorable.

"What?" I asked, turning around to the sink. I washed my hands before going over to her and glancing in the open cabinet, only to spot the wine glasses on the very top shelf. I laughed, "Sorry, I forgot I moved them up there. I used to drink wine more often, so they were always lower. But I haven't been as much the last few years, so I shifted everything around."

I reached around her and pulled the box down. I set it down on the counter while she closed the door. I could see the wheels turning. She wanted to ask. "It's okay, you can ask me anything," I said, mirroring what she had said to me before.

After she had opened up about everything with her parents, it wasn't fair of me to keep everything with Chelsea a secret from her. She needed to go into whatever this was between us completely open and understanding of where I was coming from.

She sighed, "what happened?" She questioned, mimicking my previous statement.

I took my time washing the glasses before handing them to her. "I was with someone; we had been together a few years. She moved in here, and she was a big wine drinker. Had a glass almost every night with dinner. So I went out and bought these," I held up the glass for her to see. "It was nice to sit back with a glass of wine after a long day. I worked day shift then, I had switched from nights when she moved in because she didn't like being alone every night. Used to argue that there was no point in her living here at all if I was never home. Which I mean, valid point. So I talked to the chief to get things switched around. Which meant giving up my partnership with Jacey. She was thrilled about that. Those two really didn't like each other." I shook my head before turning back to what I had been doing before she whined about the glasses being out of her reach.

"Long story short," I continued, "I proposed, in front of my whole family, her family, all of our friends. She looked me up and down and flat out said no, right there in front of everyone. And she said it in a way that made me sound crazy for even asking in the first place. Like I had lost my mind or something. But we were living together, that was the next logical step. I ended up working the night shift with Jacey that night. When I got home the next morning, all of her stuff was gone."

I didn't have to look up to know she was right there next to me; she gently placed her hand on my back, her thumb brushing over my shirt in these soft, gentle strokes. "For the record, you weren't the crazy one," she spoke softly, her tone gentle and soothing. "She was, for saying no to a guy like you. If I had met a guy like you before everything went down, I would have latched on and never let you go."

I turned to face her more at that, not sure how to take what she was saying. Was it just a hypothetical we were talking about? Did she mean it? I tried to decipher what she meant by studying her face, but she remained relatively impassive this time.

I knew I shouldn't, but the more I told myself that, the harder she was to resist. I had never been one of those people who wanted things they couldn't have. It was a waste of energy to pine after something that would always be just out of reach, but she was different in so many ways. I knew I shouldn't want her, but I did. I knew I shouldn't pursue something with her, but I really wanted nothing more. I wanted to know what it was like to hold her like I had after she told me about her parents, for that to be more than just a comforting embrace. I wanted to know what it would be like to kiss her, to explore all of that with her.

Maybe I was crazy, despite what she had just said. Even still, I couldn't help the two words that passed through my lips. I couldn't keep them from escaping. "But now?"

She watched me closely. I knew her answer before it was ever spoken. She was fighting the same war I was. She was stuck between knowing what was right and going for what she wanted. It was reassuring to know that I wasn't alone in that, but I didn't want to be the one to make the first step; that was on her. I didn't want to push anything on her that she wasn't ready for or that she didn't want. I had been raised better than that.

I swallowed as I held her gaze. I wasn't going to back down. I wanted to know the answer to that. "But now…" she said softly, shaking her head. "Now, I don't know Owen. You're the kind of guy I used to dream of finding. But everything is different. I don't know what's coming next. And you already had someone up and leave you…." Before she could say much more, the timer went off.

She turned away from me, back to the stove, to pull the fresh meatballs from the oven. After checking that they were done, she dumped them into the sauce she made. I watched her silently, begging her to turn back around and finish what she had been saying. "Dinner is almost ready," she answered, finally looking back at me.

"Oakley…" I pushed, but she only sighed.

She dumped the pasta in the boiling water, poking at it for a moment. "I'm not the kind of girl you want to get involved with," she insisted. "I can't promise that I'm going to stay Owen, I can't stand here and say I'm definitely staying in Gratin. I'm scared out of my fucking mind that if I stay it means someone is going to get hurt because of me. I'm scared you're going to get hurt. How am I supposed to live with myself if that happens? Knowing that if I had never come to Gratin, you, Jacey, Fiona, you'd all be going about your lives safe and happy and none the wiser to my existence."

I didn't know what to say to that. I could tell her that it wasn't on her to worry about that kind of thing until I was blue in the face, but she would continue to worry, regardless of what I said or did at this point, I was learning that was just who she was. She had taken on the weight of all of us, and if she didn't relieve some of it somehow, she would crumble under it.

She was right, but she was also wrong. She was precisely the type of girl I wanted to get involved with. She was sweet, she was caring, and the fact that Justice took to her so easily said everything to me. That dog knew good people; he had no reason to trust anyone, but he had trusted Oakley from the moment she walked through the front door. If I couldn't trust my own view on things, I had to trust his. Oakley was a good person, no matter what she wanted to believe about herself, and I wanted a good woman in my life.

Someone who would stand by me through thick and thin. Someone who wouldn't hold back and loudly let me know when I was doing something stupid. I needed someone just like her. I wanted someone just like her. "Do you realize how lonely my life was before you came along?" I questioned. "I was actually considering asking Liv out because I thought she was my last shot," I half laughed.

Anyone who knew the two of us knew that would never work, but being with someone who I shared some kind of friendship with was better than being alone for the rest of my life. "We don't get newcomers very often in town, and everyone else is already spoken for. I was considering going to talk to her the night I almost ran into you. If that isn't fate interfering, then I don't know what is, Oakley."

She looked at me skeptically, "Fate?"

I nodded, "I know it's lame to believe in things like fate, but I do. Every choice we've ever made has led us straight to this moment here. You could have picked any town in the world, but you chose Gratin...." She smiled slightly, "What?"

"Actually, I didn't choose Gratin at all," she confessed. "I didn't even know it existed. When I got into the cab, I told the driver to take me as far as the money I handed him would allow. He dropped me off here. When he pulled up across the street from Rudy's place, he told me the next town was a good fifteen miles away and that I hadn't given him enough to make it that far. So I got out here."

I laughed slightly; I couldn't help it. "See? Fate."

Seventeen
Oakley

As painful as it was, I had turned away from that smile to finish making dinner. I needed something to busy my hands, or else I would be pulling him in nice and close before either of us knew what was happening. I drained the pasta and added it to the sauce. "I don't know if I believe in fate because that would mean my parents were meant to die the way they did," I admitted softly. "I hate thinking that it was written in the stars somewhere, and just, no one knew how to read it. I mean, I never got to say goodbye, you know?" I turned off all the burners before looking back at him.

"But if they hadn't died the way they did, if it had been a car accident, you wouldn't have run," he pointed out to me, and as much as I hated to admit it, he was right. If I hadn't had reason to believe I was possibly in danger, too, I wouldn't have run. Every day at that manor, I had feared for my life. That I would turn the corner and come face to face with whoever it was that had killed them. "And if you hadn't run, you never would have ended up here. With me," he finished.

My stomach knotted as I stood there in his kitchen, staring up at him. It felt as if we were standing on the very edge of a canyon, nothing below us but an empty abyss. I could tell by the look in his blue eyes that he felt it, too, that this moment would define everything that would come between us. We could either leap together, holding fast to each other, putting our trust and faith in one another, and letting the moment swallow us whole.

Or we could back away slowly and pretend as if the entire evening had never even happened in the first place. No matter what, though, everything was changing between us. Whatever decision was made right then, there was no taking it back once it was out there. Even as I thought that my fingers itched to touch him, to run my hands over his muscular chest, to feel his heart beating fervently beneath his skin. Was it beating as erratically as mine was? "So is this fate?" I asked him, my eyes never leaving his as I shuffled forward a tiny step, anything to be closer to him.

He dipped his chin in a slight nod, "yeah," he answered simply. I still wasn't sure I believed in all that fate mumbo jumbo. It seemed ridiculous to think that every choice, right down to what I had for lunch the other day, led us here to this moment, that every move we made was part of some predetermined plan. I didn't like thinking that we didn't have any say in how things played out, but even I had to admit, the way I landed myself in Gratin had all purely been by chance. From the first flight out of California to the choice in direction the cab driver took all the way to Owen, being the first person in town that I met. It all seemed a little destined to happen. I was meant to find him.

My question was for what reason, though? So he could help me? It all seemed to run a little deeper than that. If I admitted we were destined to find each other, that brushed a little too close to the idea of soulmates for me.

Shaking my head slightly to chase away those thoughts, I took another careful step closer to him. Bringing my hand up to his chest, I sighed when I felt the strength there, but what captured my attention more was the way his heart thumped beneath my fingertips. The steady rhythm was quick, matching my own. So, he was just as nervous as I was.

I finally let my gaze drop from his to trace over his features. I studied each curve, every sharp line. I followed the lines from his kind eyes to his strong jaw and in toward his mouth. I wanted to take it all in, in case tonight was all we allowed ourselves.

"But what if I need to…." I started to ask, and he shook his head.

His hand came up to my cheek, his thumb brushing high along my cheekbone. "We'll figure it out, Oakley. If you let me help, we'll figure it out." I nodded. Because the idea of pulling away now seemed more painful than anything any mystery killer could ever inflict. I had to know. I had to feel his lips against mine and quell that curiosity that had been bubbling inside me since the moment I met him. I had to know what he tasted like and if his lips were as soft as they appeared to be.

I couldn't help it anymore if letting him help meant I got to push forward with this… I knew it was dangerous for both of us. If someone saw how much he meant to me, he would be the first one they'd go after. I had to douse those fears with the simple reminder that he was a cop. He was trained to deal with situations like mine. I couldn't ignore the very real fact that, again, he was right.

If I ran away again, I would be facing all of this alone. It didn't seem quite so scary knowing I had him standing behind me. The choice was made as if there was really a choice to be made at all. We would figure everything out in time when all of this was behind me. If I had to go back to Richfield Manor, we would make it work.

I wrapped my fingers in the soft material of his shirt and tugged him closer. Leaning up on my toes slightly, I met his lips in a firm kiss, and suddenly we were both freefalling over that ledge together. His arm wrapped around my waist, pulling me closer to his body. His reaction calmed the nerves that had wound themselves into a tight ball in my stomach. Releasing his shirt, I let my arms snake up around his neck and dragged him down to my level, pushing the kiss a little deeper and more demanding.

I wanted to taste him. I wanted to explore everything about him. It had been so long since I had let a man into my life I didn't know how to do it anymore. Owen was so different from any other guy I ever dated, though. This was all new territory for me in so many ways. I was used to men who were so caught up in their own appearances that they hardly noticed me there. They needed fancy cars and designer clothes. In the end, I didn't really even matter to them. I was yet another possession that made them look good.

Owen was everything those men weren't. He cared about the people around him. He cared about me – some girl who blew into his town on the eastbound winds, running from a phantom.

Parting my lips, I dared to push it further. I had to know what he tasted like. I brushed the tip of my tongue over his lips, silently begging for him to meet me halfway. I sighed into the kiss when he opened his mouth and pressed his tongue to mine. I didn't know a guy could taste so sweet and still have the hints of minty freshness burn mixed in.

I don't know how long we stood there, wrapped in that moment with each other, slowly exploring every new touch and taste. I brushed my fingers into his hair, not at all surprised to feel how soft it was. Everything about this man enveloped every single one of my senses. He pulled back first, and I whimpered slightly at the loss of his mouth against mine. Which only seemed to make him smile.

"Dinner is getting cold," he explained gently before leaning in to press a gentle, teasing kiss to my lips. "And I hear the meatballs are the best part."

I quirked a brow at him at that. "We'll see about that officer," I answered. Before I could pull away from him completely, though, I leaned up and kissed him again. Once again, getting lost in the feel of his lips brushing over mine. He laughed slightly at my second attack.

"Food," he mumbled against my mouth.

"Hmm… who needs it," I answered. He turned and picked me up, setting me on the breakfast bar so that I was a little more on his level. He pressed into me and I sighed at the feeling of him between my legs like that. Holy fuck. It had been a while since I kissed a man, but it had been even longer since I'd felt that warm heat rushing through my body.

I wanted to forget about dinner altogether, take that tour of his house, and make sure that we ended with him showing me a personal view of his bedroom. It was as if every salacious desire I had was coming out of the shadows. I wanted this man more than I wanted anyone or anything in my life.

He broke the kiss for a second time, and I almost growled in frustration until he moved instead to kiss down the side of my neck. "Owen," I breathed. Now that the dam had been broken, there was no going back. We couldn't revert back to what we had been before, and at that moment, I was more than okay with that.

My saying his name like that only seemed to encourage him, which I was more than okay with as I slipped my hands up the back of his shirt. I wanted to feel every inch of him pressed against me, preferably without clothing in the way. Raking my nails across his back, I smiled innocently when he pulled back to meet my gaze. I loved seeing that heat in his ordinarily calm blue eyes, knowing damn well I was the reason it was there.

Without a word, we both leaned back in, and our lips crashed together. His hands traveled over me, too, dipping beneath the fabric of my shirt. I had never wanted someone the way I wanted him. I needed to feel him.

Shifting on the counter slightly, I pressed against him more. I sighed against his lips at the way he felt standing between my legs.

For the second time, I found myself wishing our clothing would just vanish. It was a blatant reminder of how valuable skirts and dresses could be in these situations. I wasn't the only one who seemed to enjoy being pressed together the way we were. Owen's fingers flexed against my waist as he once again broke the kiss. One hand held me there in place on the counter while his other traveled up my side.

Meeting his gaze, I smiled slightly before lifting my arms over my head. Taking my silent invitation, he pushed my shirt up and off before dropping it on the counter next to me. Reaching for his shirt next, it was quick to join mine. He was as solid as his uniform shirt suggested.

Running my hands up over his chest, I leaned back in to kiss him again. The tempo had slowed, and our desperation to get at each other was quieting. I didn't know where this was going tonight, but I was more than happy just seeing where the night took us. Even if we just stayed like this, that would be enough for me.

His hands went back to wandering, skimming slowly over my skin. He seemed just as determined to learn every inch of me as I was to discover him. I wanted all of him, this gorgeous man who was risking it all to be with me. He deserved the world. I couldn't give him that, but I could give him me.

Then, like he knew what I was thinking, he pulled back again and sighed, his hands slipping away. Gently taking my face in his hands, he leaned in to kiss me softly once more. "We should slow down," he suggested. Before he could say any more, I was shaking my head. The last thing I wanted to do was slow down. I wanted to pick up the pace a little. I wanted him to carry me upstairs, throw me down on his bed and have his caveman way with me. He smiled, "Oakley, I don't want to rush this, okay?" he told me. "I'd like to take you out on a real first date first. I want us to build something real here, not just go at it on my kitchen counter and go our separate ways."

I huffed at that; I didn't like that plan. I didn't see why we couldn't do both. We could go on a first date and build something real after he got all carnal with my body on his kitchen counter. Both were an option. "I want to do this right."

Slowly, I nodded, "Fine. But you need to back up then, mister," I told him before rolling my hips against him slightly to emphasize my point. He tried to choke back a groan at the contact before he took a big step backward. "Arm's length away from me," I warned. "I'm going to have a hell of a time as it is keeping my hands off of you."

He smirked, "Likewise, Beautiful."

I took in the view of him standing shirtless in front of me, smirking like that. Damn, it was going to be hard not to jump him. Reaching behind me, I smiled when I found his shirt. "This is mine now," I teased before pulling it on, "You can stay like that." He raised a brow at that, but he didn't fight me on my declaration. Smart man.

I made sure he kept his distance, even going as far as snapping the cooking tongs at him when he got too close while I was serving up dinner. He laughed before moving away to shift some stuff around. I kept my focus on the task at hand, grating some fresh parmesan cheese over the top of the pasta. I couldn't start thinking about his lips on mine, about the way he had just touched me. If I wanted to survive this dinner now, I had to think about somber things, like the fact that there was still potentially a murderer out there and after me.

Nope.

Even that didn't work to calm the heat washing through me.

I turned around with both plates in hand, only to find him lighting a candle in the middle of a small table set up next to the fireplace. "You know, this could count as our first date," I told him as I walked up behind him, leaning around him to set his plate on the table.

He glanced at me and smiled; god, he had to be careful flashing that thing around like that. Every time he directed it right at me, it was a shot right to the heart. He shook his head, "No, I'd rather take you out. Plan the whole evening. Maybe a walking tour of Gratin in the moonlight," he joked. I could tell he found his suggestion funny, that it wasn't meant to be taken seriously at all, but I couldn't help but love the idea.

The town was small, yes, and I had probably seen most of it by now. Getting guided around by a local who had lived here all his life, though, and being told stories from his childhood as we strolled hand in hand down the street together. It actually sounded really nice.

"We should do that," I looked up at him as he moved to pull out a chair for me. "I mean, I get that you were joking. But I didn't grow up here. I'd love to see this place through your eyes. Get to know the real Gratin a little better. And the real Owen." Before he could pull away, I smiled slightly and leaned in to steal one more kiss.

He sighed and shot me a rather pointed look; I could see the frustration tinting that amazing blue. I laughed slightly as he walked around the table and took his spot before he bothered to answer me, "If that's something you really want to actually do, we can arrange that," he promised.

That made me smile, "Good."

We ate dinner peacefully, and the conversation flowed easily, but there was definitely a building tension between us. I saw the way his gaze kept slipping from mine and down to my lips. I couldn't help but reach out and take his hand that was sitting on the table, playing with his fingers. There was just this innate need to be touching him now, this growing necessity to feel him close.

I didn't know what he had initially planned to end the night with, but I wanted to end it curled up in his arms. I couldn't deny it anymore. Being wrapped in his arms like that, it was the first time that I felt genuinely safe since I found my parents in the study that day. Since then, every shadow was out to get me. I had heightened security on the manor to exponential degrees. Nothing was going to get in or out without my notice.

Being in Gratin with Owen was different, though. There was no high-tech security system in place. There was no security team surveying the area every day and night. There was no guard posted at every door, including whatever room I was in at the time. It was just him and me, and somehow, that was enough. I couldn't explain the feeling; it was just this sense of total calm that had come over me, like being with Owen at that moment was exactly where I needed to be, like it was fate or something.

I smiled at that and shook my head slightly, which earned a curious look from Owen. "What?"

I laughed, "Nothing."

The quiet was soon ruined by my phone buzzing in my pocket. I would have ignored it entirely, but I had told Fiona to text me when she was headed home. Maybe it was a tad overprotective, but if someone were after me, it wasn't far-fetched to believe that the first place they would look was my current place of residence.

She had been confused by my request, but she had promised to oblige. I pulled it out to answer her quickly. When I flipped it open, the message on the screen made me freeze.

"Look, I know you have your reasons for that ridiculous thing," Owen started, shaking his head at my antique phone. "But… Oakley, what is it?" I pulled in a shaky breath; it was nice to know I wasn't being paranoid for no reason at all.

I turned the phone for him to see the typed words across the screen. He looked at it slightly before his eyes widened, and he took my phone from me. "Who sent you this?" he asked me, his gaze back on mine as he searched for some kind of clue, any hint at all.

"It's from an unknown number," I answered. My hands started to shake as I pulled them back into my lap. I had known someone was out there; someone was looking for me. At the very core of my being, I had known that I wasn't running for no reason at all. Someone wanted to hurt me like they had hurt my parents.

The worst part of it all was that I had no clue who it was. It could be anyone. My father didn't have a lot of enemies, and they weren't the killing type, or so I thought. Someone had killed them, and it had been too pre-meditated and perfectly planned to be some random chance murder. It wasn't like someone had broken in; the cops had found no signs of forced entry. Which likely meant it was someone they knew, someone they trusted. My father's business associates and my mother's friends, the possible suspects were extensive. It could have been anyone. In that world, no one was truly your friend.

Now that someone was after me, too. How could I stay? How could I trust that this person wouldn't go after Fiona or Owen?

Owen shook his head, "Oakley, until we figure out who this is from… it could just be someone messing with you. The truth came out, some people have a really twisted sense of humor."

I could feel the panic starting to bubble within me. It became increasingly harder to breathe. My hand started to shake where it rested against my leg. Flexing my fingers before balling them into a fist, I pulled in a slow breath. Anything to chase away the building panic. This man had already seen me lose it once tonight. It didn't need to happen again. I stared at him, my eyes watery with the tears threatening to fall.

"Or those fucking tabloids gave me away, and now they're coming to finish what they started. Tie up any loose ends and get their hands on whatever it is they're after," I challenged. I pushed away from the table and headed back towards the kitchen, searching for my purse. I had to get out of there. Owen followed after me, hot on my heels. He reached out and grabbed my hand before I could get too far, pulling me to a stop.

"Oakley, stop," he said firmly before pulling me in against him. That sense of calm that had been over me before, that feeling of safety when I was wrapped in his arms like that. It was gone. That damned text had ruined everything.

I couldn't breathe, I couldn't think straight, my body was screaming at me to run. "We'll figure it out, okay? Jacey and I can try to trace the text. To be honest, it's probably from a burner phone. But it's a place to start, okay?" He tilted my chin up so that I had to look at him. "I'm not going to let anyone hurt you."

I nodded slightly and leaned in against his chest, letting his steady heartbeat soothe me as best it could. Up until that point, it had all been some figment of my imagination. This was proof though that it was all real. Someone wanted me dead. And worse yet, they were out to play a game with me. Those six words would haunt me for the rest of my life.

Unknown:
Ready or not, here I come.

EIGHTEEN
ASH

I set the phone down in the passenger seat as I stared across the street at the small-town diner in front of me. Fuck, this place was disgusting. Everyone always went on about charming small town life, but this place made my skin crawl. I hated that idea of everyone being in my business, but I could see why a spoiled little rich bitch thought I wouldn't find her here. It would have been the last place I'd have thought to look.

Clever, but not clever enough. She wasn't quick enough to outsmart me. The bitch would have to try harder if she wanted to escape me. I grinned at that.

When I had arrived in town a mere hour ago, I had the forethought to drive around and check the place out. After I grabbed Elizabeth, I would need a quick escape before that cop boy toy of hers caught on to what was happening. As much as I wanted to make the bitch suffer, I wasn't into leaving an even bigger mess. Killing a cop would be stupid and reckless.

Sure, the Richfield's had been important people, but authorities threw in the towel on them pretty quickly, which had been a pleasant surprise. I had been thorough, sure, but even I knew the police had their ways. I hadn't signed up for killing a cop, though. That they weren't just going to let go of. I had to tread carefully now that I was in Gratin. I had to learn all I could and make my presence known to them without giving away where I was hiding out.

I had found an empty house out on the edge of town, well secluded by the forest that surrounded this hellhole of a tiny town. It would have to do until I could find my opening to make my move. I wanted to make her suffer first. It would be too easy just to swoop in and grab her when her cop boyfriend wasn't looking. I knew I could just kill her, take her out from a distance even. I wasn't the best shot, but I was good enough. Then I could rest easy that the job was done, but that wasn't any fun for me.

I wanted to see the terror in her eyes, knowing I was out there, lurking in the shadows. I wanted her to know I was coming for her but I didn't want her knowing when I might appear. I would haunt her, make her scared of every shadow and bump in the night. I would make her regret ever pissing me off in the first place, and then I would grab her and run. There was a chance I would have my fun with her too, torture her a bit just for the hell of it. Then, I would kill her when I eventually got bored.

There was a scratching sound coming from the back of the van. Great, the old man was awake again. Was it really too much to ask that he just stay the fuck unconscious until I needed him? Or, god fucking forbid, he could just give it up and die already.

Now that I was in Gratin, It didn't matter to me if I left his body for them to find. I just couldn't do that until I was ready for them to find him. At this point, his chances of survival were diminishing. He just needed to do us both the favor and croak. Then I wouldn't have to tote him around like this. Sure, I could have killed him, too, but then I would have had a rotting body in my van. No one wants to smell that during a cross-country drive. It wasn't like I could just leave him for dead. My luck, someone would have found him, and my cover would have been blown.

So here we were; he was awake again, and I had to get out and put the old bastard back to sleep. Pushing out of the van, I pulled my ball cap low over my eyes as I rounded around to the back doors. He was tied up; it wasn't like he stood any chance of getting out, but I couldn't have the old bastard making so much god damned noise either. He was a stubborn old shit, if he thought someone might hear him, he would keep trying. Yanking the doors open, I rolled my eyes when his widened. Like he really thought I wouldn't come back here after him. Apparently, he was fucking stupid too. Climbing into the back, I grabbed the cloth that I had been using, poured a little more chloroform on it, and pressed it against his nose and mouth.

It would be more fun just bashing him in the head, but then, of course, I ran the risk of killing him. Then we were back to the very real problem of a fucking rank body that I would have to dispose of. It was a problem. I wanted the old fucker dead, but I didn't want to have to deal with the body. I couldn't win.

Though, as long as I had him with me, I could use him as leverage. She cared about the old fucker. It was a shame I never felt the same level of affection towards him. He stared up at me with tired eyes, props to him. He always tried to hold his breath.

"Just give it up," I soothed, my smile sinister. "You'll serve your purpose to me, and then I'll slice your throat," I promised. "You can be reunited with that bitch wife of yours, and all of this will be over. I'll have a new toy to play with, like a living dolly. Won't that be so much fun?" He couldn't hold his breath any longer, and I heard him take a gasp of air. Perfect. Those eyes rolled closed again. He would be out a while longer before I'd have to dose him again.

"I promise you, Daddy, it'll all be over soon," I said softly before shoving him away from me and climbing out the back of the van. I was going to have to play this smart. I knew I would be forced to interact with the town's folk. Which was going to be fucking unbearable. I couldn't permanently hide in the shadows either, though.

Locking the door on the van, I pulled the hat off, letting my long, dark hair fall down around my shoulders again. I would have to blend in. Just be another someone passing through. I had to thank my parents for one thing. I wasn't a face people tended to remember.

Pushing open the door to the diner, a small bell jingled over my head. Well, that was going to be fucking annoying. The woman behind the counter glanced up at me for a second before saying, "Have a seat anywhere. Someone will be with you in a moment." Clearly, small-town charm wasn't actually a thing. Which, admittedly, I was grateful for. If no one gave a shit that I was here, no one would ask any questions.

Moving to an empty table in the back corner, I sat down. I had sent that text to Lizzie specifically, so they now knew I was coming, but I still needed to figure out my next step. I had been able to find her house thanks to the media. I didn't understand why people complained so much about it. It was a glorious thing, really. They told me all I needed to know about my target. I wouldn't strike again tonight; I would let her stew with that text. Maybe I would even give her a day or two of peace. A false sense of security did a lot to someone, especially when it was ruptured.

It had already been determined that I couldn't go after the cop, but at the same time, he couldn't get in my way either, which meant having to dispose of him somehow. He just needed to be out of the picture. I could create some kind of diversion, call all the cops out to the edge of town somehow; there were ways. I smiled as the ideas started to filter in. I hadn't planned on bringing the town to its knees, but if that's what I had to do to catch my prey, so be it. This game of cat and mouse could be fun if I allowed it to be, but I knew too that it would likely grow tiresome after a while.

This plan was years in the making, making that bitch pay. Sure, I had a few detours along the way, but I was going to enjoy those final moments. I would savor the fear in her eyes as she begged me not to kill her. I would relish in every scream as I drained every last ounce of will from her puny body. I would make her beg for death and then make it as slow and painful as I possibly could. I would drag it out so long that she would get to see what I saw, feel what I felt when the realization sank in that the world had forgotten you. That bitch stole everything from me. She took over my life. She became the daughter they'd always wanted. She pushed me aside as if I'd never existed. So now she was going to pay, just like everyone else had.

It wasn't lost on me, though, that I could use dear Abraham to my advantage. She loved the old bastard. She had taken his name, even. Yes, I heard everything. I should have made my move then before she had the chance to run, but it wasn't worth blowing my cover. I had known if I were just patient, things would work out in my favor. Now I had all the leverage I needed to make her life a fucking living hell. If she tried to hide, if she tried to fight, I would burn this town, and I would make sure she knew it was all her fault. "What can I get you?" The same woman from the counter was now standing at my table. I did my best to smooth the hatred from my gaze. It was a mask I wore perfectly.

I looked up at her, smiling slightly, "I think I'll go with the grilled cheese. With a side of tomato soup. My mom used to make the best grilled cheese." She didn't care. I could see it in the way she rolled her eyes at me. Perfect. "And uhm, I'll take an iced tea with that too." She nodded before walking away. Maybe I would save some scraps for the old man. I needed to keep him alive if I wanted to use him to my advantage.

I ate silently, merely observing the people of this town that she had clearly come to care about. I was grateful for that. It made my job that much easier. It would make it that much sweeter when I took it all from her.

Nineteen
Owen

First and foremost, my goal was to take care of Oakley. I could see in the
way she was looking at me that the text had really shaken her and she had
every right to be freaked out. Not only did this person know where she
was, but they also seemed to know her phone number. Which considering
Austen helped her get a new one when she'd first come to town, it meant
this person, this living nightmare, was crafty.

Calming Oakley down was my only priority in that moment, though. I
couldn't get caught up in all the questions, she needed me to lean on. She
needed me to promise that she was safe. It was a promise I intended to
keep, but there was little I could do with it when we didn't know who was
after her.

I gently took the phone from her hand and set it to the side. Taking her
hand in mine, I pulled her up out of her seat and into my lap, where I
could wrap my arms around her securely. If I had to hold her together
physically, that's what I would do. She didn't deserve all of this, this fear
that something was going to rain down on her. She didn't know who to
fear. Everything and everyone was a potential threat.

She curled into me, hiding her face against my neck. I would sit there
and hold her as long as she needed me to. I also didn't want to hold off on
getting ahead of this, though. Right now, it was just a text, threatening,
sure, but threats could be empty. It could be anyone trying to scare her,
trying to mess with her because she clearly hadn't been through enough

already. "We'll figure this out," I promised, turning enough to kiss her forehead softly.

We sat there for who knew how long. She was safely wrapped in my arms, knowing that I would do absolutely anything to protect her at that point. If she were going to stay and trust me to help her, I couldn't let her down.

Jacey seemed rather amused by her, too. He had made his fair share of comments about whether or not I should make a move on her. So I knew he would be willing to step up and help, too, especially if it meant being able to keep a closer eye on Oakley's roommate. We would all step up.

I would talk to Fiona, too, about maybe getting a security system installed. My thoughts were soon interrupted when Oakley shifted in my arms. "What if we can't stop them?" She asked me, staring up at me with those big watery green eyes. Her glasses were even smudged at this point. Letting go of her, I reached up and slid her glasses off her face before using my shirt to clean them for her gently.

I needed a moment to really think about my answer. I didn't want to lie to her. There was a chance that we wouldn't be able to figure out who was behind everything. But I also didn't want her to lose hope. We had to stand together on this if she was going to pull through.

I sighed, "I don't want you thinking like that," I repeated, having said that to her once already. "We'll figure it out. If we can't figure out who's after you, then we'll come up with a backup plan. But either way Oakley, we're in this. Okay? You and me."

She looked confused by that, "Why?" She questioned. Why? What did she mean by why? "I mean, you've only known me a few weeks and most of that I've kept you at arm's length pretty much the whole time," she amended. "Why would you risk your life for me?"

There were a million reasons racing through my head in that moment.

Because I was a cop, it was my job to stand up for those that maybe didn't have the resources to protect themselves at their disposal.

Because I couldn't in good conscience stand back and let her fend for herself knowing what that could mean.

Because I was starting to fall for her, crazy or not, and I couldn't imagine losing her like that.

"Because as much as I tried to convince myself otherwise, I care about you," I answered. "I know it's only been a few weeks, but from the moment I met you, you intrigued me. I had to know who you were. But the more I tried to figure you out, the more I got to know pieces of you... the more I realized how much I was coming to care about you," I confessed, hoping that it wasn't enough to scare her away.

I didn't want to be the reason she ran, whether it was to protect me or because I freaked her out. I didn't want her out there fending for herself. She had gotten this far on her own, and for that, I was immeasurably proud of her. I could only imagine how hard it was to stand strong in the face of everything she had been through. I may not have known who she deemed to be 'the real Oakley,' but I knew this Oakley and now that she was here with me, she didn't have to fight alone anymore. There was no shame in accepting help when it was available.

There were suddenly tears in those green eyes again. I reached up to slip her glasses back onto her face before wiping one stray tear away. "That was a really good answer," she sniffled before curling in against me again. As much as my body and brain screamed for me to go into cop mode, to come up with a plan to protect her, I knew right then and there; she didn't need Officer Hale. She just needed Owen, someone she could lean on, for the time being, someone who was more than willing to help hold her together when her tape and glue patchwork heart couldn't take it anymore.

I waited until Oakley fell asleep against me, her body and mind finally settling enough to allow her some peace. I had carried her up to my spare room and tucked her into the bed before texting Fiona that she likely wouldn't be home.

I had just come back downstairs when I heard the knock at the front door. As soon as Oakley had dozed off, I called Jacey. Opening the front door, I sighed. "What the fuck is going on, Hale?" he asked me as I stepped back enough to let him in.

"Shush, Oakley is sleeping upstairs," I warned him as I closed the front door. Jacey was immediately met with a low growl from Justice. It was seriously baffling to me that he was so okay with Oakley, but even after all this time, he still didn't like Jacey. It was fine, I understood. I didn't like Jacey some days either. I glanced over at Justice, shaking my head at him in silent command that everything was okay. "All clear," I told him before he finally rested his head back down on his paws.

"About damn time you got that girl into your bed," Jacey smirked at me as he strode past and dropped onto the sofa.

I sighed, "She's in the guest room, you jackass," I told him. "Look, I don't need the comments right now, what I need is for you to do something useful for once and help me figure out where this came from." I held out Oakley's phone to him so he could read the message that had come through for himself.

"That thing is an antique from the late 1900's," he joked before taking the phone from my hand and looking at the message, "How much does she like this thing?" he asked, and I just shrugged. "Because we might be able to get something off of it, but I'm not sure a relic like this is going to survive the process."

I glanced towards the steps that led upstairs to where she was hopefully resting peacefully. "We need to figure this out."

I could feel his eyes on me; Jacey had a funny way of reading people. He was better at it than I had ever been. He'd go almost perfectly still, to the point where it was possible to forget he was even there in the first place. "You like her."

No shit.

It wasn't exactly like that was some grand secret he had just figured out. I stared at him, waiting for him to get to his point with this. I wasn't entirely sure what he was trying to prove by pointing that out. If I didn't like her, I would have had her all but wrapped around me on my kitchen counter only a few hours before. Of course, he didn't know that, though, and if I could help it, he wouldn't know that. I didn't need any more commentary thrown my way and I knew the last thing Oakley needed was jokes thrown at her.

"My point is, maybe I should take point on this one, on the actual investigation," he explained further. I wasn't about to let him do that, but by all means, I let him finish his argument. "You're too close to this one. If you're falling for her, like I suspect you are because as soon as I said it, you got so stiff it's like someone shoved a broomstick up your ass. You're not going to be thinking clearly. You're going to be focused on keeping her safe, not what needs to be done to figure things out."

Okay, so maybe he had a point there, but again, I wasn't about to admit that to him. One of the worst things someone could do was actually admit that Ethan Jacey was right about something. He'd never let me live it down if I went and did something stupid like that. "I'm not going to just sit this one out," I argued. "Especially since we don't know what we're up against with all of this."

Jacey leaned forward slightly to rest his arms on his knees as he watched me for a moment. I hadn't even realized that I had begun pacing until I saw his gaze bouncing back and forth like he was following a ping pong ball. "So why don't you start off by telling me what we do know," he requested. "I still think I should take the lead on this one," he sighed, "I'm not asking you to sit this one out, but if you're the lead officer on the case, it's going to be run by emotions. Whereas if you have to answer to me, I can hopefully correct your dumbassery before it becomes a legitimate problem."

I stopped pacing and turned to face him, pushing my fingers through my hair in frustration. The truth was, we didn't know shit and unless we could get our hands on the police files from the scene of her parents' murder, we really wouldn't know shit at all. "Someone murdered her parents," I started. "We lack motive, we know they were shot, but we don't know how the suspect got into the house in the first place. They dodged all security cameras and there were no signs of forced entry."

"Owen, listen to yourself, what do we know from that?" He asked me. "No sign of forced entry means they were let in. Do we have record of who was on staff that day? They're all assumedly still alive."

"Oakley said the PD interviewed the staff," I countered.

Jacey rolled his eyes, "Yes because a guilty party has never lied to the cops before," he shot right back. "Someone let the suspect in, or they had access to the house. So there was either an accomplice, it was someone the Richfield's knew and trusted enough to let into the house, or it was someone who was working for them. Add in the fact that they skirted the security system. They knew where all the cameras were located, which makes them familiar with the property. Which again lends to the idea that they either had an accomplice or they worked there themselves. Now we look at camera placement, in order to skirt the system, where were the cameras placed, I can only assume there was one at the front door. Which sort of rules out it being a guest of some kind. So which doors weren't monitored? Which windows weren't monitored? If there was no camera, was there possibly a sensor on the doors and windows?"

All of these were great questions that, in the scramble to get Oakley to let me help, I really hadn't stopped to think about all the holes in the case. "But without the files from the PD there, we won't know if any of this is things they looked into."

Jacey held up his hand, "Leave the files to me, I'll have them faxed in by tomorrow afternoon," he answered. "We have legitimate reason now to need those files, if the same someone who killed her parents is here, in our town, trying to harm her, they can't keep the information from us. Not if it could mean closing the case for both their department and ours."

I nodded before sinking down into the armchair across from him. I really hated to admit it, but Jacey actually sounded like he knew what he was doing with this and he had a legitimate reason for why he should head the case. I just couldn't let it go that easily, though. I didn't want to take the sidekick position in this. I wanted to find this fucker and make them pay for what they had put Oakley through.

"So where do we start?" I asked, sighing. He nodded, seeming to understand what I was saying. My heart was already involved, which meant the whole ordeal could get a hell of a lot messier if I wasn't careful. For Oakley's sake, as much as I didn't want to, I had to take that step back.

He reached for the tablet that was sitting on the table between us. "I'm going to contact the department tonight, might even call the chief to see about putting some urgency on it," he explained. "Think if we call in Austen, he can take a look at the phone for us?" he asked, and I nodded once. He was the one who sold her the phone, and given he was only the proprietor of the local junk store; he was really handy with technology.

"So we get the phone checked out. We can run it for numbers, but the text came from an unknown, which likely means it's a burner of some kind. We up patrol, not only for us but first and second shift as well. You know the guys are all going to love that, but we need to keep an eye out for anything or anyone that doesn't belong," he pressed. "As for your assignment, keep an eye on your girl, and get as much information from her as you can. I'm sure you already have, but every detail we know is another step closer to finding this fucker and making him pay. And you can also handle talking to your brother; get him to look this over in the morning." He tossed Oakley's phone back.

I felt better now that we had formulated some kind of plan and had some sort of direction to head in. Jacey pushed up off the couch and headed for the front door. "We'll catch this bastard, Hale, she may not have been here long, but she's one of us now. And she's not going down without one hell of a fight first." A few minutes later, he was out the door, and I was locking up. It hadn't been part of the plan for Oakley to stay at my place, but after the text had come through, I couldn't take her back to her house and just leave her there, knowing how shaken up she was. I turned around to start closing everything down for the night when I heard footsteps coming down the stairs.

"So what's the plan?" she asked softly, "I heard some of it, Jacey seems to know what he's doing."

"We're working on it," I promised her. "And he's got a good grasp on this, he had a point that I should let him take the lead. He's thinking a little clearer than I am with it." This amazing woman clouded my judgment. I wasn't necessarily ashamed to admit that, but I also didn't want to go running my mouth when it came to how I felt about her and possibly run the risk of scaring her off. "Jacey is headed into the station tonight to get a jump on things. But for tonight, you're safe here. I'll be right across the hall if you need me."

That seemed to make her pause in her steps, "Actually… I woke up because I had this… dream," she confessed slowly, "A pretty bad one. And if I don't have to be alone, I'd really rather not be." She stared down at her feet with that confession, and it made my heart thump that much harder in my chest. Did she want to spend the night in my room with me?

"Do you want to stay down here for a little while or…?" I asked, trying to get a feel for what she was asking.

She shook her head, "never mind, you know, I'll be fine," she turned back for the stairs.

Stepping over to her, I caught her by the hand, "Oakley, I told you. You're not in this alone. I was just trying to determine what you were asking. If you want to stay with me tonight, that's okay. I just can't read your mind."

She looked up at me with those wide eyes and smiled slightly, "Well apparently you can," she answered, "Because that's exactly what I'm asking. I know we only kissed once in the kitchen tonight. But you make me feel safe Owen, safer than I've felt in months. And tonight, I think I really just need that. I need to believe no one can get me here."

I squeezed her hand in mine. She felt safe with me. That was huge. For her to admit that, it was definitely a step in the right direction for us. Reaching up with my free hand, I brushed her dark hair back behind her ear before leaning in to kiss her softly. After our make-out session in the kitchen, I had wanted nothing more than to explore that with her, but after that text came through, I just needed to make sure she felt safe and cared for. If that meant sharing a bed with her, that's what I was going to do. In fact, I loved the idea of being able to hold her all night long if she let me. "Let's grab the boys and go to bed."

Twenty
Oakley

I never felt more protected than I did sleeping in Owen's arms, but I knew it wasn't something we could make a habit of, not right away anyway. I had never really dated for the sake of finding someone to be with. I had always dated because I needed a hot guy on my arm or because I was bored. Or simply because it was kind of fun to mess with the tabloids a little.

With Owen, though, it was different. I wanted to do this the right way. I wanted to take our time getting to know each other. I wanted that first date walking around town. I wanted to meet his family and be a part of his world. He made me feel safer than I had felt in a long time. I felt like I could finally trust someone again and I was actually starting to believe him when he said we'd figure this out together.

I felt him start to stir next to me and I tilted my head back in time to see him push his hair back out of his face. He met my gaze and smiled slightly, "morning," he said softly. "No nightmares?"

I shook my head, "no," I answered.

"Good," he nodded once. "We should get up, get breakfast," he smiled again. "This time, I'm cooking."

I laughed slightly at that. Part of me wanted to know what the plan was for today. If we were going to dig into everything or if he wanted me to stay out of the line of fire as much as I could. I didn't want the safety I felt with him to go away. The only way to make sure that didn't happen was to stay right by his side. "Only if you make pancakes," I told him.

He pretended to think about it for a moment, "I guess I can do that," he sighed. "And then afterward I'll call Austen and we can see if he can figure out that dinosaur of a phone of yours. See if we can figure out who sent that text last night. I have to go in tonight, but maybe we can get a few things squared away today before that happens."

I instinctually tightened my grip around his waist at the very thought of being alone. I knew there was a good chance I would work myself up again, but as much as I wanted to, I couldn't stay glued to his side. I was a big girl. I had made it this far without my white knight riding in to save me. I could survive a night away from him.

"Jacey and I will both be on patrol most of the night tonight," he promised, "I can even stop by the house before you go to bed." How pathetic was I, that I wanted to say yes to that? I wanted him to waste an hour of his time lying with me until I fell asleep, just to keep that bubble of safety a little bit longer. I couldn't ask that of him, though. He was already risking himself to help me. That was enough.

"I'll be okay," I assured him. "For now, I was promised pancakes." I smiled as best I could despite the growing worry in the pit of my stomach. I would be fine, I just had to keep reminding myself of that. Everything would be fine.

We spent most of the day together, save for the few hours I hung out with Roscoe and Justice while he took a nap on his couch. I had gotten to see more of Officer Hale at work as he tried to piece together the jagged pieces of the shattered mess my life had become. There was certain reassurance knowing he was good at his job, but that didn't stop the fear that his skill made him that much more of a target.

When we pulled up in front of the house I was sharing with Fiona, I sighed. "Hey," he started, reaching over to take my hand. "We've got this, try not to worry too much. I know it doesn't seem like we made any headway today, but it's a start."

I nodded, "I know," I answered. "Fiona will be home in a couple of hours and I'll feel better," I promised.

"I can take you to the diner, I'm sure she and Darian won't care if you hang out there," he offered.

"Like you said, it'll be fine," I reminded him, "I'll be fine. It's just my nerves. I'll watch TV or something until she gets home." Turning more to look at him, I smiled slightly, "Go get the bad guys," I half joked.

Leaning in, he kissed me softly. "I'm only a phone call away if you need me."

Climbing from his car, I ran up the steps and into the house, pausing a moment to look out the front window to watch him pull away from the curb. He didn't want me worrying, but that was easier said than done when I could see the worry crinkle at the corner of those beautiful blue eyes. There was also a fierce wave of determination there too, though. He was only letting me go because he was convinced he was about to go and make it all better, and I was doing my best to believe him.

With Fiona at the diner until close, I walked through the house, turning on almost every light. I wanted whoever was after me to believe that I wasn't home alone. The text had been direct, but it had also been quite vague, which made it even more terrifying to me. It basically said that they were coming for me but that I wouldn't know when, where, or how the strike would happen. They wanted me to live my life in total fear.

After hearing most of what Jacey was saying the night before and then what Owen had explained to me that morning at breakfast, I was racking my brain, trying to think of someone it could have been. Jacey seemed pretty convinced it was either an employee or someone an employee let into the house. I couldn't think of anyone, though. All of our employees had been loyal to us and had worked for the Richfield family for as long as I could remember.

The staff were all treated well, and with the utmost respect. My father paid them all generously which was why we were able to hold onto good help for as long as we had. He never looked down on anyone. As long as they worked hard, he paid them fairly for their work. So to think one of them might have been behind the gun that killed them was unthinkable. I refused to believe that good people like that harbored such a darkness in them that they could kill. It had to be someone else. That left it open to a world of possibilities, though.

I shook my head and dropped down onto the edge of the couch, resting my head in my hands for a moment. I didn't know how Owen and Jacey did this for a living. All the possible outcomes were making my head spin, and knowing that only one of them was correct, that the margin for error was so high, I sighed. Owen was right. I needed their help. I couldn't do this alone, and I couldn't keep running for the rest of my life from a ghost.

Owen had promised to check in periodically throughout the night. I had even gone as far as giving him the spare key Fiona had told me about. With her permission, of course, so that they could stop by in the middle of the night to check on things while we were asleep. He didn't like leaving me unprotected, but it was really the only option he had. What else could we do? It wasn't like I could just move in with him, though the thought had crossed my mind that being in his house, I had actually felt safe.

What about when he wasn't there, though? Would I feel just as alone and out in the open as I did in my own home? Probably. At least there I would have the boys, though. Sure Roscoe was a big dope; I couldn't help the smile that spread thinking about the big dopey dog, but Justice was a born guard dog. He didn't trust anyone. Except me, apparently. So if someone came knocking, I would have someone protective by my side.

I couldn't ask that of Owen, though. He was already doing so much for me and putting himself in the line of fire for me that I couldn't ask him to share his home too. I would just have to suck it up. I had gotten this far on my own. One night with a man didn't suddenly make me incapable of surviving independently. I just had to take it all one night at a time, one day at a time.

I sighed and pushed my fingers through my dark hair. Who the fuck was I trying to kid? I was barely surviving; I was taking it all one breath at a time. I don't know why I had expected it to end, or at least stop for a while after I left the manor. Of course, the paparazzi would find me. I was their favorite toy. I had ditched my phone, too, so it wasn't like I could call up an old friend to ask for a distraction. There was no reaching any of them, though, which was my fault.

Even if I had their numbers, I had just disappeared from their lives without so much as a goodbye. They would understandably be angry with me over it. Knowing the vindictive bitches I used to hang out with; if I did find a way to reach out, they would only find a way to make it that much worse for me. I had to find the balance between doing it all on my own and allowing Owen to step in and help me. There was no winning in any of this, was there?

I don't know how long I sat on that couch before I fell asleep, curled up in a ball. A sudden crash came from the back door and I jolted upright, my eyes now wide awake in the darkness.

Darkness?

I had turned on all the lights, though, and now there was a blanket over me, too? I fingered the material gently before I shook clear of my confusion and scrambled out from under it. I snatched the blanket off the couch and stuffed it under it. Whoever was in the house, I didn't want them knowing someone had been occupying the couch in the first place. Then they would know to look for me.

I reached for the first thing I could find to use as a weapon, the TV remote. Sighing to myself, I knew one thing without a doubt. I was royally fucked. Owen had my phone still, and the antiquated house phone was in the kitchen. Far enough out of reach that I wasn't going to be able to get to it, let alone remember the number Owen had given me.

I could hear fumbling coming from the back hallway before the door swung open. I needed to get to something, the kitchen or anywhere that would give me some kind of protection. I dropped to the floor as silently as I could and crawled for the kitchen door, freezing behind a chair, when I heard footsteps coming my way. I hoped to god it was still early enough that Fiona was at the diner. There was nothing I could do to alert her if she were upstairs sleeping peacefully.

I had no doubt in my mind that this wasn't some random break-in. This town didn't have enough people for that kind of activity and for a stranger to randomly choose this house, where I was hopefully home alone.

No.

Whoever it was, they knew I was here, and they were here for me. There was no way around that. I waited until the person slipped by the open doorway before I started to crawl again. I could feel the panic beginning to swell, a tightening in my chest that squeezed all the air from my lungs as my heart hammered away. I knew I had to hold it together, though; if I lost it now, I'd lose it all. They'd find me, and who knows what they would do to me.

I had to get to a phone. I had to get to something that would be more useful as a weapon than the damned TV remote. If I were going to go down, I would go down fighting. I wasn't about to lose everything. I had come this far; I was going to keep going.

I heard the first footstep on the steps going upstairs. This was my chance. Scrambling to my feet, I ran towards the door leading into the kitchen, trying to keep my footsteps as quiet as I possibly could. I reached first for the knife block, grabbing the first knife I could reach before turning for the phone. Grabbing it off the hook, I was once again left cursing the archaic device. It had a cord. I couldn't hide anywhere with the phone without it giving away my exact location. Seriously, how did the people of the 80s do this? How wasn't the murder rate higher?

Even still, I had to call Owen. I had to call for backup if I wanted to make it out of this alive. Dialing 9-1-1, I took the phone with me into the small pantry, hoping that whoever was in the house had no clue what a corded phone even looked like anymore.

When the operator picked up, I immediately started talking. "I need officer Owen Hale from Gratin PD sent to Fiona O'Dell's residence. He knows where it is. Someone is in the house." I rambled off to her. "I'm sorry, I don't have the address, and he has my phone, so I don't have his direct number. I don't know how else to reach him," Even I could hear the hysteria starting to seep into my tone as it all began to set in for me.

I gripped the knife in my hand even tighter as my breathing started to quicken. My hands were shaking around the phone and knife. It felt like there was… like something heavy was sitting on my chest. I couldn't breathe. I couldn't… Everything around me was starting to spin; in the darkness, I couldn't find any one thing to focus on. Even everything the dispatcher on the line was saying to me, it all sounded like I was underwater. There was a thrumming in my ears. I just, I needed Owen. I needed him to be there.

I felt the tears burning in my eyes before they finally started to fall. This was it; this was how I was going to die, like some bad B horror movie. Everything about this was so cliché, and somehow, that was the worst possible way to go. What else was I supposed to do, though? How was I supposed to handle all of this?

The operator stayed on the line with me. On some level, I could hear her telling me to breathe. Like that was so easy. I was gasping for every breath

I took; my heart was hammering away so hard in my chest it felt like it was going to explode. This couldn't be happening. Not now, not before I got the chance to go on that first date with Owen. I really wanted to see where that could go. The tears were coming harder and faster as I sat there waiting for the intruder to find me hiding in some dingy closet. I had my whole life ahead of me yet. I wasn't ready to go.

I could hear footsteps again, moving through the house. From under the door, I saw flashes of light. The killer didn't have a flashlight the first time when they walked down the hallway. Or did they? Did I miss it? On the very edges of my senses, I could hear the tickling of my name being called. How did I know who was on the other side, though?

I sank further into the pantry, trying to flatten myself against the shelves as much as humanly possible. If there ever was a time I wished more than anything to be a chameleon, it was right then. I wanted nothing more than to blend into my surroundings so that no one could see me. My elbow bumped a stack of cans, and like that, all my senses came back full force as they clattered to the floor next to my feet.

Time didn't slow down like they say. My life didn't flash before my eyes. None of that happened. Everything people always said happened. It never did, except maybe seeing the bright light. As the door swung open, that was all I saw. I didn't know what to do. I didn't know how to escape. So I did the one thing I could think to do. I dropped the phone and lunged with the knife. Catching the intruder off guard, we both tumbled to the floor, but then they laughed. Or… someone laughed.

"She just put you right on your ass Hale," a voice called.

Hale?

Owen!

I finally was able to focus in on the person I was sitting on. Fixing in on those blue eyes, a sob broke free, and I crumpled against his chest. They were here. I was safe. It wasn't until he pried the knife from my hand that I even realized I was still holding it. When he wrapped his arms around me, I could finally breathe again.

"Hale…" Jacey called again. Now I recognized the voice. I felt Owen move enough to look at him, and when he sighed, I looked up too.

"What?"

Owen looked at me, his blue eyes suddenly filled with such concern. "The knife, it has blood on it, Oakley." I shook my head. It couldn't. I hadn't used it on anyone. It had just been me in the pantry with it.

Gently, he pried my hand from the front of his uniform shirt, and sure enough, there was a gash running along my palm.

How?

When?

I didn't understand how I didn't even feel that. "Call Mason in," Owen said over his shoulder, "They're waiting outside." I barely heard what he was saying. My gaze was still trained on the slice in my skin. I knew adrenaline could make you feel less pain, but even sitting there, I still only felt a slight twinge.

Suddenly, someone else was kneeling in front of me, with those same blue eyes that I had come to love so much. "This the girl you won't shut up about?" he asked, looking more to Owen. Girl he wouldn't shut up about? Me?

"Mason," Owen warned.

Mason laughed, "I'm just saying, if you keep it up, Mom and Dad are going to want to meet her," he nodded to me as he held out his hand for mine. Mason. Owen's brother, he had mentioned something about one brother being a paramedic in town too. So this had to be him.

"Now isn't a good time Mase," Owen pushed, "Mom and Dad need to stay in Florida."

They moved me so that I was sitting more on Owen's lap. It seemed he didn't want me away from him any more than I wanted to be away from him. I knew he was going to ask me about what had happened, and I wanted to see if they'd found anything at all with the intruder. Suddenly, a thought struck me, though. "Fiona?" I asked, looking at the three men, finally wincing at the growing pain in my hand.

Jacey sighed, "She's at the diner still. She's going to stay with Liv tonight." She wasn't here, which meant she was safe. We were all safe. At that, I relaxed even more into Owen's hold on me while his brother prodded at my hand.

"It's going to need stitches, Owen," Mason told him. "We can take her in if you want so you guys can check out the house a little better." Take me in? I looked up at Owen with wide eyes. The last thing I wanted was to go anywhere without him. He was the one person who made me feel safe. I needed that right then. I needed to believe for a moment that nothing could touch me. Owen hugged me closer before leaning in to press a kiss to my forehead.

"I'll go with her," he told Mason. "Jacey can check out the house. Whoever was here is long gone now."

So someone was in the house with me, which meant that someone was in town. Our deadly game of hide and seek had officially begun.

Ducking back away from the main street, I avoided getting caught in the flashing glow of the red and blue lights. It was almost too easy, manipulating everything to my advantage. All it took was a bit of banging around, and she crumbled like the pathetic, whiny little bitch she was. The phone in my back pocket started to buzz, and I sighed. I didn't have the time to deal with his dumb ass, either. Pulling it from my pocket, I answered, "What?"

"Nice to talk to you too," he shot back, "Just thought you should know that file got sent out today. Completely intact."

So, he couldn't get to it before it had gone out. Of course, he hadn't. He had proven more than once to be a completely worthless waste of space. "It doesn't matter that you're fucking useless, I've already got a plan going," I growled in response.

Sometimes it was worth it having a man on the inside, other times he proved he wasn't worth a fucking thing to me. I had to keep him on the tether, though. If I kicked him to the curb, he knew too much. He could unravel everything for me if he really wanted to. I should have sliced his throat when I had the chance. Again, though, I wasn't in this to kill a cop. That was a mess I really didn't need.

In order to get away with what I did, though, I needed someone to keep them off my tail. I didn't like knowing that I needed help. It wasn't something I would readily admit to. For now, though, I needed to keep him happy. "I've got it handled on my end," I informed him. "Trash the files there before I get back. Otherwise, you'll be next. Cop or not," I hissed before hanging up on him.

If they had the file already, that meant they had my name. I wasn't ready for them to know it was me after her. If they asked Lizzie about me, she would put them on my ass faster than I could get out of town. I just needed to deal with the bitch. Don't get me wrong, it was fun messing with her, but things were getting messy now. I had to make my move sooner rather than later if I wanted to get out of this without any suspicions on my ass.

Stepping back into the darkness, I turned for the van. Both fuckwit cops were at the house helping her. I trusted Lizzie would keep them well occupied for me. Jumping into the driver's seat, I wasted no time in starting it up and pointing it towards the station. I had broken into a decent sized station in the Valley. That was how I'd met my accomplice. I'd gotten in and out successfully. How hard could one tiny pissant station be when both night cops were out on a call? I could get in and out completely undetected.

The one nice thing about this tiny podunk town was the fact that there were only two night cops. When a call came through at the home of the women they had it in for, they both reported—leaving their station completely empty. The only thing I had to keep an eye out for was cameras. I wasn't sure a station this small could actually afford them, but it wasn't out of the question. Not knowing where they were was going to make this a little bit harder than it should be.

If I'd had the time, I would have staked the place out, found a reason to come inside, and checked it all out. The longer I waited, though, the more likely they were to get their hands on that file. I didn't need my name out there. If they had my name, it was going to be that much harder to escape once it was all said and done. The goal was to take the bitch down and move on with my life with the satisfaction that I had finally won. I was better than her at something. It was about fucking time.

Walking across the parking lot, I tugged at the door off to the side. The chances of cameras were less likely away from the main entrance. If I could get into a back room or a hallway or something, I would be able to assess things easily. I cursed under my breath when it was locked. I thought people were supposed to trust in small town life, leave doors unlocked, and welcome strangers like family. Isn't that what all those horrid feel good movies claimed? I just needed the fucking paper. I wasn't looking to hold the place up or something. Slipping around the side of the building, I scanned the side of the building. There had to be another way in. If they had cameras, I knew they would be at the front entrance. Because most criminals today were fucking stupid. It was the whole reason they got caught in the first place.

They gave the rest of us a bad fucking name.

Not all of us were complete and total fucking idiots.

Rounding around the back side of the building, I smiled when I saw the other cruisers parked in the lot. It was as I stepped out of the shadows that someone pulled in. Fuck. There was no running and hiding now. The headlights had washed right over me. I knew I needed a good fucking story and fast. These were small town cops; they likely weren't the quickest on their feet, but they'd gotten the position somehow. I couldn't risk this one actually having half a brain. Dropping my shoulder, I placed my other hand over it. As I stepped forward, I added a limp for good measure. With the headlights still pointed at me, I couldn't see anything, "C-can you help?" I asked weakly. It was easy playing the victim. I'd have this fucker eating out of the palm of my hand.

"Everything okay?" he asked as he climbed from the vehicle.

I shook my head, fighting back tears. As he got closer, I stopped pinching my arm. I didn't need tears to actually fall. Just enough to make it believable. I wasn't the crying type. "Someone..." I choked on the word. "There was this guy..." As he stepped into the headlights, I recognized him. It was the other one. Damn. I could have almost had the chance to take him down if it had been her dumbass cop.

"Did he hurt you?" he asked, coming even closer. At my nod, he stepped forward. At his sudden closeness, I stumbled back a step. If I'd been attacked, I wouldn't trust him. Truthfully, I didn't want him fucking touching me. The smell would never come out of these clothes, and I didn't have any clear spares at the moment. "Let's go inside. I can help you," he offered.

Perfect.

Sitting down next to his desk, I kept my head tilted away from him. I didn't want him to notice the way I was scanning the walls. There was only so much I could see from my vantage point, but from what I could tell, there were no cameras in the room. Amateurs. Clearly, they weren't used to dealing with someone of my caliber. "Why don't you tell me what happened?" he asked.

I pushed out a shaky breath before nodding, "I -I was walking, I'm here visiting family and they don't have enough room at their house, so I was leaving them and trying to find my way back to the place I'm staying. It's like an inn or something," I rambled. "And I think I took a wrong turn. I told them I would be okay to walk, they offered to drive me but I didn't want to be a bother, you know? They just moved here, they're still getting settled. They don't really know anyone yet. Or the town. And I thought I would be okay..." the longer I went on, the more hysterical I sounded.

It was easy putting on a front I had grown up around. I could sound like them. All the rich bitches who looked down on me. I was better at their game than they were. If I had wanted to, I could have been one of them. The thing was, I would rather watch them all burn. It wasn't my death I begged for when I was forced to socialize with them. It was theirs. Slow and painful.

He held up his hand before placing it gently on my arm. I had to fight back the disgust that wanted to pour out of me. I wanted to rip his fucking hand off and force it down his throat. "It's okay," he said softly, "You're okay now. Can you tell me about who attacked you?" he pushed.

I shook my head, "I didn't see his face," I answered, "He came up behind me and he grabbed my arm. I - I got away. And I just started running. But then I fell too. Somehow I ended up here," I looked around. "I think he had a white van. I saw one down the street."

Great, now I was going to have to ditch the van. However, it gave me the opportunity to finally kill the old bastard in the back of it. They would write it off as another victim of this unknown assailant. Maybe I would even get lucky, and they would put two and two together. Figure out that the old man was somehow connected to Lizzie. Pair that with my story now, and they had their guy. Too bad he didn't exist.

He pulled open the drawer next to him and sighed, "I have to go get more reports, will you be okay here while I'm gone?" he asked. I nodded slowly. He needed to just fucking walk away before I couldn't fight the urge to put his head through a wall. I watched as he got up and headed for the front of the building.

Finally able to, I looked around the room and confirmed there were no cameras. Standing up, I ruffled through the files on his desk before I found the one I was after. Flipping through the pages, I stopped when I saw the suspect report. Pulling it from the file, I folded it up and slipped it into my pocket. I had just finished fixing the pile of file folders when he walked back in.

Sinking back into my chair, I watched him. I let him take me through the report step by step. I had what I had come here for. I just needed to find a way out of this. I moved my arm and grimaced, "I think," I winced again. "I think he might have really hurt my arm. Is there any way you can take me to the hospital or something? I just need a ride. I don't know where it is."

He seemed conflicted at my request. I know I was interrupting what he was supposed to be doing. Though point for him, he'd found the bad guy. Too bad he had no clue. To be a fly on the wall when he realized later on. I wouldn't want to be him in that moment. Knowing he could have stopped me if he'd only known. It was good for me, though. He couldn't be out looking for me if he was with me the whole time. "Please?" I added on for good measure.

He conceded at that. "I'll take you," he answered. I could tell there was something more he wanted to say. He shook his head, though. "Let's finish this, and then we'll go."

I stood outside the Emergency room entrance, watching him drive away. Pulling the folded up paper from my back pocket, I smiled. That had almost been too easy. Maybe there was something to be said about small town charm. They were all so welcoming and helpful that it would cost them. I was willing to burn this whole fucking place to the ground if it meant getting my hands on her. I wouldn't say no to a little extra help along the way, though.

Twenty-Two
Owen

We had spent several hours sitting in the ER patient room waiting for them to stitch up her hand. I didn't know how I could have been so stupid. Of course, whoever was after her would wait until she was alone to make a move. Jacey hadn't been able to find anything at the scene. At her house. Nothing that indicated it was anything more than just some random break-in.

Which was ridiculous. I couldn't even begin to say when the last 'random' break-in had been in Gratin. People just didn't do that around town. We had maybe one a year that wasn't linked to something else. Most of our break-ins had to do with someone either being locked out or kicked out. This wasn't random, we knew someone was after her, and no sooner she was left alone, someone broke into the house. It wasn't random. Which meant it wasn't safe for Oakley to be left alone at all.

When we left the hospital, I had insisted that she stay with me until all of this was resolved. She'd fought me on it, but she eventually gave in. At least at my place, I knew she had the boys when I wasn't there and I could see in her gaze when she was fighting against me that she really didn't want to go back to her place alone. She just didn't want someone breaking into my place either.

What she didn't know was that after we'd received that text, I had gotten Austen involved in helping me install a security system in the house. Oakley needed one place in this town that was actually safe for her. Jacey had even gone as far as convincing Fiona to stay with Liv, having filled her in on what was going on with her new friend.

If we left the house standing empty, we could watch it at night and hope that the perpetrator came back for another swipe at her. If we were correct in assuming whoever was after her was actually watching her every move, then they knew where she was, and they'd know if she was alone. It would be inevitable that she'd be left alone. I couldn't just not go to work, and she couldn't come with me every night. We could at least increase security around her when she was left alone, though.

I glanced over at her, sleeping peacefully in my bed next to me. Her hand was all bandaged up now. I couldn't help but think about how it was my fault. I left her alone. I was the one who turned off all the lights in the house when I had stopped by to check on her. How was I supposed to protect her when I was clearly only making things worse? I didn't know how to make things better for her.

Jacey had finally gotten his hands on the files from the police department in California. However, much like Oakley had promised, there wasn't much to go off of. The one curious thing was that half the interviews with the staff after the murders weren't there. The police had just written it off. They could have easily found the person if they'd kept pressing. What I didn't understand was why they'd seemingly given up in such a high-profile case.

Surely, they had the media breathing down their necks for answers, so then why did they just seem to drop the case like they already knew all the answers? If there was some kind of cover-up happening here, like it felt like there was, then why was there no scapegoat? Jacey had given me a copy of the file while we'd been at the station before Oakley's call had come through. I hadn't gotten a chance to look through it completely, but as I flicked through the pages, one fell loose in the middle of the bunch and slipped out.

Suspect: Elizabeth Richfield

Motive: Money, company, fight with father according to staff.

Accessibility: has entrance to the house. Knows where all the cameras are located.

Witness: Maid Ashland Morgan saw Elizabeth enter the house roughly ten minutes before murders.

What?

Jacey obviously hadn't seen this in the mix, or he would have brought it to my attention. This was big. Oakley was a suspect. Something wasn't adding up right either, though. Ashland Morgan was the supposed witness to Oakley returning home early. Morgan. The name Oakley had taken on when she'd come to Gratin. It all made no sense. Why would she take on the name of the witness more or less testifying against her? She'd explained to me that she took on the name from Abraham and Elisa, but then, what was the relation to this Ashland?

Pushing out of bed, I spared one last glance back to Oakley to make sure she was sleeping soundly. She had Justice laying on the floor next to the bed, and she had Roscoe curled up in the crook of her knees. I would only be right downstairs if she needed me. She was safe.

I grabbed the file from the bed and headed down the steps to my office. Flicking on the light, I turned on the computer before pulling out my phone and finding Jacey in my contacts. I needed someone with the ability to think rationally to talk me through this. I didn't want to believe the report, the way Oakley had talked about finding her parents, that was real. If she'd known they were already dead when she found them, I doubt she would have been able to describe that agony so well.

It was insane to believe that Oakley was the one behind the gun. The fear she felt, the way she'd panicked and almost taken me out at the house, that was all real. She really believed someone was after her, and we had all the evidence to back up that claim. So then the question was, who was this Ashland Morgan, and why was she pointing the finger at Oakley.

"What's up, Hale?" Jacey finally answered his phone.

I sighed. "You said you went through the file, right?" I asked. "Every last page?"

"Yeah," he answered. "There was nothing there. I mean, I didn't get a chance to look through it until I got back here to the station after I checked out the house, but nothing to write home about Hale."

"Then why do I have a paper marking Oakley as a suspect?" I challenged.

There was a pause on the other end of the phone, "What the fuck? Dude, I don't have that sheet." I could hear papers rustling as he searched for it. "There's nothing here." Then how the fuck did I have it if he didn't? "I'm coming over Hale," he warned before hanging up the phone.

I sat there studying that page until I heard a knock at the front door. I glanced up the steps to make sure the boys weren't going to wake Oakley up, but the hospital had given her some rather good pain meds to help her sleep until her hand started to heal up again. Going over to the front door, I opened it and immediately held up the page in question. He took it from my hand and read through it carefully. "I'm telling you, dude, I don't have this page," he told me.

"Then I guess the question is, who the fuck is Ashland Morgan?" I questioned. I may not have known Oakley long, but I felt like I knew her well enough to know that she wasn't the one behind the gun. I was seriously questioning if she even knew how to use a gun at all. I had a funny feeling this was the breakthrough we were missing. There was something there. "Oakley was close with the Morgan family, she said Abraham Morgan worked for her father, and Elisa Morgan taught her to cook and sew and several other things. That's why she changed her name to Morgan. Said something about them being the only family she really had left."

"Then I wonder how Ashland Morgan fits into the picture," Jacey noted. "Hale, you go be with your girl, okay?" he told me. "She needs you right now. Let me handle this, I'll look into her tonight, see what I can pull up in the database. If she's so much as even gotten a parking ticket, I'm going to find it. Got it?" He nodded for me to go back upstairs. I sighed before mirroring his nod.

I had to let him handle this, but my whole body was thrumming from this information. I had a funny feeling we'd just found our killer. "Maybe it's best not to tell Oakley about this just yet," he suggested. "She's been through a lot lately with that text and now the break in. I'm guessing if this person was staff, and part of the Morgan family, it was someone she trusted. She doesn't need that right now on top of everything else. So until we know anything for sure, keep your trap shut Hale." I nodded again. I didn't like that plan, but I had agreed to let him take the lead on this. I wanted to see what we could dig up before involving Oakley in any of it.

"Just keep me up to date," I requested as he started for the door again. He nodded once again and slipped out into the darkness, leaving me to close the door and lock up again. I knew I wasn't going to be able to sleep with this new information swirling around in my head. This person could very well be the one after Oakley. I ran back over the events of the night. Jacey had handed me the file. I started to flip through it with him when not five minutes later, the call came through from Oakley. I grabbed the file and left it sit in my car while we were at the house. Jacey had left his sit on his desk. I paused mid-step.

It wasn't random.

Someone was trying to keep information from us. The break-in had been almost a decoy, something to get Jacey and me out of the station long enough for someone to steal a few pages. Namely the ones with her name on them. It was all starting to make sense. I smiled slightly. Suddenly our game of hide and seek had turned in our favor.

I hardly slept all night. My mind kept playing the new information over and over again like some kind of movie reel. I tried to piece together everything from the file with what Oakley had told me about that day. I glanced over her way to check on her, only to find two green eyes staring back at me. "You're awake," I said stupidly.

She smiled slightly at that, "So are you."

I reached out and gently brushed back her hair, "How're you feeling?" I asked her. I wanted to make sure she was okay. She was important to me; hell, there was no denying it anymore. I'd fallen for her. I wanted nothing more than to make sure she got through this.

She shrugged slightly, "My hand hurts, the big bad world is scary, someone wants me dead," she answered. "Sounds like a normal Tuesday morning to me."

I laughed slightly, it wasn't funny, but the fact that she could find some form of amusement in all of this was astounding to me. "Well, how about we make today more of a special Tuesday?" I asked. "We can get up, make breakfast. Swing by the house so you can grab some stuff. And then we can do that walking tour of Gratin I promised you. Maybe finish out with dinner somewhere. There's this nice little restaurant in the next town over that we can go to," I suggested.

She seemed to brighten right up at that. "Our first date?" she asked me, and I bobbed my head in a nod. She needed something good in her life and like Jacey said, he wanted to keep our new developments quiet until we knew something for sure. So I planned to take her out for the day, show her around, and hopefully help her forget about everything going on for a few hours. She launched herself at me, throwing her arms around my neck. "Yes!" she giggled. "I'd love to go on our first date with you."

I laughed and hugged her back. She pulled back slightly to meet my gaze for a moment before she leaned in to kiss me. It was soft and gentle as her lips brushed over mine. Neither one of us was really asking for more than it was. We hadn't really explored all of that since the night we had dinner, and she received the text. It had only been a few days before, but it felt like a lifetime had passed since then.

She pulled back from the kiss and smiled at me. It amazed me that she found something to be so happy about even in the face of death with someone hot on her trail. It wasn't like I was whisking her away to New York or something. We were just going to walk around town. Go to dinner. It was only special because I would be doing it with her.

A couple of hours later, we were walking down the street hand in hand, "And that's where I broke my arm the second time when Mason pushed a skateboard in front of me while I was running, went down hard. Mom and Dad were not happy about that one."

Oakley laughed slightly; it was nice to hear again. I loved her laugh; it was almost infectious with how melodic and sweet it was. "So how many bones have you broken in total?" she asked, looking up at me with curiosity shining in those green eyes.

I thought about it for a moment as we continued to walk around town. "My left arm twice, right arm once, ankle once," I glanced at her, "Are we counting fingers, noses and toes?" I asked. She nodded. "Then it's too many to count. I played football all through high school. Constantly had injured or broken fingers from catching the ball wrong. Which is why I was usually the one throwing it instead," I laughed. "And you know, I grew up with three brothers, fights happen. I've broken my nose a couple of times. That's why there's a little bump right here," I ran my finger down my nose and pointed to it.

Reaching up with her free hand, the one that was all bandaged up, she ran the tip of her finger down the bridge of my nose. "I can feel it. I guess I never got any of that. With it just being me and all. And even if I'd had siblings growing up, boys would have been groomed to take over for my father, and girls would have been polished into perfect little socialites."

I smiled, "like you?"

She laughed again. If I could keep her laughing until the end of time, I would. "I was far from perfect. The perfect socialite is polite. She's proper. Not getting arrested for public intoxication. Or getting caught with another random fling in the back of her bright pink convertible. I wasn't perfect. I was the type tabloids write stories about all the time and follow around waiting for my next big screw up."

I looked her over, "Well, you haven't been arrested yet since you got here, I would know," I nodded. "You do apparently have this secret boyfriend though. I mean, that's why you ran away. Apparently, he just doesn't understand your way of life. So you're slumming it for him. The things you do for love," I quoted what the tabloids had printed about us. "And that dye job is lacking a little, looks like you did it yourself which I imagine is a huge socialite don't," I teased. She dropped my hand long enough to shove my arm. I laughed this time before taking her hand again and pulling her to a stop. "You may not be the perfect socialite your mother wanted you to be, but you're a strong woman and for that I think she'd be pretty damn proud."

Oakley smiled at that. "You know, I was really starting to question if guys like you even existed," she told me.

I shook my head at that. "We don't. I'm just a really good-looking figment of your imagination," I joked. This was what I liked about her. This ease between us when we could escape a little from the fact that someone was after her. This glimpse at what life could be like after we figured everything out.

I genuinely wanted to believe Jacey and I were enough to help her. I wanted this life with her. Everything between us just felt so natural, like it was how it was always meant to be. I knew Oakley didn't exactly believe in fate, but it was hard to ignore when the girl I'd been after my whole adult life was standing right in front of me. I wanted someone I could laugh with like this, someone I could joke with and just all around have a good time. I wanted someone who could be my best friend as much as my girlfriend, which wasn't easy to find in a town as small as Gratin.

Then Oakley had come blowing into town, and everything changed. So yeah, I had to believe this was all fate. I kept everything so safeguarded after Chelsea, but I told myself to be careful, not fall too quickly, but it was all so easy with Oakley. I knew there were risks involved. I glanced her way again, meeting that green gaze that reminded me of warm summer days, and I smiled slightly. She was worth any risk.

Twenty—Three
Oakley

I knew it was odd, the way I could feel myself already falling for him. It was all happening so quickly, but there was no denying that it felt right. I was frozen there, my retort dying on my lips. The remaining hints of laughter slowly drained from my face as he watched me. I knew I should feel bare standing before him and his studious yet gentle eyes, but it only made me feel safe.

I felt my breath catch as his gaze searched mine. I was caught in that endless blue staring right back at me. It was so easy to get lost in those inquisitive eyes. I could feel the way my pulse quickened when he looked at me like that. It was as if I was the only thing he saw at that moment, like I was the only thing that existed.

No one had ever looked at me that way before. It was like he was witnessing the real me, every crack in my heart, every bruise staining my soul. It was all out in the open and on display for him to see. I didn't dare blink until a slight smile tugged at those perfect lips. Only then did I let the breath out.

He wasn't judging me for who I was. I was just me. Nothing more, nothing less. But by the heat that slowly crept into his gaze, he wanted me. There was no denying that I wanted him too. I couldn't fight it anymore. It pulsed through me with every beat of my heart. Owen Hale had blown through my walls like a hurricane. He shattered all of my defenses and left them crumpled on the ground at my feet.

No matter what came next, I knew there would always be a special corner of my heart reserved for this man. He was everything I'd ever wanted and everything I never knew I needed. I couldn't begin to tell you which one of us started to move first, leaning in towards each other like two magnets drawn together. There was no fighting it, and I didn't want to.

Then, the first droplet hit his cheek. I smiled at the adorable wave of confusion that crossed those gorgeous blue eyes as he reached up to investigate. Tilting his head back, he stared up at the darkening sky above us just as the clouds opened up. I shrieked slightly at the sudden downpour of rain. It was coming down so hard and so fast that I could already feel it soaking through every layer of clothing I had on.

His hand wrapped securely around mine, leading me blindly through the pouring rain to a small overhang just off the flower shop. It wasn't until we were safely under it that I heard his soft chuckle and started to laugh myself. "Guess that will teach me to not look at the weather first," he joked.

I smiled right back at him. "No one is good at everything, Owen," I teased. My smile faltered when he reached up to brush back the hair that was now plastered to my cheek. As he tucked it behind my ear, my skin felt like a thousand tiny fire ants were marching across where he'd just touched.

All I could hear at that moment was the steady pounding of the rain coming down around us, mixing together with the rapid thundering of my own heartbeat echoing in my ears. It was a magic all its own, our own song of our composing.

My fingertips yearned to reach out and touch his chest, to discover if he was in tempo with me. He held my gaze a moment longer before his eyes flickered down to my lips. I nodded, nothing more than a gentle tip of my head. That was all the encouragement he needed.

His lips crashed into mine hungrily. My lips parted under the slight pressure from his tongue as he sought to explore every corner of my mouth. His fingers gripped desperately at my hips, pulling me flush against him.

There was no saving myself anymore. My fingers found the front of his shirt, gripping it tightly. I pushed up on my toes, pressing into the kiss even more urgently. I wanted him, needed him to know that I was in this, too. We were in this together. As crazy as it was, we were falling together. I was already free-falling, but it was okay. It would be okay. I wasn't alone.

Before the kiss could get too out of hand, I pulled back slowly. I felt a smile pull at my lips when he sighed in protest. I loved knowing how much this gorgeous man wanted me. We'd kissed before. I didn't understand why he still had such an effect on me, but I never wanted it to end. I wanted to get drunk on every simple touch he gave me.

"I think our walk has been sufficiently spoiled," I nodded to the side where the rain was still pouring down. "What do you say we make a run for it," I suggested. "We can go back to your place…" a slight smirk started to edge at my mouth at the very thought of what sort of mischief we could get up to in the privacy of his home, the things I wanted to do with him.

"Yeah?" he questioned, his eyebrow lifting slightly in curiosity. While his expression remained playful, I could see the heat in his gaze. He knew what I was hinting at. As much as I had enjoyed our little stroll through town and hearing all about his childhood, something else was rapidly capturing my interest. I had put up my best fight, but if I wasn't going to fight it anymore, I was sure as hell going to embrace it. He was kind, helpful, tenacious, and loyal, not to mention unbelievably gorgeous. What girl wouldn't want him?

I nodded at the thought. "We could take a hot shower," I suggested, "warm up. Curl up by the fireplace, after you've lit a fire in it of course. You can keep telling me stories about growing up here."

Some of that fire faded from his gaze at my suggestion, but there was the slightest hint of a teasing glimmer glowing in that blue. "You said a shower," he pointed out. "Not showers, plural."

"Did I?" I laughed. "Well, conserving water is good for the environment," I nodded, a smirk pulling at my lips. I wanted this. I wanted to forget everything else and just be here, in this moment, with this man. Owen stepped back from me and held his hand out.

"We're going to have to make a run for it," he tilted his head towards the rain. I squeezed his hand in response, and together, we took off into the downpour. I could barely see a foot in front of me, but I could see the way the raindrops plastered his shirt to his broad back. I could see when he glanced back at me, laughing. I trusted him to lead the way.

We made it to his car and then back to the house in record time. By then, the rain had slowed to a steady fall, but that didn't seem to slow Owen down at all. We headed toward the house, and he fumbled with his keys, trying to unlock the door. I reached out and ran my hand down his back. He paused enough to glance over at me and smile before opening the door.

The dogs barely acknowledged our entrance; it was as if they knew it wasn't a moment to interrupt. Taking my hand again, he pulled me towards the stairs, tripping slightly when he collided with the bottom step. I couldn't help it. I had to laugh.

Everything about this man was pure perfection. It was like he'd been chiseled by the hand of God himself, but he couldn't seem to walk without tripping over his own two feet. It was oddly adorable.

He shot me a look for giggling at his misfortune before more successfully leading me up the stairs. To the right was his bathroom and the promise of that hot shower together. To the left was his bedroom, where just about every x-rated fantasy I had about him could possibly come to fruition. Dropping his hand, I reached for the hem of my shirt and pulled it over my head, tossing it towards the tiled floor of the bathroom.

The way his hot gaze traced over my skin, it was as if I could feel it. Every inch burned as he studied me. When his eyes flickered back up to meet mine, there was something else hinting at the edges, something that needed to remain unspoken for the time being. If we got through whatever was coming, then maybe we could look into those three little words. I shook my head ever so slightly, but it was enough; he seemed to understand. I didn't want to think about any of that. I just wanted to enjoy whatever it was between us.

I stepped closer to him, though; I wanted to see more of him, too. I wanted to touch him and explore his body for the beautiful masterpiece it was. I wanted to trace my finger along the ridges of his muscles; I wanted to feel his heartbeat beneath my lips. I wanted us to connect on a level I had never reached with a man before. There was so much more to all of it than just the physical dance. I knew, somehow, we were speaking the same language. Every flicker of his gaze, every twitch of my hand, we could read each other, hear each other. Know each other. He knew what I wanted.

Reaching for my hand, he led it to the hem of his shirt in a silent okay. Pushing it up slowly, I sighed at the sight of him, at the way the wet fabric tousled his already messed up hair when he pulled it over his head. Running my hand down his chest, I leaned in to kiss him again, gasping in surprise when he returned the favor and reached out to touch me, too. The warmth of his palm against my skin was the most fantastic feeling in the world.

"I think we should forget the shower," he mumbled against my lips; I barely caught half of what he was saying. I smiled at that, though. Once again, he seemed to read my mind. I pulled away again, and he groaned. "You've gotta stop doing that," he teased, causing a bubble of laughter from me.

"Well, you've already proven to not be the most graceful," I countered. "I'm only thinking of your safety here." I traced my finger over his pec in a small circle, "I do think we should take this into your bedroom, though," I told him, purposely avoiding his gaze. Instead, I focused on that small pattern my finger was drawing. "Onto your bed, lose the rest of these clothes," I added.

"I'm liking the sound of this," he nodded. He stepped back, though, before holding his hand out to me. "In the interest of safety," he joked.

I laughed again. He made it all so easy. It was the first time I felt like I could really and truly be myself in a long time. The way he looked at me too, he didn't just accept me for who I was, he lo- no. We weren't going there. I took his hand, squeezing his fingers. He squeezed back. We were in this together, whatever was to come.

Owen led me to the left, to his bedroom, pulling me into the inviting darkness. He had the shades drawn so the remaining daylight barely soaked through. But it was just enough that I could still see him. He took me over to his bed and I dropped down onto it, immediately reaching for him and pulling him down with me with a giggle.

His lips found mine again in the dark. His hands grazed over my skin, igniting a trail of tingles in their wake. He traced his way up to my shoulders, then down my back, and reached for my bra. My heart hammered away in my chest as he unhooked the clasps holding it in place, and I sighed at the release of pressure as my breasts fell free.

He paused to brush his thumb over a nipple, causing it to harden under his touch. I arched my back, pressing myself more firmly into his hand. I could feel his low chuckle rumbling through his chest as he felt my reaction. He flicked his tongue lightly over the firm nub, and I gasped softly.

His hands resumed their exploration, gently heading further down my body, and I squirmed at his gentle yet insistent touch. His fingers hooked under my waistband, and I lifted my hips so he could pull the sodden material down and off of my legs. I pushed at the back of his pants, wordlessly communicating my need to feel his skin against my own. He obliged, and suddenly we were both naked, touching from shoulders to feet. I was no longer chilled. I was on fire. It felt like any residual dampness must be turning to steam where we touched.

His hand trailed down between us and gently stroked over my sensitive folds. He dragged a teasing finger along the edge, wetting it, and I moaned with anticipation. He slid a gentle finger in, dipping it into my center, before pulling back to find the bundle of nerves that was aching for his touch.

He started tracing lazy circles over me, and I moaned. His touch was gentle, and I wanted more. I wanted him. I wanted to feel all of him as we moved together. I knew how ready he was for me. I could feel that much against my leg. But he didn't appear to be in any sort of hurry to get there. I was fine with that; it was a sweet kind of torment. I shifted beneath him, trying to press my hips more into his hand, anything to increase the pleasure of his touch.

The pressure only lasted a few seconds at best before he pulled his hand away. Finding his eyes with mine, I shouldn't have been surprised to see amusement there. "Cruel," I accused.

He leaned in and kissed me once, "Or not," he challenged, his hands slipping lower still before he pushed his finger back into me. "Is this what you want?" he asked, moving to kiss the side of my neck instead.

"I want you," I countered, sighing as he pumped his finger languidly. He added a second one and I almost came undone.

His gaze wandered down over my body before meeting mine again. There was a silent question there in his eyes about whether or not I was sure about this. But the truth was, we were already too far gone to go back now. My body needed his touch; I felt safe in his arms. We belonged together.

I nodded slowly, and he leaned over me, reaching for something in the drawer beside me. Readying himself, he looked deeply into my eyes again before leaning in to kiss me. Everything became electric at that moment as he lined himself up so our bodies could join. I felt the weight of him settle over me gently as he pressed against me. His hips met mine as he slid into me easily. He filled me completely, my body accepting his eagerly.

I groaned into the kiss that hadn't yet broken and shifted against him to take him in even deeper. I needed to feel every inch of him, and he complied without hesitation. We started moving together, somehow already in sync with each other. At first, every thrust forward of his was gentle, but I wanted that teasing fire I had seen in his gaze. I wanted him to give over to everything he wanted to do with me.

Pulling away from his lips, I shifted my mouth to his ear. "Faster, baby," I breathed against his skin. I gasped when he responded with an increase in speed, my nails digging into his shoulder as he moved against me. Each stroke was coming faster, gliding more smoothly.

It was everything I had imagined it would be. Feeling him like this, knowing I had tapped into his primal instincts, made me feel powerful and alive with sensation. His every thrust was deep. He rolled his hips into me again and again, and I met him just as enthusiastically.

"Oh…" I groaned as he shifted slightly and hit the perfect spot. "Yes… don't stop…." I breathed before finding his lips again, covering them with my own before he could say anything.

He pulled away from me suddenly, sighing my name, "Oak…." He was there. I could hear it in the way his breath hitched, and I could feel it in the way his rhythm became just a little erratic. He was ready to explode, and I wanted to watch the fireworks as they went off.

"C'mon baby," I whispered, moving to kiss his neck, "Let go." I reached down between us and cupped him gently. He moaned into my shoulder and reached for me, his fingers finding my sensitive bud as he continued to pump into me. The fire was back in his eyes as he looked down at me again.

The added pressure was enough to have me gasping. "Owen," I cried out. Unable to resist any longer, he went off inside me. I could feel him pulsing with each continued thrust. His free hand trailed along my body, touching every part of me he could reach while his lips traveled the skin of my neck and shoulder.

He seemed to manage to assault all of my senses at once. There was no resisting the charms of Owen Hale. I felt my body tightening before the waves of completion crashed over me, pulling me under. I cried out into the dark room. Pleasure I had never known rolled through my body, all of my nerves singing his praises. I shuddered, utterly spent when it finally subsided.

My breathing was heavy when Owen pulled back enough to look at me again.

As he rolled off of me and to my side, he immediately reached to pull me in against him. I sighed, content, as our hearts slowly returned to their normal rhythms.

In the dark at his side, my mind began to sort through the implications of what we had just done. I had always prided myself on not being 'that girl,' the one that fell at a man's feet with one glance her way. But when it came to him, I was totally that girl. I was that pathetic soul they wrote love songs about. And I was oddly okay with that.

I could still be me, strong and independent. Someone who didn't need a man to provide for her. I was making it on my own, after all. But I was still allowed to get weak in the knees when my prince charming walked into the room. I could be both, couldn't I?

Yes.

The answer was really that simple. I could be, because laying next to me was what every songwriter, every romance writer, and every poet envisioned. A man who, given a chance, could possibly love me for everything I was and in spite of everything I wasn't. A man who could promise me the happily ever after that every woman dreamed of finding. It was insane to think like that, but there he was beside me. When I looked into his eyes, every promise was shining there.

He rolled gently to his side and kissed me again. There was no hurry this time, but there was a fire to that kiss that hadn't been present before. Maybe it was the promise that was blossoming between us.

I didn't like the idea of him putting himself in harm's way for me; it scared me to no end. The way my parents had been murdered, whoever was behind it was cold-hearted enough to take him out, too. I didn't know what this was, what it could be if we allowed it to grow naturally between us, but I did know that I was in deep enough that I couldn't lose him, too. I couldn't survive losing someone else.

We didn't know how this was going to end for us. We still had no idea who was behind everything. There were no leads. The only thing we knew for sure was that they wanted me dead. I wanted to believe in this small-town police force. That Owen Hale and Ethan Jacey would somehow find a way. But I also had to accept the possibility that this was just outside of their realm of expertise.

There was someone after us, yes, but it only made me want to appreciate the time I had with him all the more. So, I wanted to make the most of whatever time I had left. If death came for me, I needed to be able to say I lived every day to its fullest.

I pulled away from his kiss, needing to catch my breath. "You're really good at that," I mused softly.

I could hear the smile in his voice when he spoke. "Not the only thing I'm good at," he promised me. I liked the sound of that.

He nuzzled into my neck, nipping the skin where it met my shoulder. I leaned into his touch, my body already craving more of it. He chuckled at my eagerness and brushed his nose across my collarbone. His hand was roaming across my skin. It seemed as though he were trying to memorize every curve, every plane, down to the smallest dimple.

Everywhere his hands moved, his mouth followed. He trailed fingers and lips over me, igniting sparks in his wake. He brushed his fingertips over my ribs and down my stomach. He kissed his way down the trail of goosebumps he had raised, taking a moment to swirl his tongue over my navel.

I gasped. He shifted so that he was lying between my legs, and I rocked my hips lightly in anticipation. He hooked his shoulders under my thighs and kissed softly down over me. He took his time, lips and tongue exploring everywhere but my center. When I whined in protest, he gently scraped his teeth over my inner thigh.

"So impatient," he scolded. His voice was light, teasing me almost as much as his kisses. "Let me have control for now. I promise you're safe with me."

I could feel the honesty in his words. I knew he wouldn't hurt me, just as much as I knew he couldn't guarantee my safety. My body screamed for my brain to stop overthinking, stop overanalyzing, and just be. I melted into his touch, and I let him guide me where he wanted me to go.

He moved at a leisurely pace, still focused on learning the map of my body. I squirmed beneath him, reacting to every new sensation with a fresh wave of desire. He kissed down one leg and up the other. He paused as he reached his eventual goal.

He gently kissed me where I needed it most, and I writhed. His tongue parted me delicately, and I moaned my pleasure. He gave a long, slow lick, sweeping over every nerve ending. His mouth found my nub and he lavished it with attention.

As my cries got louder, he added first one, then a second finger, probing me sweetly. The room began to spin. We might have fallen into a hole, swallowed up by the earth itself, and I wouldn't have noticed. There was only room in my senses for this man and his skill, driving me closer and closer to a second sweet release.

I could feel it building again. That heat in my belly, curling my insides, growing warmer with every flick of his tongue. My hand found the back of his head and I twined my fingers into his hair. His arm across my hips was the only thing holding me down, preventing me from thrusting into his mouth.

I felt the heat coalesce into a single point, centered right below his mouth. Within seconds, I could feel the heat explode. It raced through my veins, and I bucked against his restraining arm. I cried out as I climaxed again, and my voice echoed in the darkness.

When I couldn't take it anymore, he finally released me. I shivered, and he came to lay beside me, drawing the blankets over us both. He held me close as I drifted in a daze, my worries unable to take control back. Whatever I was worried about would still be there in the morning. I let myself pretend, just for tonight, that I was a normal girl with a normal life. I fell asleep in his arms, listening to his heart beating steadily under my ear.

Twenty-Four
Owen

I lay there for a while, just watching her sleep. I was grateful that she felt safe enough to sleep. I knew after everything that sleep wasn't exactly going to come easy for her. Just looking back on the night she'd gotten that text message, the fear in those green eyes when she told me about her nightmares. I wanted nothing more than to keep her safe.

I wanted to just curl up with her, fall asleep with her wrapped safely in my arms, knowing I would do anything to protect her. There was only so much Jacey and I could do, though. We could pull in help from the other shifts or maybe ask Graff and Langley for assistance. They were detectives. Maybe they'd think of something we hadn't. Just because we had a name now, that didn't mean we'd be able to stop her.

I was going to settle in and try to get some rest, but just as I closed my eyes, my phone chirped on the nightstand next to me. I wanted to ignore it, but with everything going on, I knew I shouldn't. What if Jacey had found something? Then again, he knew to call if he had. He'd promised to look into Ashland Morgan, but I hadn't heard anything more on that. I didn't like keeping things from Oakley, But Jacey was right. There was no point in worrying her about this if it was nothing.

Just the stark reminder that someone was out there, wanting to kill her, had me instinctively tightening my hold on her, making her sigh against my chest. I loosened my grip at that. I didn't want to wake her. When I glanced down, though, I saw those green eyes watching me. There was contentment in her gaze. I could feel the way she just completely relaxed against me. I couldn't take that away from her just to ask a few questions about some maid.

Trailing my fingers up and down her arm, those words were right on the tip of my tongue. I loved her. I was in love with this woman, but the look she'd shot at me before was enough to keep me quiet. For now, anyway. I didn't know what she had against me saying it; it wasn't like I was expecting her to say it back. Whether I said it or not, it didn't change how I felt. "Oakley," I started, shifting enough to look down at her. Those wide green eyes met mine, and I sighed.

"Don't say it Owen," she all but begged me.

Biting into my bottom lip for a moment, I shook my head, "Why not?" I asked her. If she wanted me to keep it in, I needed a damn good reason. I had learned the hard way not to keep things bottled up in the past, and I was really struggling to see how it was a bad thing.

"Because," she almost whispered. Closing those impossibly green eyes, building a wall between us with the broken eye contact. "Because if you say it and I don't…" she paused for a moment and I could feel her tense back up in my arms. "And I don't survive all of this…."

"What?" That wasn't what I was expecting at all. How could she possibly think she wouldn't survive? I had managed to protect her this long; I didn't understand how she thought I wouldn't keep doing just that.

"It's something we have to consider, Owen," she insisted as she pulled away from me enough to sit up. Her short hair was messy, sticking up in different directions as her natural curl showed through from the rain. "Why are you smiling at me? This is serious," she whined. I was smiling? Sure enough, when I took stock of everything my body was currently doing without my permission, I was indeed smiling.

"I know it is," I sighed, pulling the smile from my lips. I wanted her to know that I was taking all of it seriously. "But Oakley, I'm not going to let anything happen to you. We'll figure this out. We'll catch whoever it is."

"Will we?" she asked, searching my gaze. "I'm tired of running Owen, I'm tired of fighting a ghost."

Sitting up more in the bed, I readjusted the pillows behind me to lean back against the headboard more. It was hard for me to wrap my mind around why she would even think for a moment that she wouldn't survive what was possibly to come. She had to know I would run with her if I needed to. I wasn't about to just give up on her like she seemed to believe

I would, but then something clicked into place for me, a slow shift in understanding as I watched her. Worry suddenly smothered my gaze. She thought she wouldn't survive because she planned to go at it alone. "Oakley…"

Tears suddenly filled her green gaze as she shook her head, "They're after me Owen, not you," she whispered. "I-I can't lose you too."

No.

She couldn't honestly believe I was going to just let her go through with whatever insane plan she was concocting. I wasn't going to leave her high and dry. I couldn't lose her either. That simply wasn't even an option. Reaching for her, I pulled her in against me again. This wasn't the conversation I had been hoping we'd have after what we had done earlier.

We were both still very naked in my bed together, and I wanted nothing more than to tell her how I felt and make her mine, but that clearly wasn't the way this was going. I could all but taste the goodbye in every kiss. Thankfully, she didn't fight me when I pulled her in. Instead, she sank in against my side, letting me wrap my arm around her again.

"What makes you think at this point that I could lose you?" I asked her. "I know it's all a risk. One of us could get hurt again or worse. But they'll keep coming unless we do something about it. I can't. I won't let you do this alone because it's already too late for me, Oak," I confessed. She could avoid the words, but I wasn't about to let her pretend that the feelings weren't there. I wasn't going to make it easier for her to walk away. If saying it kept her with me and allowed me to help her, I would selfishly shout it from every rooftop in town. I would tell every soul I walked past on the street. Whatever it took to keep her with me. "I-" but now that she wasn't immediately jumping to stop me from saying it, the words seemed to catch in my throat.

What if I lost her? There would be no coming back from that.

No.

I couldn't think like that. If I let the doubt in, then there was a far greater chance of our mystery assailant winning. I had to believe, more than anyone, that we could figure it all out before it was too late. I had to hold onto the faith that our small-town police department was just badass enough to bring down a high-profile murderer. Thinking about it like that, though, was enough to give me pause again. What if we weren't enough? Jacey and I did our best, and I knew we were a damn good team with him at my six, but we weren't trained like the swat guys were. Hell, even Austen was better equipped for this sort of thing than I was.

Dammit!

I had to stop that. I could sit there and question our skill and our ability and resources as a department, but there was one thing I knew I couldn't even begin to question. How I felt about her and just how far I was willing to go to protect her. She deserved to know how I felt. She needed to understand the lengths I was willing to go to if it meant keeping her safe. Even if she didn't want to hear it, I had to say it.

Even in the darkness of the room, I could see the way her brilliant green eyes watched me expectantly. She was waiting for me to finish that last thought. Reaching up, I brushed back her dark hair, tucking it gently behind her ear. I couldn't help but smile at the way the misbehaving curls wrapped around my finger. Leaning in, I kissed her softly. "I love you," I whispered against her lips.

She likely needed to hear those words just as much as I needed to say them. She needed to know how far gone I already was and that there was no saving me from getting hurt in all of this. There were a thousand and one different outcomes to our current predicament, and only one seemed to end with neither of us getting hurt in any way.

The odds weren't exactly in our favor; in fact, they were pretty stacked against us, considering our attacker had sights on us, but we still didn't know for sure who it was. I knew the outcome looked grim. I understood why she was scared. I was scared, too. The fact that we were both scared, though, gave us a reason to fight for each other.

My words had been soft-spoken, but I could tell by the way she was watching me that they had hit her like a ton of bricks. She parted her lips for a moment before closing them again. "You don't have to say anything," I assured her. I didn't want her to feel any added pressure just because I had said it first.

She held her hand up to quiet me, though, "I can't say it yet, but know, it's there. Everything just feels so right when I'm with you," she smiled slightly. It seemed once the dam had been broken, there was no preventing the floodwaters. There was no escaping this now. Live or die; we were in this battle together until the very end.

I could see the fight in her gaze, too; somehow, by some miracle, she seemed less hellbent on taking all of this on alone. Maybe it was because she now knew how deep I already was. Maybe it was something else I had said that had gotten through to her. I couldn't be sure of anything at that point. All I knew was that we were in this together.

She reached for my hand and laced our fingers together again before shifting so she could kneel over me. With the words so newly admitted, she leaned in to kiss me. She wasted no time in finding my tongue with hers. Sighing into the kiss, I pulled her closer, all but forcing her to straddle my waist instead. It seemed she had other things in mind for how we could spend the rest of the night together. Not that I could say I minded.

Oakley Morgan was unlike any woman I had ever known. She had a way of jump-starting my heart while simultaneously taking my breath away. Rolling over on the bed suddenly, she landed beneath me, a gasp coming from her when the change in position pressed me up against her. Of course, it was then that my phone's shrill tone filled the darkness, lighting up on the nightstand behind me. Dropping my head down against her shoulder, I groaned in disappointment.

"Ignore it," she encouraged, lifting my face so she could lean in to kiss me again. With everything going on, I couldn't just ignore it. It was almost painful to pull away from her, but I knew if I didn't answer it, it could spell all sorts of consequences for us with everything we were up against. I sighed when I met her gaze before leaning in to kiss her again once.

"I'm sorry," I all but begged forgiveness as I pulled away from her and stood up to grab it. I needed to put space between us, or there was no way I was leaving my bed. "Hale."

"About damn time you answer the damned phone," Jacey grumbled on the other end, "I just thought you should know we got a hit finally. That white van turned up again. Except this time it was left abandoned. With an old man half beaten in the back."

I started to rummage around the room for clothes to put on. "What do we know so far?" I asked.

"Nothing. Some rando reported the van to 911, hung up before the operator could get her name or any information. Which if you ask me sounds exactly like my visitor last night. Who also mentioned the white van. But what do I know? Preliminary reports on the old man is that he's out cold. You can thank your pain in the ass little brother for that high tech medical examination. We're hoping to talk to him when he comes to."

I nodded; looking back at Oakley, I tried to write the apology all over my face, but her unamused expression told me she wasn't buying it. "Text me where you are," I told Jacey before hanging up. I didn't have time to listen to him protest and bitch like a little baby. Knowing him, though, I was going to hear it for hanging up on him in the first place. Reaching out, I cupped Oakley's cheek in my hand. "I'm sorry, but I… I have to go. They found the white van with someone in the back. This might be it, baby. We might finally be able to put this whole mess to rest." Shifting in, I kissed her softly. "But that means I have to go meet up with Jacey."

She pulled back the covers, revealing that perfect naked body of hers, and I could only sigh, "I'll come with you," she told me, causing my gaze to snap back to hers.

"Oak. You don't have to," I protested. "You can stay here, I can lock you in with the boys," I offered.

"We're in this together Owen," she threw my words back at me. "If I'm not allowed to go at it alone, neither are you. I know you're the cop, but I'm the one they're after. Chances are probably fairly good I have some idea of who's in the van."

She was right. If the older man didn't wake up anytime soon and if she recognized him, that was still a step in the right direction. But I hated the idea of her being out there again in the open. I knew I couldn't keep her hidden away, but the only thing I wanted more than to end this finally; was to keep her safe. Safe was at home with Roscoe and Justice. "Fine," I huffed, "Get dressed. But we're taking Roscoe with us. He may be a police dog reject, but at least he learned a thing or two before they threw him from the program."

"And you know he'll protect me," she insisted.

I sat back and watched as she gathered her clothing from the floor. "I should grab my bag. These are still wet from our impromptu shower in the rain," she sighed. "Are you just going to check out the van?" she asked.

I shook my head, "Jacey is already on that. I mean I want to look it over myself, but the suspect is already on his way to the hospital with Mason and one of our daytime cops. So it's mostly just Jacey filling me in on what they found." I looked down as my phone chimed. "In fact he just told me to meet him at the station instead."

She shook her head, "Then maybe I will just stay here, do some laundry so I have clothes to put on. And you can take me to see this person in the morning?" she requested.

I nodded, "Of course. I'll lock the doors on my way out. Keep the boys close, please?" I asked. "I shouldn't be gone more than an hour. There's only so much they could have found in the van." I paused, "Don't let anyone in," I requested. "Even if you know them." I know my request was likely strange to her, but I didn't want to chance it. If Ashland had something to do with this, if the old man was another fake out, I needed to know she was safe. I trusted the security system I had in place. I just needed to make sure she didn't let someone in.

Climbing onto my lap, she took my face in her hands. "It better be quick," she insisted. "And if I'm not allowed to let anyone in, you need to make sure you come home safely to me. You got that officer?"

I nodded, "Yes, ma'am," I answered. We shared another heated kiss, one that I really wish I could have explored further with her before she moved from my lap and allowed me to stand up again. I spared her one last glance before I headed down the stairs and out the front door, making sure to lock it tightly behind me.

Five minutes later, I was pulling in at the station. I had promised Oakley an hour, which meant I had to be home no later than 9:15. And maybe I would stop off at the diner and pick up something for a late dinner. The way she was looking at me before I'd left the bedroom, we would be up late. Not that I was complaining. Heading into the station, I found Jacey sitting at his desk. "What do we got?" I asked, dropping down into my chair across from him.

He turned the computer screen towards me so I could see the pictures from the inside of the van, "looks like we've got a shrine to you and your girlfriend."

I studied a few of the pictures that had been posted up on the inside of the van. "Are we thinking a stalker?" I asked.

Jacey shrugged, "Unless we've got one of those 'If I can't have her no one can' situations," he suggested. "there was no indication on who's actually behind it all. And Mason said the old dude was well and truly still out like a fucking light when they got him to the hospital. So we may have to wait on questioning the old bastard. The way he was beat though, I don't think he's our guy."

I sighed and pushed my fingers back through my hair in frustration. It felt like we were sitting on a fucking gold mine of clues, but none of it was adding up. How did all of this connect back to her parents' murders? Did it even link back at all? Was it possible that it was just a coincidence? I wasn't sure I believed that it could be merely a coincidence. Whoever was after her was definitely out to kill, but that didn't discredit the stalker theory.

"I'm going to take Oakley to the hospital tomorrow morning. Maybe she can ID the victim you found in the van. If she knows who he is, it might push us in the right direction. It might jog her memory about someone who might have it out for her family."

"They were a family of money, Hale, chances are the whole fucking world had it out for them in some way or another," Jacey shook his head. "No matter how we spin this, we might not be able to come up with the why. At this point as long as we get this bastard before he puts a bullet through either of your heads, I'd say case closed."

"The problem is, figuring out the who before they do just that," I retorted.

He nodded, "We found some prints. I sent them off to the city to have them run through the system there. If this person so much as shoplifted a candy bar and their prints are in the system, we'll find them. Tonight was a win. We possibly have a second victim and a witness to who it is. If he wakes up, we have prints. We've got the creepy mural dedication to your girl. It's finally a starting point."

He was right, but something almost seemed too easy about all of it. Everything just seemed to fall into our laps all at once, and it just wasn't sitting right with me. How had we gone so long with nothing to show for it, and now, all of a sudden, we hit the jackpot with evidence?

No.

It was almost like they wanted us to find all of this, but why?

Twenty-Five
Ash

Well, that had been easy.

It was almost too easy, really. I hadn't made it this far into this by being stupid. As far as the California State Police were concerned, I was clean. They had checked me out and bought into my pleas hook, line, and sinker. The poor, dumb bastards. Though to be fair, I had taken the time to make sure there was nothing for them to find.

Smirking to myself as I watched her precious officer Hale jump into his cruiser and turn over the engine, firing it to life, I knew I had to time it all exactly right. If I was too quick to jump the gun, he might return. If she heard a noise outside, if one of the dogs barked, she could call him back. If I waited too long, though, he might be headed back from the scene I left them. Though I was thorough enough that I knew darling daddy Abraham wouldn't be saying much of anything to anyone for quite a while. Plus there wasn't a print to be found in that van. I was no amateur at this after all.

Heading back down the road towards town, I made it about half way before stopping. Digging in my pocket, I pulled out the book of matches I had. Striking one, I casually tossed it into the brush around me. If he did come back too soon, at least he wouldn't be able to get through. Striking a second one, I tossed it off to the opposite side. Grinning to myself, I walked away from the growing flames and back towards the house.

Now it was just her and me.

This was the moment I had been waiting for. My whole body thrummed with the sheer anticipation of having that pretty little neck wrapped tight in my grasp. I was finally so fucking close I could almost taste the sweetness of victory. I wanted to see the fear in her innocent green eyes as she realized that once again, I had won.

I had watched the very life drain from her parents that day. Victory came again the moment I drove in the knife with Elisa, watching her choke on her own blood. Now this. Possibly the sweetest victory yet. You bet your fucking ass, I was going to savor each and every painful second of it for her. I would make that bitch feel every ounce of betrayal and pain I had felt since she had dared step foot into my life.

I wanted her to suffer the way she had made me suffer, but most of all, I wanted to keep her alive just long enough for her to understand that her cop wasn't coming to her rescue this time. I wanted to watch as that realization struck. She had an irritating flare for indignance. With that said, of course, it would take a lot of restraint on my part not to snap her neck the moment I had her within reach. I could refrain, I suppose, as long as she didn't dare open that mouth of hers. She'd always struggled with controlling her tongue. Always had something smart to say.

I mean, there was only so much restraint one could expect of a person, and whether or not I got my fun out of it or not; in the end, the results would ultimately be the same. The bitch responsible for ruining my life would be dealt with. She would be dead, rotting in hell where she fucking deserved to be. A world without Elizabeth Richfield in it, well, that sounded like a damned utopia to me. Paradise on earth.

As much as I wanted to make her pay, as much as I wanted to make her suffer, as much as I wanted her to feel pain like she'd never felt before in her pitiful little existence, if it came down to listening to her run her mouth or just driving the knife in… It would go in. Hard and fast. The goal here wasn't to drive myself to the brink of insanity after all.

I kept watch over the house, tracking her movements through it with each light that turned on and then off again. All the while, I kept an eye on the time too. Reaching out, I fiddled with the police scanner I had swiped. Finding the channel the Gratin PD used, I waited for him to call his arrival on scene.

He wasn't technically on duty, but it was more or less his case. Once he called through, I would know I likely had about twenty minutes before he packed up and headed for home. The two of them were inseparable right now. It was fucking nauseating. I should have left just enough to keep him occupied longer, but I wouldn't need long once I breached the house.

Digging in my bag, I found the dog treats I had bought. Surveillance had shown the cops two idiot dogs begged for them. I could only hope that they would take the bait. I wasn't a monster; after all, I wasn't going to kill the dogs if I could help it. They had done nothing wrong in all of this.

Glancing at the radio again, I sighed. What the fuck was taking so long? I was starting to question if he had turned back in favor of being with her instead. It wouldn't surprise me after all. I had to get creative to find a way to get him away from her. I figured a seemingly dead body would do it. Especially in the white van they had seen skulking around town, always empty. I couldn't make it look more suspicious than I had. Plus now they had someone within reach. How the fuck was he not chomping at the bit to end this already?

Shaking my head, I all but growled to myself, slamming my hand against the steering wheel. If this didn't fucking work, I was just going to have to take a cheap shot from a distance. Then she wouldn't know that I was the one behind her parents' deaths, though. She wouldn't know that it was her fucking fault they were dead! Or the truth about Elisa. That Abraham was left to rot in that van. All because of her. Her demise would be quiet. She would be mourned. Painted the victim instead of the fucking villain she really was.

No.

I couldn't have that.

She wasn't going to get off that fucking easy.

Before I could get myself too worked up over it, though, the radio to my right crackled before I heard the magic words come through the speaker.

"10-97, Hale on scene."

I felt the pull of a smile on my lips. About fucking time.

Pushing the door open, I tried not to move the brush too much. I knew enough about Hale's dogs to know the one had the hearing of a fucking fox. He heard everything and was quick to sound the alarm. If he spotted me, the whole plan went to hell. Somehow, I had to figure out where they were in the house and make a move. If I were too slow, that fucking rottweiler would rip my arm clear off.

From where I stood I could see the light turn on in the kitchen, and the side door opened, both dogs bounding out into the darkness after something was thrown. It was like fate was shining down on me tonight. I had my in. I just had to jimmy the lock on the front door before she let the dogs back in, and I was home free. This was seriously turning out to be a lot fucking easier than I had thought it would be. I watched the door close again, the dogs wrestling in the enclosed side yard.

Stepping gingerly, I made my way through the darkness in silence. I still couldn't risk alerting the dogs to my presence. If they sniffed me out, they would go off, and then it would all blow to hell again. Skirting the halo of light from the front porch light, I slipped into the darkness along the side. The light was a problem, but if I worked fast, it wasn't like Hale had any neighbors closer than a mile away. His desire for solitude made it all that much simpler.

Climbing up over the porch's railing, I dropped soundlessly onto the wooden frame. Sliding over to the door, I started to work at the lock. I likely only had a few minutes before she let both dogs back into the house. The lock was a simple single-cylinder deadbolt. It didn't take long before I heard all the pins click into place, and I was able to turn the lock open. Now the one thing I hadn't been able to figure out from my distance was whether or not he had any kind of security set up. If the door chirped the minute I opened it, she would be alerted, and I couldn't have her knowing I was there before I wanted her to know.

Slowly, I pushed the door open, grinning to myself when it silently swung open. Perfect. Slipping into the house, I stuck to the shadows. If it weren't for the dogs and their ability to sniff me out in a second, I would have loved to haunt her. I would have enjoyed every second of slowly driving her crazy, letting her think it was just her imagination getting the best of her, again and again, every time she heard a bump in the darkness. I would have relished in her growing hysteria.

Unfortunately for me, though, it appeared his security system was those dogs. Which meant I couldn't play with her the way I really wanted to. At least not in the house. There would be time enough to play my games once I had her free and clear of here.

I could hear movement in the kitchen as she milled about doing god knows what. None of that mattered anyway. I knew I had to strike before she dared to open the side door, though. Slinking along the wall, I kept to the darkness, but I needed visual to know what I was up against. Where she was in the kitchen. I also couldn't risk her reaching for a knife. Bitch always thought she could fight back. As if she actually stood a chance at winning. Part of me wished I had brought my gun instead; it would have been one quick pop, and she would be down. The deed done.

I suppose that would have been a satisfying outcome too. Watching him come home to find her brains splattered all over his kitchen walls. Oh, the ways I had fantasized about killing her. The pleasure it brought had almost the same effect as watching some raunchy porno. I got off on the idea of her gasping her last breath. Slipping against the wall just outside the kitchen, I finally got the visual that I needed.

She was alone, of course. Her back turned to me. I knew once I stepped out of the shadows, there was nowhere to hide anymore. If she turned at all, I would have to make my move against her, and unfortunately, she would have a greater chance at fighting back if she saw me coming.

I watched her, studying her every movement as she fixed herself a bowl of cereal. So mundane. If this was her life, I was almost doing her a favor by ending it. God, that put a bad taste in my mouth. The last thing I wanted to do was do something that was actually beneficial to her. I felt the grimace pull at my lips at the very idea. She didn't deserve to live, but she sure as hell didn't deserve the out of death either.

The desire to torture her pulsed through me. I wanted to make her scream; I wanted her to believe that she could escape, that she could win if she just fought hard enough. Because that would make her fall that much more glorious to me. It would likely take every trick in my arsenal to break her will, but I would. I would have her begging for death, and then just for the fun of it, I would deny her that too. At least for a little while. I wanted to see her so defeated and beaten down it would be a mercy killing.

When it came down to it, though, I wanted her to understand one crucial thing above anything else.

No one fucked me over and got away with it.

Twenty–Six
Oakley

Something prickled at the very edge of my consciousness, raising the hairs on the back of my neck, standing at attention like little soldiers issuing a warning to me. Something was off; I could feel it like two eyes staring right through me, cutting me to the core. The very atmosphere around me changed completely.

Owen's house was the one place in this whole town where I felt completely and truly safe. His presence was preserved within these walls, and it was like he surrounded me even when he wasn't physically here with me. It was only seconded by actually being wrapped in his arms where nothing would ever touch me.

There was something here, though, something that was sucking the very life from the warm home. Part of me wanted to reach for my phone sitting at the other end of the counter. This feeling twisted itself up inside of me, screaming for me to just reach out for help. Owen had told me to call before he left. He'd specified to call if I needed anything at all.

Except, my imagination had gotten the best of me before, creating vivid stories of someone in the house with me. Giving birth to monsters lurking in the shadows. I had overreacted then. Not only harming myself in the process – I glanced down at my hand where the wound was still healing, leaving behind an angry red line stitched together, but I had almost hurt Owen too. In my hysteria then, everything was out to get me.

Taking a deep breath in through my nose and out through my mouth, I tried to calm my increasingly frazzled nerves. There was nothing really wrong, right? It was just the fact that I was in the house alone at night for the first time. Not having Owen here gave the darkness eyes that seemed to bore right through me. If there was something completely wrong, Owen was likely already on his way home, already knowing about it.

He'd installed the silent alarms for that very reason, and he'd made it clear to me before he left that he'd planned to set them all, locking me in for the night. He had the whole thing set up to alert him every single time a door opened or closed while the system was armed. If there were really something off, he would have at the very least called to check in. Make sure it wasn't just me letting the dogs out like I had promised to do. He would have called.

I glanced towards my phone again. There was nothing there. Because there was no reason to be panicking. That seemed to be enough to start calming my racing heart, at least ever so slightly. I could breathe a little easier. I just had to keep telling myself that, a mantra to keep repeating. If something were really and truly wrong, Owen would call. He would likely know before me, and he would come racing right home. Because he had promised me. He had vowed that nothing could touch me here.

Turning back to my cereal, I poked at it. Suddenly I wasn't hungry anymore. Maybe I could just leave the bowl sit out; it would be something for him to eat when he got home again before heading upstairs to crawl back into bed with me. I had finally managed to calm myself back down when I heard something behind me. Turning, I glanced back over my shoulder. I didn't know what I was supposed to do if something was actually there, but glancing into the dark living room, there was nothing more than a collection of menacing shadows.

Part of me wanted to grab the dogs, turn on every single light in the house and go upstairs and lock myself in the bathroom until Owen got home. If he didn't already think of me as crazy, that would definitely push him to that point. I had already fallen for him, quite hopelessly. I wasn't about to scare him off now.

No.

I had to handle this like a mature adult. I'd grab the dogs, and we'd check the house out. When it proved that there was nothing really there, I would just go back to bed. I should never have moved; it would have saved me a lot of energy that was being wasted on my anxieties. Sighing to myself, I turned back to the bowl of cereal. Maybe it was simply the fact that Owen wasn't in the house with me. I had gotten used to the way his presence seemed to soothe every frayed nerve ending in my body. I had been so on edge for long enough that it had become my new normal. I had forgotten what any form of peace felt like. Now that I had been granted some semblance of peace in the form of a very sexy cop, I wasn't used to the same level of chaos anymore.

It was a rather jarring realization, though, that I had come to rely on Owen to that degree. I knew I couldn't depend on him for everything. I had to find my footing again. Everything was so back and forth and upside down that I was clinging to whatever shred of sanity and normalcy I could find. In the wake of everything, it wasn't like anyone could blame me for that.

The incident at the house had sent me into a complete tailspin. Owen had been the one thing to hold me steady through that. He'd been so calm and unwavering; he was a life raft keeping me afloat in the torrent of everything that was going on, but it wasn't fair for me to lean on him completely.

I had been raised to rely on everyone else completely for everything in my old life. I wasn't allowed to do much of anything because we had people for that. Then I had taken most of it on myself, letting everyone who worked for my parents go because I couldn't afford the level of upkeep my parents could. I'd still had Abraham and Elisa to hold me steady in the wake of my parents' deaths, though. I had managed to successfully stand on my own for a few weeks before I'd fallen helplessly into Owen's arms like some sad damsel in distress from those romance novels my mother had always read.

To be fair, I hadn't given Owen my heart right away, but I had handed over complete control to him. Yes, it made sense because he was a cop. He had the training and the resources required to handle the job the way it needed to be handled. It had been almost too easy for me to step back and hand over the reins to him, though. For once in my life, I had to take charge and figure things out for myself.

I had gotten so caught up in my own thoughts, though, that I had all but forgotten my anxieties about being left alone in the house, but they all came rushing right back when something scratched at the door. The dogs. Fuck I had forgotten about the dogs. Pushing away from the counter, I moved towards the door when something grabbed my arm.

Next, I felt the unmistakable bite of a sharp blade against my throat. "Don't even think about it," an almost sinister voice hissed in my ear. My whole body froze as tears threatened my eyes, burning at the corners. I didn't know what was worse, the cool metal against my skin or the fact that I recognized the voice.

"Ashland…" I managed to choke out her name. "You…" she pressed the knife harder against my skin, and I whimpered quietly when I felt it break the skin.

"I what?" she sneered, her grip on my arm tightening to the point where I was more than sure I would have bruises from her nails. "I don't have to do this? Funny, your mom said the same thing." God, I could hear the grin in her voice. She was proud of herself for killing them. Just like she would undoubtedly be proud of herself for killing me too. In all the things Owen and I had talked about, all the ways he'd taught me to defend myself, we'd never covered this.

My whole body started to shake at the very idea that I might not get out of this one, that I might not ever see Owen again, that everything he'd done for me and risked was for nothing. "But yeah, I do," she smirked. I could tell that she really believed that. Which meant I didn't really have a chance to escape. She would slice me open without a second thought. "Now you're going to do exactly what I say, Princess," she instructed, the last word drenched in complete disdain. That's what Abraham had always called me when he wasn't working. "And if you fight me," she continued, interrupting my train of thought, "I won't stop with you. Got me?"

I nodded, crying slightly as the movement pressed the knife harder against my throat. "Don't hurt him, please," I all but begged. It was one thing for her to come after me. She was delusional enough to believe that I had genuinely ruined her life, but Owen had done nothing. There was no reason for him to die in all of this too.

"Don't give me a reason to," she answered coldly. With a hard yank, she pulled the knife away from my throat and turned me so that I could finally see her. The look in her eyes struck me hardest. They were lifeless. There wasn't a hint of remorse in them. There was no warmth. There was no bringing her back from this. I would have to apologize to Abraham and Elisa after it was all over if I lived to see them again.

Her grip on my arm was unrelenting as she dragged me to the front door. I knew my chances of survival diminished if she got me out of the house. The town was small, but it was surrounded by woods and mountains that she could take me into, and if that happened, they weren't going to find me alive. I didn't know how to fight. Despite Owen showing me a few moves, I knew Ash was stronger and completely unhinged. She had nothing to lose.

With a hard, sudden twist, I was able to pull my arm free. Without the knife pressed against my neck anymore, I actually stood a chance. If I was going down, I was going down fighting, and I wanted Owen to see that much when he got home. She shrieked at the lost hold on me. A sound bubbled from within that wasn't human, flourishing from a pain that had festered in her for far too long.

Stumbling back a step, I turned and ran. My legs were weak beneath me. I knew I wouldn't make it far before she caught up, but what other choice did I have? Owen had told me where he kept his guns in the house; I just had to get to them first. He'd gone out of his way to make sure that I knew there was one gun, kept away from the others that defied all of the safety procedures. He kept it loaded just in case he ever needed it. If I could just get my hands on it and out the back door before she caught up, I knew I had a fighting chance.

My heart was pounding in my chest. I could feel it reverberating throughout my whole body as I tried to run down the hall. A hand wrapped around my ankle, followed by an enraged, guttural scream as she yanked me to the floor. The pain from the brutal hit was instant, rocketing through my frame. Kicking back, teeth clashed beneath my heel. It was enough to break free and scramble to my hands and knees. Glancing back over my shoulder, eyes wide, I screamed.

Twenty–Seven
Ash

I wasn't sure where she'd suddenly gotten her scrappiness from, but I was going to beat it out of her before I finally put us both out of our misery. Fuck my jaw hurt. She was going to pay for that. I was going to make the bitch suffer, slow and painful. Regaining my bearings, I took off up the steps after her. I wasn't about to let Lizzie Richfield get the best of me.

Maybe I would have to do something about that cop of hers, payback for teaching her how to defend herself. This would have been so much easier if she was still the useless socialite I was after in the first place. No, I had to make it fun. I had to make it a fucking game, and she had risen to the challenge.

Heading down the hall, I kicked open the first door on my right. This house wasn't that big. She had to be here somewhere. The next door was on my left, and I slammed it open. I grinned when I heard her shriek. At least some things never changed. Walking into the room, I found her on her knees, trying desperately to put in the code on a safe.

Oh fuck no.

Going over to her, I grabbed a fist full of her hair and pulled her away from it. There was no fucking way she was going to get the best of me again. I wasn't fucking stupid. Of course, he had something hidden away, and maybe he wasn't as dumb as I thought he was. He'd told her where to find it if she needed it.

She squirmed in my grasp, trying desperately to pull away from me. She wasn't fucking going anywhere this time, though. She tried to swing on me, but I caught her hand in my free one before she could. "You've gotten feisty," I sneered as I dragged her across the floor. I hated having to improvise, but my knife was downstairs. Bitch had knocked it out of my hand. Just something else she was going to pay for.

We reached the top of the stairs, and she really started fighting my grasp. Reaching up with her free hand, she dug her nails into the hand still wrapped in her hair. I wasn't fucking letting go. She could fight all she wanted. Getting her to the edge of the stairs, she screamed again before suddenly throwing all of her weight against me. Knocking me off balance, I let go of her and tumbled down the stairs.

Laying at the bottom, I looked up just as she moved by me, making a run for the back door. I couldn't let her get outside. Reaching out, I wrapped my hand around her ankle, and she crumbled to the floor with me. I could hear the sobs shaking through her before she weakly tried to kick at me again.

Not this fucking time.

I yanked her towards me, hellbent on just fucking ending her right there in the middle of his living room. Leave that for him to find when he got home later. I could hear the dogs at the side door, scratching to be let back in. They knew something was off. If she got away from me again and let those dogs in, I wasn't going to have a choice.

Moving so that I could turn her over and sit on her, I wrapped my hands around her neck. This wasn't how I wanted this to end. I wanted her to suffer. She deserved to suffer. I hadn't wanted this to end so quickly for her. She was leaving me no choice, though. She clawed at my hands again, trying to fight back as much as she could. It wasn't as satisfying as slowly draining the life from her, but it would do.

Her eyes darted around her. She wasn't giving up. I could say she came by that naturally. Her mother had been stubborn, too. She had fought to hold on, struggling to breathe. Her little Lizzie had the same fire. Fuck, I was going to enjoy putting that fire out. I squeezed a little harder and smiled when a strangled sound slipped from her.

She let go of my hand and started reaching for something around her. I had to stay focused. If I let myself worry about what she was doing, she would fucking win. I couldn't let her fucking win.

Nothing about how all of this had gone down was going the way I had planned. She was supposed to be there the day I had gone into the manor. She was never supposed to run. She was never supposed to fall in with some white knight complexed night cop. She was never supposed to fight back like this. She was supposed to fucking die.

All of it. Everything that had happened since that first day was her fucking fault. Her blood was the only one I wanted staining my hands. Now I had killed three other people because of her. Four, if the old bastard died too. Five if I had to go after that cop of hers. He knew too much.

There were too many variables at play, too many what ifs. I would have to burn the whole fucking town to the ground to be able to get away with killing her. She'd caused such a fucking mess. I squeezed a bit harder and smiled when I felt her go limp in my hands. I watched as her eyes rolled closed. It was about fucking time. Slowly, I uncurled my fingers from her skin, relishing in the marks left behind.

I sighed in relief and sat up a bit straighter. It was over. I had done it. The bitch was finally dead.

All of a sudden, I felt movement beneath me. Before I could react, something hard slammed into the side of my head and shattered around me. Looking back down at her, I saw those fucking green eyes watching me as she coughed. She swung again, and everything went black.

TWENTY–EIGHT
OWEN

Pushing my fingers through my hair, I took in the scene around me. No sooner I'd made it to the station, Jacey had told me we needed to go back out to the scene. The old man that had been found in the back of our mystery van was obviously a victim. He'd been tied up, beaten and drugged. The place had been completely wiped down, though we were still waiting on the prints that had been found to come back.

I had already known that we were dealing with someone of a caliber the Gratin Police Department hadn't ever seen before, but this just solidified that. Glancing towards Jacey, he shrugged. I didn't know what else we could do for her. Whoever it was stayed at least one step ahead of us the whole fucking time. They seemed to know what we were going to do next before we even did. That sided with the current working theory that we were possibly up against a dirty cop. How else could someone outsmart the whole of the California State Police?

At the same time, though, things didn't add up with that theory either. What would a cop want with a vineyard owner and his socialite daughter? The whole thing was turning into some massive cluster fuck, and I was really starting to worry that Oakley would think better of it and take off again.

"He's still out cold, Hale," Jacey shook his head as he stalked back towards me with his phone in his hand. "He's the only one who might be able to give us any inkling of a lead, and the doctors can't bring him back around."

Something about all of this wasn't adding up. Until this point, this van had been a ghost, people kept reporting seeing it, but by the time we got there, it was gone. Even the one time I had seen it myself, it had been there one minute, and the next, it was like it had vanished into thin air. It made absolutely no sense that it would just turn up abandoned like this in the middle of town with a victim tied up in the back.

They'd wanted us to find the van, but why? What good did it do them to leave it unattended now? All of a sudden it struck me like lightning, hitting me down to my very core. "Fuck!" I yelled, barely noticing Jacey jump next to me. Turning on my heels, I bolted back towards my cruiser. Digging through the papers that were piled on the passenger seat, I continued to mutter curses under my breath. We'd fallen right into it. How the fuck hadn't I seen it?

"Hale!" Jacey yelled from over my shoulder.

No.

No, no, no.

Fucking no!

Finally finding my phone, I pulled up the home screen. There was nothing there from Oakley, but there was a series of alerts from the security system. The side door opened and closed, not long after a key unlocked the front door.

"Goddammit!" I threw my phone across the car. Turning back to Jacey, I knew I looked half-crazed. "We have to get back to the house. This was all a fucking setup!" That seemed to be all I needed to say to kick his ass in gear too. There was no telling what was waiting for us back at the house. All I knew was that I had left Oakley there like a sitting duck.

"Hale!" Jacey yelled at me, looking pissed off at everything, "Get in the car!" I started patting myself down, looking for my keys before he pulled up next to me. Without a second thought, I jumped in with him. He hit the sirens and peeled out of the parking lot, squealing the tires as we left.

I would never forgive myself if something happened to her. She'd trusted me to keep her safe. I had promised that I would do everything in my power to protect her. I had even gone as far as installing that security system. What good did it do me, though, when I left my fucking phone in the car. I should have known better. What if… "Goddammit, Hale, fucking focus, I said call it in!" Jacey ground out through clenched teeth as he pushed the SUV faster still.

Reaching for the radio, I realized my hands were shaking. I needed to get a grip if I was going to do Oakley any good. If I fell apart before we even got there, I wasn't going to be able to do shit all to save her. Whoever was behind this was going to pay now. I tried to do it the right way. I tried to find them and let the courts do their job, but this was all-out war now.

If I got the chance, I would put a full round of bullets right through them. I didn't care anymore about keeping my job or what it would all mean for me. The only thing that mattered now was that Oakley came through this alive and no worse for the wear. So I did as Jacey had demanded. I called it in to dispatch, knowing we would need back-up if we were going to end it tonight.

I also knew that having back up there would keep me in check. There was a white-hot rage simmering in the pit of my stomach and pumping through my system at the very thought of what this sick fuck could be doing to her. She was a good person; she didn't deserve the hand she'd been dealt. I couldn't trust that I would do the right thing in the moment, I would make the fucker pay for putting her through all of this.

It didn't matter that all of this had brought us together, I couldn't see the sliver of good in it anymore. I was glad she was here, I was happy I could help. However, if never getting the chance to know her meant that amazing woman never had to suffer through all of this, I would give it all up in a heartbeat.

Jacey squealed the tires again as he turned the truck onto my road, the momentum throwing me into the passenger side window. The impact barely phased me as my gaze zeroed in on what was up ahead. The hot, red, angry flames that were blocking the road between Oakley and me.

"I don't know that I can get through it," Jacey shook his head, his tone almost defeated after he'd slammed on the brakes. I didn't hear what he had to say next, though. I didn't want to hear what he had to say. They weren't going to win this easily.

Jumping from the truck, I heard a door slam behind me as I stalked towards the flames. "What the fuck are you planning on doing, Hale? Walk through it?" He snapped at me. "I get it, you'd walk through fucking fire to get to her, but what good are you going to do her if you look like fucking fried chicken when you get there?" He grabbed my arm to stop me from moving, "I'm calling in fire. Don't. Move."

He didn't understand what it was like knowing the woman you loved more than anything in this world was slipping through your fingers. I actually glanced down at my hands at that. Why the hell would she come blazing into my life like this, only for it to end like this? No. We still had a chance.

Looking to either side, the fire hadn't spread that far off the road yet. It was growing at an alarming rate, but I could get around it on foot if I were quick enough. Before Jacey could stop me, I took off into the beginning brush of the woods surrounding my house. The flames licked at my skin with an angry heat that could only rival the fires of hell itself. The smoke seared my lungs; it felt like I was burning from the inside out, but it was a small price to pay.

Finally finding a patch that the flames hadn't touched yet, I started to sprint through them. I didn't know where in the woods I was in relation to my house, but something was guiding me, pulling me in the right direction. Jacey had said it best, I would walk across hot coals for her, I would literally run through flames for her, and I knew in my heart that if it came down to it, I would die for her too.

Breaking through into a clearing, I had surpassed the flames enough that I was finally gasping in fresh oxygen again. Doubled over, with my hands on my knees, I fought to catch my breath, knowing I had no time to waste. I didn't know how far out of the way the flames had taken me, but I had to keep pushing on. It was either that or admit defeat, and that wasn't an option.

Behind me was the low crackle of the flames as they started to spread in my direction again, and somewhere ahead of me, I heard a scream. That was enough to kick my ass back into gear. The low-hanging branches continued to pummel me as I sprinted through the woods. Some scratching me, some poking at me. I followed the direction of that scream, using it as my north star through the darkness. Then I heard Roscoe and Justice, and I felt myself smile.

Running for the back gate, I pushed it open. The front door had been locked again after whoever entered the house, and my keys were no longer in my pocket. I didn't know where they were, but that didn't really matter anymore. The dogs immediately ran over to me, both poised for whatever was to come next, waiting for my command. I didn't know what sort of weapon, if any, the intruder had. Part of me didn't want to risk the dogs, that something could happen to one of them if I let them into the house, but they were both trained to protect.

Throwing the side door open, the dogs took the lead. Roscoe immediately ran for the steps as Justice started sweeping the first floor. The kitchen was empty, and it was almost eerily silent, aside from the pitter-patter of the dog's paws against the hardwood floors throughout the house. I started to scan the kitchen for any signs of anything amiss. Oakley's stupid flip phone sat on the counter, just inside the door. There was an untouched bowl of cereal on the counter. There was a single droplet of blood on the white floor. Looking around for something more, I found another droplet, and then another one smeared across the tile. I tried to imagine exactly what had happened in the kitchen, if Oakley had managed to fight back at all.

Before I could start to piece too much together, I heard Roscoe coming back down the stairs. He came around the corner, and if it were possible, I could see worry in his eyes. He knew something bad had happened here. Out in the living room, though, I could hear Justice whimpering. Following after him, I found the back door hanging wide open. The boys had been trained only to leave the house when I directed. Reaching down, I scratched his ear, "Good boy," I answered.

I didn't know if this meant Oakley had been taken or if she was on the run. Either way, she needed my help, and I needed to get the boys out before the flames got any closer to the house. Turning around with a new fire inside, I reached for their harnesses. Hooking them both up to their leashes, I grabbed the first thing I could find of hers. The one thing people didn't know about Justice was that before he had come to me, he'd been a search and rescue dog. He'd been one of the best, able to find almost anyone whose scent was put in front of him. I was hoping now that those skills hadn't diminished at all, because out in the darkness, I knew he was my only hope at finding her.

Reaching back, I felt for my gun tucked into the waistband of my jeans. Feeling the familiar smooth finish, I sighed. This ended tonight, once and for all. Kneeling down next to Justice, he seemed to know what I needed from him. "I'm counting on you, buddy," I told him. He watched me with such precision, waiting for the command. Holding out the sweater for him to sniff, I nodded, "Search."

Twenty-Nine
Oakley

I didn't know where I was going. I didn't know where I was. I didn't know which way town was. I had to keep running, though. The lamp I had hit her with had only momentarily knocked her out. By the time I got out the door, she was right behind me again. I didn't know what else to do, I just had to get into town. If I could get to the diner or Austen's shop, I would be safe. I didn't know these woods, though; I didn't know which way to go.

I could hear her, hot on my heels. I didn't know how she was still standing, how she was coming after me still with such little energy exerted. I barely felt the stabbing pain in my feet as I kept moving forward. Stopping wasn't something I could risk. I just… The tears were streaming down my face, blurring my vision. The cut on my neck was throbbing. I could feel the blood as it started to dry against my skin. I couldn't stop the thought before it completely encumbered my mind.

I was going to die out here.

It had been a mistake to leave the house. At least there, Owen would have been able to find me. I could have opened the door, so it looked like I had gone outside and just found a place to hide in the house or something. I should have doubled back to the side yard where the dogs were. Hindsight. My heart was racing in my chest. It hurt to breathe; every muscle in my body was screaming in agony. I couldn't keep running forever.

The more I let those thoughts take over, though, the slower I moved. This was it. After everything I'd been through, after everything I survived, this was how it was going to end. Owen didn't deserve this. Maybe… I had come to a complete stop. There were no footsteps behind me, though. Had I actually managed to lose her in the woods? Daring to glance back over my shoulder, my eyes searched every tree, every bush, every twig looking for signs of movement from her. I searched for anything, but in the harsh darkness, there was nothing. Only the sounds of my labored breathing surrounded me.

Everything felt heightened out here. I felt her gaze on me long before I heard her, long before I could pinpoint which direction she was coming from. She'd slowed to a steady pace, like a mountain lion stalking its prey. I was the frightened deer, running for my life, and she was letting me. "Come out, come out, wherever you are. Princess." She called through the darkness. Her voice seemed to come at me from all sides as it bounced from tree to tree. I couldn't even fully tell which direction it was all coming from in the first place. Which meant I didn't know which way to run to get away from her.

"You know, as much as I enjoy the chase, I'm really going to revel in snapping your neck, should have done it back at the house when I had the chance," she called out with a cackle. "Lizzie…" she added in a sing-song type of voice. I didn't dare move; I had a feeling that she would hear even the quietest rustling of leaves. Remaining rooted to my spot, I tried to watch from every angle possible.

It was useless, though; through the tears and the darkness, I couldn't actually see anything, and I knew I wouldn't be able to until she was standing right in front of me. By then, it would be too late to run. Completely on my own, I had to figure out my next move. "Do you realize just how satisfying it was for me to finally put a bullet in your pretty mother's chest?" she asked, "She was always so fucking demanding. Everything had to be perfect at all times. And your father, he was a trip. It was fucking hilarious the way he tried to save her. Standing in front of her. Telling me I wasn't going to touch her until I put a bullet in his head. Most amazing feeling in the world. You should try it sometime, really. Total high." I knew what she was doing. I couldn't take the bait she was throwing out. "But god damn, even as priceless as that all was. Nothing will top the look on your sweet Abraham's face when I drove the knife into his precious Elisa's still beating heart."

I couldn't hold it back anymore at that. I tried to contain the sudden rush of pain. Elisa was… No. She couldn't be because if she were, that meant it was all my fault. If I had just stayed there, I could have protected them. I could have… if they had come with me, maybe we'd all be happy and alive.

The sob started softly as I tried to fight it back. I tried to hold it all in as best I could. I could let it all out after this was over. The more I let escape, though, the harder it was to contain. It squeaked out of me, and I heard her footsteps halt. "You know that's where your pretty boy cop is right now. Attending to daddy Abraham. After I'm through with you, I'm going to go back for him. And then, just for these games, I'm going to burn this fucking town to the ground. And it will be all your fault." There was a certain sneer to her voice. Now that she was getting closer, I had a good sense of where she was. If I stayed completely frozen to my spot, I knew I had a slight chance that I could get the jump on her.

I wasn't stronger by any stretch; I didn't have the fighting skills I knew I would need to take her down. In an all-out fight, she would win. I wasn't fooling anyone, least of all myself, into thinking that I actually had shot at beating her. I had gotten away from her, though. I had put up a good fight so far. I was just so tired. I could only hope that if I went up against her again there was enough of me and enough hatred for her bubbling inside of me that I could take her down with me.

I wasn't coming out of this alive. Somehow, I had come to peace with that. Because if we both went down, it meant everyone else got to continue on with their lives. They would get to live. Too many people I cared about were dead because of her twisted animosity towards me. No one else was going to die because of me. I heard her footsteps getting closer, and when she was within sight, I lunged.

Thirty
Ash

That. Fucking. Bitch.

Together we crashed to the ground. I had to admit I was impressed that the little princess had it in her to keep fighting back. There was part of me that was really enjoying watching her struggle. It was going to make watching that light die in her eyes that much fucking sweeter. Somehow, when she didn't first respond to my taunting about her parents, I had known that bringing up Elisa would do the trick. She'd loved the old hag. God knows why.

I cackled, though, as she pulled away and scrambled to her feet. "Why?" she asked. It was sickening how she was so desperately trying to understand me. As if everything in life had some sort of sugary sweet fucking answer. News flash, it didn't. The answer was really fucking simple. I. Didn't. Like. Her. Thought that much was clear.

"Why what?" I shot back; my hand clenched around my knife. Oh, what I wouldn't give to just slice her open from navel to neck. Should have just slit her throat when I had the chance, but no, I had to make it fun. Yeah, this was real fucking fun right now.

"Why are you doing this Ashland?" she pushed. "Your parents sent you away to help you," she pleaded. "They sent you away because they loved you, not because they were trying to replace you, not because they hated you. Or whatever twisted reason you keep telling yourself. They loved you." She shook her head, "They loved you. They only wanted what was best for you. They wanted you to get help so that you could come back and be a family again."

She needed to shut her god damned mouth. She thought she knew me. She thought she had me all figured out. Just like those fucking doctors that kept feeding me pills to make me better. What the fuck did they know? Stepping closer to her, she didn't have time to react before I had my hand around her throat and shoved back against a tree. A satisfied grin touched my lips when it knocked the wind from her.

"Whatever game you're playing at, it isn't going to fucking work," I warned her. "The longer you try to stall, the more you run, the worse it's going to be for all those precious fuckwits you love in this piece of shit town," I hissed at her. "I'm going to stand back and watch it all burn. And I'm going to enjoy every last fucking second of it." Squeezing her neck a little tighter in my grasp, my grin only grew as she clawed at my wrist, gasping for air. There was genuine fear in those eyes, and nothing had ever felt more right. "No one is coming to save you," I told her softly, but the fucking bitch just wouldn't die. Suddenly a knee slammed into my stomach, causing me to stumble back a step. At that point, I was barely even feeling the pain she was so desperately trying to inflict on me.

Growling at her, I lunged this time, my knife at the ready. I was done playing games, she was going to fucking die, and then everyone else would pay for her mistakes. I wouldn't be satisfied until this whole town was a pile of smoldering ash, and I would make sure each and every person knew that they could blame her for it. She grabbed my wrist, still coughing from the loss of air. Wrestling for the knife, I managed to break free and swing, catching her with the blade across the cheek. Before she could register what had happened, I was swinging again.

The only way they were going to be able to identify her was by her dental records, and that was if I didn't knock those perfect teeth back into her skull first. Once again, she made a play for the knife, pulling at my arm. She managed to get a foot up enough to kick me back off of her. I'd be so fucking close, three times now I'd had her neck in my hand, and I didn't just snap it. I was ready to dive for her again, letting my anger fuel a fire unlike any other when I heard them in the distance. Footsteps coming our way.

There was no fucking chance that someone had actually found us. She'd led me on some sort of wild goose chase through the woods, and yet… if I had to take a guess, it was that fucking cop of hers. Probably shoved a GPS up her ass. Reaching out, I grabbed her arm again. "You say a fucking word, and I'll kill him first and make you watch," I hissed at her before dragging her behind me. Hearing them coming seemed to renew that spark of hope in her eyes. God damn, that thing was almost harder to kill than she was. It didn't matter which way I took her though, the sound of footsteps through the brush stayed right behind us.

Fine.

If he wanted to play it that way. Spinning her around, I pulled her in against me, pressing the blade of my knife to her throat again, enjoying the way she winced in pain as it glided along the cut and growing bruises from before. I knew I should just do it, let him find her bleeding out on the ground when he reached her, knowing that he was too far away to save her. I could hide as he watched her die.

I couldn't do it, though. I was too far into this now to take the easy way out and run. I wanted to inflict as much pain and torment as I possibly fucking could. I wanted him to watch me slide the knife along her throat. I wanted her to know just how close he'd come to saving her. I wanted that hope to reach a level where they both believed they could beat me and then I wanted to fucking end them. So yeah, I could have killed her, but where was the satisfaction in that? Holding steady, I waited for them to find us.

Thirty-One
Owen

"Keep moving, Justice," I encouraged as he kept on the scent. He was getting up there in years, but the old dog still knew a thing or two about tracking someone. He'd barely looked up as he followed her path through the woods. There was a sinking feeling in the pit of my stomach that whoever was behind all this was hot on her heels too. Holding both dogs' leashes in one hand, I reached behind me for my gun. If they didn't already have her, they could be anywhere waiting to pounce.

Part of me knew I should have waited for back-up, that going at this alone was stupid and reckless and could very well end with me in a pine box covered in a flag, but it was a risk I had to take. If I had waited for back-up to arrive or sat around until the fire crew had shown up to put the flames out, there was no telling what irreversible damage could have been done in that lost time. I was already looking at possibly losing my home to the fire, I would have lost the dogs if I'd waited, and I sure as fuck would have lost Oakley.

Pressing on, right on Justice's heels, I almost tripped over him when he stopped. He looked back at me before looking ahead of him again. Roscoe started to pull on his lead, a low growl sounding deep in his throat. Bingo. The only issue was that I didn't know who they'd found. Roscoe's warning growl told me it wasn't someone so friendly, but Justice's pointed stare into the darkness and his stiff frame told me that his trail had led here, which meant Oakley was nearby.

"Good boys," I told them both quietly, bending down enough to scratch them both behind the ears, my gaze still trained on the spot that Justice was staring at. He saw something I didn't. Hunched down into the lower brush of the wooded floor, I scanned the area. I had to hold steady here. I had to let my training take the lead on this and not my emotions. Though, to be fair, flying by the seat of my pants had gotten me this far. Maybe it was due time to say fuck protocol in all of this.

I wasn't a cop right now. I had the training of one. I was an excellent marksman. I couldn't squelch emotion in this, though. I couldn't think like a cop and have that front dropped into place. A crash sounded just in front of me, twigs snapping, leaves rustling, and a loud grunt as if someone had taken a somewhat hard hit. Pushing up again, both boys pulled at the leashes in my hand, poised and ready to attack at a second's notice.

Before I could let them go, not knowing if it was Oakley, her assailant, or something lurking in the woods, I heard the distinct sound of soft footsteps running towards me. Pulling my gun from its spot, I clicked off the safety, watching for whoever was coming my way to emerge. Justice started to wag his tail, though, just before I saw her. She was turned back and looking over her shoulder. She didn't see me until she crashed right into me, sending us both tumbling to the ground.

She looked back at me, her eyes wide and frantic. There was a cut on her neck that was bleeding and a gash down her cheek, but I couldn't think of anything else other than the fact that she was alive. She was scared, yes, but she was still fighting. She pushed off of me and scrambled to her feet again, "Oakley," I started as I followed her lead.

She shook her head, her short hair waving around her face at the movement. "No, we have to go," she all but begged me. "She won't stop, and if she sees you, she'll kill you too." She reached for my hand to pull me with her, but the boys both lunged forward, yanking me away from her. Roscoe's low growl had turned into a full-on deadly bark with Justice backing him up. "Please Owen," she cried. My gaze had transfixed back on the spot the dogs were barking at as she stepped out of the shadows and into the moonlight that was shining down through the trees.

"Well, if this isn't the sweetest treat," she sneered. "Two for the price of one." I could barely hear her over the dogs, and I knew if I let go of the leashes, they'd tear her limb from limb. The most disturbing fact of all, though, was that when faced with two large dogs like mine, she wasn't even batting an eyelash at them. That's when I saw the glint of the knife she was holding in her hand. I could only guess that's what was responsible for the cuts Oakley had.

"Leave him alone, Ash," Oakley warned from behind me, her hand reaching for mine that held the gun. Right. Gun. I had one of those. Something had been knocked out of sorts when Oakley crashed into me. I had gotten so caught up in the fact that she was still alive and, for the most part, still safe that I had forgotten all the training I had gone through over the years. I stared her down, the one responsible for everything Oakley had gone through, everything slowly started to click back into place in my head. Raising my arm with the gun, I didn't hesitate in aiming for a kill shot. "Don't come any closer, or I will shoot," I warned. If I could go about this the right way, I was still going to, but it was only just now dawning on me that I was in the woods with nothing but my gun. I didn't have handcuffs with me. I was sure Oakley and I could get creative in a pinch, but it would undoubtedly make apprehending her that much more difficult.

Instead of backing down, though, she smiled at me. The kind of smile that sent chills down my spine. She didn't care that she was staring down the barrel of my gun. She didn't care that one wrong move on her part, one flinch of my trigger finger, and she would be done for. She was completely deranged, but that had to be the case, to commit the atrocities she'd committed. "It's sweet really, how you think you can still save her," she mocked. "I will never stop coming for her. Not until I've severed her pretty little head."

My trigger finger twitched at that. God, it was so fucking tempting just to put a bullet in her brain and deal with the consequences of it later. I could spin some story about it being self-defense. It wasn't like Oakley was going to go off about it.

I watched her every move; my other arm pulled tight as Justice and Roscoe fought my hold. If it weren't for the fact that she could hurt them in the process, I would let them go. I knew she couldn't take both of them on at the same time, and they would tear her limb from limb if it meant keeping Oakley and me safe. They had taken to her almost as quickly as I had. "Put the knife down," I ordered, my aim never wavering in the slightest.

"Or what?" she smirked, "You'll shoot?"

I could feel the way Oakley held tight to the back of my shirt. She was ducked down behind me; she was counting on me to protect her, but I couldn't do that with one hand. "Oak…" I started softly, her grip tightening slightly in response. She was listening. "I want you to reach around me and take the leashes. They're fighting, but they'll listen to you. I want you to take them and go. Justice will lead you back."

"Owen, no," she finally answered. "I'm not leaving you here with her!"

I sighed, I didn't want to be left with her either, but the odds were stacked in my favor here. I was the one with the gun, after all. She'd have to get close enough to hurt me with the knife, and if she even dared to move an inch, I would end her. "Do it, please," I ordered firmly. I didn't like telling her what to do, but it was either that or risk something happening to either her or the boys. I wouldn't be able to live with that. "I can't do anything while I'm holding onto them like this. If I let go, they'll attack, and I have a funny feeling she has nothing against using that knife on them."

She heard me. I first heard her chuckle, "I resent that," she feigned offense at my words, "What do you think I am, a monster?"

I did my best to ignore her though, "Please Oakley," I added, "You need to take them and go. Jacey was just out past the house." Fuck, I hoped they'd gotten the fire out by now. "But be careful. There was a wildfire, one I'm starting to think wasn't an accident." I met Ash's gaze at that.

"Bravo! They should make you a detective with skills like that," she ridiculed.

I wasn't sure that Oakley was going to leave. She seemed hesitant to listen, but then she reached around me and took the leashes from me, allowing me to bring my free hand up to help steady the gun.

Thirty-Two
Oakley

He wanted me to leave. He wanted me to take the dogs and just leave him behind with a psychopath. He had to understand that there was no way I was doing that. I couldn't just walk away from him knowing what she had done to my parents, to Abraham and Elisa. She would take no issue with taking him from me, too. I knew he was trying to protect me, but without him, I truly had nothing in this world. I had barely survived losing my parents. There was no way I was going to survive losing him too. "Owen, I..." I started. I didn't know how to make him understand that it wouldn't matter if he saved me if I lost him in the process.

"Oak, please," he whispered. I saw the way the muscles in his back tightened at that. His finger slipped over the trigger easily. He was the one with a gun. He was a trained police officer. I had to trust him that he would come out of this okay. I had to believe that maybe he just didn't want me to see him do what we both knew he needed to. "I need you to go find Jacey," he told me. I wanted nothing more than to just wrap my arms around him and refuse to let go. "I can't do this alone. I need help. You can go get me help." I knew what he was trying to do, but how could I tell him no? How could I force him to handle this on his own?

Leaning in, I pressed a gentle kiss between his shoulder blades. There was a sinking feeling in the pit of my stomach that I would never see this man again if I walked away. I needed him to know everything. I couldn't walk away from him without him hearing those words from me. I felt the tears brimming as I rested my forehead against him. "I love you," I whispered softly. Before he had a chance to say anything, I gave the leashes in my hand one sharp tug, and both dogs heeded my silent command. They both retreated to my side as I stepped back away from him. I couldn't see his face, but I knew this was killing him just as much as it was me.

Turning away from him, I urged the dogs back in the direction he had come from. I still didn't know where I was, but he had said Justice would be able to lead me back home. If I got back to the house, I could call for help. Jacey and whoever else the Gratin Police Department had at their disposal could come out here and find Owen before it was too late. He could hold Ash off. I had to believe in him because if I let myself think otherwise, I wasn't going to make it back to him. "Justice," I said, my voice a bit strangled. "Get us home," I pleaded. He seemed to understand what I was asking and started through the woods. With each step, I was reminded of the pain and damage Ash had already inflicted. If she took Owen, too...

No.

I had to stop thinking like that. I would get back to the house, I would get to Jacey, and Owen would be fine. I was so caught up in my thoughts, though, that I didn't see the tree root sticking out of the ground. My foot hooked on in, and I pitched forward towards the ground. I dropped the dogs' leashes in the process and tumbled down an embankment. Landing in a small stream with a splash, I tried to regain my bearings. Both dogs were looking down at me from the top of the hill. I sized up the hill I had just tumbled down. After everything with Ash, it was nothing in comparison. I was already so banged up and bruised. What was one more?

I had to stay focused, though. I had to get out of this mess and keep moving. Reaching for another tree root, I tried to pull myself back up the hill. It was steep enough that I was just going to be able to walk back up it. I was getting somewhere when it gave out, and I crashed back into the stream. Slamming my hands down into the water, it took everything I had to not completely lose it right then and there. I just wanted to give up. I hadn't been enough to save my parents. Elisa was dead, and it was all my fault, and now I might lose Owen, too. All of these people who had taken me in and cared for me were all better off without me. Part of me wanted to go back and beg Ash to just do it, leave him alone, and just end it. I knew there was no way he would let that happen, though.

I could do this. I fought off Ash in the house and then again in the woods. I could get up this damn hill! Standing up again, I tried to find something to grab onto that would get me out of my current predicament when a hand reached down. Looking up, I felt the tears swelling again when I met that same blue gaze I loved so much on Owen. Reaching out, I took Austen's hand and let him pull me up the embankment. As soon as I was on my feet in front of him, he wrapped a jacket around my shoulders. I looked behind him to see Ethan holding onto both dogs. "Where is he?" he asked.

I looked around me, "I don't remember which direction we came from, he told me to take the dogs and get help, but I-" I tried to figure out where I was.

Austen nodded, "Jacey, you get her out of here, I'll go and find Owen," he directed.

I shook my head, "No, let me go with you," I begged. "It's me she wants, he was holding her off enough that I could get away, but I can't leave him there, Austen!"

He looked at me, "He'd want you out of the way, where you're safe," he directed. The next thing I knew, Jacey had his arm around me, pulling me closer against him. I knew what Owen wanted, but when it came down to it, he was in this mess because of me, so fuck what he wanted. I wasn't going to leave him to handle this on his own. We were a team. He broke that promise when he asked me to leave. We were supposed to be in this together. I leaned into Jacey, almost like I had given up. I hugged him just enough but sighed when my hand bumped against his gun. Without really thinking through what I was doing, I pulled it from his hip and stepped away from both of them.

"The fuck do you think you're doing?" Ethan asked me.

I shook my head, "I'm not going home without him. I know Owen, he wants to do this the right way. He wants back up so that the three of you can take her down and send her to jail," I huffed. "But what proof do we have that she had anything to do with my parents murder, or Elisa's?" I looked between them, "And I'm still fucking alive so what you have her on assault, kidnapping, breaking and entering... that's not going to fucking hold her. I've watched enough cops shows to know." I turned my gaze on Ethan, "He won't kill her. He's too good. But that bitch has destroyed my life and she won't stop until I'm dead too. It's the only way."

Stepping back away from them, I guessed at which direction I had to go. Maybe I was going the completely wrong way, but I had to try. I had to do something. If I could take her down and just end this, then that was what I was going to do. Because any hope Owen and I had of a future together hinged on Ash no longer being an issue in our lives. The rest we could figure out. I could hear Ethan behind me, yelling my name. Maybe he was following me, maybe he wasn't. If I had been smart, I would have brought Justice with me. He could have led me straight back to Owen. I just had to figure this out on my own.

Finding that fight in me again, I started running. I wasn't the girl who just gave up and let someone else save the day anymore. This was my problem to figure out. Owen and I were in this together. I never should have left him, but he also never should have asked me to leave. After a moment, I stopped running, looking around. I wasn't entirely sure of where I was. There was a chance I was headed in the completely wrong direction. I just needed something, a gut feeling, anything to point me back to him.

Thirty-Three
Ash

I was officially fucking over it. This had gone on long enough, and at first, it had been fun. Oh, I enjoyed making the bitch squirm like a worm on the end of my hook, but I was over the cat and mouse. It was about fucking time for the mouse to die. I didn't care anymore if it was quick. Just as long as she was six feet under.

I had been surprised with how easily she had listened to him. After the level of tenacity she'd shown so far, I figured she would stand by his side. She had listened, though, and now her stupid fucking cop was standing between me and my prize. It had crossed my mind as she was retreating that I could throw my knife and bury it hilt deep in the back of her skull. I would have risked missing, knowing damn well that he would have fired on me. It was too dark, though, and as good as I was, I'd never hit a moving target with that kind of accuracy. As much as I wouldn't want to admit it, his aim was likely better than mine.

This whole thing was wearing on my last fucking nerve. "You can't fucking save her," I sneered. I was so done with playing their games. "I will keep coming for her. No shadow will be safe. No corner of this ungodly hell left unturned. You can't protect her forever." Except that he seemed to be delusional enough to think he could. Clearly, I wasn't going to get out of killing him. More blood on my hands, great, that was just fucking great.

They had sucked all the fun out of it. It was almost like work now. I had wanted to make them suffer, yes, but I was the only one fucking suffering.

I'd had her in my grasp so many times already. I could have ended her pitiful existence over and over again, but no, I just had to fucking play games with her. She had to keep fighting like she actually stood a chance at beating me.

Hope. It was the hardest fucking thing to kill.

If she'd never made it to this trash heap of a town, I would have won. All these people here, this dipshit cop, they'd all given her hope that she could have a normal life. She didn't fucking deserve it. Not after everything she'd done, and I was going to make her pay, one way or another. First off, though, I had to deal with the cop. Tightening my grip on my knife, I waited. He was going to break his eye contact with me sooner or later. He was going to check to make sure she'd really left. Because she was more important to him than his own wellbeing. They were all like that. It was revolting.

Her father had done everything in his power to save his wife. Abraham had begged me not to kill Elisa. Now, like a lamb to the slaughter, her cop was laying down his own life to save hers. Men were pitiful, putrid creatures. They liked to accuse women of being the emotional ones, but really it was them that were so weak-willed and let their hearts lead the way. They were all so quick to claim they would die for someone. Women were smarter than that. They at least had some sense of self-preservation.

"Well, well, look who couldn't leave her man to die," I shook my head, staring over his shoulder. It was time to move this along. As predicted, he turned, pulling his gaze from me for a fraction of a second, but it was all I needed. With a scream fueled by every ounce of rage I harbored, I ran at him. He turned back too little too late. I slammed into him, knocking him to the ground. I still had my knife, but I wanted the gun. I wanted to blow that pretty boy face of his clean off. I wanted to make sure he didn't have it anymore.

Reaching for it, I wrapped my hand around the barrel, swinging with the hand that still held the knife. I managed to catch him just below his hairline as he turned away from me. Keeping the gun pointed away from me, he struggled to get it back. He was at a disadvantage. I was on top, I had the leverage, and if he so much as weakened his hold on the gun, let alone let go with even one hand to fight back, I would win. He had strength on me, but I was only using one hand.

Finally dropping the knife, I reached for his throat, squeezing the air from him. He gasped for air, his hands dropping the gun to claw at my arm instead, fighting to break free from my hold. I was content to just choke the life from him. To watch him struggle to breathe. He deserved a slow, painful death.

"Just think," I said softly, leaning down over him, holding his gaze. "After I kill you, there will be no one to stand between her and me, and I'm going to make her suffer when I find her again. I'm going to make sure she knows that you died because of her. That everyone died because she existed, and that pesky hope you fuckers filled her with, I'm going to squash it like the rotten little bug it is." He managed to pry my hand away from his neck with unexpected strength, coughing as he struggled to take in air again. Fine. If he wanted to play it that way, I would.

Reaching for the dropped gun before he could, I pushed to my feet and aimed it down at him. I was done with the games. Clearly, they weren't just going to give up. Which, admittedly, was fucking annoying. So this was how it had to be. Without a second thought, my finger slipped to the trigger, and I pulled. One down, one to go.

A gunshot rang out through the darkness, and I froze in my steps. No, no, no, no, no, no. Owen wouldn't have used his gun unless he absolutely had to. My grip tightened on the gun in my hand. Owen wasn't the type to shoot someone, he wasn't a killer. Which meant… I felt the tears start stinging my eyes again, but this time there was no fighting them. I dropped to my knees right there in the brush.

What if he?

I couldn't even think it, the thought that maybe she'd gotten the best of him the same way she'd managed with my parents and Elisa… I couldn't keep losing people like this. If she had gotten the best of him, then what hope did I have? She would keep coming after me until she won. What use was running anymore? Owen had been right, I couldn't live a life like that, always on the run and looking over my shoulder.

The tears streaked hot down my face, with or without Owen by my side, I had to end this. I had to push aside every fear I had and I needed to keep moving forward. If he… No. I couldn't think like that, not until I knew for sure. If he was, though, I owed it to him to keep fighting. It was what he would want me to do. He wouldn't want me to just give up.

Pushing up onto my feet again, they screamed in protest. Running through the woods barefoot had done a number on me. But I didn't have any other choice. I looked around me, trying to figure out which direction that shot had come from. My grip tightened on the handle of Ethan's gun, there was nothing I could do other than just pick a direction and hope like hell that I could find them again.

Trudging through the underbrush, I paused when I heard a laugh. I was getting closer. My heart was racing in my chest, I wanted to get to Owen because what if he was still okay? That laugh told me that Ash was still out there. "Come on out, Lizzie," she called out in that taunting tone again. "I know you're still around." I cringed, trying to not think about Owen bleeding out on the ground. If she was okay enough to taunt me, then Owen really was... I shook my head, I just needed to keep moving. For once it was okay to just stop thinking.

Coming up on them a few minutes later, I stifled a cry when I realized Ash was still standing over a lifeless form. Tossing the gun to the side, she started to dig around for something. I caught the glint of her knife's blade as she tucked it away safely in the top of her boot. She had no idea I was there. If I could just get close enough to Owen, close enough to the gun without her noticing me, I could end this.

Slipping around the tree, I waited for her to turn her back, looking away from me as she seemed to assess which direction she needed to go. Slipping from one tree to the next, hiding behind each one as best I could, I tried not to make a sound as I crouched down low to the grassy floor. She'd dropped the gun next to Owen. He really needed to move. I needed to know that he was alive. I needed something to keep me moving forward.

If he was still alive, I would fight, fight for him, and fight for myself, for everyone she'd already hurt or killed. I would fight until there was nothing left in me to continue. I would pull together what little strength I had left and I would go another round with her, because I didn't trust I would be able to hit her from here. If Owen was still breathing I wasn't about to chance it that she might take another shot at him.

If he was already dead, though, I would take that shot and just pray that I hit her in a spot that would stop her. If I missed that's when I would turn and run again because he would have died to save me. I wasn't about to let everything he sacrificed for me be in vain. At that point, the only thing I could do was find a way to keep going for him. God, please, I needed him to be alive. I needed to believe we still had a chance. Never in my wildest dreams would I have thought I'd meet someone like him.

Creeping closer to where he lay, I watched him closely for the steady rise and fall of his chest. A twitch of his fingers. A flutter of his eyelids. Anything at all to signify that he was still with me. Focusing in, I saw it, the proof I needed. He took a breath; I was sure of it. It was shallow and I could tell he needed help. I was the only back up he had for the moment, I hoped that was enough. I just had to keep reminding myself of the simple fact that he was still alive; we could still win this.

I didn't have my phone on me. I hadn't had the chance to grab it before I sprinted from the house with Ash right behind me. There was no way to call Ethan for help. Not unless I was lucky enough that Owen had his phone on him. I just had to get to him without calling attention to myself. If I could get to a phone, I could call Ethan or share our location with him, anything so he and Austen would know where to find us.

I was going to do everything in my power to help him, but it wasn't lost on me that Ash was barely breaking a sweat with all of this. I was up against someone with a lot more strength than me. I tried to creep closer to him, but I was behind the last tree big enough to hide me from her view, and I was still a good three or four feet from him. I would have to take the chance that she'd notice me as she started to walk away, having opted to follow me, I could only assume.

Stepping forward and out from the shelter of my tree, I heard a twig snap beneath my foot. Having heard it too, Ash whipped back around and caught my gaze. As she moved around Owen and towards me again, something sinister touched her expression. "Couldn't just let him die, could you?" she smirked, her voice cold. I tripped back a step away from her. I was so tired; I wasn't sure I had it in me to go another round with her.

My grip tightened on the gun in my hand, I just had to make sure she didn't make a move for the one still laying by Owen. "That's fine by me…" she moved to step closer to me. I raised the gun, my hands shaking. I wasn't sure I had it in me to kill someone either. She seemed to falter slightly at the sight of the weapon in my hand. "Well, this is interesting," she noted, but it hadn't escaped my notice that she'd stopped moving towards me. Taking a careful step forward, I stepped over Owen and kicked the gun by his side closer to him. "Guess we're not so different after all," she mused.

I shook my head at that, "I'm nothing like you!" I yelled. "I..." I couldn't do this anymore. If we let her live, she would never stop. She would make every waking moment of my life a living hell. I just had to pull the trigger.

She smiled again, seeing me waver. "You're right," she agreed. "I would have already taken the shot. You could bleed out right there next to your boyfriend. You don't have what it takes to put me down." Her smile slipped into a sneer and she came towards me. Closing my eyes, I braced for impact and squeezed the trigger.

I opened my eyes again in time to see a hint of unadulterated glee in her gaze, but it gave way to shock when another gunshot rang out through the woods, the sound ricocheting off of every nearby tree. I screamed as she stumbled forward a step before collapsing next to me. What the...? I didn't do that. I looked down at the gun in my hand and dropped it in disgust. I had only fired it once. I didn't... I looked around me, trying to figure out if maybe the others had caught up, but there was no one there. Turning around, that's when I saw him. Owen was sitting upright, breathing heavily but very much alive, with the gun still in his hand. Running at him, I stopped short when I saw the blood soaking through his shirt around his shoulder. Dropping to the ground next to him, I choked on a sob. He sighed and with his good arm, pulled me in against him.

THIRTY-FIVE
OWEN

She was safe. It didn't matter what else happened now. That thought was the only thing going through my mind. She was safe now. I didn't want to let go of her, but she gently pushed back from me and met my gaze. "Owen…" she started softly as she assessed my injury. "You're going to be okay," she promised before moving to pull her shirt over her head. She balled it up and pressed it against my shoulder, apologizing at my almost instant grimace. "We have to stop the bleeding," she told me. "Lay back down."

I shook my head at that. I could already tell the shot had gone completely through. The idea of laying back down in the brush made me cringe. Her shirt was already soaking through with blood, and I could see the worry in her gaze as she looked me over. "My phone," I said, looking at her. "It's in my back pocket. If I lean towards you, can you grab it?" I asked, and she nodded. I knew it was going to hurt to move at all. Just sitting up to take down Ash had taken what little energy I had in me.

With her assistance, I leaned toward her, and she reached behind me to slide my phone from my pocket. She moved to unlock it and smiled slightly, "Point for my little flip phone," she teased slightly before turning my phone so I could see the big crack running down the screen.

I sighed. Guess a new house and a new phone were in my future. "Code is 0926," I told her, and she typed it in. Without me telling her to, she found a number and pressed call. Bringing it to her ear, she watched me closely.

"Austen," she started, "It's Oakley. I'm going to share our location with you. Owen is hurt and we need help." Austen? Why had she chosen to call my brother and not Jacey? He would have been the logical one. Austen was still in town. She must have seen my confusion. "When I left you here, Austen was with Ethan. They have the dogs." I wanted to nod at her explanation, but there was something moving behind her.

"Oak..." I warned softly. Fear suddenly washed over her gaze at my change in tone. There was a cough behind her, "Take my gun," I instructed. She did as I told her and looked back over her shoulder just as Ash pushed up to her knees. Seeing us still there, she smiled before diving for the gun Oakley had shown up with, and despite the pain that shot through my chest and shoulder at the sudden movement. I raised Oakley's arm with the gun. "Squeeze the trigger," I told her.

I didn't want Ash's blood on her hands, but if Ash got that gun, even in her state, I wasn't in a position to protect Oakley. Following my command, Oakley fired the gun. With my support, the shot landed right where it needed to. Ash crumpled back to the ground, and I was pretty damn sure she wasn't going to be getting up again. "Good job," I whispered. She let out a shaky sigh before turning back into me. She rested her head against my good shoulder for a moment before she turned her attention back to my makeshift bandage.

"Do you think you can get up and walk?" she asked me. "I don't know what else I can do for you..." She shook her head, and tears instantly formed in those green eyes. "We have to get you help." I wasn't about to tell her everything would be okay because I knew I wasn't in good shape, but I had to try for her.

"If you help me up..." Before I could finish that sentence, though, Mason came walking through the trees.

"You can sit your ass back down is what you can do," he directed. "Austen sent the coordinates to me," he explained. "We've got a chopper waiting to get you out of here." Coming over, he kneeled down next to me. "Seriously, Owen?" he asked as he pulled away Oakley's bloodied shirt. "Mom is going to be thrilled you're alive, but then she's going to kill you herself," he told me. Pulling out his radio, he called everything through, "28 year old, caucasian male, single GSW to the chest," he sighed, looking at me. "You're lucky to be alive."

He started work on getting me bandaged up enough for transport when I heard Justice barking. It didn't take long before Jacey and Austen came through into the clearing as well. "Shit Hale, you look like hell," Jacey said to me. Ignoring him, I looked at Austen and nodded towards Oakley, standing behind Mason, hugging herself. He walked over to her before shrugging out of his flannel shirt and draping it over her shoulders. He wrapped one arm around her, and she melted in against his side. I couldn't help but feel a little glad that she was finally letting others care for her.

Jacey looked between us before walking over to where Ash was lying in the dirt, "I take it this is who's been after you?" he asked, glancing more toward Oakley.

She nodded at that, though she was desperately trying to avoid looking in Ash's direction. I couldn't blame her. The second shot had been a direct hit. There was blood everywhere. I didn't want her to focus too much on the fact that she'd been the one to pull the trigger. She let out a shaky sigh before focusing her gaze on Jacey. "Ashland Morgan. She was the daughter of my father's valet, Abraham. Her parents sent her to a facility in Chicago when we were just young teenagers. She needed help. I guess she didn't get it," she explained. A sadness touched her gaze, then, "She's the one responsible for my parents' murders. She also murdered her own mother, Elisa, and she said something about Abraham too…."

Jacey held up his phone to her, "Older guy? This him?"

Oakley closed her eyes at whatever picture Jacey was showing her, "Is he?" she asked.

"He's alive; he's at the hospital. Which is where your boy over there is headed too as soon as we get him out of here," he answered.

Mason shot me a look at that, "We won't be getting him out of here if he doesn't stop moving," he grumbled.

I cringed as he continued to try and bandage the area. Every time he poked at me, I pulled away. "Well, whatever you're doing fucking hurts," I threw back at him.

"Owen," Oakley said softly as she pulled away from Austen and came back over to kneel next to me. She reached out and took my good hand, "Let Mason do what he needs to do," she pleaded with me. "I can't lose you to your own stubbornness." How was I supposed to argue with that? I had made her go get her hand looked at the other night. I was just so worn down I just wanted to lie down and sleep. Squeezing her hand in mine, I nodded.

"Too bad Wyatt isn't in town too, he might have been able to help save the house," Jacey noted. "Austen led the way to find you, Mason is here patching your ass up..."

Oakley glanced back at Jacey before turning back to me. "What does he mean by save the house?" she asked me. My guess was she didn't know the full extent of what Ash had done. I had mentioned the fire when I'd first caught up to them, but even I hadn't been aware of the extent of the damage done.

"The fire Ash set," I started, "It was spreading towards my house when I ran after you," I explained.

Jacey nodded, "Dude literally ran through fire for you," he told her. "I think that means you need to marry him," he joked.

I shook my head at that, "So the house is gone?" I asked, looking at the three of them.

Austen tipped his chin in a slight nod, "by the time fire got everything under control, it had already gotten the house," he told me. That stung. I had been hoping that there would be somewhere safe Oakley and I could return to after all of this was over. It was just a house, though, I could rebuild. We could rebuild. What mattered most was that both of us and both of the dogs were safe. We would be okay in time.

Mason finished up what he was doing and glanced at me, "We're going to get a backboard out here for you, I don't want you walking with the blood loss you've had." He turned to Oakley, "I want you checked too, okay?" He moved her hair away from the cut on her neck, "This will need to be cleaned up and stitched. If done right, hopefully you won't have too bad of a scar." He reached for the radio again. "We'll get you guys out of here and Jacey can deal with the rest of it."

Jacey sighed at that, "Thanks Mase."

It had taken time and teamwork to get Owen out of the woods. They had to not only worry about his injuries and mine but also about how to get around the hot spots that the fire teams were still working on putting out. I knew that Owen wouldn't want me thinking any of this was my fault, but I couldn't help it. If I hadn't come to this tiny mountain town, none of this would have ever happened. I had thought if I had found some small, no name town, that whoever was after me would never find me. They would have thought to look in places like New York or Miami. I couldn't help but wonder if maybe everyone would have been better off if I had.

The people of this town didn't deserve the hell I'd put them through. I should have left when I'd had the chance, as soon as the news broke of where I was. Maybe that would have meant living my life on the run, but that had to be better than sitting here watching the man I had come to love suffer the pain I'd put him through. He could be living his life worry free right now. Because of me, though, he was hooked up to several machines. The doctors had said he would be okay. I had no reason not to believe them, but there was part of me that refused to believe it until he woke up and told me himself.

As soon as we'd gotten to the hospital, they'd rushed him right into surgery. Not only did they have to repair the general damage the bullet had done, but they found out pretty quickly that his collarbone was shattered, too. It really made me wonder how he'd managed to push through the way he had. I knew he loved me, but the amount of pain he had to be in through all of that. There was no way I was ever going to be able to repay him for what he'd done for me. Jacey was right. The only thing I could do was marry him. That's what happened at the end of these types of stories, right? The white knight rides in, saves the princess, and they ride off together in some form of happily ever after.

The only thing was, this wasn't some fairy tale. This was real life, and real life dictated that there was still a chance of infection that could take him from me. The doctors had said the first twenty-four hours would be the most touch and go. It was when an infection might show itself. I sighed and leaned back in the chair I had been sitting in since they'd brought him back to his room. I couldn't even begin to guess how long it had been. How many hours had ticked by? I wanted nothing more than to curl up next to him and sleep all of this away. I wasn't going to do that, though. I couldn't sleep yet, not until I knew he would be okay.

There was a soft knock at the door. Looking up, I sighed as Austen walked in. "How's he doing?" he asked.

I shrugged, "No change, still asleep. I'm guessing that's a good thing. The doctors and nurses don't seem too concerned," I answered.

He looked at me, "You should get some sleep too," he suggested. "You need to rest too."

I shook my head, "I can't sleep," I told him. "Not yet. Not until I know he's going to be okay."

Walking over to me, he knelt down in front of me, "He's going to be fine," he promised. "The doctors all say he's going to make a full recovery. They just go over every possible outcome so that we know the risks. That doesn't mean that's what's going to happen."

Looking back at Owen, I squeezed his hand. I hated seeing him like this. He'd been this strong, solid force I could lean on through everything. He never wavered. To see him in a hospital bed; it broke me. That was a big part of why I hadn't gone to see Abraham yet, either. How was I supposed to face him? I let out a sigh as I turned back to Austen. "I know," I answered. "But that doesn't change the fact that I can't sleep." I didn't know how to explain it to him. I couldn't find the right words to explain to him that I was terrified to close my eyes. "Right from the night I met him, Owen has made me feel... safe. I didn't understand it at first, and I did everything in my power to push him away. Because my problems were mine to deal with, and I knew getting involved with a cop would only make him want to help me more." Bringing my foot up, I rested it on the seat of the chair and wrapped my arm around it. I just needed something to hold onto. "But it was useless to try and keep him at arm's length. I don't know if you know this or not, but your little brother is seriously fucking stubborn," I half teased.

He laughed at that, "Yeah, I've learned that a time or two," he agreed.

I smiled slightly, "I never meant to fall for him. But now he's the one place I feel safe. The only place I feel safe. I can't sleep until I know he's okay because I can't face the nightmares alone. Every time I close my eyes I feel her there behind me, her knife pressing against my neck. I immediately go right back to that moment and all that fear and worry I felt." I shook my head.

Austen reached out and put his hand on my arm. "You guys have been through hell," he agreed. "And that's going to have its consequences. But you'll get through it together. He's not the only one you have now. You're with my little brother, which means you've got the rest of the Hale family standing behind you too. And Jacey. He's that annoying little tag along you just can't shake," he joked. "So, while I know I'm not my brother. I can stay here so you can get some sleep too. We can ask the nurses to bring in a cot, and I'll watch out for both of you. When he wakes up, he's going to need you too. As you mentioned, he's stubborn. He's not going to like that he doesn't have use of his left arm and he's going to try to do everything himself. You're going to have to be stern with him." He squeezed my arm. "But that means you need to get some sleep too. So you have the strength and patience it'll take to take him on."

I could understand what he was saying, but at the same time, I knew sleep wouldn't come easy. I'd already had issues sleeping before everything. How was I supposed to sleep now? I nodded, though, "If you can get the nurses to bring a bed in, I'll try," I promised. It was the most I could offer him. I knew he was just looking out for me the way Owen would want him to, but I wasn't sure he understood the extent of my fears.

Austen nodded, "I'll go talk to them and see what we can do," he told me. Standing back up, he watched me for a moment. "Do you want me to let the others in?" he asked. When I looked up at him, confusion written across my face, he tipped his head towards the door. "Everyone has been here just as long," he explained. "Fiona and Liv even closed down the diner. Pretty sure that's never happened before."

I glanced back to Owen, still sound asleep. "Maybe after he wakes up," I suggested. He accepted that answer and turned for the door. When had that happened? When had I become the point of contact for Owen? Were we so enmeshed together that people were just turning to me now? I wasn't sure how I felt about that. I still had to figure out where I stood with Richfield Winery. Did I go back and take over? Did I just let it all go and start fresh here with Owen? I wanted to be able to talk to him about this.

I didn't like not knowing what was coming next, but ever since losing my parents, everything about my life had been unsure. Now, I might be able to solidify things a little. I needed something to be sure of. Sitting up, I leaned forward onto Owen's bed. I needed to be sure of him. I wasn't sure I could do this whole life thing without him by my side. I didn't know what that meant for us. I knew most people would tell me to just get through this next step and then figure out the rest, but I needed something I could hold onto.

Resting my head down against his hand, I sighed. I knew he was going to wake up. The doctors had said as much several times. They said he was sleeping as much as he was because he needed to recover. If he needed the sleep, then I wanted him to get it, which was a big reason I had asked Austen to keep everyone out. If people were in and out of the room, there was no way either one of us was getting the sleep we needed.

I was tired. There was no denying that. After the adrenaline had worn off, it had hit me like a ton of bricks. I couldn't quiet my thoughts, though. They kept going, a hundred miles a minute. What was I going to do about the manor? What was I going to do about Owen? Where did we stand after everything? What about his house? I was the reason it had been burned to the ground. I couldn't shake the million and one questions that just seemed to pound through my head. How was I supposed to sleep?

It wasn't more than twenty minutes later that the door pushed open again. Turning my head slightly, I saw it was just Austen again. "They're bringing in a second bed," he told me. "They said they can put down the railings on both and push them together so you can curl up with him and maybe get some rest."

"But..." I started, sitting upright. I didn't want to hurt Owen.

He held up a hand to stop me, "If you stay on his right side, he'll be okay. They've got him on some pretty good pain meds, too. You said you feel safe with him, so I found a way that you can stay right here with him and still get the rest you need." Before I could argue with him further, a nurse pushed the door open behind him. They brought in another bed, and after moving everything, including me, out of the way, they lined it up with his.

"I know we've already discharged you, but if you're going to be on our floor, we're going to take care of you," the nurse told me as she handed me an extra blanket. "Get some rest."

I watched as they left, and Austen smiled slightly. "You can't argue with nurses' orders," he teased. "I'll hang around until you fall asleep, and then I'll just be a text away if you need me," he explained.

I shook my head at that. "My phone was in the house," I started. "And Owen fell on his phone and broke the screen." I didn't have a way of texting him.

He nodded, "I figured you'd say that," he smiled before holding out a box to me. "Now that no one is after you, I figured we could bring you back into the 21st century. Same number as your old phone, I already programmed Ethan, Fiona, Liv, Owen and the rest of the Hale family into it for you."

Standing up, I walked over to him. I took the offered box before wrapping him in a tight hug. "Thank you," I said softly.

He hugged me back but then nodded to the bed, "Go get some sleep. I'll be right here if either of you need anything." He moved to sit in the chair I had been in before as I crawled onto the bed with Owen. Lying down only made it that much more apparent how exhausted I was. I just hoped sleep would come easy.

Thirty-Seven
Owen

There was this intense pressure. It felt like someone had laid out weights along my body, holding me down. Everything was hazy at best; I didn't know where I was or really what had happened. The last thing I could clearly remember was sending Oakley away in the woods, telling her that it was okay to run. Then, a shot was fired, and everything went black. I tried to focus on the chaos that was swirling around in my head. I needed to zero in on something.

Not having opened my eyes yet, I started with what I could feel. There was a dull ache in my left shoulder that I knew if I dared to move it, it would likely wake an angry beast within, and it would hurt like hell. The rest of my body felt stiff, like it would hurt to move, but nothing I couldn't handle. It was that post-workout feeling, that burn of overworked muscles. A little movement would sort all of that out.

Most importantly, though, something was holding fast to my right hand. Something I didn't dare pull away from. I knew who it was without looking. I squeezed her hand gently before moving on.

Next, I tried to focus on the sounds around me. There was a steady beep coming from my left. It was following in time with my heartbeat. There were the soft murmurs of people talking quietly. Lastly, I could smell nothing but that sterile hospital smell. Maybe Ash was right. With deduction skills like that, I should be a detective.

I couldn't remember much of how I ended up here, but that was okay because if I were here with Oakley holding tight to my hand, that meant one thing: somehow, we'd won. I felt the gentle pulls of sleep again. My body felt as if it had been run over multiple times. I was beyond exhausted. If I knew my girl, though, she was worried sick about me. As much as I wanted to sleep, I had to give her something to show her that I was okay, that we would be okay.

I tried to open my eyes slowly, but the room's bright lights caused me to cringe back. I was left suddenly taking note of just how much my head hurt, too. In response, I squeezed her hand in mine again, this time a little more firm. I could manage that much for her. It got her attention this time, and she moved to sit up; gently, she brushed back my hair from my forehead. "Don't tell me I went and did something stupid," I said softly. I was almost surprised at how hoarse I sounded and how much speaking made my throat hurt.

I finally forced my eyes open enough to look at her, though, trying not to let her see me cringe against the light. She looked beat up, too, but otherwise, no worse for the wear. We were both alive. That was what mattered above anything else. "Stupidity is usually Jacey's job."

Oakley laughed, but there were tears in her green eyes as she stared down at me. "You were shot. They rushed you right in for emergency surgery as soon as we got you here," she explained. "But it's over, Owen," she added, "We're safe." I knew we would have to sit down and review everything that had happened in the woods. We would have to figure it all out together, but I didn't even want to think about it for now. There was a lot that needed to be sorted through: the fire and whether or not it had gotten the house. What had actually happened, the dogs, and where they were. I was sure we had covered all of that already, but again, everything was fuzzy.

Squeezing her hand again, I couldn't take my eyes off of her. Bruises were staining her light skin, and there were stitches and bandages throughout. I just had to keep reminding myself of one fundamental fact: no matter the recovery we'd both have to go through physically and mentally. She was alive. We were both alive, and I would be there for her as long as she'd let me. I would help her through this.

Taking my hand back from her, I tried to push up on the bed, grimacing with pain when the movement jostled my shoulder. "Owen, stop trying to move," she scolded me. I just shook my head at her, though. Reaching for her, I pulled her in enough that I could kiss her. No amount of pain would ever stop me from kissing her, especially when I had honestly started to believe that I would never get the chance again. Her soft lips responded to mine as she leaned into it. My good hand tangled in her hair. I never wanted to let her go.

"Hey, hey, no making out," Jacey's voice called from the doorway, "Especially not when the parentals are in the building."

I pulled back at that and looked at him. "My parents are here?" I asked. "You called them?"

He held his hands up in surrender, "Don't look at me, dude. I'm not the one who made the call. That was Austen and Mason; you can blame them. They also called Wyatt, but he won't be able to make it here for a couple of days. He basically said as long as you're good and not dead, there's no rush." He laughed. Of course, Wyatt would have said that. It was the same thing my parents should have said. Hell, Mason and Austen should have never called them in the first place. Mom liked to worry about all of us, a little too much if you asked me. She meant well. She loved all of us, but it had been a bit of a relief when they'd decided to move to Florida.

I looked to Oakley, "My parents are here."

"I heard," she smiled at that, though. "I was going to have to meet them eventually," she added. "Given that you're all in love with me. And I don't have any parents to introduce you to, so we only have to go through this once."

Leaning in, I kissed her again, but of course, it was interrupted by none other than my mother. "Owen Jacob, you shouldn't be sitting up like that."

The full name usage caused Oakley to giggle against my lips before she pulled back. I sighed though at that; my mother knew too much. I had only just managed to convince Oakley to ignore everything coming out of Jacey's mouth. I doubted I would be able to convince her to ignore my mother. "Hi mom," I answered, returning to my former position on the bed. She walked over and handed me the remote to bring the head of the bed up.

"For when you want to move, but shouldn't," she noted. I laughed slightly, wincing at the pain it caused in my shoulder. "See?"

Glancing towards Oakley, I sighed, "Mom, this is Oakley Morgan…Elizabeth Richfield?" I looked at her. Now that everything was over, would she go back to her family name? And she was still the heiress to the Richfield family business. It had occurred to me before now that it was safe for her to go home, but the question had remained unanswered. Would she?

"Morgan," she answered my question. "Oakley Morgan."

I nodded. That was just something else we'd have to figure out. "And this is my mom, Chrissy Hale," I finished introducing them. "I assume dad is around here somewhere," I looked back to my mother, and she nodded.

"He's talking with your brothers. Getting a few of the details from them as to what happened. We figured it was better to ask them. You two have been through enough. They're also trying to figure out what to do about your place."

"My place?" I asked. Everything was starting to come back. I remembered asking about my house. The fire had reached it. "How bad is it?"

She exhaled slowly. "It's still standing, but it's pretty much inhabitable," she told me softly. "They think it can be fixed up. You should get some money from insurance…." Oakley's hand tightened around mine again, pulling my attention away from my mother and what she was saying. Yes, it sucked, but it was just a house. The main thing was that we were all okay. The boys weren't in the house; Oakley and I weren't in the house. Everyone was still alive.

"If the insurance doesn't cover the repairs," she started before shrugging. "Maybe I could help."

"Oak, you don't have to do that…." I argued, shaking my head.

She smiled, though, "I know I don't. But she was after me. She set that fire because of me. And I have my parents' money. I want to do something good with it."

I could see in the way she was watching me that she meant it. She believed putting that money into a new home for me was a good thing she wanted to do. "Fine. On one condition," I told her, "You move in with me when it's done," I countered. "And in the rebuild process, we make it ours. Not mine. I know living with three boys isn't the kind of life you're used to…."

Her smile only grew at that. "I wouldn't have it any other way," she answered. "Yes," she nodded.

I couldn't help it. I pulled her in to kiss her again. She was staying. She was willingly moving in with me. We could build a life together. And who knew, maybe somewhere down the line, we'd take that plunge together. "I love you."

I could feel her grin against my lips, "I love you too," she answered just as softly.

"Okay, okay, enough of that, you two," my mother scolded, but I could tell even she was smiling. All four of us had put careers above finding a family. Three of us hadn't ventured away from Gratin, really. It was the same women we had all grown up with, known our whole lives. There hadn't been many to pick from. Until Oakley came blowing into my life and turned it upside down. Everything had gotten so predictable before she'd come along. She'd brought some color back into my world. "It's nice to meet you," my mother added, directed at Oakley.

She hadn't pulled away from me. In fact, she made the move to scoot in closer on the bed with me and curl into my side.

"It's nice to meet you too, like I told Owen, with my own parents gone this is the only 'meet the parents' we have to go through. So despite his apprehensions, I'm happy to be meeting you."

My mom nodded again, "Austen filled us in on some of what was going on," she confessed. "I'm sorry about your parents."

"Thank you," she nodded.

Over the next few hours, people came and went. There was a lot of talking about what came next, about getting someone out to look at the damage done to my house for the insurance claim, all of it. Everyone around us had jumped right into recovery mode, looking to patch things up for us so that we could all just move on. When all was quiet in the room again, I hugged Oakley close against me. "So what now?" I asked her. "What'll become of the Richfield name?"

She shrugged slightly, not answering me for a long moment. I was okay with the silence as she figured it all out. It was something she needed to consider, though, something I could help her figure out. "I don't know how to run a business like that," she confessed. "My father had been grooming me to take over one day, but then everything happened and truthfully, I hadn't had any interest in taking all of it on. I wanted to party, to date, to have fun. But it's the last thing they left me. I don't know that I can just turn around and sell it. My dad put everything he had into that business. My mom poured her heart into being a good wife to him, being a top-notch socialite. And I was supposed to fall somewhere in the middle. But since moving here, meeting all of you. I don't want to be some businesswoman with some crazy plan. I'd love to just… be. Figure out for myself what I really want out of life and not what I'm expected to want. I could keep the business, be a silent owner, I guess. But part of me really wants to take it back to the very roots, where it started before it became this big corporate conglomerate. My family started it to share their wine and jams with their neighbors."

"Sounds to me like you have a vision for the company," I pointed out. She said she wasn't some businesswoman who could head up a corporation, but it sounded to me like she was on some level.

She laughed, "Yeah, but the investors and my father's team would never go for it. To take Richfield back to all of that, to bring the heart back into it, it would cost them their cushy paychecks. They'd never go for it."

"You're the one in charge Oakley," I reminded her. "You're the one with the power here. Not them. But if you were to do that, what would that mean for us?" I asked. It wasn't a question I wanted to ask, but it was one I had to ask.

She paused at that, looking up at me. "It would mean maybe spending part of the grow season out in California. We already have the vineyards. But after everything is picked I could have it shipped here. I could start over the way my family did. With a little shop here in Gratin. Take the brand out of all the big chain stores and take it back to what it used to be. Little shops with people who really loved the products. Elisa used to work for us too. She'd been one of our cooks. But then my father did away with the jam selections and focused entirely on the wine. He said that was where the money was. And he wasn't wrong. But he took the love and care out of Richfield when he did that."

"If you take the brand out of the chain stores, won't it kill it?" I asked. The truth was, I didn't know much about business, but I knew most people worked their whole lives to get their products into chain stores.

She nodded, "It might," she answered. "It's something I have to dig into. Maybe when we're both healed up you can go with me?" she asked. "Back out to California, I can start sorting through my parents' things and figuring out where all of it stands. I might have a fight on my hands with

Dad's VP. He stepped up and took over when my father died. But only because I let him."

"I'm going to be sidelined while I heal up anyway, so I'll have some time off," I answered. "Yeah, I'll go with you. Once you feel up to going, just say the word."

She nuzzled in against me more, "Maybe in a couple of weeks," she answered. "Right now I just want you to focus on getting better again. Fiona said I could move back in with her, Austen offered up his spare room too. So you can go live with him, I'll move back in with Fiona and when our house is done, we'll officially move in together." Tilting her head back, she looked up at me and smiled, but there was a glint of mischievousness in those green eyes that I had come to love so fucking much.

"Gonna hold out on me, huh?" I asked her, and she nodded. She was going to make me wait to live together until we could actually move back into our house.

"I can't possibly move in with you already. I hardly know you," she teased, but I knew she was right to make us wait on some level anyway. We had rushed into so much with everything going on that I couldn't even say I'd taken her out on a proper date yet. We had done dinners and our walk through town but not much else, and she deserved better than that. Once I could, I would take her out on the town; I would wine and dine her and show her exactly what a life with me could be like because she deserved all of it. Her kind heart had been damaged, and I would do everything I could to fix it.

There was a knock on the door before I could answer her teasing remark. A young nurse clad in blue scrubs stood there. "I'm sorry to interrupt, but I thought the two of you might like to know. Mr. Morgan has woken up." Oakley sat up at that, pulling away from me.

"Abraham is okay?" she asked. He'd been unconscious the last I had seen him when I left the scene where he'd been found. Mason hadn't had high hopes that they'd be able to bring him back. By the way Oakley choked over the words; I knew this was a good thing. He was likely the only family she really had left. From the way it sounded, she was now the only family he really had, too. They were going to have to lean on each other through their recoveries.

The nurse smiled softly, "He's having trouble recalling some of the details of what's happened over the last few weeks. But that's to be expected. The doctors are predicting he'll make a full recovery, that it'll all come back in time. So yes, he's okay."

She turned and looked back at me, "You should go, talk to him," I ran my good hand up and down her back. "I'll be right here when you get back if you need me," I promised. She wasn't in this alone, and I wished I could go with her to see him, but I knew this was something she had to do on her own. They shared something I would never be able to understand fully. They were going to need each other through this.

Oakley nodded and pushed off the bed slowly. I could tell by her movements that I wasn't the only one in pain, but she needed this. "Okay."

Thirty-Eight
Oakley

Pushing off of Owen's bed, I really didn't know what I was going to have to face when I walked into Abraham's room. I was the reason he was here in Pennsylvania. I was the reason his wife was dead. I was the reason his daughter was dead. Ashland had her problems, yes, but Abraham had always loved his little girl. That's why they had gone out of their way to get her help, hoping that they could find their sweet little Ash again.

I knew I wasn't to blame for Ash's disease. There had been something severely mentally wrong with her, and Owen killing her had been out of defense for not only his life but mine, too. I wasn't sorry that she was gone, but I was sorry that Abraham now had to live with the fact that both his wife and daughter were dead. I wouldn't blame him if he never wanted to see me again.

I let the nurse lead me down the long hallway, each footfall sending another shot of stabbing pain through my heart. How was I going to explain everything to him? I hadn't even made an effort to save Ash for him, and she'd made it more than clear that she blamed me for Elisa's death. Even though she was the one who'd done it. I wasn't sure that I would ever get rid of the guilt I felt. If I had just stayed in California, if I had just fought back there, maybe none of this would have happened.

Yes, I likely would have ended up dead, just like my parents. At least Abraham's family would have been left untouched, though. That man loved them above anything else, including me. I was just his boss's daughter, whom he'd felt obligated to look after when my father died. He

"

didn't owe me anything, but I owed him everything. Starting with an apology that he'd had to go through all of this at all. The nurse stopped just up ahead of me and motioned to an open doorway. "If the two of you need anything, just hit his call button," she told me, and I nodded.

I stopped just outside his door, just out of sight, off to the side. I didn't know what to say to him. An apology wasn't enough. It was never going to be enough. I couldn't hide out in the hallway either and refuse to face him, though. He deserved an effort, at the very least. Taking a deep breath to calm my completely fried nerves, I stepped into the open doorway and knocked on the frame softly.

He was sitting up in the bed. That was a good thing. At the sound of my knock, he looked up at me. It took a moment for him to assess me; taking the bandages and bruises into consideration, I probably didn't look like myself. "Elizabeth?" he asked softly, "You changed your hair," he noted. Right. God, that felt like forever ago now. Cutting it off and dying it a different color. "Or are you going by Oakley now?"

I smiled and nodded slightly, "It's still Oakley," I told him. Reaching up, I brushed my fingers through my short hair. "Abraham…" I started as I stepped into the room.

He shook his head, though, "Don't, princess," he told me. "None of this is your fault." How'd he know I was here to apologize? I guess the guilt was probably written all over my face. I'd never been particularly good at hiding how I felt.

"But she was after me, she blamed me for everything that happened with her," I argued.

He weakly held a hand out to me, not saying a word until I walked over and took it. "Ashland was sick," he reminded me. "She had a twisted sense of reality where you were to blame for everything that happened. It was never your fault. If anything, we can only blame the disease for what it did to her." He shook his head again. "She didn't want to take on any of the responsibility for herself. But the truth is, only she could have helped herself. The doctors all tried, and she had them fooled that she was well enough to be released. But Ash has always been good at twisting things to get her way. She's the one who hurt your parents; she's the one who…." I squeezed his hand, knowing what he meant. I wasn't going to make him say it. "She's the one who hurt me. She made those choices. You didn't make her make those choices, okay? I don't want you blaming yourself for this. And neither would your parents or Elisa." He returned the gentle squeeze on my hand.

"I'm still sorry," I told him softly. "I thought if I left, maybe whoever it was would just give up. I don't know. And we didn't know it was Ash behind all of it. It was stupid of me to believe that." I should have known that whoever dared to kill my parents the way they had would stop at nothing to kill me, too. She'd made it quite clear that she wanted me dead. I don't know why I actually believed running away would change that. I had only issued a challenge by running, and she'd taken to that challenge like a dog to a bone. She stopped at nothing, and I knew it would have continued if it hadn't ended the way it had. She would have done exactly as she promised. She would have burned the whole town to the ground to find me. The only way to stop her, to finally end it, was to kill her the way we had. I would never regret what Owen did. He saved my life and his own.

"Oakley, it's okay, it's going to be okay," he promised me. Abraham had always been that wise father figure. He'd taken me in and did all the things with me my own father was too busy to do. While my parents had been quick to teach me all about business and being a woman of society, Abraham and Elisa had given me the escape just to be a kid. I would be forever thankful to them both for that. They let me experience things and try things my own parents would have recoiled at.

"With…" Again, I started knowing it didn't need to be said; he understood. "I've decided to stay in Gratin. I've made friends here. I want to build a life here. And I met someone, someone really special who; it turns out, loves me. And I love him too. But I was wondering if maybe you'd want to stay too. My parents are gone. You're the closest thing to family I have left. And I hate the thought of you going back to California alone."

He watched me for a moment, and I could tell that the wheels were turning in his head. "I built my life out in California with my wife," he answered softly. "We picked out that house together; we raised our little girl there. As lonely as it might be, that's where all of my memories are." He sighed, though, "And she burned it all."

"You can make new memories here," I told him. Ash had taken everything from him, too. "I'll help you find a little house; I'll get you stuff for it. I can give you a job if you need one, I'm thinking about holding on to the vineyard. I have some ideas. And I could use a partner who knows a thing or two."

He stared at me at that, "Partner?" he asked. "I'm an old man, Oakley, past my prime."

Shaking my head, I smiled, "You're the same age my father was. And he was only closing in on his mid-fifties. Stop talking like that. You still have years left in your prime. Please, Abraham, I want you here." He sighed, and I could tell that it was a tough call for him. It wasn't as easy for him to walk away from his life in California as it was for me. I recognized that I had nothing there.

The life I had lived before everything, that wasn't who I was anymore. I would only be fooling myself if I thought I could just turn around and go back to it. Abraham's life, he couldn't go back to how it was, but his life hadn't been a lie. He was the most honest man I'd ever met. I couldn't force him to move here. It wasn't his job to look after me anymore. I wasn't his daughter; he no longer worked for my father. I couldn't make him stay if he didn't want to be here with me.

Pulling over the chair next to his bed, I sat down and watched him for a moment. "If you want to go home, though, Owen and I are going out there in a couple of weeks to start to sort things out for the Richfield Estate. I have to figure out what to do with the manor. We can all go back out there together, so you don't have to face it all alone," I offered. He nodded. There was a lot that he would have to deal with; there was a lot we would all have to deal with to be able to heal and move on from it.

I wanted us to be able to do that together, but if he felt best going back to the life he'd built with Elisa, then that's what he needed to do. I started to pull away from him, "I should let you get some rest; you've been through a lot the last few weeks." He wasn't the same Abraham anymore; he'd experienced things that had changed him completely, and I couldn't fault him for that. "Owen is waiting for me. He hasn't been able to rest without knowing I'm close by."

"Elizabeth…" he started as I pulled away from him. His use of my former name had me pausing. "I'll think about it," he nodded.

Walking back down the hall to Owen's room, I tried to go over everything and what I could have done differently to save some of the people Ash had hurt. If I had done anything differently, though, I wouldn't have met Owen, and despite all of the hurt Ash caused and all of the things she blamed me for, I couldn't bring myself to regret running the way I had. It had brought me to this whole new world outside of the one I had been used to. It gave me a place where I felt like I truly belonged. I had found a family outside the one that had raised me, and somehow, these people meant more. They chose to be in my life. Owen chose to love me when he didn't have to. Fiona, Jacey, and even Liv had all taken me in and cared for me without asking for anything in return. It had taken some getting used to that they weren't after anything in return.

To be fair, they didn't know who I really was, but even once they did, all they wanted to do was help me. These were the kinds of people I wanted to be around. I wanted to build a life for myself here with Owen. Who knew, maybe one day we would have a little family of our own. There were so many things that I would do differently from my parents.

I grew up with expectations, not dreams. I wasn't allowed to be anything other than a savvy businesswoman. I was the only heir to the Richfield business. My father had to pass it on to me to keep it in the family. I sighed. It was no use dwelling on how they wanted me to turn out because losing them knocked me off that path. I wasn't the perfect daughter they wanted. Especially not now.

Stepping back into Owen's room, he was sound asleep on the bed. Going back to my extra bed, I slipped in next to him and gently curled into his side, careful not to wake him. No matter what was thrown our way now, I knew we'd get through it if we were together. It was amazing to think it had only been a few weeks now since the night we met when he almost ran me down with his cruiser. I couldn't help but laugh slightly at the mere memory.

"What's so funny?" Owen's mother asked, stepping back into the room with me.

I shook my head, "I was just thinking about the night Owen and I met. And how I knew that if I wanted to keep my secret and lay low that I had to avoid him at all cost. I couldn't risk getting tangled up with a cop. Especially one who looked at me the way he did. Like I was this mystery he had to figure out."

Chrissy laughed at that, "He always was a… curious child. Asked the most annoying questions on the face of the planet. Why is the sky blue?

Why does the grass grow like that? Why can birds fly but he can't? All those impossible questions that parents hate answering because we don't actually have the answers to them. And no sooner you'd get him off one question, he was on to the next. It was endless." I laughed at that; it was adorable to think of little Owen all curious about the world like that. "From what I understand, he still asks annoying questions like that. Are you sure you want to take him on?"

I looked back up at the man safely asleep in the bed next to me. The heart rate monitors steady beeping, letting me know that he was safe and sound. He would make a full recovery, and we would rebuild everything. I felt myself smiling softly as I watched the steady rise and fall of his chest. "I'm more than sure," I answered his mother. There was nothing I wanted more than to take him on. He could pester me with annoying questions for the rest of our lives, and I wouldn't care. Because having someone who loved me the way Owen did, it made the rest of it just melt away.

I could feel her watching me as I watched him. I didn't know what she thought of me, but after everything Owen and I had been through together, there was nothing she could say to chase me away from him. She could hate me and despise the fact that I was with her son. She could think I was the worst person on the face of the planet for him. I wasn't going anywhere. As long as he loved me and as long as he wanted me around, I would be.

"You know, of all my boys, Owen is the one I worry about the most," she confessed. "He's always acted like things don't bother him. But at the end of the day, I know they do. They cut through to him. And when Austen told me he'd gotten caught up with a girl in trouble, I was genuinely worried that something would happen to him," she admitted to me. "But seeing the two of you together today when we got here. I just want to say thank you to you, for taking care of him. I'm guessing you've seen just how gentle his heart is behind that grump exterior he can put up front. And now that everything you've gone through is over, I'm hoping you find a way to move on together."

I smiled slightly, "I'm not going anywhere. We're going to figure out this house thing together. And he's going to help me figure out what comes next," I promised her.

Time slipped away from us once again. People came and went to check in on Owen. He slept through most of it, but I didn't. As tired as I was, I couldn't fall asleep. I didn't want to risk that it was all a dream. I didn't want to lose him again. Walking away from him in the woods was one of the hardest things that I had ever done, and then hearing that gunshot ringing through the trees, knowing that it could have been him on the receiving end of the bullet, knowing that I could have just lost him. She might as well have shot me, too. I didn't think it was possible to find someone like Owen. I didn't think guys like him existed outside of some fictional world.

Slowly, he started to stir again, opening those amazing blue eyes and finding mine. Smiling slightly, he moved to wrap his good arm around me. I could see the grimace cross his face at the movement, but before I could say anything, he leaned in and pressed a gentle kiss to my forehead, "Have you slept at all?"

I shook my head as I buried it against his neck, "I'm afraid to," I admitted to him. "I'm afraid that all of this is just some dream, and I'm going to wake up, and you won't be here anymore."

He hugged me tighter against him. "It's not some dream, Oak, I promise. We're safe now. And we're going to figure this all out. Now, please, get some rest." That was easy for him to ask of me. He was on painkillers that knocked him out every couple of hours, but I could try. I knew if there was one place I was safe, it was in his arms. Nothing could touch me as long as I had him around me, holding me together. I was hoping that went for any nightmares as well. Even if they came, though, he would be right there beside me, holding me together as he promised. The road to this point had been broken and battered; it had been rough getting this far. Though, every bump and bruise had been worth it. Because it led me to a home, I never knew I was missing.

It had been a week since everything had gone down. They'd only let me out of the hospital two days before, and I had been putting this off. It was easier to face and handle without seeing it. Standing outside my house, I sighed. My mom hadn't been wrong. It was still standing, but it wasn't inhabitable. I had already reached out to the architect who had designed it in the first place, and he was already on board to start us over. It was still a tough pill to swallow, though, knowing that everything was gone.

Coming up next to me, Justice nudged my hand. I looked down at him and shook my head, "We'll figure it out, buddy," I told him.

"We will," Oakley said as she came walking over with Roscoe. "We'll rebuild, it won't be what it was, but we'll rebuild," she promised.

"It'll be better," I nodded. She was right; it wouldn't be what it was, but that house had been built by a young guy just starting out. I had a spare room put in, but it wasn't designed for a family. I think there was part of me that had always known things with Chelsea weren't forever. We never talked about building a family together. This house had been enough for what we had right then and there. I wanted to marry her, but that was also the next logical step: hindsight and all.

Now that I had what I had with Oakley, I could understand that what I had with Chelsea wasn't the real deal. What I had with Oakley was. Maybe it was everything we'd gone through together to get to this point, but I couldn't imagine my life without her in it. I couldn't wait for the new house to be built and for us to finally start our lives together. We would be okay.

Stepping in next to me, she wrapped her arms around my waist. "I know this isn't easy," she started, looking up at me. "But before we get too far into talks with this architect of yours, we should probably figure some things out."

Leaning in, I pressed a soft kiss to her lips. It was hard to resist her, especially after everything that happened. Sending her away in the woods like that, I hadn't known if I was ever going to see her again. Now, I didn't want to take anything for granted. Having her here in my arms meant everything. She smiled into the kiss, which made me smile, too, and I pulled back. "Okay, what do we need to figure out."

She dropped her gaze shyly before forcing herself to meet my gaze again. "I know it's only been a few weeks, but we're building a house together. So like, I think we should talk about… you know…" She was stumbling over her words, and while it was adorable, she didn't have to be nervous about asking me anything.

"Oak, it's fine, just say it," I encouraged, squeezing her closer.

She took a moment to look away from me and back over the burnt wreckage that was the remains of my house. "We should probably figure out if… if we want kids," she finally said, looking back at me. "You know, so we have enough room. Wouldn't be smart to build a two-bedroom like you had, if we want kids. Someday."

I smiled and nodded, "Well, I'm one of four," I pointed out to her, "Yes, I want kids. And I think if we go for a three bedroom, that should be big enough."

She dipped her head in a slight nod, "okay," she returned my smile. "Three bedrooms sounds good to me. Because I'd want more than one. At least. Being an only child sucks. It's lonely. It's crossed my mind more than once that all of this would have been so much easier to get through if I'd had someone in it with me." She met my gaze again, "But if I'd had a brother or sister, I wouldn't have run." She shrugged, "either way, I don't want my kids to ever feel like they're in something completely alone."

"So then at least two. And if we decide on more, they can just share a room," I answered. "My parents had a three bedroom for us. Austen and I shared most of our childhood. Then Mase and Wyatt shared the other room. It was annoying at times, but I think it made us all closer."

I liked this, talking about what might come in the future for us. It might have only been a few weeks, but I knew without a shadow of a doubt that I wanted to marry this woman. I wanted that family with her. We would have it in time. I couldn't dwell on the things that I had lost in the fire. They were just things. What mattered most was that Oakley and I were both okay, and both of the boys were okay. We could start over.

Five weeks later…

Tossing Oakley's bag into the backseat of my car, I turned around and looked at her where she stood, giving Austen all sorts of directions on how to take care of the dogs while we were gone. I didn't have the heart to tell her that he'd taken care of them for me before. He knew how to take care of them better than she did, but she had insisted that I let her handle the arrangements for them. I had to hand it to him. Austen was taking her instructions like a champ. He'd even gone as far as pulling out a piece of pen and paper to write down everything she was saying. He was so unbelievably full of shit; he and I both knew he was only going to throw that paper out once he got back inside. At the very least, it was nice that he was appeasing her, though.

"Babe, we've got a flight to catch," I called over to her. "We still have to pick up Abraham yet." He'd made the tough decision to stay in Gratin with Oakley. So, along with packing up everything of Oakley's, we were also going to be seeing what was left of Abraham's old home as well. Oakley waved her hand at me, not turning around to look at me. She wanted to make sure Austen was taking care of our boys the way she deemed they should be taken care of. I had to admit. They were spoiled rotten now that she was around. They loved her more than they loved me, but she was also the one who fed them things they shouldn't have.

Leaning back against the car, I tucked my good hand in my pocket and watched her. I was still in a sling, and I would be for another couple of weeks until my shoulder fully healed up. It was the price I paid for what happened that night, but it was all worth it to be standing there watching her order my older brother around the way she was. I was happy to say that much. My whole family had taken to her almost right away. Dad was already calling her his daughter-in-law; he didn't want to hear that it wasn't something we'd barely even talked about yet, but I knew he wasn't far off base with that one. I was going to marry her someday. I just wasn't in any big hurry to get there. As far as I was concerned, we had all the time in the world.

Oakley, however, seemed to have other ideas in mind. For now, though, we needed to figure out a few other things before we could start looking at the possibility of a wedding. I wasn't going to argue with her, though. There had been a lightness to her since everything ended. I would have expected her to need some time to sort through everything. I know I had needed that time to cope with the fact that I was the reason someone was dead. Good or bad, a life was still a life.

Somehow, though, Oakley had found and chosen to look toward all the positives that came out of everything that happened. Her favorite to point out was that it had brought her to me. I had to admit, though, that one was probably my favorite, too. Knowing what could have happened if she had stumbled into another small town, anywhere else in the country. Knowing Ash would have found her either way. I was glad for what happened because it meant that she had stumbled into my tiny town that night. She'd met me and let me help, and now we could do crazy things like talk about weddings.

I was just going to let her go, let her dream, and plan all she wanted because it wasn't like we were actually getting married any time soon. She was having fun. There was no harm in that. When Austen glanced back at me again, I couldn't help but laugh. The big, bad military man needed help escaping my petite blonde. Because, yes, she'd dyed her hair back when the roots had really started to come in again. As gorgeous as she was before, I had to admit, I loved the blonde on her.

Pushing off the car, I ran up the front steps of Austen's small townhome and placed my good hand on the curve of the small of her back. "Babe, we really have to go. And if I could drive, I'd leave you here to boss Austen around more and go get Abraham before coming back. But I can't. You have to do it. If we're much later, we're going to miss our flight." She grimaced at me before smiling.

"I just want to make sure Roscoe and Justice will be fine," she told me, and I couldn't help it. I had to laugh.

"They will be," I promised her, "Austen has taken care of them before for me. He knows what he's doing."

"But he won't take care of them the way I do," she argued.

Leaning in, I pressed a soft kiss to her forehead, "That's a good thing, babe, maybe by the time we get back they won't be fat anymore."

She swatted my stomach at that, "They're not fat!" she argued, but I shot her a look at that, and she just smiled, "Fine, let's go," she huffed. Then, reaching out, she stole the keys from the front pocket of my jeans. "Bye, Austen," she answered, leaning up to press a kiss to his cheek. "Just remember…" she shook her head, "You know what, never mind. They'll be fine."

"I'll take good care of them," Austen promised. "Now go get everything squared away. And no stopping off in Vegas either. You know Mom would kill you if you did that," he directed more to me. Everyone was so quick to make jokes.

Oakley shook her head, "Oh we are so not getting married in Vegas, it's so tacky," she wrinkled her nose at the very idea of it.

"Let's just go," I laughed. She waved once more to Austen before running down the steps to the car. Climbing in, I glanced over at her as she turned over the engine, and the car fired to life. "Are you ready for this?" I asked her. She looked over at me before pulling out onto the road, not answering my question, but she didn't have to. I knew her well enough at this point that I could tell what she was thinking. She just had to remember that no matter how hard it was going to be for her to revisit her old life, I was going to be there every step of the way, holding her hand.

We were all situated on the flight three hours later as it started to back away from the gate. Oakley reached over and took my good hand in hers, lacing her fingers through mine. I could tell by how both she and Abraham were sitting that they were tense. It just seemed to radiate off the both of them. Abraham didn't talk much, which I'd noticed. He mostly kept to himself. Once he'd been released from the hospital, Fiona had offered up her den to him while they found a new home for him. When I was over at the house, he mostly kept to the den, not really talking to any of us. Of all of us, though, he was the one going through the most. Oakley had filled me in on everything that had gone down between Ash and her parents leading up to her end. As much as she blamed Oakley for everything wrong in her life, she seemed to have harbored a special hatred towards her parents, too. To go as far as killing her own mother while her father watched on. I squeezed Oakley's hand at the thought. We weren't married, we weren't even engaged, we didn't have any children, and just the thought of losing her like that was like a hot knife to the heart. I could only imagine what kind of agony Abraham was suffering through.

However, Oakley glanced my way at how I held onto her hand. Shaking my head, I sighed. I didn't want to get into it with Abraham sitting just on the other side of Oakley. It wasn't fair to bring it all up when he had no escape from it. So, instead, I covered it all the best I could with a little white lie. "I hate flying," I told her.

She leaned in and kissed my cheek, "It's a long flight, maybe you should try sleeping through most of it," she suggested. She'd already told me that's what she planned on doing. However, she'd made it clear that she could sleep almost anywhere as long as I was with her. Nuzzling down against my shoulder, she settled in for the long flight. Leaning over, I pressed a kiss to the top of her head. Looking up, I caught Abraham watching us. He nodded once before turning his attention back out the plane window as we took off into the air.

It didn't take long before Oakley was fast asleep against my shoulder. I felt a pair of eyes watching me as I flipped through the magazine the airline provided. Looking up, I caught Abraham watching us again. "The two of you remind me so much of Elisa and I, when we were just starting out. So in love, it was like nothing could touch us," he spoke softly. "I want you to promise me that you're going to take good care of her. Because this girl right here, she's special. And she deserves to be treated right."

I nodded; I already knew all of that, but Abraham was the closest thing she had to a father figure in her life. There was no big brother to give me the speech; her father had already passed on. I was just glad that there was someone who was willing enough to fill the role to give me that 'you better not hurt her' speech. Because it meant she had someone who cared enough about her to give it.

"I know how special and amazing she is. And believe me, I know how lucky I am that she chose me to help save her, that she trusted me to do my part. But most of all, I'll always be grateful that despite everything she's been through, that she can find it in her heart to love me the way she does," I told him. "So you don't have to give me some speech about how amazing she is and how if I hurt her, you'll hurt me," I smiled at that. "Because I already know. I knew from the first time I got the chance to talk to her."

That seemed to appease him enough that he turned back to look out the window, and I went back to my magazine. For Oakley's sake, I was glad that Abraham had opted to move to Gratin with her, that they could share that bond together. Neither of them seemed to blame the other for what Ash had done. It would have been easy to get caught up in the blame game and ruin what they had, but thankfully, they both saw it for what it was. That the only person to blame in all of it was Ash.

Glancing down, I watched her sleep for a long moment. Everyone joked about us running off to Vegas despite her clear show of total disdain at the idea, and I didn't know that I was ready to take it that far. When we got back from California, the house would be well underway. She would be moving in with me soon, for good, and I, for one, couldn't wait to start my life with her.

Standing outside the Richfield Manor the next morning, I looked on at what had been her life. There was a small pink convertible parked in the now open garage. Her room had been a shrine to designer everything. I was having a hard time connecting who this home had belonged to and the woman she was now, though.

She'd told me just to pack everything, that we would go through it all once we were home again. She'd said something about donating most of it, but I wasn't going to let her throw away everything. Whether she wanted to admit to it or not, at one point in time, all of this stuff had meant something to her.

Maybe it was materialistic, and maybe she'd learned the hard way that material things weren't what made her happy, but that didn't change the fact that all of it had once been a big part of who she was. I wouldn't stop her from getting rid of the clothes or the shoes or anything that was now genuinely worthless to her. We didn't need her past cluttering up the basement, but I didn't want her getting rid of everything.

Pushing back through the front door, I went to head for the steps when I found her standing outside her father's study. She'd pointed out the room to me, but as far as I knew, the door had remained shut the entire time we'd been in the house. She had her arms wrapped tightly around herself. Stepping up behind her, I wrapped my good arm around her waist and hugged her tight, pressing a kiss to her shoulder.

Despite all of her positivity, I knew it would catch up with her eventually, and standing outside the room where her parents had been killed was the final blow to the wall she'd erected around herself. Her whole body started to shake as she stood there and cried. I did my best to hold her together and be the rock she needed me to be. She had to know that I would do anything for her.

"I can't," she breathed after several minutes of standing there while she cried. "I can't go in there Owen. I can't relive that again."

I hugged her tighter, "Why don't you give me the key? I'll go in and pack everything up and leave the boxes sit out here," I suggested to her. "We'll load them into the truck, and when we get home, we'll put them away. When you're ready to look at them, we'll pull it all out, okay?" She managed a nod at that. Spinning around in my good arm, she threw her arms around my neck. I knew she would have struggled with facing all of this alone. I was still benched until I was out of the sling and able to return to work fully. Of course, I wasn't about to let her face all of this alone.

I didn't know what I had expected to find in there, but everything looked neat and orderly. If I hadn't already known better, I wouldn't have had a clue that two people had died in this room. It had obviously been professionally cleaned several times by the looks of it.

Grabbing an empty box, I started to load up all the files that were in the desk first. Like I promised her, I would help her go through everything when the time came. Moving on to the top drawer, I went to pull it open, only to find it locked. I wasn't sure that Oakley had the key to the desk, and if the drawer was locked, that told me that there was something important in it. Looking around the office, I moved a few things around. A key had to be somewhere.

I was about to give up when I noticed a small figurine of a ballet dancer slightly off-kilter. Going over, I picked it up, only to find the key I'd been after. It was a little odd to me that a businessman of Jonathan Richfield's status had a ballet figurine in his office, but I wasn't one to ask questions. He had a daughter; after all, maybe it had been a gift.

Going over to the desk again, the key slipped easily into the lock. Pulling the drawer open, I don't know what I expected to find, more files that held more pertinent information, I guess, but the only thing in there was a white envelope with Elizabeth scribbled across the front.

I knew by now that Oakley was actually her middle name, so I knew it was for her, but there was no telling what could possibly be in that envelope. Whether it would wreak havoc on her life again or not, folding it in half, I tucked it away in my back pocket. Something like that, I didn't want to get lost in some box that got tossed into the basement.

I would find the time to show it to her. I didn't know when the right moment would be. Maybe it was just best to give it to her and let her figure it all out. It wasn't my place to make that decision for her, but she was already so upset about just being near the office… we just needed to get through this process so that we could all close this chapter and move on.

Forty

Oakley

Leaning back against the wall outside the closed office door, I tried to fight off the rush of emotions I was feeling. I couldn't keep breaking down like that; we would never get anything done. I hadn't known how I was going to feel coming back here. I had been so caught up in the panic and fear when I left that I hadn't stopped to think about if I was ever coming back.

I could still feel them here, and there was a part of me that felt like I was abandoning them by moving away. I knew if I asked, Owen would move for me. I wasn't going to ask, though. I needed to move on, and that meant leaving them behind. Leaning my head back against the wall, I sighed. Coming into this, I knew that none of this would be easy on me, but I hadn't expected it to be this hard, either.

I couldn't help but wonder if they were still proud of me. If I was the daughter they'd raised me to be. I was stepping up, but I was also completely changing things. I had taken charge of my life, though, and I think that was all my father ever really wanted from me. It didn't stop me from wondering, though. If they were proud of the woman I'd become, against all odds. If they would love Owen the way I did.

I had to believe the answer to all questions was yes. I couldn't dwell on the ifs because they weren't here to tell me otherwise. I sat there against the wall, so caught up in my own thoughts that I barely heard the door open next to me.

When Owen walked back out, I saw him let out a heavy sigh before he noticed me sitting there on the floor. "I thought you went back upstairs," he said when he noticed me.

I shook my head, "I couldn't," I answered. I owed it to my parents to see things through with the estate and company. "Did you find anything in there?" I asked. I wasn't sure I really wanted the answer to that. While I'd been gone, the cleaners kept coming; I had demanded that. I wanted all traces of what had happened in that room gone. I just... I didn't know if that stain was still there.

He held his hand out to me and pulled me to my feet first. "I grabbed everything from his desk," he answered, "I found the key to his desk under some old figurine on the bookshelf." The ballerina. I'd forgotten he still had that. "I also found this," he held something out to me. "I wasn't sure if I should give it to you now or not. But that's not for me to decide."

Taking the envelope from Owen's hand, I sucked in a breath when I saw my father's handwriting across the front. "Did you grab it?" I asked him, not looking up from the envelope and the way my father's chicken scratch handwriting made my name hard to read.

"Grab what?" he asked. I could tell by the tone of his voice that he was confused.

I smiled slightly before looking up. "The ballerina figurine?" I corrected. "We did one of those paint your own ceramic things on vacation the one time. He let me pick one out for him to paint. It was that figurine. He didn't say anything, he just sat there happily painting away. It's sat on that shelf in his office ever since," I explained to him.

He nodded, "Yeah, it's packed. I wrapped it up with some old newspapers he had sitting on his desk," he answered. I looked back down at the envelope in my hand before folding it back up and slipping it into my back pocket. We still had work to do, and if I was being perfectly honest with myself, I didn't want to be in the house any longer than I had to be. It was one thing for the ghosts of my past to haunt me when I was on the other side of the country. It was another entirely to subject myself to every single haunting memory.

It was as if I were being dropped into a dunk tank. Repeatedly. With no real chance to catch my breath. I would look at the letter later when we were safely back at the hotel. Maybe I would never look at it. I wasn't entirely sure. I couldn't even begin to imagine what my father had to say to me before everything. It wasn't like he knew he was going to die that day. It wasn't as if there had even been any threats on his life that he knew to be prepared in case it happened. Which only fed the curiosity that much more.

No.

It was too dangerous for me to get caught up in what he might have said. There was too much going on. We had to finish packing up the house and get the truck loaded. We had to help Abraham yet. He needed to go see what was even left of his house, if there was anything to pack up at all. I knew going to the small house he shared with Elisa would be hard on him. I'd been the one to find my parents after they'd been murdered, but he'd had to sit there and watch his daughter kill her mother.

I couldn't even truly begin to imagine how hard all of that was going to be on him. Knowing there was an incredibly good chance that every memory he had with her burned when Ash set fire to the house. We would do it, though. Owen and I would both stand strong next to him and help him sort through everything. When we were done with that, we needed to hit the road back across the country.

It also didn't help that I had a secret of my own weighing on me. Something I had been trying to figure out how to tell Owen for the better part of a week now. He'd made it quite clear where he stood with our relationship; we were moving in together officially when we got back to Gratin, but he'd already stated that from there on out, he didn't see the need to rush things. He just wanted to enjoy what we had together.

I couldn't say that I disagreed with that, but I knew what I had to tell him would likely change his mind. I shook my head. That had to wait, too. I couldn't get too caught up in thinking about how or when I would tell him when we still had so much work ahead of us. Besides, I wanted to wait until after we were done packing everything and loading the truck. I didn't need him going all protective over me when he was the one with currently only one working arm.

There was too much that still needed to be done, though, before I could even begin to worry about any of that. I shook my head, trying not to think about the letter in my back pocket or the secret I was carrying around. I hated carrying around a secret like this from him if I was being honest. After I'd finally opened up about everything, I'd made a promise to myself that I wasn't going to keep any more secrets from him. It had only led to more issues for us.

If I had been upfront and honest with him the night he'd almost run me over, we might have been able to get ahead of Ash. I didn't like that he didn't know, but I would tell him in time when we weren't in the middle of rooting through my past. "We should get a move on it. I'm sure there's still a lot to do over at Abraham's house," I nodded. He seemed to accept the change in subject easily enough. He knew I would come to him in time if I needed him.

Hours later, I was sitting out on the balcony of our hotel room after a long day of packing and moving things around. I sipped at the bottle of water in my hand. I couldn't put the whole thing off much longer. He was soon going to start noticing signs that something wasn't exactly as it should be. Then, as if he knew I needed to talk to him, the glass door to our room slid open, and he stepped out in only a pair of shorts. God, the man was gorgeous. I swear, half the time, he didn't even know it. "Everything okay?" he asked, dropping down onto the bench next to me.

I nodded slowly. Yeah, everything was fine as long as he took the news well. It wasn't like it was bad news. I wasn't dying or anything. "There's just something I've been trying to figure out how to tell you. And knowing we were coming out here, knowing what I had to get through, I decided that it was best I focus on one thing at a time," I started. "But now that's over and done with. The house is packed up; the timeshare people will get it ready for next season. Now there's nothing else to distract me from telling you. The issue is, I still don't know how."

Reaching out, he wrapped his arm around my shoulder. "What's going on, sweetheart?" he questioned. "You know you can tell me anything." Yeah, I knew that, but most things that I had to tell him wouldn't completely upend both of our lives the way this would. We'd had enough excitement lately. This would change everything, and there was no denying the fact that we were still very new in this relationship. We had both fallen fast for each other. It was likely some white knight, damsel in distress thing that my therapist would have a field day with, but this solidified what we had to a degree I wasn't entirely sure we were ready for.

"The thing is. I was having some issues, I was late, and I was having some discomfort as well. So, thinking it might have been linked to what happened with Ash, I went to get checked out because stress can cause a cycle to be irregular. I went to the doctor about two weeks ago. They called me a week ago to tell me what it was." I sighed, leaning into him more. "I'm…" I started, but I couldn't quite get the words out. It was like ripping off a bandage, though. I just had to say it. "I'm pregnant."

Owen pulled back from me and stared at me for a moment, "As in…."

"We're having a baby, Owen," I nodded. I knew all of it would come as a shock to him. It had been a shock to me, too. We had been careful the one day we had been together, but no birth control was foolproof. If one of the condoms broke and we didn't notice…

I sat there watching him for a long moment as he seemed to try to process the information. It was a lot to take in, but then his face broke out in a slow smile, "I'm gonna be a dad?" he asked, looking at me again.

Laughing slightly, I nodded, "You're going to be a dad," I told him. "So you're okay with this?"

His smile only grew at my question, "Of course I'm okay with this, I love you Oakley," he insisted. "And I know I've been against too much wedding talk but that's only because I don't want to rush anything. But that doesn't mean I don't want a family with you or that I don't want to marry you someday. Yes, okay, this is faster than I would have liked. But that doesn't change how amazing this is. We're gonna have a baby," he grinned again.

I loved how happy it seemed to make him feel that he was going to be a father. "We're having a baby," I repeated before leaning in to kiss him.

At first, he seemed to return the kiss just as enthusiastically as I was, but then he jerked back. "Wait a minute, you're telling me you're pregnant and you were moving around those heavy boxes so concerned about me lifting anything because of my shoulder?"

I laughed; I couldn't help it. It was kind of adorable when he got all protective over me like that. I knew it was coming. It was just in his nature to watch out for the people he cared about, and now it wasn't just me he needed to watch out for; it was our little one, too. "Your shoulder needs to heal," I scolded, "And it won't heal if you keep using it. Don't act like you don't want to go back to work with Jacey."

He grimaced at the idea, "You're right, I'm totally doing it on purpose, I don't want to go back to work," he chuckled. "This is really happening for us, isn't it?" He reached up with his right hand to brush my hair back behind my ear. "Everything is going to be good now Oakley, I promise.

Yes, we're going to face some tough times, we're going to fight, and life isn't always going to be easy. But this baby, it's a good thing. We're going to have a family. And one day, probably sooner than planned now, we will get married."

I smiled at that; I couldn't help it; leaning in, I kissed him again. Then, taking his hand, I placed it over my stomach, where our little peanut was growing. He was right. Everything was going to be okay.

Everything was packed up. We were getting ready to leave, but I had told Abraham and Owen that I wanted to do one last walk-through of the house before I locked it up and walked away from it. This had been the house that I grew up in. Somewhere in the kitchen, a door frame marked my height as I got older. I had run these halls and fallen down the stairs more than once in a pair of my mother's heels. My whole childhood happened within these walls.

It was hard to let go of that. At the same time, though, I knew I had to. Not just for my own sanity but for my baby's sake, too. I knew our baby would grow up in an entirely different world than I did, and for that, I couldn't be more thankful. The real reason I had come back into the house alone, though, was that I wanted to put to rest the ghosts in my father's study. I would never not see the image of the two of them on the ground like that. I knew that would haunt me until the day I died, but I couldn't be afraid anymore.

Pulling in a deep breath and then pushing it out in a sigh, I reached for the door and pushed it open slowly, the old hinges creaking with the effort. Instantly, I braced myself for the memories, but instead of being bombarded by images of them lying on the floor, covered in blood. Every other memory hit me hard. Skipping into the office to ask for money for the ice cream truck, coming in on meetings with investors, and interrupting those meetings much to his annoyance. I was met with everything good because as bad as that one bad day was, it didn't outweigh years of memories.

Stepping into the office, I rounded around the desk and dropped into his big leather chair. God, how I used to love spinning in this chair when he wasn't home. It was the most incredible thrill there was. Not only did I spin until I couldn't stand up straight, but there was the added adrenaline rush that he could catch me at any moment.

Digging into my back pocket, I pulled out the letter that Owen had given me. Part of me didn't want to open it. I wanted to leave whatever sage words he had a mystery. I wanted to leave him as he was: strong and stern. The little girl in me, who just, simply put, missed her daddy. She had to know what he said. With a shaking hand, I reached out for the letter opener that was still sitting on the desk. Owen had packed away the nice one that my mother had bought him. This one didn't matter so much. Slicing open the envelope, I tugged out the folded-up sheet of paper with a steadying breath. I started to read.

My little Lizzie,

You frighten me. You were born just a few hours ago, and I'm terrified that I don't know how to do this whole fatherly thing. My father wasn't exactly a warm and comforting man. He was tough. He provided for his family. He took care of things and did everything a father should. But he lacked a little in being a dad. I want to be more than that for you. I want to learn from his mistakes and make sure you never question how I feel about you.

So I'm making a promise to myself now: no matter what, there will always be a hug goodnight at the end of the day. Because I've found that a hug can make a world of difference in your day, don't you think?

I promise to be your fiercest protector. My father wasn't too thrilled when he heard you would be a little girl. He asked who I would pass the company on to if I didn't have a son. That I had best get on that because there was no way I could possibly hand it over to my daughter someday. However, that's the third promise I'm going to make; I'm going to make sure you grow up to be strong enough to take on anything in this world, including this company. There is nothing in this world that you can't do if you set your mind to it. I can already tell you may have my eyes, but you have your mother's spirit. It's there, this faint spark when they handed you to me and you first looked up at me. You are going to be a force to be reckoned with, Lizzie.

The will is already written. If anything happens to me, Lizzie, it's all yours. No one will ever be able to take that away from you. You're only hours old, and I already have faith that you will grow up to make me proud. Maybe one day you'll have a child of your own and know this feeling. I don't know if you'll ever even see this, but if you do one day, know that, above all, you are my greatest treasure. I love you with everything I have, Elizabeth, and I can't wait to see the gorgeous young woman you'll undoubtedly grow up to be.

Love,
Daddy

I found myself wiping away the tears as I read through it a second time. I had always known on some level that my father loved me, and the hug every night had always seemed a bit out of character for him, but he'd keep those promises to me. At the end of the day, that hug sometimes did make all the difference.

If my grandfather was pushing for a grandson to take over, it explained so much about why my father pushed me. Because he wanted everything for me, he wanted me to stand strong. I could only hope that he was looking down on me, proud of the woman I'd become. Because I knew now what he was talking about.

Digging through the drawers for a pen and some paper, I started to write.

A little while later, there was a knock on the door. Looking up, I smiled slightly when I saw Owen standing there. "I was just coming to check on you, make sure everything was okay?" he asked before laughing slightly, "And I'm just now realizing how much I've been asking you that lately."

I pushed up from the chair, shaking my head at him, "Never stop asking me that," I told him as I walked over to him. Leaning up, I pressed a soft kiss to his lips.

We were bound to face a whole myriad of challenges as a couple, as individuals, and as parents. We were going to make mistakes and mess up sometimes. My parents did, and I was sure that Owen's parents had their moments too. It was what we did with those mistakes that mattered most. My parents hadn't been the most affectionate people, but I could always count on that hug goodnight.

Stepping in, I wrapped my arms around Owen's waist, and I felt the calm surround me. No matter what was swirling around me, he was the eye of the storm, the calm in the middle of all the chaos. I couldn't help but smile against his chest at the thought that my father was right. A hug, especially from the right person, could make a world of difference. I knew that as long as I had Owen to turn to at the end of each and every day, I would be okay.

Pulling back from him, I looked up at him, "Let's go home," I told him softly. He nodded before reaching out to take my hand and leading me out of the manor. I was stepping out on my own. I didn't know what I was doing in this new world. I was forging my own path instead of following the one that my parents had taken the time and care to pave for me. It had been bumpy and hard to follow at points. I had gotten lost more than once, but through all of it, I had discovered that sometimes it was the broken roads that led to the most beautiful destinations.

To my little girl,

We only just found out today that you're going to be a little girl and I now understand the fears my father had the night I was born. It's scary, becoming a parent, knowing this little life is going to depend on you to take care of it. But I'm going to make you the same promises that my father made to me. No matter what happens, I'll always end the day with a hug and an I love you. Because I do, baby girl. There is nothing you could say or do that would ever make me change my mind on that.

I'm going to take the promises a step further though. I'm not going to burden you with the responsibility of being a Richfield by blood. The company is yours for the taking, should you want it. I will have it ready to hand over to you when you feel you're ready. But there's no family obligation here. You can do whatever you want with your life. You aren't some heiress, I want you to just be a kid. I want you to have the childhood I never got to have. My parents meant well, but it's my job to do better for you than they did for me. That's how we grow.

There is nothing you can't achieve, if you put your mind to it. And I am going to make sure you know that. Nothing is out of reach. I want you to have that same fire my mother passed on to me. I want you to have the confidence to know you can do anything, and your dad and I will be your biggest support.

I hope you never get to read this letter, because as long as I'm around, you don't need to see this. If you're reading it, it means I'm gone. I promise to do everything in my power to be there for you every step of the way, baby girl.

Your dad and I, we can't wait to meet you. Our little Audrey Elisa. We love you.

Love,
Mommy

Ten Years Later
Owen

Walking into the kitchen, I slid the belt through the loops on my pants and fastened it in place. "Have you seen my badge?" I asked Oakley. She turned from the stove where she was making the girls breakfast.

With a slight laugh, she unclipped it from her pocket, "Savanna was trying to arrest the dog again this morning," she told me. Leaning in, I pressed a gentle kiss to her lips. "I found the badge, because she was waving it in his face telling him to freeze, which he wasn't doing a good job of – she made sure I knew that. But I wasn't able to find the cuffs."

I sighed at that and shook my head, the last time my cuffs had gone missing we'd found her trying to handcuff the poor cat to the handle on her lowest dresser drawer. This was why I now kept a spare pair in my desk at the station, and I usually tried to keep them out of my youngest's reach at home. Savanna was something of a little terror though. I liked to try and blame Oakley for that, but my mother took great pride in reminding me that I wasn't exactly the picture perfect angel child growing up either. "They'll turn up when she tries arresting her sister," I half smiled.

It was still hard to believe sometimes that this was where life had taken me, taken us. Audrey looked like me in almost every way, except she had her mother's mischievous green eyes. Looks was the extent of our similarities though, she was all Oakley, brimming with fire and passion that would burn this world to the ground if she so willed it.

Despite her penchant for trying to arrest every living creature in our household, Savanna was her polar opposite. She had her mother's blonde hair and bubbly personality, but she made it well known that she wanted to help people when she got older, she wanted to be a cop like me. Or find missing people like her Uncle Austen. At one point in her short seven years, she had also declared she was going to save lives in the back of an ambulance like her Uncle Mason. Though she had made it perfectly clear she didn't like fire, so she wasn't going to be like Uncle Wyatt. Which he had taken great offense to.

"I'm rather hoping to avoid that today of all days," Oakley laughed. "You know Audrey will hold it against Savanna until the end of time if she tries arresting her on her tenth birthday." It was hard to believe that it had been ten years already since Audrey had come along. That Oakley and I had been married nine years. My life with my girls was anything but boring, but I wouldn't have it any other way.

"We're still doing dinner tonight?" I asked and Oakley nodded. We had promised Audrey a special dinner on her birthday, but what she didn't know was we had a surprise party planned for later on in the week. My parents were flying in and everything. Everyone would be there to celebrate with her and she would soak up every second of it, I was sure.

Oakley sighed, "She hasn't decided yet where she wants to go, but I feel like it might be that play space over in Colcannon." She looked back to me, "Also fair warning, she's not too happy that you're still going to work today, she says if she and Savanna can take the day off from school, and I can take the day off from work, so can you." She shook her head, "I heard rumor that they were going to find a way to make you stay," she laughed.

We had explained to the girls numerous times that Oakley could take time away from the Winery because she owned it, even with it thriving, she had a team who could step in when she wasn't there. That gave her the flexibility to work around the girl's school schedules.

Whereas I couldn't just drop everything, being a cop meant I might have to work birthdays or holidays sometimes. The girls didn't want to hear it though, but for the most part they would pout at me but still send me off with a hug. That didn't stop them from trying though. I wasn't sure I wanted to know what their latest scheme was.

Leaning in, I pressed a kiss to Oakley's cheek, "I should go, I'll try to get done early, we don't have much going on at the station anyway."

She smiled and shook her head, "You're not getting away that easy," she laughed before pulling on the front of my shirt to tug me in for a kiss. Giving in to her demands, I met her in the kiss. That was something we had always promise to each other, that we never part ways without a proper goodbye. Not that we thought anything would happen, it was more of a just in case type situation.

When the kiss broke, I smiled at her before adding, "I love you."

"Love you too," She answered. "Good luck getting out of the house," she teased. She clearly knew more about the girls scheme to keep me home than she had previously let on.

Grabbing the last of what I needed from my office I headed for the front door. I stopped though when I saw what was waiting for me. Both girls were laying on the floor up against the door. There was no getting around them without going out the back and around the house.

"What are you two up to?" I asked, walking over to stand over them. Savanna immediately broke and giggled, which earned her a nudge from her older sister.

"We're protesting," Audrey answered.

I nodded, "I see," I tried to stifle my own laugh, "And what exactly are we protesting?"

Audrey still didn't even look my way, she kept staring straight up at the ceiling. "Today is my birthday and I don't want you leaving."

"I'm sure we can come to some sort of agreement, since this appears to be a peaceful enough of a protest," I agreed. When she didn't answer me though, I sighed. "Though refusal to negotiate might result in the use of force," I warned. That earned me a side glance, but still no response. Without hesitation, I bent down and tossed her over my shoulder.

"Dad!" she whined. "Get him Savanna!"

Ten Years Later
Oakley

Less than ten minutes later, Owen came walking back into the kitchen with our now ten year old thrown over his shoulder and our seven year old wrapped around his leg. I could tell by Audrey's silence that she was trying to act tough, but I knew my daughter, she was desperately trying not to laugh. Especially with Savanna giggling up a storm with every step he took. Pulling Audrey from his shoulder, he set her on the counter. Then bending, he pried Savanna from his leg and set her next to her sister. He then aimed that impossibly blue gaze at me. "Did you know our daughters were protesting?" he asked me.

I tried to hide the smile, Audrey had come to me first thing and asked how we'd convince him to call out of work today so we could all do something special for her birthday. I may or may not have given her a few ideas. Wasn't my fault she took them and ran with it.

My non answer was apparently answer enough for him. "You just had to teach them to fight for what they believe in, stand up for themselves, and others," he teased, watching me. "Just had to raise them to be strong, independent, willful little women."

We had both done that. I watched him, knowing that with his little girls protesting his departure that he wasn't going to work now. Not today. Kohl would understand and let him off the hook. As far as I knew, there wasn't much for either detective to do. Gratin had gone back to its normal quiet. Things still happened, but not to the degrees of stalkers, murderers, and serial killers. He could take the day off.

I looked at the girls, "And how exactly were you protesting?" I asked them.

"We were laying in front of the door so he couldn't leave," Savanna answered, looking back at me.

Owen glanced my way again, "I had no hope of getting out of the house and since they were unwilling to negotiate, force was used," he nodded. "Though now that the situation has been contained, we can revisit the idea of negotiations," he turned back to our oldest. "I understand your stance, perhaps we can reach some sort of agreement."

Audrey looked up at him, the same blue gaze as her father. He liked to claim that she was all me in how she handled things, but then there were moments like this that I had to argue she was definitely part Officer Hale too. "I'm listening," she answered.

Owen was trying hard to keep a straight face as he held her gaze. "There is some paperwork that has to get done by the end of the week," he started, "I propose a half day, in which I go to work and get done what I need to do and you two have a spa day here with Mom. Then when I'm done, we can celebrate together."

Audrey stared him down and I could tell she was contemplating his offer, but I knew my little girl, she wasn't going to let him win that easily. She glanced to Savanna and then back at me. I gave the slightest shake of my head. She turned back to her father and sat up straighter, "No," she answered firmly. "You can go get what you need at work and then come back," she started. "You can do whatever in your office for… two hours. And! You have to take Savanna when you go get your stuff, so that you have to come back. When your two hours are done, then we can go to a movie."

I watched Owen carefully, he wanted to blame me for how strong willed she was, but the truth was that was something we had both wanted for her. We never wanted either one of our girls to find themselves in a situation like mine. I never wanted them to be dependent on someone else to save them.

"You drive a hard bargain kid," he sighed, pushing his fingers through his dark hair. "Fine. How about you call Detective Langley and tell him I won't be in today. He's more likely to say yes to you. Or better yet, you go with me, he won't be able to turn you away."

I laughed at that, from the moment he had walked out of the kitchen I had known he wasn't going to work today. We normally didn't give into the girls if we could help it, and for the most part they understood that sometimes their dad had to work. Today was different though. We always tried to do something special for their birthdays, Audrey just didn't know that her something special was happening on Saturday instead.

Audrey didn't answer his proposed offer right away, but Savanna bounced on the counter next to her, "Can I go too?"

Owen leaned in and pressed a kiss to the top of her head, "of course you can." He looked to me next, "You coming too?"

I nodded and smiled, "Admitting defeat so quickly," I teased.

"We both know there's no way I'm getting two hours of peace in this house. I'll just catch up with work tomorrow."

That seemed to shake Audrey's silence, "Deal," she held her hand out to him for a shake.

Owen laughed slightly and shook his head before shaking her hand. "Go get your shoes on, we'll take breakfast to go." Helping them both down off the counter, he watched as they ran from the room. "Think we can pack this up?" he nodded to the pancakes I had made.

I turned and grabbed a bag to put them in, "This is why she requested pancakes, so when you caved they'd be easier to travel with," I told him with a laugh. "I'm honestly surprised you even tried to fight it."

He stared at me for a long moment before letting out a defeated sigh, "How am I supposed to say no? It's her birthday."

Before I could say much else, Audrey came skidding back into the kitchen with Savanna hot on her tail. Except Savanna hadn't tied her shoes. I didn't have a chance to say anything before she went tumbling into Owen. Catching her with ease, he put her back on the counter.

"Tie your shoes kid," he told her. "Then we'll go."

Acknowledgements

To say this process has been a challenge is probably the understatement of the century. There was a time when I truly once believed that I would never be able to write a novel. I thought I was only cut out for short stories. Which is why I first want to thank everyone who's ever believed in me and pushed me to do better. Without you, none of this would have been possible.

Next, I would like to thank those that supported and helped me through this process. Not only did Mandy share some of her resources with me, making it that much easier to answer simple questions as I wrote. She also took on the great task of editing and rewriting some of the more intimate scenes. They're not quite my strong suit yet, but I'm working on it.

Leah not only read it and offered her critique, but she is also the mastermind behind my cover. I wanted something more subtle, but I couldn't figure it out. Without much guidance at all, she figured out exactly what I was after. I couldn't have done it without you.

Renee asked me every day if I'd managed to write anything. While the question was annoying to say the least, she kept me moving forward.

Simone was the first one to read this book, as I wrote it. Her constant questioning of what happens next really brought back a level of joy in my writing I hadn't felt in a long time.

To my editors and beta readers, I can't thank you enough.

Linda was kind enough to read the really rough first copy of an aspiring author she'd never met. Her advice and kind words really encouraged me to keep going.

Nichole, she not only read it, keeping me up with text messages half the night, but she also put up with me day in and day out at work complaining about it. Truly, just having someone to bounce ideas off of really helped.

Steph, for giving me the readers perspective. She helped me make it all make sense. Which is a real challenge some days. She caught things everyone else missed. Including myself. Repeatedly.

Finally, to my dear intern, Anna. I'm sorry I haven't written more for the next one. I'm working on it. But look, this one is finally done! Your help has been immeasurable. From helping me with possible cover designs to yelling at me in the park to keep writing.

People often view writing as a solitary endeavor. Writers work alone. But without the support and team standing by us, helping us through each painful step, we'd never get anything done. So to my support, an endless and forever thank you.

VICTORIA

Coming Soon!

Don't Miss What Comes Next for the Gratin County Police Department:

Shattered Trust

Follow Ethan Jacey and Fiona O'Dell as they come face to face with the dirty cop out to destroy them.

About the Author

Victoria grew up just outside of Philadelphia Pennsylvania, only just over two hours from the Pocono Mountains. She resides with her writing assistant, Poe, in Pottstown. She began writing at fourteen, never dreaming that one day she would be publishing her first novel. With a mess of short stories behind her, this is her debut novel.

www.ingramcontent.com/pod-product-compliance
Lightning Source LLC
Chambersburg PA
CBHW022113310726
48972CB00007B/2012